CAIN LAKE

ONE

SIN EATER

SIN EATER

CAIN LAKE

BOOK ONE

www.TerryFisherBooks.com

ISBN 978-1-7364107-7-6

This book is dedicated to my sister Tina,
who encouraged my talent and creativity
since I was old enough to hold a crayon.
I miss our talks, your laugh, and
never-ending positive spirit.

1
FORTY YARDS

The female victim wore nothing more than a tattered bathrobe and a thin blanket of snow. Last night's squall was beginning to melt away, revealing the truth of the brutality. She must have sprinted through the woods to evade her killer, but either ran out of steam or was just outpaced. He was probably faster and stronger. She was caught just forty yards from the road. Forty more yards might have saved her life. She would have been out in the open, near traffic and possible witnesses.

Forty yards.

She lay on the ground, outlined by a terrible rendition of a snow angel comprised of blood and mud, with raised edges from her thrashing and panic. She had put up a hell of a fight, but her strength had failed to be enough. With her hands bound by paracord in front of her body, it was the only outcome anyone could expect.

"Poor girl didn't stand a chance," the state trooper commented. He scribbled something on a notepad and didn't bother looking at the sheriff when he spoke. "Running through the woods barefoot with her hands tied in front." He waited for the sheriff's response. The sheriff had just arrived at the scene and stood stunned when he saw the victim. He had been afraid that this day would come and had been trying to prepare himself.

He hadn't prepared enough.

Sheriff Jeff Bourbon was clean-shaven, broad in the shoulders, and soft with his words. He lowered himself into a squatting position, since his knees felt like they were about to give out, and rested on his heels. Close enough to smell the dead woman on the ground, he removed his wide-brimmed hat, which he only wore in the winter months. Living in the foothills of the Adirondack Mountains, the hat kept the brutal winter snow off his face and shielded his head from the cold wind. He wore that hat from dusk to dawn, removing it only when his shift was over or when he ate a meal. But today, he took the hat and placed it over his heart to keep it from falling out of his chest. With his glistening eyes, he peered down at the beautiful woman who'd lost her life in such an ugly manner.

"Willa," he whispered. "My God, girl, what happened to you?" Staying on one knee, he resisted the urge to take her hand and fought a losing battle with his tears. His efforts to keep his emotions in check and stay strong were futile and exhausting. Upholding the law in his little town was usually a simple job, but now he had two difficult jobs to do—find a murderer and solve a crime.

The state trooper stepped forward—a freckle-faced giant of a man with round features and red sideburns. "Sheriff, are you telling me that's Willa Savage, the woman who's been missing for two days?"

"Three," Bourbon wheezed. He cleared his throat to achieve more volume, and peeked at the black watch strapped to his wrist. "Fifty-nine hours."

"You knew her?"

Bourbon nodded. "She's Annabel's daughter." He threw his hand to his mouth to keep himself composed. Admitting how he knew the victim was like swallowing gasoline. "She's my girlfriend's daughter." He took his phone out of his pocket. Three missed calls from the victim's mother in the last two hours. Calling her back would need to wait until he could muster the strength to hear her voice. He needed to be her rock—a comforting fire in a cold, dark nightmare. The news of Willa's death would shatter her, and he would need to be there to collect the pieces.

"Goddam, Sheriff, I'm sorry," the trooper said in a tone constructed more from formality than sincerity. "So sorry for your loss." The trooper stepped over Willa's legs and noticed her left ring finger. "She was married. I assume you know the husband, too?"

Bourbon gave a nod.

"Do we know his whereabouts? He could be our killer."

"Yeah...no...he's probably at home waiting for a phone call. His name is Cody—Cody Savage. He's going to be crushed."

"Savage? Jesus, his name even makes him sound guilty. You think he's capable of this? She was stabbed in the back several times, then twice in the front. Stabbing is usually a crime of passion. They have a history of domestic altercations?"

Bourbon regained his feet and donned his wide-brimmed Stetson. "No. No, they were a perfect couple. They were great for each other. I've never seen two people more happily in love."

"Yeah, well, you know as well as I do that the husband's always the first, and most likely, suspect."

"Cody's not capable of this," Bourbon countered. "No way he could ever hurt this girl. He put her on a pedestal. Worshiped the ground she walked on."

"That's what all the neighbors say just before we find a bloody hammer in the hubby's toolbox." He scanned the trees as if he were looking for one adequate enough to piss behind. "My money's on the husband."

Bourbon refrained from debating or decking the young trooper. Right now, Willa needed his attention more than Cody needed a defender.

The state trooper wrote more words in the notebook, presumably Cody's name, and then retrieved his buzzing cell phone from the left inside pocket of his light jacket. Excusing himself, the trooper stepped away from the body and began speaking to whoever was on the other side of the conversation.

Sheriff Bourbon stared at Willa's feet. It was easier than gazing into her cloudy eyes with the cold blue sky reflecting in her irises. Those unrecognizable feet could belong to any woman, so he pretended she was someone else.

Frostbite had turned her toes black. Orange nail polish—left over from Halloween—cracked and peeled from the frantic run through the woods with no footwear. A late-autumn snow had covered most of her body, but not enough to keep her hidden until spring. Luckily, a local school bus driver had been turning the big yellow vehicle around on an abandoned logging road when she saw her in the rear-view mirror wearing a lilac-colored bathrobe. The bus driver parked with the engine idling and the heat on while she called her supervisor.

Last night's November rain had stopped at 11 pm. The snow squall started around 3 am, dumping 1.5 inches of wet snow on the crime scene. There were no tracks in the snow to or from Willa's body, which meant she'd been killed before the weather changed. The rain probably washed away any scent for the tracking dogs, but Sheriff Bourbon wanted them called in anyway.

Without a scent or tracks, Bourbon would have to solve this horrible crime with hardcore evidence and science. He hated to depend on microscopic traces and invisible clues. He'd much prefer a bloody knife with distinct fingerprints. But the murder weapon was nowhere to be found. With the early morning snow squall, it could have been three feet away. Hopefully, he'd find it under the snow near the scene, and the pathologist could pull the killer's DNA from the handle.

Bourbon's thoughts jumped back and forth from evidence to the victim—a mess of strategy, grieving, and guilt. He shouldn't have to break this news to Annabel and her son, Levi, who awaited his call. He took his phone out again, hesitated, and put it back in his pocket. He wasn't ready to make the most harrowing call of his life.

And Willa's husband, Cody, would not take this well. Bourbon had seen Cody Savage angry in the past. He was a capable fighter with fast hands, strong legs, and a temper like a Roman candle. If he found out who murdered his wife, there would be severe retribution, possibly a bloodbath. Secretly, Bourbon hoped he'd be there to witness it.

The snow muffled the sound of footsteps approaching from behind. Sheriff Bourbon didn't have to turn around to recognize his deputy's gait and cadence. The deputy followed the footsteps through the snow, slipped on the muddy bank of the ditch, cursed out loud, and joined the sheriff at the crime scene. Deputy Charlie Archer stood shoulder to shoulder with his boss, staring at the unfortunate victim.

"Damn. Fuck, Sheriff, I really thought we'd find her alive," Deputy Archer said.

Bourbon just nodded. His feet were frozen to the ground, and for the first time in his twenty-seven-year career, he didn't know what to do next. He felt like a victim, cold and empty, as if he were the motionless body that lay before him.

"I don't wanna fuck this up, Arch," Bourbon said. "I want to make sure we find the sick bastard that did this."

"We will, boss." Deputy Archer reassured the sheriff. "What do we have?" He knelt to take a closer look at Willa's face. "Goddam, I've seen her picture a hundred times in the last few days. I knew she resembled my Charlotte, but holy shit, she's just as beautiful."

"She was a true beauty, inside and out, just like her mother." Bourbon reflected on the first time he'd met Willa. She was a spunky fifteen-year-old girl working on her mother's small farm, throwing hay bales to the horses and shoveling manure in the barn. Nothing seemed to faze her, and Annabel thought Willa would never find a man who could match her wild spirit until she came home one day with Cody Savage.

"Their eyes are a different color, but they—" Archer had to breathe deeply as he thought about his wife, Charlotte. "They look like they could have been sisters."

Sheriff Bourbon thought about the deputy's wife, Charlotte. He had to rummage through his memories to recall her features. He finally found the right image. He couldn't deny it: there was a remarkable resemblance, and the two women could have nearly passed as sisters—fraternal twins. And then he shuddered, thinking about Charlotte Archer's death. Charlie Archer had only been a deputy with the Stoneville Sheriff's Department for a month when he got the call that Charlotte had been hit and killed by a vehicle while she'd been out on a morning run to Cain Lake.

The accident had happened quite early, even before the sun rose in the east. There were no witnesses, and the vehicle's driver fled the scene, never identified. Deputy Archer had been the responding officer to the scene that morning, a brutal way for him to begin his life in Stoneville. When he arrived, he found his wife with a broken pelvis and back, and a fractured skull. She lay there lifeless, taken from him just two years into their marriage—practically newlyweds. Since that day, the memory of his dead wife chased Archer like a shadow. Bourbon knew Archer's perseverance had taken strength. He worked long hours, took extra shifts, and built a house on the lake to keep himself busy. The ability to endure was something to admire, even though it occasionally made Charlie Archer bitter. Thankfully, he'd been in therapy ever since.

The sheriff of Stoneville knew that Deputy Archer couldn't be a part of this investigation. Archer would lament Charlotte's death and try to find closure by arresting the first suspect in Willa's murder. He'd go down a rabbit hole, spiraling out of control to make up for all the loose ends in his wife's murder, and that young temper of his would jeopardize the case.

As he replayed Charlotte Archer's case in his mind, Sheriff Bourbon watched the state trooper who was still on his phone describing the scene to whoever was on the other end of the call. A supervisor or detective, no doubt. Bourbon could only catch a few words of their conversation.

Deputy Archer stepped over Willa's body, and pulled her robe down slightly to examine the wounds, exposing her left breast.

Bourbon's focus turned to his deputy, but quickly looked away. He was still grappling with the notion that this was real and not some horrific nightmare he could soon wake up from. Seeing Willa as anything other than the spitfire beauty she was, rather than this empty corpse on the ground, still hadn't entered his reality.

Willa stared back at Deputy Archer. Something cold occupied her eyes that couldn't have been produced by the chilly autumn morning. The look on her face was hatred and fear, frozen in time, as if a clock had expired during her ordeal. Archer took her hand to inspect her fingernails. He checked the ropes around her wrists.

Charlie Archer looked into Willa's eyes. "Her eyes are green. Charlotte's eyes were blue. My God, the resemblance is uncanny." He sniffled and wiped an eye with his sleeve.

Seeing Charlie Archer break nearly propelled Sheriff Bourbon into a level of empathy he'd never experienced.

Archer barked through tears, "How could he do this? How could Cody Savage viciously murder his own wife, Sheriff? I swear—"

"Easy now, son," Bourbon stepped closer. "We don't know if Cody is the murderer here. We can't assume anything until we get more evidence. I've known Savage for—"

"Sheriff!" The state trooper shouted from behind Archer. He marched back to the scene, holding his phone against his chest so the person on the other end of the call wouldn't hear him shout. He yelled in a whisper, an aggressive finger pointing at Deputy Archer. "Sheriff, your man's not wearing gloves. Get him the hell away from the body before he contaminates the scene."

Archer covered the breast and jumped up, realizing his mistake. "Oh, gee, fuck. Boss, I'm sorry, I just got caught up—"

"I know, son. I know. It's okay, Arch." Bourbon put his arm around Archer's upper back and turned him toward his patrol car. "Go back to the station? I'll take point on this. The coroner should be here any minute to process the body. She'll probably need a DNA sample from you, though." He put a hand on Charlie Archer's shoulder. "I know this can't be easy, so just go. I've got this."

Archer glanced back once, and scuffled away in tears with his head down, like a kid who'd been scolded by a teacher. Bourbon watched him leave, not surprised by Deputy Archer's reaction, and had hoped the young deputy would lead the investigation. But now it was on him to find Charlotte Archer's hit-and-run driver and Willa's killer. The weight on his shoulders had doubled.

I've got this. I've got this.

He dialed Annabel Thompson's number to tell her they'd found her daughter in the woods, sparing her the details that Willa's hands were tied and she'd been stabbed to death.

Annabel had lost her voice on the other end of the line when she heard the news, and Bourbon could hear the phone fall out of her hands. She finally composed herself...a little.

"D...did...did she suffer?" Annabel asked between breaths.

"No," Bourbon lied.

"Was it Cody? It couldn't have been Cody, could it? Would he do this? Oh, fuck, Jefferson. Why did this happen?" He heard her crumble on the other side of the call.

"I don't think Cody Savage is capable of this. You know that."

"But people are talking, sayin' he's the only one who's been with her. She never left his side. I want that fucker hung by his balls! His balls!"

"Okay, hon, I'll do what I can. Listen, I've got to get the coroner on the line, and the DA, and make a few more calls. I'll swing by as soon as possible. Are you alone?"

"No. No, the Ladies Auxiliary is here, and the new pastor's coming by. Don't worry about me...you just go find the sonovabitch that did this."

"Okay, good. I'll call you again soon and get there as soon as possible."

I've got this. I've got this.

The second call was to Willa's husband, Cody Savage, who was now the only suspect in her murder.

2

GATE MONEY

Four years later.

Cody Savage experienced what life in prison was all about. Reform and repent of your sins—that was the lie that prison life promised, but he saw right through the bullshit. Prison life broke a man down, fed his ire toward the outside world, and fueled his anger.

Prison turned most rock-hard men into cold steel. There was little reform, especially for those inmates who believed they'd never see the outside world again. There were only men pretending to find God and men who knew they never would.

Because of his rage, Cody had almost killed another man four years ago. After his wife was brutally murdered, he was hounded by a reporter—he hated reporters—and the tenacious veteran of the press kept printing fake stories about Willa's death. Cody erupted in rage when the reporter showed up at his doorstep and had beaten him senseless. Since that incident, he'd been locked up in Dalton County Correctional Facility to "reform."

The rage was still there because no amount of therapy or incarceration could take that away. But Cody had learned to control the anger that sometimes struck like a viper. Age, not the prison system, had taught him how to stay in control.

He hadn't lost his temper in over a year—ever since Lefty Dumas left a number two under his pillow. That night, all 315 pounds of Lefty went to the hospital, and Cody spent three days in solitary confinement. Lefty was never a problem again, and the other inmates stayed clear of Cody. Hell, he'd even made a few friends while doing time.

Today, he said goodbye to those friends and exited the prison with nothing but the clothes he wore and about eighteen pounds of new muscle. He was no longer the skinny, twenty-five-year-old kid who went into Dalton prison for assault.

The heavy glass doors opened, and Cody stepped out and raised his eyes toward the sky. He wasn't sure why he looked up, but it felt natural and respectful to the universe that had returned his freedom. The doors closed behind him, like scissors cutting an umbilical cord and liberating him from his ugly mother. It was time for him to leave the womb and face this world reborn.

It was quiet outside the concrete walls amid the open yard and parking lots. The little sounds he did hear failed to echo off brick and mortar, and for a moment, Cody thought there was a problem with his hearing. The wind juggled a few dead leaves, bouncing them up and down off the coarse blacktop, and whisked them under a small blue car parked at the curb. The driver of the car honked and gave Cody a little wave. The now ex-con approached the car as the driver lowered the passenger-side window with the push of a button.

He was met by the biggest smile he'd seen in years. "Get in, son," the driver said. "The state is providing you a ride to the bus station."

Cody climbed into the passenger side of the vehicle. The little blue Toyota pulled from the curb and drove away from the concrete and steel bitch that had held Cody Savage for forty-four months.

Cody studied the building from the outside. It appeared so differently from this perspective. He hadn't seen the outside of Dalton County Correctional since the day he had been brought in. He decided the exterior view was much better than the interior and vowed never to see the inside again.

"Nice to be free?" The elderly driver asked, still smiling.

Cody said nothing for a moment. He swallowed hard and willed his eyes to dry, trying to be as stone-cold as a prison wall. His eyes stopped watering once the prison was out of sight, and nothing but tall trees filled his window's view. The sensation was overwhelming, and it took a few minutes before he could speak. Cold steel melted like ice cream. "Feels damn nice."

The driver grinned, remembering that feeling himself from twelve years prior. Now, it filled him with joy to see these young men freed from the constrictive grip of Dalton's walls. Unfortunately, he witnessed a large percentage of these men return.

The driver twisted the fan-speed control knob clockwise. "Be about twenty-five minutes to the bus station. Need anything before we get there? I'm gonna stop at the Sunoco Gas Station and grab me a coffee."

Cody considered all the merchandise inside the little store. Nothing seemed essential, and nothing in the store would make his day better. He wanted to get on the bus and go home, so he assured the driver he was content.

The driver pulled the vehicle into the gas station's parking lot. Cody waited patiently while the older man used the restroom, made a coffee to go, and picked out a box of mini donuts. When he returned to the car, he offered Cody a donut. "Bought you a bottle of water. Thought you might be thirsty."

"Thank you, sir."

"Thomas. You don't need to call me sir." He reached out with his right hand, and they shook.

"Cody," the passenger replied.

"Oh, I know who you are," Thomas said. "I remember reading about you a few years back. They say you killed your wife over in Stoneville. How come they didn't lock you up for that?"

"Well, because I didn't do it."

Thomas chuckled, "Every boy come outta this prison say he didn't do it. I suppose you're different, ain't that right?"

"Damn straight."

"And why should I believe that?"

Cody spun hard toward the old man. "I don't give a shit what you believe—"

Thomas cut him off with a hand gesture and a laugh. "I'm just messing with you, son. You best get used to questions like that, mmm-hmm. So far, that sheriff up there in Stoneville, what's his name? Bourbon. Sheriff Jeff Bourbon. Sounds like a damn drunk to me. Anyway, he ain't got any new suspects or evidence on who killed your wife."

"I know. The police think Willa's killer is locked away."

Thomas steered the car onto a busier road and didn't say another word for the next two miles. He kept his chatter to a minimum to concentrate on the heavy traffic. When they exited the highway, he resumed the conversation.

"A little advice?"

"You're going to give it to me anyway, right?"

The little car rolled to a stop at a four-way intersection. Thomas kept his foot on the brake and looked Cody square in the eye. "I don't have to go straight here," he said, nodding to the road ahead. "I can turn left, or I can turn right. Point is, we all choose our direction and the roads we take." That toothy smile returned to the old black man's face. "You, young man, get a fresh start. Fresh out of prison. Tell me which way to go. It don't have to be to the bus station. I can take you anywhere, or I can take you nowhere. All you gotta do is point."

Cody looked down each road that formed the four-way intersection and considered Thomas's suggestion. "So, you don't think I oughta go back to Stoneville?"

"Up to you. I don't give a rat's booty where you go, son, but Stoneville might be a step back in time, back to your past. That could be a good thing, but based on my experience, the past is a place where previous correctional residents, like you and me, should avoid. Ain't nothin' in Stoneville but the past, and you need to have a future. You know what I'm sayin'?"

Cody thought about Stoneville and the events that had led him to prison. He thought about his deceased wife and her unsolved murder. She was buried in Stoneville. His mind also drifted to memories of his best friend, AJ, and his old biker gang. He thought about the night the police arrested him, and the whole town cheered about it. No one wanted him back in Stoneville.

No one.

Even if Cody could prove his innocence, they would always look at him as a murderer, a convict, a nobody. He was none of those things, and it was time to set things right. Running from a fight never got him anywhere, but fighting for what was right was ingrained in his DNA.

"Straight," Cody nodded toward the windshield. "I've got some unfinished business in Stoneville."

*****

They drove for eight minutes without speaking another word. Thomas wished Cody had chosen differently. He could see that Cody was a fighter, which would ultimately bring him back to Dalton. Maybe Cody's next prison sentence would be another forty-four months, or perhaps he'd be a gray-haired old man by the time he became an ex-con for the second time. Thomas had seen it repeatedly: young men hell-bent on returning to their past, thinking they could pick up right where they left off. Young men who thought that time stopped while they were on the inside and never realized that their absence seldom made a difference to the world they'd left behind.

Thomas knew from personal experience that Cody wouldn't find his answers or solve his wife's murder. Stoneville wouldn't accept him as an ex-con suspected of murdering his wife. No one in town was going to give him respect.

Respect was for the dead.

They arrived at the bus station at 7:40 am. Cody jumped from the car, closed the door, leaned through the open window to thank Thomas for the ride and his words of wisdom.

Thomas nodded in return. "You're welcome, son. Good luck, and God bless, Cody. I hope I never see you again."

"No promises, but I'll do my best."

With that, the two parted ways, and Cody made his way inside the bus station. He stepped to the ticket counter, where a pretty woman in her fifties greeted him. The thin brunette smiled and instantly recognized that Cody had just left the prison system—his shyness was evident, as he kept his head down and his eyes up, aware of his surroundings. The muscles to form a smile seemed to be in a state of atrophy, but Cody tried anyway. He could feel his face contort to the right and felt stupid for the attempt.

The ticket agent leaned forward. "May I help you?"

19

"One ticket to Stoneville, please."

"One way or round trip?" She already knew the answer.

"One way."

"Going home, sweetie?"

"Yes," Cody replied. "Been a few years. I hope things haven't changed too much."

"This is northern New York," the ticket agent said. "Nothing changes around here but the color of the leaves, and that's only once a year."

Some of the atrophy wore off Cody's face. "What time is the next bus?"

"9:30."

Cody finished the transaction using a preloaded debit card provided by the state, which had just enough to cover the bus, a night in a sleazy hotel, if necessary, and some groceries. He took his ticket, thanked the nice lady, and told her to have a great day, then proceeded to a row of uncomfortable chairs to sit and wait. Despite the cleanliness of the waiting area, the air was musty, like someone had cleaned the floor with a moldy mop. A Coca-Cola vending machine hummed in the corner while fluorescent lights flickered annoyingly above the exit.

He leaned back and tried to get comfortable, but the plastic chair forced him to sit up straight. He resisted the chair's form, sat on the edge of the seat, and leaned his body backward. Comfort eluded him, but he was used to that.

A boy, not more than four years old, knelt on the floor across from him, racing a toy car in circles. The boy made a humming sound to mimic a car engine, although he sounded more like a motorcycle. It made Cody smile, but the boy failed to notice. The boy's mother, however, did notice Cody and glared at the ex-con with protective eyes. Cody gave her a respectful nod and looked away. The young mother held a phone to her ear, so Cody assumed she was on hold with whoever was on the other end of the call. The little boy spun in circles as fast as he could when he inadvertently let go of the small metal car, which sped across the freshly mopped floor, under Cody's legs, and disappeared under the vending machine.

"Uh-oh," the boy said.

"What happened?" Mom asked. She was wearing a worn-out base-ball cap and large-rimmed glasses. Cody guessed she was trying not to look attractive while traveling with her young son, without being pestered by creepy men in the station or on the bus. Despite her effort, she was still pretty.

"*Perdí mi auto, Mami,*" the boy replied as he ran to the vending machine.

He knelt and peeked under the Coke machine, but darkness shrouded the toy car. "I can't see it, *Mami.*"

The exasperated woman switched the phone to her right ear. "Well, I guess it's gone forever, isn't it? You need to be more careful with your things." The boy wasn't listening to his mother's lecture or accepting the car's fate. He reached until his shoulder was against the machine, but his tiny fingers fell short of his goal.

"Maybe this will help," Cody said. He held a broom and pointed the handle under the vending machine.

"Yeah," said the boy. "That will reach, won't it?"

"I think so."

Cody knelt beside the child and used a broom handle to sweep under the vending machine. Several dust bunnies, three Skittles, a bottle cap, and an earring came out with the toy car. Cody seized the car, blew the dust off, and handed it to its rightful owner.

"We got it," the boy proclaimed to his mother. "We got my car, *Mami.*"

"I see that. *Buen trabajo.* Did you thank the nice man for helping you?"

"Thank you, mister."

"No problem, little *amigo,*" Cody said. He took his place back in the uncomfortable chair, and the boy resumed playing. He was so free, so innocent and trusting.

The mother finally began speaking into the phone, and Cody couldn't help overhearing her conversation with a bank or credit card company. Her card had been declined when she tried to purchase her bus tick-ets, and now she and her son were stranded at the bus station with no money. The Uber driver who had dropped her off was gone, and she had no money for another.

"Mommy, when is the bus going to leave for Grandma's house?" The boy inquired.

"I'm not sure, honey," the mom lied. Cody could see the tears swelling in her eyes, and it was apparent she was trying to muster the will to break her son's heart.

Cody pulled the debit card out of his pocket—the gate money for his expenses. He'd hoped to have enough to get a cheap phone, but he knew he could get by without one. He handed the card to the beautiful stranger.

"What's this?"

"I'm sorry, but I couldn't help but overhear your conversation. I'd like you to take this."

Confused by Cody's gesture, she adjusted the ball cap that held her hair and pushed her glasses higher on her nose. She wondered what the catch would be.

"This is my gate money—from prison," Cody said. "The state gave it to me this morning when I left, and honestly, it's more than I need. There should be a $78 balance on the card. I hope that's enough—"

"No. No. I can't take your money."

"Truthfully, it's mostly taxpayers' money, so it's more of yours than mine."

"Still, don't you need this to get where you're going?"

"I already bought my ticket. Plus, I don't need a hotel. I'll be all right. I insist."

The mom teared up a little more. The kindness of a stranger, an ex-convict, overwhelmed her. She mouthed a thank you because she'd momentarily lost her voice. Cody didn't think much of it until he watched them board the 8:55 bus to wherever they were going.

"*Adios.*"

3

JESSE LEWIS

Jesse Lewis knows the taste of a gun barrel because he's put a pistol in his mouth five times in the last two years. The result is always the same—someone or something interrupts his suicidal intentions. On two occasions, he just lost the nerve to pull the trigger. Jesse assumes it's a sign from God that his life is too valuable to cut short, or maybe he's just too much of a coward to actually do it.

Once, Jesse drove his truck toward the Cascade River, hoping to plunge into the frigid winter water and drown. However, the ice covering the river was thicker than he had anticipated, and the truck just slid across the ice until it crashed into a group of box alders growing on an island the size of a basketball court. A family ice fishing witnessed the whole thing and towed him back to the mainland with their four-wheeler.

Jesse had even tried carbon monoxide poison to end his life by attaching a hose to his car's exhaust pipe. It should have been an easy and painless death as the fumes began to build inside his garage and rob him of oxygen. He hacked and coughed a couple of times and was ready to enter eternal sleep when the car's timing belt broke and the engine seized up and quit. He cursed God for a moment and Toyota for two hours.

Today was going to be different. Today, there was no stopping Jesse from silencing the voice—a woman's voice—and ridding himself of the evil urges that had plagued him for so long.

Today, Jesse Lewis would die.

Alone in the hayloft of his barn, Jesse tied a thick rope around a hemlock beam twelve feet off the floor. The rope hung down to form a noose at the bottom. Below the loop, Jesse placed an old sturdy table that was strong enough to support his weight. It had thick legs with mortise and tenon joints that would easily support his weight. The edges around the top were worn dull from generations of use, and had been there ever since Jesse purchased the property twelve years ago.

The hayloft was dim, but the evening sun shined through a pair of open dormer windows. Dust swirled in the beams of light as Jesse prepared the rope. A pigeon, perched upon a beam that crossed the wall, watched with nervous anticipation. She didn't seem to care about what Jesse was trying to accomplish but wanted him to finish and leave her barn. Her mate would return from time to time, landing noisily on the sill of the open window, but lacked the courage to stay and watch the human.

Jesse stepped onto the table and tested the strong rope with a good pull, and everything seemed capable of withstanding his weight.

Nothing could fail or stop him now. He slipped the noose into place and cinched the knot tight around his throat. He whispered a little prayer in case anyone else was paying attention.

Before he could take his ultimate step off the table, an engine whirred outside, and he could hear the loud vehicle slow down and turn up his driveway. He recognized the sound of a four-wheeler approaching his house. He removed the noose, jumped off the table, and peeked out the window of the northern gable.

Annabel Thompson steered the four-wheeler up Jesse's driveway, kicking up dust and gunning the throttle like she was on her way to a fire. She veered to the right, where his driveway formed a Y, and stopped in front of the porch and killed the engine, but she remained sitting on the four-wheeler. Thick black mud covered her boots and jeans up to her knees.

"Pastor Jesse!" Annabel yelled. She looked around and noticed Jesse's truck parked in the driveway. "Pastor Jesse? You home?"

Jesse looked skyward in frustration, only to see the perched pigeon staring back at him. He leaned out the window and waved his right hand. "Up here, Annabel. Everything okay?"

Annabel restarted the vehicle and shifted into drive. She gunned the throttle, accidentally slinging gravel from the driveway into Jesse's fresh-cut grass. When she reached the barn, she shut the ATV down again.

"Jesse, I'm sorry to bother you this late, but I was wondering if you could help me."

Annabel Thompson asking for help was a strange notion to Jesse Lewis. Annabel was well known throughout Stoneville. At the age of thirty-six, she assumed the responsibilities of the farm her husband had inherited and transformed it into a successful small business. The little farm consisted of sixteen head of cattle, a dozen chickens, four horses, and six alpacas. She also tended an acre garden where she grew the best vegetables in town. There wasn't another soul in Stoneville with Annabel's work ethic or determination. At forty-one, she served as a town councilperson, where she met Sheriff Jefferson Bourbon, and the two of them began a romantic relationship that was still going strong eight years later. Although they were rarely seen together due to their demanding schedules, everyone in town was aware of their relationship.

"Is everything all right, Annabel?" Jesse asked.

"I just came from the swamp, and my cow Pearl is stuck up to her belly in mud. I think she went in there to cool down, and now she can't get out." Pearl was more like a member of the family to Annabel rather than a farm animal. Before her death, Annabel's daughter Willa took care of the cow like a pet dog, and the big bovine didn't eat for days after Willa disappeared from her life. "I thought you'd be able to come down with your big tractor and give her a pull."

"Don't you have a tractor, Annabel?"

"Yes, but the dang thing's at Curt Davie's garage. He's welding some cracks in the tire rims for me."

"What about Dunkelberg's? Have you talked to Kip?"

"Kip's out of town. Having surgery on his back in Burlington."

"Jesper—"

"Gone to hunting camp for the weekend to work on the roof."

Jesse glanced at his Kubota tractor, with its front-end loader, and realized it had been a while since he had fired up the machine. "Sure.

I'll be right down."

"Oh, thank you, Jesse. You're a lifesaver."

Jesse just smiled.

"Oh, Jesse?" Annabel shouted from the ground.

"Yes?"

"Would you happen to have a good, heavy rope? Pearl's a heavy bitch, you know."

Jesse looked at the noose he had fashioned, which now dangled empty above the rustic table. "Yeah, I got a rope."

*****

Jesse removed the rope from the overhead beam, untied the noose, and threw it into the tractor's front bucket. Annabel gave him directions to locate the stranded cow and assured him that her farmhand, Connor Bayley, would meet him at the edge of the swamp to assist. Annabel was sorry she couldn't help the two men, but she needed to change her clothes and get to a community meeting. She was already running late.

Jesse assured her that he and Connor could set Pearl free and advised her not to worry. He followed Annabel's directions: half a mile up the road, turn left through the open gate; follow the trail past the cedars on the edge of the field; turn right at the tree stand; another 100 yards, you'll find Connor.

Jesse drove his tractor down the road to Annabel's farm. When he reached her property, he steered the four-wheel-drive machine through the woods until he saw a tall, blonde-haired man standing amongst the long shadows of the fading daylight. Connor leaned against a dying ash tree riddled with beetle holes and watched Pearl with amusement, taunting the cow with crude remarks, and Jesse was glad Pearl couldn't understand his words. Jesse stopped the tractor and turned off the diesel engine.

"You must be Connor."

"Hey."

Jesse expected a more mature salutation, but brushed it off as fatigue rather than disrespect. After all, it was Friday night, and Connor had been working since sunrise. He was probably exhausted and reluctant to finish the day in mud up to his waist.

Less than ten feet away, Pearl was in mud up to her belly. The big girl could have made it out on her own if it weren't for the embankment she had slid down. Now, the cow was stuck, and every attempt to climb out had created more mud. Jesse could see where she had worn the bank away, with nothing for her to gain traction, since the spring thaw had left the swamps full and the banks soft. Nature's gift of warm sun and fresh water had created the perfect trap for a clumsy cow.

"Quite a mess she's gotten herself into, huh?" Jesse said.

"I guess so. Stupid cow."

"Well, there's a rope in the tractor's bucket. If you can tie that around Pearl's chest, I think she'll come out without much fuss. You may need to get on the other side and coax her this way to keep her from going in deeper."

Cursing under his breath, Connor skidded down the bank and into the sticky muck while dragging the rope behind him. Jesse could hear the suction of the black mud with every step Connor took. The young man was used to getting dirty on the farm and wasn't bothered by the thick black mud. His protest was for the time they were wasting trying to free the hapless animal.

Connor pulled one end of the rope around the cow and tried working it through the mud and under her belly. Pearl, confused by the attempt, swung her head from side to side and let out a moan. Tired, hungry, and stressed from her entrapment, she inadvertently knocked Connor sideways, and he came up with an ear full of mud.

"Calm down, stupid bitch!" Connor yelled. He threw a fist, hitting Pearl behind the ear, and threatened her with his cocky attitude. "I'll turn you into beef fuckin' jerky."

"Take it easy, son—"

"To hell with that! You want to get down here in the mud and tie the rope, old man?"

Jesse ignored the question but not the insult. Although he was only in his mid-thirties, he knew that was probably ancient to a young adult like Connor.

Connor continued his rant. "I didn't think so. It's Friday night, and I've got better things to do, man. I told Annabel I couldn't work late. She's no smarter than this damn animal."

Irritated by Connor's insult of Annabel, Jesse was seething on the inside, but kept a calm demeanor. "Going out to party with friends?"

Connor ignored the question as he worked the rope through the mud under Pearl and started to tie it back on itself so it would cinch around her chest as the tractor pulled. "Aren't you dating that Poole girl? What's her name? Tabitha? Tammy?"

"Darcy," Connor corrected him.

"Oh. She came into church last week with a nice shiner on her eye. Swollen lip, too."

"Yeah, well, I don't know anything about that. She probably got high and passed out somewhere. She ain't much smarter than a fence post."

Jesse felt the heat rising under his collar. He gripped the steering wheel a little tighter. "Well, that's not a very kind thing to say about your girlfriend."

"She ain't my girlfriend. Bitch is a little pot-monger, is all."

Connor didn't seem to care that he was speaking to the church pastor or that Jesse knew almost everyone in town—most by name only. Most people respected the church's pastor, but Connor didn't seem to respect anyone—not him, Pearl, or even Darcy. Jesse kept pressing the subject.

"Yeah, I know. Darcy came to confession after church and admitted that she'd stolen some marijuana from her boyfriend, and he nearly broke her ribs with his boot. You know anything about that?"

Connor smirked in the same manner he had when he was watching Pearl struggle in the mud. "Some people get what they deserve. Anyway, she wasn't talking about me 'cause I'm not her boyfriend anymore."

Jesse stared Connor down, nodding his head to feign approval.

"Listen," Connor said. "I don't go to your church, and there ain't no steeple out here. So, mind your own damn business, and let's get this friggin cow out of the mud so I can go home."

Jesse wasn't sure how to react to Connor's attitude other than to block out his irritating voice with the sound of the tractor. He turned the tractor key, engaging the high-pitched starter motor. The engine sputtered quickly and then settled into a deep, rhythmic thump, thump, thump as the diesel engine idled. Then he pulled a hydraulic lever on the forty-seven-horsepower machine and lifted the front bucket skyward. The slack disappeared in the rope, and a confused Pearl bellowed in fright. Once the tractor supported some of her weight, Jesse threw the transmission into reverse and began backing up cautiously, pulling Pearl toward the embankment. Once the animal realized she was drifting toward salvation, she started digging her hooves into the ground to free herself of the swamp's grip. The smell of earth and diesel fuel filled the air as Jesse gave the throttle a little push to generate more power. All four wheels of the tractor tore through the sod, creating more mud but doing their job.

Pearl fell to her front knees, slipping in the mud, fighting for freedom. She got back up, dug at the dirt some more, and found the strength to hop to the top of the bank, leaving the black mud and Connor behind.

Pearl was free.

Jessie lowered the bucket to put slack in the thick rope and then shut down the noisy engine to allow Pearl to calm down. He climbed off the tractor and removed the thick rope from the bovine's ribcage.

Pearl turned away and wandered back to Annabel's field, meandering in and out of the deciduous trees and forgetting about the two men who had just saved her. Jesse watched her for a moment as she headed for home. He wondered if Pearl knew he'd saved her life. Did she even care? Maybe the old cow had wanted to die, and this was the only way she could think of to do it. Less than an hour ago, Jesse stood on a table with a noose around his neck and ready to rid the world of another sinner, but this good deed made him feel just a bit heroic—for a moment.

Connor, on the other hand, was now hip-deep in her place. "Now you gotta get me, I'm stuck," Connor bellowed. He wiggled in the mud, but the suction of dirt and water just grew stronger as he sank deeper. His legs were nearly out of sight.

Jesse coiled the muddy rope and tossed it into the tractor's front bucket.

That's when the pain began.

Immense pain crushed his skull like it was a dog's chew toy, awakening a part of Jesse he wished were dead. He closed his eyes for a moment and flashed back to Connor putting his boot into Darcy's ribs. It was a hazy scene playing out in his mind, but Jesse could see Darcy cowering with fright as Connor balled his fist and screamed in her face. Jesse couldn't make out the words, but the tone in his voice and the spit he emitted were full of rage.

This wasn't just a thought. It was his ability to detect and see the guilt of anyone, from their sins. "No, not now," Jesse whispered. The pain swirled around his brain, stirring his thoughts and clouding his judgment.

"Hey! You coming or what?" Connor shouted.

"Just a minute."

Connor wiggled in the mud once again, fighting a useless fight. He could see the pastor's agony and became more impatient. "You having a stroke, old man?"

Jesse pushed the pain aside and the tractor's throttle arm forward.

The sun had dropped behind the horizon, casting a dark blanket across the swamp. Jesse, impaired by the ultra-migraine crowning his skull, flipped a switch on the tractor, illuminating Connor and the marsh with the tractor's lights.

The noise of the tractor was unbearable to Jesse, who squinted to find Connor in the headlights. He drove the tractor forward anyway. Connor motioned with his hands, directing the operator who would pull him from the thick earth. Jesse followed the hand signals.

"Whoa!" Connor yelled. He raised his hand and kept a thumb pointed at his boots. "Bring the bucket down. A little more."

Jesse was gentle at the controls, pushing the lever to lower the large bucket on the tractor's front until Connor could reach the rope inside. He held the rope and flipped his thumb skyward to indicate to Jesse to lift the tractor's bucket.

Jesse reversed his movements, and two large mechanical arms began to lift the tractor's bucket. As the rope became taut, Connor began to rise from the earthly stew.

"A little more, and then start backing up," Connor shouted over the puttering engine.

The pain struck Jesse again, and with full force this time. The closer he got to Connor, the more intense the pain. He could sense the evil within the young farmhand, an evil that was innate and gruesome, and Jesse hungered to know what it was. The sinner was guilty of something worse than just smacking his girlfriend and selling marijuana.

The pain traveled down Jesse's neck, through his shoulder, and ignited the nerves of his arm. He shouted with agony, and Connor heard the howl.

"What the hell's the matter with you?"

Jesse's arm spasmed, and the bucket dropped six inches.

"Jesus! Be careful, you friggin' idiot. Pull me out!"

The pain kept rising, and Jesse's breathing became shallow.

"Pull me out!"

The bucket lowered slowly, and Connor sank back into the mud, screaming profanities at the pastor behind the tractor's controls. The screams intensified Jesse's pain, feeding it like a hungry dog.

Jesse couldn't take any more. He slammed the hydraulic lever downward. Hydraulic hoses filled with oil and the powerful cylinders on the machine pushed the bucket downward. The force of the tractor would have crushed even Pearl. Jesse watched Connor vanish under the mud, buried in the cool earth in an instant.

Balance.

The pain began to subside, and Jesse's mind returned to its previous state. The numbness in his arm subsided, and he regained his strength. He turned the tractor off and sat in silence. A light breeze from the west pushed the engine's heat, wrapping him in a blanket of soothing warmth. Only then did Jesse realize how cool the swamp had become as night encroached.

Three sounds carried across the dead swamp: a tom turkey gobbled from his roost 200 yards away, a cacophony of frogs chirped at high pitches, and the sound of Connor's hand protruding from the mud and slapping and pawing at the steel tractor bucket that pinned him down.

After one minute, there were only two sounds in the swamp.

*****

Jesse drove the tractor back to Annabel's farm and parked on the edge of her field. The lights were off at the house, and Annabel was still gone. Jesse knew the black truck parked beside the barn was Connor's. Annabel's other farmhand had left hours before, and Connor's Silverado was the only vehicle left. Jesse climbed inside, disgusted by the smell, the dirt, and the tacky stickers on the back window, and drove the truck away from Annabel's house.

He sent a text message to Annabel, "Pearl is free. Tractor ran out of gas. Connor drove me home. I'll stop by tomorrow to pick it up."

His stomach growled in protest after he sent the message, begging for food, which was the last thing on his mind a couple of hours prior. Now his body needed nourishment. He decided to go home, take a hot shower, and then drive to town for dinner.

32

4
EXTRA PICKLES 

Cody Savage hadn't visited his Uncle Bruce's house since his parents were alive. Christmas—no, it was Christmas Eve. He remembered sitting on the third step of the stairs to the second floor, unwrapping a few gifts from his aunt and uncle while the adults drank whiskey and soda, cheap wine, and schnapps. They were all loud, intoxicated with holiday cheer as they exchanged gifts and reminisced about old stories that only made half sense to a teenage boy. Cody unwrapped a remote-controlled car, although he'd already lost interest in such hobbies, and feigned appreciation to his aunt and uncle.

Cody and his younger brother Michael were the only children present. His two cousins, Jacob and Iris, were much older and didn't make it home that year. No one ever saw Iris after that winter. She married a man with money, and they moved to Arizona. She never spoke to her parents again. Jacob made a career in the Army, and this week would be the third anniversary of the helicopter crash that had claimed his life.

Cody and Michael were the only living relatives on his mom's side. Uncle Bruce was gone and put to rest next to Aunt Deb at the cemetery on Timberland Road.

While in prison, Cody received the news of his uncle's passing and, to his surprise, the inheritance of his aunt and uncle's house. It was a modest home built in the 1970s on a two-acre parcel on the edge of town. Cody's favorite feature of the house was that it overlooked the Cascade River that weaved through the county, flowing north toward Canada.

"Damn, Uncle Bruce," Cody whispered, standing in the driveway. After signing deeds, papers, and other forms that he didn't understand, he'd been dropped off by a lawyer who worked for the village. Taking the keys from his pocket, he made his way to the front door. There were boards on the windows, preventing break-ins or vandalism, but they failed to stop some jackass from painting graffiti on the porch. The village had done its best to paint over the words "Murderer" and "Killer" spelled out on the siding, but the text was still visible through the cheap paint.

I guess everyone in town knows who the new neighbor is. The transaction had been in the local paper under "Property Transfers," and the townsfolk weren't shy about protesting Cody's ownership of the home.

Still, this was better than a prison cell, and Cody was proud to call it home. The house needed a lot of maintenance, and Cody looked forward to keeping his hands and mind busy with the chores. He just needed to find a job so he could afford the renovations.

A light spring rain began to fall as Cody made his way to the covered porch wrapped around two sides of the building. The stair treads creaked as he climbed them with a hollow thump as each boot dropped. The top tread gave way and broke under his weight.

The railing around the porch leaned inward, and last year's leaves littered the deck. The lawyer had been considerate enough to give Cody a small pry bar, so he quickly went to work removing the plywood nailed over the entrance and windows on the first floor.

He worked the nails loose on one side of the plywood and pulled the entire piece off with his hands. The plywood might come in handy for repairs, so he set it against the deck railing for later use.

When he walked inside, he was surprised to find it relatively clean, but someone had taken a baseball bat to the drywall. Cody counted eight holes that would need repair. The air was thick and musty, and despite the rain, he opened a few windows to allow a cross breeze to freshen the house's interior. He was extremely grateful to find the utilities fully functioning when he flipped a light switch. A smile formed on Cody's lips when the ceiling fan turned on. More satisfying was the discovery of hot water at the kitchen sink. Hot water, electricity, and a roof over his head. He felt blessed and choked back a couple of tears. Having essential utilities lifted his spirit and his sense of freedom. He owed someone his eternal gratitude.

That someone pulled into the driveway.

AJ Timmons, Cody's best friend since seventh grade, exited his Dodge Charger. He was tall and thin, dressed in khaki pants and a T-shirt. The sunglasses covering his eyes were ridiculously overpriced, and his sneakers were as clean as the granite-colored paint of his muscle car. AJ always had a way with money and making things work out. Cody used to tease him, "You could fall in a pile of shit and come out with a hundred-dollar bill."

Overwhelmed at the sight of his friend, Cody dashed through the door and to the driveway. The two old friends shook hands, followed by a firm hug.

"Damn, AJ, it's good to see you."

"You too, buddy. I missed your ugly face," AJ said. "How's the new house look?"

"Much better than the old house."

"I'm sure it is. You going to invite me inside?"

"What's the matter? Your hair getting out of place in the rain?" Cody laughed. "Come on."

Cody led AJ to the door and gave him a quick tour of the first floor. There wasn't much to the upstairs except two bedrooms and a small bathroom. Cody flicked a light switch twice. "Somebody had the electricity turned on. Do you have any idea who that was?"

AJ knew he was busted but lied anyway, "Nope. Must have been the electricity elves."

"Sure, elves. Thanks, man."

"Well, no sense having a house you can't friggin' see in or take a hot shower, right? Besides, you're going to need them with all the repairs and cleaning you'll have to do." AJ backed up a little. "Is that mouse shit on the counter?"

"Yeah, I'll have to evict them."

"Jesus, let's get out of here," AJ said. "You hungry? Dinner's on me."

"Sure, I could eat."

"Good. I've got us a reservation at the steak house in an hour."

"The Blue Onion?"

"Hell yes. We can get a steak, lobster, or how about surf and turf? What are you hungry for?" AJ asked.

"Cheeseburger...With pickles. I could never get pickles in prison."

AJ felt terrible for what Cody had endured. He couldn't imagine what it must have been like to miss something like pickles. What else did he miss? There must be a list longer than the river that flowed past the house.

"Is The Mineshaft still open?" Cody asked.

"Hell yeah, buddy. Still the best burgers in the state, too," AJ said. Now he forgot about steak and lobster. "Alyse still works there, too. She's bartending tonight, I think."

"Who?"

"Oh, shut up. Like you don't remember Alyse. The girl from Louisiana with the green eyes and dark hair. Southern accent."

"Doesn't ring a bell. Come on; you can introduce me when we get there."

The duo got into AJ's car and made their way to the other side of town, AJ filling Cody in on all the changes in Stoneville, but that was a short topic. Then he explained some of the political issues that had come up since Cody's arrest. Both men seemed to ignore the one conversation that Cody was eager to talk about: not tonight, though. Tonight was a celebration.

Cody admired the Charger, but AJ didn't even try to impress him with the 700-horsepower engine. AJ was driving a $70,000 sports car, and all Cody wanted were some friggin pickles on a cheeseburger. AJ always admired Cody's ability to be satisfied without material possessions. Cody was a minimalist before being a minimalist was cool. He didn't desire extravagant things or try to keep up with the neighbors. All he ever needed was a fishing pole, a good song on the radio, and a bonfire.

But AJ had been taught that success was based on income. His parents preached to him about his grades and appearance, and that money equaled power, so he spent his life pursuing wealth rather than happiness. Although he earned more money than anyone else in town, AJ was modest about his work and income, but there was a void within him that no amount of money could fill.

Maybe that was the difference between the friends. Cody's parents were never present in his life, even when they were alive. Cody pretty much raised himself and his brother. Sure, his parents brought home food and made sure the boys went to school, but they never checked his grades or went to his sporting events. They seldom took a family vacation or went camping or fishing. Cody learned from an early age to be grateful for what he had, even if all he had was the ability to breathe.

They pulled into the parking lot of The Mineshaft. It was a unique establishment because a family could sit in the restaurant side while adults enjoyed the separate barroom. Cody and AJ each claimed a stool at the far end of the bar and weren't sitting for long when an athletic brunette walked into the bar from the kitchen. She balanced a large tray heaped with nachos and chicken wings and took it to a table behind the two new customers.

The brunette returned but didn't go back to the kitchen or behind the bar. She stopped behind Cody and threw her arms around him. "Hey, stranger! Welcome home."

"Hey, Alyse. How have you been?" Cody asked. He could see AJ's jaw hanging.

"Great. Living the dream, right?" She waved at the surrounding bar like Vanna White turning letters on Wheel of Fortune.

She yanked the bar rag off her shoulder and hit AJ with it playfully. "Hey, TJ, how are you?"

"AJ," he corrected, but he was sure she didn't hear the difference. "Good. I'm good."

She worked her way around the bar until she stood in front of the two men. She reached into a cooler tucked under the counter and presented Cody with a bottle of Busch beer.

"You remembered."

Alyse just gave him a wink.

"I'll just have my usual, too," AJ said. He took a fifty-dollar bill from his wallet.

"Fat Tire draft?" Alyse asked. Her face squished to one side in doubt.

A disappointed AJ corrected her. "Samuel Adams in a bottle. Winter

Lager, if you have it."

"Winter's over, sweetie," Alyse teased. "You can have a Summer Ale."

"How about a Cherry Wheat Ale?"

"How about a Summer Ale?"

"Summer Ale will be fine," AJ conceded.

Alyse was beautiful and confident, with green eyes that nearly glowed in the dark. Her skin was flawless except for one little scar on her eyebrow that appeared to be placed there on purpose. It was difficult to determine her heritage, but she could have belonged to many nationalities and represented them all well. She walked like a dancer to the other end of the bar to take another order while Cody and AJ both admired her stride.

"Damn, I've come in here once a month for five years, and she still can't get my name right," AJ pouted. He took a sip of his Sam Adams, satisfied with the light lemon flavor. "You've been gone what, four years?"

"Forty-four months."

"Forty-four months," AJ continued, "and she still remembers that you drink piss in a bottle."

Cody laughed at his jealous friend. "Maybe she remembers because Alyse is just like me."

"She drinks piss in a bottle, too? Or does she remember you because you have that face every woman notices?"

"No. Well, maybe, but Alyse appreciates the simple things," Cody said.

"Why? She must have tried all these beers," AJ waved to the glass coolers with the numerous brands displayed.

"Because it's cheap," Cody said. "She's trying to save money to go back to college and get her degree in Human Resources."

"Holy shit, you two had a thing together, didn't you?"

Cody just gave him a smile and finished his drink. He set it on the edge of the bar for Alyse to replace it with another. "We had a little thing."

AJ put some cash next to Cody's empty bottle. "When did this happen?"

"Forty-four months ago."

"Really?"

"Yup. It was a few months after Willa died. During the trial and through the whole mess, she kept me sane. And she drove me crazy."

"Did she visit you? In prison?"

Cody remembered the last time Alyse had come to Dalton Correctional to visit him. She sat on the glass panel's free side and spoke through a phone with tears in her eyes. They said their goodbyes, and then a guard escorted her out the door. That was three years ago. It was his idea that she not come back, not waste her life waiting for his release.

Alyse returned to the bar, switched the empty beers for a couple of full ones, and took their orders for a couple of cheeseburgers.

"With extra, extra, pickles," Cody pleaded. When Alyse left to turn in the order, AJ excused himself to visit the restroom. For the first time that night, Cody was aware of the environment. The same pictures adorned the walls from the last time he'd eaten here. There were black and white portraits of local miners who'd dug into the earth before color film was invented. There were also portraits of primitive elevators that took men to the bottom of the mines, images of carts full of talc, garnet, and sandstone, and dump trucks that grew larger with each year they were built. Oil lamps, headlights, shovels, picks, and other equipment were mounted on the wall freely and filled shadow boxes. Red lights reflected off faux stone walls, giving the bar the sense that it was deep underground. He loved this place.

As Cody's eyes scanned the room and the mining memorabilia, he could sense the other patrons' eyes watching him. There were whispers and pointing, which came as no surprise. This was how he had anticipated his homecoming. He wasn't welcome here in this town that couldn't forget. People watched him in silence, side-eying him and whispering across the tables. Cody contemplated leaving—but not before he had his burger with pickles. He'd waited a long time for this.

When AJ returned to his seat, Cody's focus narrowed as the two reminisced about some of the good and bad times they'd had at The Mineshaft.

The kitchen door squeaked open as Alyse pushed through with AJ's cheeseburger.

"The cook is bringing yours out, Cody."

"No problem," Cody said.

Six seconds later, the cook pushed through the door and placed the burger in front of Cody, dropping the plate hard enough that it nearly broke. "You order a cheeseburger, Savage?" The burly cook asked. He was at least three inches taller than six feet, and his arms were thick. Cody could tell that the muscles under several inches of fat were well-developed. He'd seen a thousand men in prison with the same build.

"With extra pickles. I ordered a cheeseburger with extra pickles."

The thick cook looked at the burger. "Well, let's make sure I didn't forget the pickles." He lifted the top bun to reveal a healthy number of bread-and-butter pickles. "Yup, there's the pickles, but I forgot one thing." He bent forward, spat on the burger, and then replaced the top bun. "*Bon appétit*, asshole."

Alyse gasped in disgust and disappointment, "Brody! What the hell?"

Brody stepped back and folded his arms, satisfied with himself.

Cody refused to give Brody the reaction he wanted. That's what the bully wanted. Instead, he grasped the burger with both hands, took an enormous bite, and then set the food back on the plate, giving the cook a thumbs-up. Speechless and defeated, Brody flipped his middle finger at Cody and returned to the kitchen.

Cody had been harassed in prison for forty-four months. He'd had his food spat on, stepped on, and topped with cockroaches. He learned that when he was hungry enough, the taste or look of food didn't matter. You just needed to get it into your body for nourishment to survive.

"Buddy, you don't have to eat that," AJ said. "We can go somewhere else."

"It's no big deal," Cody assured him. "This is my first day of freedom, and I'm not about to let that dickhead ruin it. Besides, I'd get the same treatment anywhere we go."

AJ lifted his beverage. "To the best burger in town." Alyse joined in with a drink of her own, and all three bottles clinked together.

Alyse took a sip of her beverage and then set the two men up with another round. "This one's on me, fellas," she said.

The two men occupied the barstools until midnight after switching to fountain sodas at eleven. They laughed with Alyse and a couple of other girls from out of town. Cody forgot about the burger incident and the other patrons who had watched him earlier. The alcohol in his blood made him forget about prison, and it felt good to feel like a free man again.

Tucked behind the jukebox and hidden by a large ficus tree sat a man with a splitting headache and a numb arm. Pastor Jesse Lewis didn't expect the pain to return so soon—not after soothing it with the farmhand's sins, but it hit him halfway through his order of chicken wings.

Jesse didn't understand this hunger that possessed him. He'd lie awake most nights wondering if he was doing God's work or if he was a pawn of the Devil. Either way, he hungered for the blood of sinners and then nearly drowned in the guilt afterward.

Connor Bayley had been a band-aid, relieving the pain for a few hours, but Jesse needed more. He needed to claim a sinner who would satisfy this demonic hunger for months or years. He required a sinner guilty of a more heinous crime, and he was looking right at Cody Savage.

A female voice invaded the pastor's skull, taunting him with the solution to ease his pain. "You can kill the ex-con, but at what cost? He may be more than you bargain for. There is another sinner here. Easier prey."

Jesse Lewis scanned the restaurant with his telepathic insight. He took a long sip of his beer while he observed the flock of patrons and answered the voice quietly. "They're all sinners."

5

SHERIFF BOURBON 

onnie? When the hell did the price of coffee jump twenty-five cents?"

"Two months ago, Sheriff."

Sheriff Jeff Bourbon stared at the menu at Tabitha's Diner. The sun was getting some traction and rose above the gray clouds that had brought fresh showers to Stoneville. The morning light peeked through the blinds, watching the sheriff's back as he sat at the counter. After scouring the menu, he removed his reading glasses and asked for the same thing he ordered every time he ate at Tabitha's.

Connie brought Bourbon's order out within forty seconds. She knew what the sheriff was going to order and had sent the ticket to the kitchen the moment she saw his patrol vehicle drive into the lot.

Bourbon was a man of habit, and he'd been coming to this diner every other day for fourteen years. He'd lived in Stoneville most of his life, after his parents moved here from out west. When the previous sheriff had passed away from a heart attack, Bourbon was elected to fill the vacancy. He'd run unopposed ever since.

Connie reached under the counter and pulled out a special dish with a sweetener that was just for her favorite customer, who only liked the green packets because the yellow packets left a bitter aftertaste. The gray-haired waitress poured a coffee, hid the salt from her customer, and grabbed a ketchup bottle. Sheriff Bourbon liked ketchup on his scrambled eggs.

"Where's the salt?" Bourbon asked the waitress.

"Fresh out of salt, hon," Connie replied. She wasn't sure which would elevate his blood pressure more—the fact that they were out of salt or that she was lying about it. It was a little ruse that Annabel had asked of Connie.

Bourbon began scouring a newspaper abandoned on the counter, even though its print date was two days prior and he'd already read it. He checked the obituaries, which he read daily out of respect for the dead. It made him think about how his own obituary would be written someday, and he hoped people would find it worth reading.

Bourbon was fifty-three years old, rugged in the body, with some gray in his beard and more on his head. His eyes were warm and brown, and people could hear the honesty in his voice, even if it was a bit gruff and candid. Bourbon didn't hash his words or his feelings. The man couldn't afford for Stoneville's residents to think he was anything less than unbreakable and relentless.

He was halfway through his scrambled eggs and ketchup when his only two deputies walked through the diner door.

Charlie Archer had been a deputy since the town voted to expand its police budget. He was a hot-headed man who loved how he looked in a mirror. Archer had an athletic build only because he valued the aesthetics more than the health of his body. Despite his narcissism, Archer was dedicated to his work, especially since his wife Charlotte was hit and killed while jogging near Cain Lake. So far, the only black mark on his record was contaminating the crime scene at Willa Savage's murder. Hence, the DNA samples from the scene were thrown out, and the case was never solved.

Deputy Eli Birchcraft had joined the department six months after Charlie Archer. He came highly recommended by Annabel Thompson when she was on the town council. No one had ever met the man, even though Birchcraft had been a resident of Stoneville for twelve years. Deputy Birchcraft had a degree in criminal justice but was working for a car dealership before getting the opportunity to join the Stoneville Sheriff's Department. Just past his thirty-fourth birthday, Birchcraft was built like a bulldog and just as loyal, with dark skin and a fading hairline. If Birchcraft had a sense of humor, neither Bourbon nor Archer had ever seen it. He took his job seriously and was hyper-focused during every shift.

Sheriff Bourbon was a mentor to both men, although he knew

neither would qualify to take his place. That's why he hadn't yet retired. He would give his career a few more years, and hopefully, a suitable candidate would run against him. But he'd never recommend either of the deputies who came and sat beside him.

Charlie Archer looked at himself in the stainless-steel napkin holder, fixing a strand of hair as the sheriff finished his toast. Both men had learned not to interrupt the sheriff during breakfast. His motto in the morning was, "If it's not on a plate, it can wait."

"Well, what is it?" Bourbon asked, wiping his chin with a paper napkin.

"Sorry, Sheriff," Archer said. "I just wanted to let you know who was spotted last night at The Mineshaft."

Bourbon gulped his orange juice and pulled a toothpick from his shirt pocket. "Cody Savage?"

Archer side-eyed Birchcraft and returned his focus to Bourbon. "That's right, Sheriff. How'd you know?" His voice was too high for a man his age, and he always spoke so fast that Bourbon only understood half of what he was saying. If Archer weren't a deputy, Bourbon would swear he was on speed.

The sheriff turned the newspaper over and pointed to an article with his toothpick. "You boys should read more."

Archer leaned toward the paper and read the headline aloud, "Suspected Killer/Husband To Be Released."

"That was two days ago," Birchcraft said. "Why didn't you warn us Savage might be back in town?"

"Because I didn't think he'd be dumb enough to come back here, that's why. Look, there's nothing we can do about Cody Savage being in Stoneville. He's done his time for one crime, and he's never been proven guilty of murder, so as far as we're concerned, it's just another day in paradise, all right, boys?"

Deputy Archer slapped a hand on the paper. "We can't just let that sonovabitch walk around like he's done nothing wrong." He lowered his voice so the other seven patrons wouldn't hear him. "I was at the crime scene with you, Sheriff. As soon as I saw Willa dead, I knew who killed her. We know that bastard is guilty. We need to find a way to prove it."

"We've tried, Arch. The state investigators tried. The federal investigators tried. No one has turned up any evidence against Savage." Bourbon sipped his coffee and thought about the Savage family. Stewart Savage, Cody's father, was intelligent, but his drinking had kept him from stable employment most of his life. When he wasn't working, he performed odd jobs. When he was employed, Stewart drank away most of his earnings. Every Friday, he'd drive down to the grocery store and purchase an overpriced 30-pack of beer. Stewart would return to his garage, and no one would see the recluse until Sunday evening. He spent most of the weekend working on his cars and old machines. If it had a motor, it had his full attention. His two boys took a back seat to all things mechanical.

Ida Savage was a mean and nasty woman, and truthfully, probably where Cody inherited his temper. Despite hating children, Ida was a part-time school bus driver and made extra money by sewing. After the boys had eaten dinner, Ida would bring a plate of food to the garage and sit with her husband while he devoured his meal. Sometimes, she would stay out there for a few hours, watching Stewart work, giving him an extra pair of hands, and smoking her Salems.

Sheriff Bourbon remembered getting the call the night Stewart and Ida had died. Cody must have been about fourteen, and the younger boy—Bourbon forgot his name—was nine.

It was a chilly September night, and all the garage doors must have been closed. Ida Savage sat in a lawn chair watching her husband work on an old generator he'd bought at a yard sale. She was sleepy and eventually passed out in the chair. Stewart checked the engine, making minor adjustments to the carburetor, and replaced the fuel line and a rusty gas tank. He had finished his ninth beer when exhaustion had taken its toll on the mechanic. He idled down the generator and listened for any knocks in the engine or skips in the timing. Taking the empty chair beside Ida, he slipped the burning cigarette from her still hand and finished the last few drags, listening to the generator purr behind him. As the old motor hummed a single-cylinder lullaby, Stewart drifted off to sleep. The small engine sang for an hour until it burned through all the fuel in the gas tank and stalled, but not before it filled the garage with poisonous carbon monoxide gas that killed the husband and wife as they slept.

One mystery always surrounded the Savages' deaths: Why would Stewart Savage, a knowledgeable mechanic, leave the garage doors closed with an engine running? There were rumors, of course, that somebody closed the door. Some people blamed Cody Savage for that, too. Other people gossiped that it was a double suicide, which seemed more likely.

Bourbon snapped back to the present. His two deputies exited the diner and waited for him to meet outside. Bourbon presented a debit card to Connie, and the hardworking waitress snatched it immediately to ring up his bill. When she handed Bourbon back his card and receipt, she grabbed his hand. "Jeff, that sonovabitch doesn't belong in Stoneville. He's a monster, and who knows what he'll do next."

"He's a free man—"

"Find him! Send him packing." She lowered her head and whispered, "Put a bullet in his damn skull if you must, but don't let him stay here. Do it for Annabel."

The old sheriff was speechless. He saw the fear and rage in Connie's eyes and wondered if she was right. Bourbon wasn't worried that Cody might be dangerous. He wasn't afraid of the hot-headed man who had returned to Stoneville. What he feared was how the town's population would react when they found out. Luckily, most people read only obituaries and classified ads. The little article tucked in the back of the paper was barely noticeable, but now that Connie knew, the news would spread like wildfire.

The townsfolk were about to lose their minds, and Bourbon would be caught right in the middle of it.

He needed to be proactive: maybe visit Cody and tell him to keep a low profile. Maybe warn him to leave because his life was in danger. Maybe tell him there was no future for him here. Tell him he's stupid to return to a town where he's the lead suspect in a murder. But that was a lot of maybes.

The sheriff's thoughts were interrupted by Deputy Archer, who stood by his patrol car holding his cell phone, with a look of horror on his handsome face and waving urgently to Bourbon. Bourbon pushed the diner door open, stepped into the sunlight, and met his senior deputy halfway across the small parking lot.

"What is it, Arch?"

"I just got a call from a girl who works in the kitchen at The Mineshaft."

"Yeah? You gonna be a daddy?" Bourbon joked.

"No. She called me about Brody Sherwood."

"The big guy who cooks there?" Bourbon asked. "What did he do this time?"

"He died. Murdered at The Shaft. They just found his body behind the dumpster."

"Jesus. Isn't he a member of the Road Barons?" Bourbon asked.

"The biker gang?" Birchcraft added. "Think they had something to do with this?"

"No," Bourbon said. "But they won't take this lightly. If someone killed one of their members, then they're going to be on the warpath—blood for blood."

"Frig, who would be stupid enough to mess with one of the Barons?" Birchcraft asked.

"Savage, that's who. He used to be a Road Baron before he got married."

The thought made Bourbon sick.

"It's been years since we've had a murder in Stoneville," Archer said. "This is no coincidence, Sheriff. Savage is connected to this somehow. I say we go get that piece-o-shit."

Bourbon raised a hand to calm his deputy. "We can't jump to conclusions, Arch.

"And Savage was at The Mineshaft last night, too," Birchcraft reminded them.

"Let's get over there." The deputies started for their vehicles. "And boys—"

Archer and Birchcraft stopped in their tracks and waited for the instructions they knew were coming.

"Not a word to anyone, ya hear?" Bourbon went to his truck and watched his deputies peel out of the parking lot. He dialed a number on his phone and waited for Annabel Thompson to pick up.

"Hello?" Annabel answered.

"Hey, hon, it's me."

"I know. Caller ID, remember? How's your morning going?"

"I've had better. Listen, there's been a murder in town."

"Oh, my goodness!" Annabel exclaimed. "Are you kidding? Who?"

"I can't discuss the details right now," Bourbon answered. "I'm on my way there now. I just wanted to call and let you know...he's back."

"What? Who?" She knew as soon as she asked. "Savage? Are you sure?"

"Yes. Just keep an eye out and let me know if he comes around the farm. I don't think there will be any issue, but just in case, keep your gun handy."

"My gun? Bourbon, don't you think you're overreacting?"

"Please."

"Okay. Okay, I will."

"I don't know what Savage is capable of doing. It can't be a coincidence that there's a murder in town the very same night he comes home." Bourbon checked his mirrors out of habit. "I'll stop out to the farm this afternoon, but I may have to cancel our dinner plans."

"Okay, I understand. Be careful."

"I will. Love you."

Bourbon threw the Jeep truck into gear and sped off to the murder scene. He wondered how long it would take before the town went crazy. How long until the press had a field day?

But his biggest concern was where the hell was Cody Savage now?

6

THE PURGE

Pastor Jesse Lewis was one of the few people to experience Cain Lake's secret. The lake had a supernatural power that could not be explained, affecting some the minute the water engulfed them. If fully submerged, the swimmer's darkest emotions and psychological demons were intensified. For Jesse, the lake exacerbated his desire to rid Stoneville of its sinners. He didn't want to just exorcise the sins. He wanted the sinners to suffer and cease to exist. That was the only true way to cleanse the town.

He stepped into the cool waves that seemed to disappear into the sand. The water was dark and empty except for a few minnows that played in the shallows. But once he stepped a little deeper, the lake revealed its true self, its secret power that Jesse had discovered almost three years ago. Little organisms of light swam through the ripples and danced around Jesse Lewis's ankles. Jesse was almost up to his knees in Cain Lake with the gentle waves kissing the bottom of his rolled-up pant legs, but he didn't care. He scrunched his toes into the gritty sand that supported his weight and watched the little glowing bugs swirl in the cool water. The hungry minnows darted in and out of the shallows, chasing the lights that were impossible to catch.

Jesse watched the minnows and lights play like school children in a chaotic game of tag. He wished he knew more of the lake's history. The water of Cain Lake had collected from the mountains for eons. The ancient lake was settled in the late 1700s by a French commandant, Laramie Cain, and his Iroquois bride. The couple built a school and a church and filled their home with nine children. The lake population grew, but when two of Laramie Cain's children were murdered, people

51

began to move away. Laramie caught the slayer and punished him for his sins. He rowed a small boat to the middle of the lake with the killer, hands and feet bound, and threw him overboard.

Jesse wondered if the madman had infected the lake or if the lake had infected the man. The latter seemed the obvious answer.

Cain Falls migrated north, closer to the mines, and was renamed Stoneville after Morris Stone, the town's civil engineer and biggest philanthropist. Laramie Cain, his wife, and his murdered children have long been forgotten.

Jesse Lewis was one of the few people who knew the true history of Cain Lake. He studied that history when he'd taken the pastor position at the church perched on the hill overlooking the water. Now, he stripped all of his clothes from his body and tossed them on the wooden dock. He slowly made his way deeper, hesitating when the cold water reached his testicles. He turned around and let himself fall backward. The lake swallowed him, and the little blue lights followed.

The Purge, as he called it, had begun, as the lake pulled the evil energy away, feeding on it, leeching it from his skin like a sponge.

The little blue lights swarmed the pastor as he swam for twenty minutes.

As Connor Bayley and Brody Sherwood's sins were cleansed from his body, a dark cloud left his mind. Normalcy returned, and it was intoxicating. He passed the end of the dock, swam over a row of seaweed, and into the deep, chilly water. He laughed out loud as he splashed in the water and felt better with every stroke. He was free of the sins he'd eaten.

He swam further.

It wasn't until he started to swim back to the church that he noticed her—a woman, alone, walking with a tall stick and a tattered backpack. She watched Jesse approach the shore as she sipped water from a thermos. She was sweating and dirty, so Jesse ascertained that the older lady had been out here for days, maybe even weeks.

Without embarrassment, Jesse strode out from the lake dressed the same as the day he was born, with the addition of a few tattoos. He was giddy with freedom and wondered if the woman was as insane as he.

"Good morning," Jesse said.

"Morning, Pastor Jesse," the woman responded.

Jesse wasn't surprised she knew his name. He'd been in the local newspaper, *The Stoneville View*, many times. "May I help you with something, ma'am?"

"Just passing through. You haven't seen a medium-sized black dog with pointy ears, have you?"

Jesse scratched his left ribs with his right hand. "No, sorry. We could post some fliers at the church if you'd like, though." He nodded to the white chapel on the hill.

"Hm." The woman removed a handkerchief from her jacket and wiped her brow and neck. "No, thank you for the offer, son. That will be okay. I'll just keep circling the lake until I find him. He don't usually go too far unless he gets a scent. Then he's off like a jack rabbit."

She was dressed in a parka and rubber boots, which were more appropriate for fall rather than June's heat. Jesse could see the shirt under the coat was flannel, and a pair of gloves stuck out of her pocket. The backpack looked quite full, and Jesse contemplated that she might be homeless.

"Do you live around here?"

She ignored the question as if it were irrelevant. "Who the hell swims buck naked in Cain Lake?" There was a little giggle in her tone.

"You'll have to pardon my jubilation, ma'am. I'm sorry," Jesse laughed. "I just got a little carried away. I didn't mean any harm." He scrambled to the dock and began to dress.

She raised a hand and smirked, "Aw, don't go apologizing on my behalf. I don't own a bathing suit myself, so I mean, I do the same. Maybe we're the only ones, but damn, it sure is exhilarating."

Jesse slipped his pants over his thighs, skipping his underwear completely to speed up the dressing process."

"Don't get dressed on my account, Pastor. I didn't mean to interrupt."

"Oh...No, you didn't inter—"

"The purge. I didn't mean to interrupt your purging. You gotta let the lake feed off your sins, or it will poison ya."

A knot formed in Jesse's throat. How does she know? He grasped for an excuse to leave and kept his clothes close to his body. He gazed towards the woods, wondering if he was being recorded. He took three steps backward as if he had someplace to go. Overhead, a crow flew by and landed in a dead evergreen tree that was void of any needles. The corvid perched above the woman's head. Jesse could sense the bird's curiosity as it cawed and flapped, all while keeping an eye on the half-naked pastor. The strange woman paid no attention to the creature.

"The purge?" Jesse said.

Her thin, dry lips formed a decadent smile that revealed perfect teeth, although stained with age. She took a few steps closer, swinging the six-foot walking stick like a shepherd following her flock of sheep. She stepped forward twice to catch up with it. "It's okay, son. I've been here since the beginning. I know what this lake can do and what it can make you do. What you're experiencing—it's nothing new."

Jesse finished dressing. The senior wanderer seemed lucid, but she was talking crazy. Could it be that others felt the same as he? Did Cain Lake inflict pain and suffering on its victims so they would murder the guilty and feed the energy back to the lake?

"Well, I'd love to stay and chat, but I'd best be going," the woman said. "I'll see you again sometime, Jesse Lewis."

"How do you know my name?" Jesse asked. He'd met most people in town but couldn't recall this woman. "Do you have friends in the church?"

"No," she nearly snorted when she laughed at the notion. "I don't have any friends, and I don't go to church." She stated the last sentence as if she were trying to win an argument.

"Well, I hope you change your mind someday."

"I won't. This lake is my church, my peace. It's my home." She pointed her walking stick from west to east to encompass the entire lake.

"So, you come here to what? Meditate? Or pray, maybe?"

She laughed a little. "No. No, I come to purge, just like you, Jesse. I bathe in the lake's power, and it gives me strength I cannot explain. When I'm submerged, these mystic waters invigorate me, and I am reborn." Her eyes were closed, her head high, and she looked at peace.

Jesse understood what the woman was referring to, but still felt that she was bat-shit crazy. He, too, felt the power of Cain Lake. It began three years ago, when he started performing baptisms in this very spot. He thought using the lake to baptize his congregation would be more memorable than just a few drops of water at the altar. With each baptism in the lake, Jesse could hear Cain Lake calling to him, permeating his skin and diluting his blood until he felt as though lake water filled his veins.

"You know who I am. May I ask your name?" Jesse asked.

"I've had many names," she sighed. "But now I go by Flesti. Flesti Thaed."

Flesti walked to the shoreline and gave the fluid a swirl with her hand, which produced a blue glow that the pastor recognized. She took a sip from her hand and then shook it dry.

She said goodbye and started to march east toward the woods. She stepped lightly, her powerful strides indicating that her legs were strong and durable. Jesse guessed Flesti walked around this lake for a thousand miles and wasn't ready to stop yet. The crow sprang from its perch and flew in the same direction, skimming along the water and ascending to the trees. Jesse watched them leave until they were out of sight, merging into the dense flora.

The dock creaked and rocked under his weight as he sluggishly walked to the end over the water. He peered into the water. An image of himself stared back while minnows darted away. The blue lights had drifted into the deep and were consumed by the dark. All the sins that Jesse had stolen had satisfied the lake, for now, but Jesse knew it wouldn't be long before it hungered again. The lake would compel him to kill again and lure him back to the water for another purge. It would be an endless cycle.

As he pulled on his right shoe, a morbid realization formed in his mind: How many more people had, or were, purging in Cain Lake?

7

RIDE AGAIN

The pounding on the door at eight a.m. vibrated right through Cody's skull. He was awake, sitting at the kitchen table. The effect of last night's impromptu celebration at The Mineshaft left him with a thick head and thirsty mouth. He poured hot water into a ceramic cup that already had a heaping teaspoon of instant coffee grinds. He ignored the obnoxious knocking until he had the right amount of cream and sugar in his cup, and then he approached the door while stirring.

"Jesus, just a minute. I'm coming." Cody stopped as he passed a window and saw Sheriff Bourbon's blue Jeep parked in his driveway. He removed the spoon from the coffee, set it on the windowsill, and opened the front door.

"Morning, Sheriff Bourbon," Cody said. He made it obvious he was faking his hospitality.

"Savage," Bourbon nodded. "I need to ask you a few questions." Ever since Cody was a teen, Jeff Bourbon had a distaste for the boy. Whenever he spoke to Cody, he referred to him as 'Savage,' as if it were a descriptor rather than a name. He never really approved of Cody and Willa's marriage, but he knew the couple were madly in love and perfect together.

Cody preferred to close the door but remained polite. "Come on in. What can I do for you?" He opened the door wide and backed away. "Would you like some coffee? It's some shitty instant brand, but the water's still hot."

"No. I've already had two cups this morning. This isn't a social visit, anyway." They both knew that.

Bourbon did a quick inspection of the interior of Cody's new home.

It was somewhat of a shit hole, but primarily because of the neglect it had suffered since the previous owner had died. The house had good bones, and the sheriff considered what it would take to renovate it for rental property.

"Nice place," Bourbon said. "Interested in selling? Has the potential to be a steady income stream."

"Sorry, it's not for sale." Cody leaned against the counter and sipped his hot drink.

A mouse scurried across the living room floor, bringing Bourbon back to focus on the reason for his visit. He took mental notes of the home and its occupant: no dishes or appliances on the counter, no furniture except a single folding chair at a two-person table, and no food visible other than the jar of cheap coffee.

When he finished surveying the house, he quickly sized up the man facing him. Cody was not the same person the sheriff had arrested for trespassing as a kid or the same one he had pulled over for doing 118 mph on a motorcycle. Cody had filled out since going to prison. He stood shirtless, every muscle showing. Cody wasn't a big man, but it was a mistake to underestimate his strength and skills in a fight. Bourbon recalled an old memory of when he had to break up a fight between Cody and three rival players during a high school basketball game. At half-time, Cody didn't follow his team into the locker room. Instead, he provoked a few players from the visiting team because they were throwing cheap elbow shots at a small guard. Bourbon stopped the fight before anyone was seriously injured, but he remembered being mostly concerned about the kids on the rival team getting hurt.

The memory made Bourbon smile for a moment. He loved watching high school basketball teams play. Cody's voice interrupted his memory.

"Did I do something wrong, Sheriff?"

"Where were you last night, Savage?"

"Mineshaft—with AJ Timmons. Had a burger with extra pickles and extra spit. Service has gone to shit since I was there last."

"Brody Sherwood," Bourbon said the name and waited to gauge Cody's reaction.

"What about him? 'Cause I'd like to catch that asshole in a dark—"

"He's dead, son. You're not going to catch him anywhere."

Cody went silent. He looked out the window, walked over to the counter, and set his coffee cup down. "That's too bad," his tone sincere. "Is that why you're here? You think I had something to do with Brody's death? That I killed him?"

"I didn't say he was killed."

"No, but why else would you be here? An ex-con comes back to town, goes out for a burger, and kills the man who spits in his food, right?"

"Brody spat in your food? Jesus, I might've killed him for that," Bourbon said. "Look, you've got to admit, it's kinda suspicious. We haven't had a murder in this town—"

"I know. Since Willa. I know. And don't you think for a moment that I've forgotten?" Cody said, grinding his knuckles into the counter. "Not a day goes by that I don't think about her."

"I know. Me neither. And I don't know how Annabel manages to maintain such a positive attitude, but she thinks about her daughter every day as well. She'll grieve until we know the truth. Only then will she be at peace."

"The whole town thinks I killed her." Cody stared out the window, hoping the bright light would burn up the tear forming on his eyelid. It didn't. "I loved her. She was my everything."

Bourbon was silent.

Cody continued, "I came back here to find the truth. I'm going to find the piece of shit that murdered my wife, Sheriff."

"And then what? What will you do when you find him?"

"I'm not sure, but you'll probably be the first to know."

"Savage, we've been looking for years—"

"Have you?" Cody interrupted. "Have you been looking, or did you assume the murderer was locked up in Dalton?"

"The whole town thinks you're behind your wife's death, Savage. You're not welcome here." The sheriff jingled his keys and looked at his watch. "But that's not why I'm here. I'm here to eliminate you as a suspect in Brody Sherwood's homicide. You don't have any idea what happened last night?"

"No."

"Did you see anything unusual or suspicious?"

"Other than him spitting in my food? No."

"Did you know he was a member of your old biker gang?"

"Yeah, I think he'd been a Baron for about a month prior to my exit."

"You mean when you were kicked out?" Bourbon asked. Cody didn't respond to the correction.

Bourbon was taking notes on a small notepad. He paused, making sure he was asking the right questions. "Did you see anyone else from the Barons there last night? At The Mineshaft?"

"No. But Alyse told me Brody was no longer in the Barons. He was too much of an asshole and had the wrong impression about what they stood for. Brody Sherwood hid his criminal past—armed robbery, stolen property, narcotics."

"Is that a problem for the Road Barons? Don't they all have shit to hide?" Bourbon was curious about Cody's relationship with the old gang.

"Nothing major. A lot of the guys have priors, but mostly misdemeanors and petty shit. All in all, they're a bunch of good Samaritans."

Bourbon knew Cody was telling the truth about the Road Barons. The gang was formed primarily of older men and women who did charity rides and promoted local businesses that needed help. They liked their drinking and weed, but if a Baron had a run-in with the law, it was probably for excessive speed or an expired motorcycle registration. The gang did more good than harm for the community. However, everyone knew that a few members had hidden agendas and found creative ways to make money, so they didn't have to work their day jobs.

Bourbon was standing back in the open door. There were fresh tire tracks in the muddy driveway. "Who dropped you off last night? BJ Simmons?"

"AJ Timmons."

"AJ Timmons," Bourbon repeated as he printed the name. "He a Road Baron?"

Cody laughed at the notion. "No. AJ keeps to himself mostly. But the Barons would be lucky to have him. AJ's the kindest, most benevolent soul in Stoneville. Other than Annabel Thompson, of course."

"You and AJ were together all night? Until he dropped you off?"

"Yup. About 12:45."

"Were you intoxicated?" Bourbon knew he wasn't going to get the truth this time.

"Nope. Gotta stay sober."

The sheriff stepped onto the porch and tapped his pen against the pad. He looked around again and finally put the notepad in his shirt pocket. "I guess that's all I have. We'll be keeping an eye on things around here, son."

"Good. Maybe you'll catch the little dicks that spray-painted my house."

Bourbon smirked. "Keep to yourself and stay out of trouble. If I have any more questions about Brody Sherwood's death, I'll be back."

"No problem. I'll be glad to help."

"And one more thing." Bourbon stepped down on the first tread of the stairs and turned to face Cody. "Keep that temper of yours in check. I've seen your blind rage when you get pissed off. I don't ever want to see it again in this town. Am I clear?"

"I'm not the man I used to be, Sheriff."

"I've heard that from every ex-con I've ever met. I know you want to believe that, but there's an innate animal instinct in you, Savage. Your dad had it. Your mom had it. You have it."

With that, Cody closed the door, and Bourbon drove away. Cody knew that once Brody's homicide became public knowledge, the whole town was going to be out for his blood, again.

After a shower, he threw on some not-so-clean clothes and headed for the streets. He hoped to find some work and groceries before coming home that night. AJ had been generous enough to give him a little cash, but he wanted a job, not handouts.

He left the residential neighborhood and meandered along the outside of the business district, following broken sidewalks and cutting through alleys. He wore a light hoodie and a pair of cheap sunglasses that he'd found in a drawer. It was a little cooler today, and he enjoyed the weather and freedom. Every section of town, every building, and every park brought back memories from his teen years. He'd lost touch with many friends over time, and all he had now were memories of this town—and AJ. He was thankful for AJ, who never judged him and never questioned his innocence regarding Willa's death.

Cody passed his old employer's office, only to find the construction company was gone. "Probably went bankrupt, you friggin crook," Cody said as if his old boss could hear. There were a couple of other construction companies in town, and perhaps one of them needed a certified electrician.

By noon, Cody had covered several miles and visited twelve businesses. He completed one application but struck out everywhere else.

By 1:30, he surrendered to his stomach and stopped at Five Guys for a burger and a cream soda. Sitting at a table outside, he heard a rumble in the distance. The sound grew louder and closer, and as he finished his cheeseburger with extra pickles, three Harley-Davidson motorcycles circled the building. They parked in front of the restaurant, taking as many parking spaces as possible. Cody recognized two men before they even parked—Levi Thompson and Jeremy "Cricket" Morrison. The third rider turned out to be a woman. Her gender was difficult to discern until she removed her helmet. The Red Baron leather jacket she wore hid her curves.

Levi Thompson dismounted the thick black motorcycle and removed his helmet and sunglasses. A gray T-shirt stretched around his chest and shoulders, swollen from years of hard labor on the farm and hours at the gym every other day. An eagle, printed on the front of the shirt, spread its wings wide. Levi wasn't any taller than Cody, but he always wore motorcycle boots with thick soles that added almost two inches to his height. He was an imposing figure.

Levi was Annabel Thompson's son and Willa's brother. Cody and Levi were close before Willa died, but for six months following her death, Cody never saw Levi. Instead, he spent every minute looking over his shoulder, waiting for Levi to put a knife in his back. That moment never came, and Cody wondered why. Why didn't Levi avenge his sister? Maybe he knew Cody was innocent. Perhaps Levi wanted Cody to live in fear, constantly checking his reflection on shiny surfaces like cars and windows to ensure Levi wasn't behind him. Maybe he wanted Cody to go insane from sleepless nights and paranoia.

Levi and Cricket entered the restaurant without noticing Cody, who sat outside on the red round table. Or, maybe they did notice and paid no attention to the former Red Baron. Cody quickly tucked his empty burger wrapper in the greasy paper bag it had been served in and dumped it into the trash can beside his table.

The sight of his ex-brother-in-law stung Cody's soul more than he had anticipated. He missed being a part of the Road Barons. There was only one way he would ever find his way back among their ranks. He would have to find the truth about Willa's murder and prove to Levi that he didn't kill his sister. He'd have to find the real killer, and then, maybe, he could ride again.

8

CIVIC DUTIES

Brody's body lay on the ground partially behind The Mineshaft's dumpster. He'd fallen against the building's wall, and his limp body had twisted as it dropped. The large metal dumpster blocked the view of Brody's body from the back door, and any employee taking the trash to the large metal bin wouldn't have seen the body in the dark. A homeless man and his dog, scouring the dumpsters for food that morning, found the dead cook. The man flagged down a passing Uber driver, who called the sheriff's office to report the crime.

At The Mineshaft, Sheriff Bourbon let Archer and Birchcraft do most of the initial investigating while he went to interview Cody. Now, Bourbon sat in his vehicle after hanging up with Annabel and watched the two deputies work. He thought about the building's layout, the darkness that concealed the violence, and the possible motive for such a crime. Nothing made sense. When his thought process plateaued, he exited the Jeep Gladiator and approached the scene.

The two deputies had cordoned the area with yellow tape, and Bourbon was pleased that there was not a single member of the press there—yet. The coroner had come and gone, but an ambulance stayed and waited to haul the body away. A couple of local volunteer EMTs with the rescue squad stood around and watched law enforcement do their job.

Birchcraft approached Bourbon and gave him some updates.

"What's the cause of death, Birch?" Bourbon asked the burly deputy.

"Severed spinal cord—back of the neck. Someone hit this kid with an ax or something sharp. It wasn't a knife because there's some bruising around the wound from the impact. The coroner thinks it was an ax or machete. It appears our victim exited the building and was struck from behind when he passed the dumpster."

"So, you think the murderer was waiting behind the dumpster?"

"Yup. Whoever it was must have been targeting Brody. Two waitresses left just four minutes before Brody and made it to their vehicles safely."

"How'd he know when the victim would be leaving?"

Charlie Archer entered the conversation and, as always, took over for Birchcraft. "Because Alyse probably told him."

"Told who?" Bourbon asked.

"Savage. Obviously, Savage did this. Brody Sherwood spat on Cody's burger, so Cody killed him for it."

"Jesus, Arch," Bourbon said. "That's a pretty flimsy motive. The man had just been released from prison. Why would he jeopardize his freedom over a friggin cheeseburger?"

"We know Savage is a stone-cold killer, Sheriff. Let's go arrest that piece-of-shit."

"No." Bourbon shook his head and stared at the body from a distance. "I'm not buying it. I'm not saying Savage is innocent either, but I want all the facts and evidence we can get." He watched Deputy Birchcraft snap pictures for evidence and thought about his next step. "Birch, you go talk to any of the staff working last night. Arch, I want you to interview PJ Simmons."

"AJ Simmons," Archer corrected.

"Timmons," Birchcraft corrected Archer.

"I'm going to take a look around here. Meet me back at HQ at fifteen hundred hours. We'll go over everything we have and go from there."

The three officers parted ways, and Bourbon waited before he approached the body. Visually scanning the parking lot first, he made his way toward the dumpster. The Mineshaft's owner was standing with some EMTs, shaking her head and wiping tears from her eyes.

"Are you okay, Ms. Brigham?" Bourbon asked.

"I'm…I'm fine. I just can't believe this is happening to me."

"To you?" Bourbon asked.

"Yes. Jesus, this is going to shut me down for a week, isn't it? I can't afford to be closed, Sheriff."

"Well, sorry, Nicole, but this is a crime scene. Until we find out who murdered this young man—"

"Sheriff, you work for us taxpayers. I expect you to solve this by the end of the week, or I'll take it to the town board. I'll lose revenue every day you and your men don't solve this thing."

"We'll do our best, ma'am, but I can't make any promises. We'll need your whole staff to cooperate with our investigation. The more they help, the faster this will go."

Nicole scowled, "I'll let them all know that you'll be asking questions." She started to walk away, but Bourbon stepped backward with an outstretched arm to corral her.

"Do you know if Brody had any enemies?"

"Enemies?"

"Yeah, rival gangs? Ex-girlfriends with jealous boyfriends? A current girlfriend with a jealous ex? That sort of thing."

"I'm not his goddamn mother, Sheriff. I barely knew the man. He worked nights, and I'm usually gone by seven o'clock. Alyse might be able to answer those questions."

"And she's the bartender?"

"Yes. Alyse Burns. She was working last night. Maybe she knows something."

Bourbon turned and scanned the asphalt near the business again, finally realizing what was bothering him. "Do you know where Brody lived?"

Nicole said, "Shit-side of town, on Partridge Street. I recall seeing that on his application. I didn't think anyone from the east side could cook anything other than a can of beans or meth. But Brody was quite talented in the kitchen."

"That's about four miles."

"Your point?" Nicole said.

Bourbon pulled his notepad from his shirt pocket and wrote a few lines. He turned back to Nicole Brigham. "Who owns that Nissan Maxima?" He pointed toward the employee parking area.

"That's mine."

"So, where is Brody's vehicle?"

Nicole couldn't answer that question. She wasn't aware of what vehicle Brody drove, other than it might be a truck with large wheels. She remembered seeing it there often but never really paid attention. But this was Stoneville, where a lot of people drove trucks with big wheels.

"Ms. Brigham, do you have any security cameras out here near the dumpster?" Bourbon was studying the building now.

"No. Why would we? We've never had anyone steal from the dumpster other than that freak that reported this."

Bourbon looked over his shoulder at the homeless man sitting on a concrete barrier and watching the scene. "That's Elliot Osgood. He used to be a physics teacher. Nicest guy in town." He looked back at Nicole with a disapproving expression. "So, you have cameras inside? I'm going to need a copy of the video footage from last night."

Nicole sighed. "I'll have the security company make you a backup copy. But it could take a day. They're not the fastest people to work with." With Bourbon's permission, Nicole Brigham crossed the parking lot, got into her vehicle, and left the property.

Bourbon was sickened by the corpse lying on the ground, not from its physical appearance, but because it reminded him that Stoneville had some disturbing residents. There was a dark side to the little town that appeared squeaky clean on the surface. Hopefully, the psychopath who killed this young man wasn't a resident. And more importantly, Bourbon hoped this was a one-time event.

What he did know was that the entire town was going to think Cody Savage had murdered again. But this time, Bourbon was quite certain that Savage had no part in this crime.

*****

"What the fuck do you mean Savage is innocent?" Archer barked at Bourbon. Bourbon was sitting at his metal desk, and Archer stood over him, leaning on his knuckles. His stance would have intimidated most people, but Bourbon paid no attention.

"Exactly what I said. Savage had nothing to do with Brody Sherwood's death." Bourbon opened his top drawer and removed a file. Then he fumbled in the back for a small bottle of Dr. McGillicuddy's schnapps and took a sip that burned as it dropped down his throat.

Birchcraft was sitting in the corner, calm as usual, when he lowered his coffee from his lips. "So, in other words, we have a new killer in town?"

"Yes, Birch, we do."

"Jesus, Sheriff," Archer snapped. "This is bullshit! Savage is guilty as hell."

"What did you find out from that CJ guy, Arch?"

"Same story Alyse the bartender told. Cody and his friend stayed at the bar until around one a.m. They never left or went outside, other than to the restroom. I think she's full of shit. Brody finished work and left long before them, so chances are he didn't hang around out by the dumpster that long. Cody left with DJ—."

"AJ," Birchcraft corrected.

"—And no one saw them after that," Archer finished. "I think Brody came back later that night, just as Savage was leaving, and the two tussled outside."

Bourbon ignored Archer's theory.

Birchcraft flipped a page of his notebook and read a few notes, "Actually, there is video surveillance of them stopping at the convenience store at 1:08 a.m. Clerk said they were acting normal and were overly courteous. They bought a couple of waters, a medium pizza, and a can of Pringles."

Bourbon swallowed another ounce of schnapps, stuffed the bottle back in the drawer, and stared out the window. He leaned way back in his chair and changed his gaze to the ceiling. "Okay. So, we know Cody Savage didn't do this. Nobody saw any of the Road Barons in the area, and word is they were all at a wedding reception for one of the members."

"There is something else," Birchcraft added.

Bourbon raised an eyebrow, waiting for Birchcraft's elaboration.

"The store clerk mentioned that someone was outside, following

Savage. The clerk noticed a truck pulled in behind Savage and Timmons. He waited for the customer to pull up to a gas pump or come inside, but he never did."

Bourbon leaned forward, straightening his back and the chair that supported him. "What the hell are you talking about, Birch?"

"The security video supports his claim. I can't make it out or tell who it is, but someone in a black truck pulled in behind Savage and Timmons and just watched them. It's difficult to see in the dark, but I think it's a Chevy Silverado. Then, the black truck pulled out behind Savage and Timmons."

"Alyse? The bartender?" Archer asked. "Maybe she followed them home, and they all—"

"I don't think so," Bourbon said, cutting Archer off with a hand gesture. "She worked until two a.m. when the bar closed. No, our suspect has an interest in our returning citizen. Birch, did you get a copy of that video?"

"Working on it. The store's going to send you a copy as soon as the manager gets back in town. Maybe tomorrow."

Bourbon looked at his watch and dismissed himself from the meeting. He instructed his deputies to finish their reports and make a few more calls about the mysterious vehicle that had followed Savage. He needed to go home and shower so he could meet Annabel for dinner while the two deputies would be on the clock for three more hours.

Bourbon drove like the ice cream man on his way home, meandering from block to block, watching for traffic and pedestrians, and crossing town like he had nowhere to be. It was customary for him to drive like he was lost. He patrolled and thought about cases simultaneously. Once he cleared the underpass of Highway 26, he gave the V-6 engine more gas and passed the speed limit. His brain zig-zagged in the same pattern as the vehicle. Who wanted Brody dead? Where was his truck? What was Cody Savage doing back in town? Was he guilty of Willa Thompson's murder? Only time would give him the answers, so tonight, he was going to leave it all at work and enjoy his dinner with Annabel. The two hadn't seen each other all week, and she deserved his full attention and a nice night out.

*****

"Dinner was amazing."

Bourbon looked across the table at Annabel. The rough-and-tough farmer had morphed into a beauty queen with a bit of makeup and a pretty dress. She wore her hair down for the evening and covered her muscular shoulders with a sweater. The candle on the table created a twinkle in her eye that kept Bourbon thinking about dessert.

"You've been quiet as a fox outside the hen house this evening. Everything okay?" Annabel asked.

"Everything is perfect."

"Something's on your mind. Work, I presume? Can you talk about it? Is it Savage?"

Bourbon looked from the wine rack on the far wall to his equally intoxicating date. "It's you, actually."

"Me?"

"Yeah, I mean...Well, are you okay? I'm worried that Savage's return is going to stir up some old hostility."

"'Old hostility'?" Annabel echoed. "Listen, when someone murders your daughter and gets away with it, your hostility never gets old. It lingers there, waking up with you in the morning. It follows you like a tail. It becomes part of you. It's not old hostility, it's just hostility that you learn to live with and try to hide like an ugly birthmark."

"I get it, really, I do." Bourbon gulped his wine. "But I think you've been at ease for the last couple of years because he was behind bars. And, now—"

"Now that he isn't, you think I'm going to go all cookie on you and crumble, right? Well, no, sir. I refuse to live that way. I've grieved enough."

Bourbon reached across the table and took her hand. With her free hand, Annabel poured the rest of the wine bottle into their glasses.

"What if he didn't do it?" Annabel asked.

"I know. I've been thinking about that too. Savage is a smart guy, but I don't think he's smart enough to cover all the evidence that should have been there. How would he do that?"

71

"Well, if he didn't, then whoever murdered Willa has been running free all this time."

"Enough of this," Bourbon said. A playful smile appeared on his face. "Why don't we get out of here and head back to the farm?"

"Why, Mr. Bourbon, you read my mind. Dinner's on me tonight." Annabel pulled the check toward her, and Bourbon knew there was no point in arguing. As Annabel dug through her wallet for a debit card, Bourbon's phone buzzed. He answered on the second ring.

"Bourbon," he answered. Deputy Birchcraft was on the line. Bourbon straightened in his chair. "What? Jesus, Birch, since when…Where was the last… Uh, huh…How old…Fuck…Anybody had eyes on Savage lately…Yes…No, it's okay, we were just finishing up," Bourbon gave Annabel a solemn look that she understood right away. He continued on the phone. "Okay, I'll meet you there in about twenty minutes."

He hung up the phone and dropped his head. "I gotta go," there was a croak in his voice, and Annabel knew it wasn't just fatigue or frustration but something serious. Bourbon stood and came around the table to kiss his love.

She gave him a supportive smile. "It's okay, I know. Go. Be the sheriff we all love and need."

"I'm tired of being everyone's sheriff. I just want to be yours for a while."

"Well then, don't go. It's your choice."

"I have to. Mary Poole called the station. Her nineteen-year-old daughter hasn't been home since Thursday night."

"Darcy? Oh, dear, she's such a sweet girl. I'd better swing by the Poole's house and see what I can do."

Bourbon loved the way Annabel cared so much about every living thing. It's what made her such a good farmer: how she cared for people, animals, and plants. She'd sacrifice a little of herself for a dying tomato plant if she had to. Annabel would give her life for any other human without hesitation. Bourbon knew she'd go to Mary Poole's house and stay all night if necessary. She'd make food, do laundry, or just hold Mary's hand. How could he not love her?

Bourbon straightened, inspired by Annabel's generosity, and knew he needed to perform his civic duties. He touched her cheek as he walked away, just to feel her skin for a few more seconds before disappearing through the exit.

Driving into work, he wondered if there was any connection between Darcy Poole and Cody Savage. There was nothing. The Pooles lived on the outskirts of town on an eighty-acre lot, where they sold firewood all year round. Greg Poole, Darcy's father, used to be a supervisor for a local tree company until a log fell on his leg and destroyed his knee. Now, he was unemployed and squeaking by on his disability checks. There didn't seem to be any way Cody Savage had ties to this family. Maybe he was overthinking it. Maybe there was no foul play involved in Darcy's disappearance, and the girl simply ran away. Either way, somebody in town knew where she was, and he wasn't going to stop until he got some answers.

9
JESSE & ANNABEL 

Annabel Thompson downshifted her old Ford truck from fourth to third, second, and finally neutral and put her foot on the brake. She cranked the driver's side window down by hand. Driving the fifty-year-old truck was an experience, and Annabel liked how it rattled and shook going down the road. She felt connected and in control and preferred it over her Range Rover. Going through the gears seemed more natural, and she could envision all the mechanisms working in harmony as part of a system. The Range Rover was more of a computer on wheels, and Annabel had a distaste for technology.

It was nearly late enough to kiss the evening hours goodbye and start turning on the lights. Annabel steered toward the sunset, keeping the old truck centered on the road that lacked any paint to identify lanes. She crossed a bridge, slowing to wave at a couple of neighbor boys fishing for trout, and then stopped to talk to another neighbor walking her dog. It was an opportunity to gossip and spread the news about poor Darcy Poole.

She passed Jesse Lewis' little farm and then noticed a medium-built man trekking alone along the roadside.

She stopped 300 yards from her house to speak with the man.

"Howdy, Pastor," Annabel said.

"Hello, Annabel, how are you?" Jesse answered.

"Better than Mary and Greg Poole."

"Oh? What seems to be the problem with the Pooles?"

"Mary and Greg are all right, but their daughter Darcy has been missing for two days. Too young to go off on her own, I think."

"I'm sure the girl is fine, but I'll say a prayer for her anyway. We can have a mass prayer tomorrow during the congregation."

"I'm sure Mary would appreciate that." Annabel looked at the road ahead. It was getting dark now, and the pastor was not carrying a flashlight. "May I give you a ride somewhere?"

"Sure. Actually, I'm on my way to your house, anyway. The tractor ran out of gas last night when I was helping Pearl. I had Connor drop me off at home. Nice kid."

Annabel gave him a look of confusion, "Connor Bayley? That kid's a pain in my ass. Works like a machine sometimes, but that boy is as wound up as a wolf in a cage. He's not very dependable, either. I never know when he's going to show up for work."

"I think he means well," Jesse said. He walked around the front of the Ford and climbed into the passenger side seat. He worked the window crank until he was able to rest his arm on the door with his elbow hanging outside.

Annabel put the truck in gear and began to move forward. "Did Connor say anything about Darcy? I think he was dating that girl for a while. Maybe he knows where she is."

"Uh...no, I don't recall him mentioning her name." Jesse lied, and then changed the subject. "How's Pearl doing?"

"Pearl's just fine. Back where she belongs and happy as a duck in a puddle."

They drove to her farm, and Annabel veered to the left, staying along the side of the pasture. Jesse was thankful she was taking him right to the tractor behind the field.

"Did you already put gas in it?" Annabel asked.

"Yes. I stopped by while you weren't home and gassed it up. I just drove my truck back to the house and parked it. That's when you came along."

"I'm sure I had diesel fuel in the garage. You should have just helped yourself. Least I could do after you saved my poor Pearl."

Annabel pulled up to the abandoned tractor and exited the truck, wanting to be sure the pastor got the machine started. While Jesse climbed on top of the Kubota, Annabel pushed four feet of muddy rope hanging from the bucket back into the remaining coil so it wouldn't fall out and drag down the road. She slapped her hands together to knock off some of the mud that transferred to her palms, careful not to get the muck on her dress.

"Jesse, thanks again for your help with Pearl," Annabel said.

"Anytime, Annabel."

"I don't know what this town would do without you. Lately, things seem to be spiraling out of control around here. Did you hear about the murder at The Mineshaft last night?

"A murder? At the Mineshaft? That can't be true, Annabel."

"The cook there—just a kid. Killed out back after his shift."

The pastor shook his head. "What a shame. The sheriff must have some suspects."

"Not that I'm aware of, but there's an ex-con in town they're keeping an eye on." She refused to let Cody Savage's name cross her lips.

"Well, I'm sure Bourbon and his men will find whoever is responsible. Maybe it was one of those bikers who frequent that place."

"Everybody goes to The Mineshaft. Best burger in the state."

"Really? I'll have to try it sometime," Jesse said. "I hear their smoked chicken wings are fantastic."

"You've never been to the 'Shaft? Well, I'm going to have to take you to lunch sometime. You pick the day, and it's a date."

"Oh, you don't have to do that, Annabel." Jesse felt a tightness form in his shoulder. He rattled a hydraulic lever with his arm, hoping the movement would relieve the tension in his joint.

Annabel walked to the side of the tractor, stepping closer to the driver, "Nonsense. It's the least I can do after you helped me."

Now the pain was spreading to the nape of his neck, and the pastor knew it wouldn't be long before his head felt like an egg cracking. He needed to escape, "Okay. Maybe next Wednesday, then. My schedule is wide open on Wednesdays." It was a desperate attempt to end their conversation.

"Oh, that sounds great. I'll give you a call that morning, and we'll decide on a time."

Once the tractor engine fired, Annabel waved goodbye and climbed into her truck. She backed up fifty yards before finding a place to turn around.

Jesse left the scene, thankful that his tractor was no longer parked where he had snuffed the life out of Connor Bayley. He went straight home, iced his shoulder and neck, and watched reruns of M*A*S*H to forget the night.

He thought he'd purged in Cain Lake long enough to rid himself of the pain he was experiencing. Perhaps he was wrong. Or was there a hint of a sinner in Annabel?

Impossible. As the pain subsided, Jesse speculated what had agitated his senses. It had come from Annabel, and though he could not see her sins, Jesse was sure she was hiding something big, indicated by the amount of pain he had felt. He hoped he was mistaking the source. What could Stoneville's super-woman be hiding? Annabel was incapable of harming anyone or anything, and her honesty would make George Washington jealous. His curiosity grew, and he knew the only way to be sure Annabel was the catalyst for his pain was to join her for lunch.

Wednesday couldn't come soon enough.

10

BEAR SHIT

Sheriff Bourbon searched for Darcy Poole for two days. Two days of hell in Stoneville. Eighty-four volunteers searched the woods, the lake shore, the alleys, dumpsters, and roadsides. Any clue would have made Jeff Bourbon feel better, but so far, they had turned up nothing.

He was frustrated and tired as hell. He'd put twenty miles on his boots in that time, eating almost nothing, and had slept a total of three hours. He was ready to snap at the first person to cross him and hoped no one would try his patience until after breakfast.

Bourbon lurched through the door of Tabitha's Diner, a little bell announcing his entry and annoying him simultaneously. The rest of the patrons stared at the man who hoped to perform a miracle and bring nineteen-year-old Darcy Poole home. He'd never felt so defeated. He never looked so shitty. His pants were stained from the cuff to the knee, torn across the thigh, and etched with wrinkles. His elbows were bruised and scratched from climbing through bushes and briers, and his shirt was torn in four places. The sweat stains on his shirt were two days old. A filthy bandage snaked around his left hand, protecting the laceration he received searching a dumpster, and his bloodshot eyes burned from the bright lights of the diner.

"Jesus, Sheriff, you look like shit," Connie said. She set a plate of food, his usual, in front of him. "It's on me today, hon. Any luck?"

Bourbon couldn't look her in the eye and just shook his head in defeat. Connie shook her head with him and walked away before her eyes began to drip. Bourbon could sense everyone in the diner staring at him, and he felt like he'd let them down. In truth, they were staring out of respect for the man who refused to give up on Darcy Poole.

He wanted to lash out, scream so loud that it would blow the windows out of the diner in a cascade of little shards. He wanted an excuse to relieve some of his anger and felt sorry for the first person to cross him.

Bourbon stared at his plate. He was so hungry that he would have eaten the food right off the floor, and yet, he was so upset that the thought of food made him want to vomit. He wondered if Darcy had eaten since her disappearance or if she was even more famished than he was. Had she starved to death by now, or was she 500 miles away eating seafood by the ocean? He pushed the plate a couple of inches away and decided to start with his fresh coffee. The rich brew would provide a few calories to get him through the morning if his appetite didn't improve.

He lifted the cup of java to his lips and saw the blood and mud on his hand. There was no excuse for sitting to eat with such dirty hands, so he left his stool and made his way to the men's restroom to wash up. As he made his way to the back of the diner, he saw a face he'd never seen before—a woman, young and pretty.

The strange woman watched the sheriff make his way past her table and took notes in a journal every few seconds. Now, she held her pen near the corner of her mouth, as if she'd run out of words. A Dell laptop was open on her table, and she sipped a tall, overly sweetened coffee. Bourbon could tell she was there to work, not eat. Her brown eyes looked away from the sheriff, and he was close enough to see a name badge pinned to her shirt.

Damn, Bourbon thought. *Another reporter taking advantage of poor Darcy's story.* He smiled at the woman politely anyway. "Morning, miss."

"Good morning, Sheriff."

Bourbon entered the men's restroom.

The female reporter knew the sheriff was exhausted and worn out from days of searching. He had managed to gain her respect in seconds, which wasn't an easy feat. She stirred her beverage with a thin wooden spoon and planned to boldly confront him when he came out of the restroom. Or maybe she'd let him eat his breakfast first and catch him on the way out of the diner. Or, perhaps, she'd drop her business card—.

The dinging bell interrupted her planning, and a young man, visibly shaken, burst through the door brazenly, aiming a pistol. He was at the counter in four strides and pointing the gun at Connie. Silence fell on the hometown diner once again as everyone stayed low and out of sight. No one screamed, but panic emitted from every booth. This was such a new occurrence in the small town that no one knew how to react, or if a reaction was even required. A few businesses were robbed every year, but those were typically all-night convenience and liquor stores where the robber operated under the cloak of darkness. No one had ever held up a greasy spoon diner in the morning.

The man with the mask was so nervous that he had missed the sheriff's Jeep parked among the other vehicles in the side parking lot. He had approached from the opposite end of the building.

Connie raised her hands and side-stepped to the cash register, anticipating the young robber's intentions.

"O-open the reg-gister. Open the register," the shaky gunman ordered. Nervous lips could barely put the words together. His thin legs shook uncontrollably, and Connie wondered who was going to piss themselves first—her or him. She pushed a button, and the register drawer sprang open with a ding. She dug for paper bills and piled them on the counter beside her.

In the corner, the journalist crouched in fear at her booth. Stealthily, she slid her phone out of her laptop bag and started recording the incident. She intently watched what was happening and didn't notice the big man who walked out of the bathroom and past her table until he came into view on her phone screen.

"You sure you want to do that, son?" Bourbon said softly to the gun-yielding thief.

The man spun around, pointing the pistol toward Sheriff Bourbon, who never flinched. Once he saw the uniform, his shaking worsened, so he put two hands on the gun, hoping to steady the barrel. His effort was in vain.

The young man was tall and slender. His face was covered with a red bandanna that contrasted with the dark blue hoodie he wore. The ball cap on his head was pulled downward at the bill to shade his face. The effect would have been more effective at night. He had intended to wear sunglasses, but his nerves were rattled before he left his car, so he forgot them on the vehicle's dashboard.

Bourbon put one hand on the back of a barstool and the other out to the side to keep them visible and not inadvertently spook the jittery kid into pulling the trigger. He could see one of the cooks in the kitchen on a cell phone, presumably calling 9-1-1, so he needed to buy time before one of his deputies arrived, without escalating the situation.

The young man waved the pistol back toward Connie.

"Keep that pistol pointed at me, son," Bourbon said. "She's no threat to you. Relax, no one here is going to hurt you."

Connie pushed the crumpled pile of cash a little closer, tempting the gunman to grab it and go, but Bourbon kept talking. "You must need this money pretty badly to pull a stunt like this, am I right?"

"I'm hun…I'm just…hungry. I…w-won't hurt anyone. J-just don't do anything stupid."

"Nobody's going to do anything stupid. And nobody's going to stop you. Here," Bourbon slid his plate of food toward the kid. "I'll trade you this plate of food for the gun. Then we'll call this a big misunderstanding, and we can get you some help."

"One p-plate…one plate…isn't…going to help," the boy stammered.

"I know. I know," Bourbon said. "I know what it's like to be so hungry you can't think straight. It was the worst feeling of my life once. I was in the Army when I was about your age. They took us to the mountains, not far from here, and left us for a week to survive in the woods."

"Yeah, but you probably took food with you, right? Nobody's giving me shit."

"We had a little, but you know, they don't teach you to keep it away from the bears. I was partnered up with two other boys my age, and we ate half the food the first night, then a bear ate the other half 'cause we were too stupid to hang it from a tree out of reach. Well, we went for five days with nothing to eat except beech nuts and a few rotten wild apples. But one of my partners thought that you could eat bear shit to survive if you had to."

Bourbon could sense Connie's disgust, but the kid was smirking under the handkerchief. He began to relax a little and had to ask, "So, what'd you do? Did ya shoot the bear?"

"No. But my buddy found a pile of the bear's shit," Bourbon couldn't help but smile from the memory. "That sonovabitch ate almost half of it. You ever seen a pile of bear shit, kid? I'm talking a big bear that will leave a pile the size of that breakfast platter."

The kid lowered the gun slightly and continued listening, seeming to forget why he had come to the diner.

Bourbon continued with his story, "So he ate half that pile of bear scat, because supposedly, bears have a fast digestive system and their scat is hardly digested apples and berries, and full of nutrients, right? Well, my partner ended up vomiting for four hours straight after that." Bourbon was laughing now from the story and exhaustion. "That kid vomited to the point he was completely dehydrated, and after he threw up on his boots, we called our training officer on our emergency radio and had him sent back to base. To this day, the Army has to remind the recruits that it's not a good idea to eat bear shit."

The kid was smiling under his handkerchief now, realizing how self-ish he'd been for being hungry and willing to rob the diner.

Bourbon scratched his beard. "I'm surprised you never heard that story before." His tone was serious and genuine.

"Why would I have heard that story, Sheriff?"

"Because the guy that ate bear shit was your dad, Andrew."

Andrew's eyes widened, and he realized his disguise was too thin to fool the wise sheriff. Now, he wished he'd remembered his sunglasses to hide the weakness in his eyes. "You knew my dad?"

Bourbon watched Deputy Birchcraft pull into the parking lot, so he slid his breakfast closer to Andrew to divert his attention. "My offer still stands. I'll trade you this plate of food for that pistol. Your dad would be disappointed in both of us if he were here."

Shame overtaking him, Andrew placed the pistol in Bourbon's open hand and moved shyly to an empty seat at the counter. Bourbon sat next to him and sipped his coffee. "Before he passed away, your dad asked me to check in on you occasionally, and I did, too. I've been to about twenty of your soccer games, followed you home from prom, watched you graduate, and saw you at your mom's wedding. I thought I didn't need to check on you after you went to college. That's on me. Nobody in this town should go hungry—not on my watch."

Just as Bourbon predicted, his deputy entered from the back of the diner and stood in the kitchen assessing the scene. Bourbon motioned for him to hold a minute. He wasn't going to haul Andrew Mills away until the kid had a full stomach.

Connie brought Andrew and Bourbon two big pieces of pie, and the two sat and talked about Andrew's father and some of the other crazy things he'd done. When they finished their food, Bourbon motioned behind him, and Deputy Birchcraft gently set his meaty hand on Andrew's shoulder.

Andrew, feeling full and not-so-alone, didn't flinch.

"Andrew, this is my deputy, Eli Birchcraft. He's going to take you down to the station, and then he'll take you home, okay?"

Andrew nodded and stood. With a full belly, he was calm enough to understand the seriousness of his actions. "I'm sorry. That...I was so stupid. I knew this was a stupid idea. I don't know what I was thinking. I guess...well....I wasn't thinking clearly, sir. Thank you."

"Come on, son," Birchcraft urged. "We just need to do a little paper-work, and then you can go home."

Bourbon walked the two men to the door and watched Birchcraft lead Andrew to the patrol car.

The diner's patrons erupted with applause. Bourbon motioned with his hands to settle down, thinking it was no big deal. He took his seat, exhausted physically and emotionally. Connie poured him another fresh coffee.

The female reporter, in awe, had recorded the entire incident on her phone. Now, she was inspired and eager to interview Stoneville's head lawman. Approaching cautiously, she took a seat at the counter, leaving one empty stool between them.

"That was amazing," she said as she took her seat. Bourbon rolled his eyes a little as she sat down—a reaction she was getting used to—but he smiled anyway. She put her hand out to introduce herself, "Sheriff Bourbon, I'm Daisy Torrez, with The Stoneville View."

"Nice to meet you, Ms. Torrez. And it was nothing."

"Nothing? You just completely talked a would-be robber out of his gun. You traded a piece of pie for a pistol, had him in tears by the time he left, and most astonishingly—you did it without ever drawing your gun."

Bourbon sipped coffee in modesty.

"May I ask, how did you know who he was?"

"It's the eyes, Ms. Torrez. You can recognize anyone just from their eyes. I've known that kid for eighteen years. He just didn't know me, or his father for that matter."

"Will he be locked up?"

"No. What good would it do? Andrew knew he was in the wrong."

"But he pointed a pistol at you and the waitress."

"He wasn't going to shoot anyone."

Daisy was holding her phone on the counter, recording the conversation. She slid her hips another stool closer to the sheriff. "How can you be so sure? Didn't he seem a little crazy?"

Bourbon was bothered by the question, "'Crazy?' Have you ever been hungry, Ms. Torrez? I mean, stomach-shriveling, dizzy spells with every movement, a never-ending migraine, and delusional thoughts, kind of hungry?"

She gently shook her head, but in truth, she was hungry right now. She'd only been working for The Stoneville View for a week, and she was too proud to admit the tall coffee she was sipping was all she could afford.

"I didn't think so."

With a stern look, Connie wiped the counter in front of the journalist with a dirty dish towel, hoping the pesky reporter would get the hint to stop asking the overworked sheriff any more questions. It didn't work.

Daisy took note of the sheriff's pistol still nestled in its holster. "Why didn't you pull your gun? You approached him from behind, unarmed. You had the upper hand."

Bourbon was happy to answer. "Thirty-three years. That's how long I've been in law enforcement, Ms. Torrez. Do you know how many times I've had to draw my weapon?"

She shook her head. "No, how many?"

Bourbon held his right hand up, forming a zero with his thumb and index finger. "Never."

Daisy found this hard to believe. "You have never pulled your weapon in the line of duty?"

"Nope." He finished his coffee and threw Connie's tip on the table, but Connie pushed it right back at him. He stood, and Daisy put her hand on his forearm.

"How can that be? Most law enforcement officers seem to have blood on their hands, even in large departments. You have a department of three deputies, right? So how do you do it? What's Sheriff Bourbon's secret?"

"No secret. Nobody cares about the suspect. They're instantly a piece of garbage that needs to be removed. Well, if you'd take the time and talk to them, you'd realize they're usually a victim too."

"What do you mean?"

"I mean, somebody probably walked all over them first. Someone beat them up first. Someone probably stole from them first. Nine times out of ten, they just want to be heard. They want someone to care, to listen, and to empathize."

"So, how did you know that Andrew wasn't going to shoot anyone?"

"Did you see how scared that boy was?"

Daisy nodded.

Bourbon looked out the window, replaying the scene in his mind while Deputy Birchcraft pulled away with Andrew Mills in the back seat. He continued: "When you see someone shaking like that—in fear—it's because it's not in their nature to harm. He wasn't scared of me. He was scared that he might hurt someone."

Daisy sat back, slumping in her chair with a smile as she regarded Bourbon's wisdom. She wished they could talk longer; she'd been so impressed with Bourbon's reaction to Andrew that she completely forgot about the original reason she'd come to interview the Stoneville Sheriff—the return of Cody Savage.

Bourbon turned to make one last comment. "When I face a man with a gun who isn't nervous—who isn't shaking—that's when I'll know he's a cold-blooded killer. That's when I'll draw my pistol for the first time."

Daisy knew she'd gotten all the story she could from Bourbon, but she tried to push her luck like a veteran reporter anyway, "And what about Cody Savage, Sheriff?"

Bourbon turned cold as he turned to face her, "What about him?"

"Is he just a victim himself? Or is he a cold-blooded killer?"

"Why don't you go find out for yourself, Ms. Torrez? Formulate your own opinion of Mr. Savage and put it in your paper." With that, he walked out, dinging the bell as the door closed.

11

FRESH PAINT

Two days had passed since Cody left his house. In an impromptu yard sale, he'd sold some furniture that his uncle had left behind. One antique table fetched $700, and the other items he sold made for a total of $915. It was enough to send AJ to the local hardware store to pick up some paint, cleaning supplies, and light bulbs. The house didn't just need cosmetic upgrades, so AJ also purchased three plumbing valves, four light switches, plastic sheeting to cover the broken windows, and a toilet seat.

Cody worked until midnight that Sunday, and AJ and Alyse joined him on Monday with a twelve-pack of beer and two dozen chicken wings. They cleaned, painted, and fixed everything they could. Alyse danced around the house, dusting and cleaning windows, and then was the only one willing to climb into the attic to empty the mousetraps. When she came down from the ladder with a fresh corpse in a trap, she playfully chased AJ around the house with it until he ran outside.

Once Cody and Alyse stopped laughing, AJ returned and painted the inside trim and polished the kitchen appliances. Cody rolled paint on the walls, fixed some lights, and replaced two breakers in the electric panel.

"This is looking great," Alyse said as she made her way down the stairs. She stopped to rub fresh paint off the banister.

Cody handed Alyse a cold beer. "Let's call it a night. I appreciate all the help, though." She gladly accepted, and the two clinked their bottles together.

Cody took a large swig of his beer, stepped to the middle of the living room, and stared at the blank walls with pride.

Alyse sat on the second step of the stairs. "Whatcha thinking about?"

Cody looked around, "This. These walls. I love how blank they are. Is that weird?"

"No, not at all. They're a clean slate—a fresh canvas. You can hang or paint anything you want now. It's all up to you."

"'A fresh canvas.'" The words didn't seem to make sense. Being in control of his own life seemed surreal, a day he felt would never come when he was incarcerated. Painting the walls and working on the house made it his, when just a week ago, he owned nothing more than a toothbrush.

Cody loved Alyse's perspective of what they had accomplished. He took a seat on the plastic cooler not far from Alyse and admired her. She was so pretty, but the spark between them only flickered now. They had a friendship that seemed unbreakable—two kindred spirits, too much alike to be in love. Cody had a great deal of respect for Alyse and knew that she deserved someone who could give her the world and more, but Cody knew that would always be out of his capabilities.

"I think AJ fell asleep upstairs," Cody said. The sound of his voice echoed off the empty walls, followed the stairs, and reached AJ.

"I'm awake, just putting the last outlet cover on," AJ shouted from the bedroom. His voice boomed down the hall despite the poor acoustics. He clambered down the stairwell, joined his friends, and turned up the volume on an old radio. Located this far north in New York, most Stoneville residents preferred to listen to Canadian rock stations out of Ottawa and Kingston. A fast rock tune by The Headstones filled the room, as lead singer Hugh Dillon sang "Tweeter and the Monkey Man."

AJ twisted the top off a bottle of beer. He tried to hide his grimace when he tasted the cheap beer, but the second sip was better, and the third was quite good.

"Not bad for a day's work," AJ said.

"Let me know if you ever want to sell," Alyse said. "This would make a cute little bed and breakfast or rental property."

"With a lot more paint and a bunch of upgrades," Cody said.

"But you could—"

A knock at the front door surprised them all. Cody froze for a second. He looked at the time. 7:35. He remained frozen. They'd had a productive day with no worries about the sheriff or his deputies. No nosy neighbors had stopped by to meet the new homeowner. It was too late on a Sunday for any salesmen to be soliciting. Cody wondered who was standing on his porch, ringing the doorbell and knocking, but remained sitting on the cooler.

After the second knock, Alyse sprang to her feet and peeked out the window to see who was standing on the porch. She walked into the kitchen and opened the door.

"Hi, I'm looking for Cody Savage. Someone said that he owned this house, and I—"

"Come on in," Alyse greeted the attractive woman and motioned her inside.

Cody watched from the living room as Daisy Torrez stepped inside. He walked into the kitchen to greet the stranger. "Can I help you?" His tone was a bit raw.

Daisy's eyes grew like two dark bubbles. "It's you."

"Well, of course, it's me; I own the place."

Daisy composed herself, put out a hand, and started fresh. "Mr. Savage, my name is Daisy—Daisy Torrez. I'm with The Stoneville View."

Alyse backed away at the mention of the newspaper and went to Cody's side, knowing he'd need the support.

"*The View*, huh?" Cody smirked. "How's Dale Talbert these days?"

"I'm afraid I don't know who that is."

Alyse answered the question, speaking softly to Cody. "Talbert quit the paper five months ago and moved to Florida."

"Good," Cody said. He gripped the neck of his beer a little tighter. His jawline became visibly rigid. "So, you haven't been with The View for very long, then, have you?"

"Not at all. I just started working on Saturday, actually. I was wondering—"

"You're too old to be just out of college," Cody interrupted her. "What did you do before this? Before working at *The View?*"

"Well, I went back to college after my—" Daisy stopped, realizing that *she* was supposed to be asking the questions. *Damn, how did he turn the interview on me?* She composed herself, not wanting to exploit her past. "If you and your girlfriend don't mind, I'd like to ask you both some questions about the incident that took place four years ago."

Alyse chugged the last quarter of her beer and set the empty bottle on the counter. "I'm not his girlfriend. Just a friend who is leaving. He's all yours. Come on, AJ, we gotta go."

"Why do I gotta go?" AJ protested. He was staring at the pretty reporter, but she had just now realized he was in the room.

"Because you're going to give me a ride," Alyse ordered. She leaned in to hug Cody and whispered in his ear, "Fresh paint."

Cody thanked his friends several times and said goodnight twice. AJ closed the door behind them, leaving Cody alone with Daisy.

Daisy peeked out the window where the sun was getting low and reflecting off the narrow river that passed the house.

"Pretty," she whispered, not realizing it was aloud. "This would be a cute vacation rental for southerners during the summer. Maybe rent it by the weekend or week."

"Why does everybody keep saying that?" Cody shook his head.

"Well, you'd have to get rid of the graffiti outside first. Kinda looks like a crack house when you pull in."

"Yeah, I'm working on it. Don't have much money right now."

"Are you looking for work?" Daisy asked, knowing it was a stupid question.

"Hard for us ex—" he stopped himself, remembering Thomas' words the day he drove him to the bus station. "Hard for us previous correctional residents to find jobs. Even harder when the whole town thinks you're a murderer. That's why you're here, right? You think I'm a murderer, too?"

"No. If I thought that, I wouldn't have come in. I don't form opinions with my job. Give me just fifteen minutes of your time, and I'll only report the truth."

"Like Dale Talbert? He was supposed to report the truth, too." Cody opened two beers and handed one to Daisy. She was reluctant but needed to gain Cody's trust, so she accepted the drink. They sat at the small kitchen table, which now had two mismatched chairs. Cody turned his chair around and sat on it backward.

"Okay, Mrs. Torrez, ask your questions," he said, taking a long gulp of his beer.

"It's Ms., I'm not married. But, anyway..." She flipped through a little notebook and then set her phone on the table to record their conversation. "Okay, where are you from, originally?"

"Right here. Born and raised in Stoneville."

"How old are you now?"

"Twenty-nine."

The interview started as personal, with Daisy asking about his family, work history, and his affiliation with the Road Barons. He retaliated with his questions, and she kept the trust going by answering each one honestly. After their third beer, the questions grew more intimate, and they began to smile at each other's answers.

When Cody cracked a joke about the neighboring town, Daisy erupted in laughter. Her stern and flawless expression was replaced by a beautiful smile, not unlike a blooming flower.

They stared into each other's eyes without realizing it, but guilt overcame Daisy as she thought about Darcy Poole and Willa Thompson. Angry with herself for getting so distracted, she cleared her throat, and a more professional demeanor came over her.

"Back to the more relevant questions."

"Oh, you're going to ruin my mood, aren't you? Gotta keep it professional, right? Okay then." He sat straight in his chair and tried to appear more serious.

Daisy's voice softened, "Tell me about Willa." She gently bit her bottom lip.

It had been years since anyone had asked him about his deceased wife, but her memory made him smile. "There's not much to tell, honestly. She died—everyone in town thought I killed her because the husband is always the first suspect. I think that's a rule or something. End of story."

"That can't be the end of the story. Do the police have any new leads? I mean, my God, what's it been? Four years?"

"Mm-hmm."

"So, if you're innocent, how'd you get locked up in Dalton for...what, four years?"

"You sure you wanna know?"

Daisy nodded and stood. She crossed the kitchen, opened the refrigerator, and brought two fresh beers to the table. She handed both of them to Cody, who twisted off the caps and handed one bottle back to her.

Cody stared at the label of the Busch bottle. "I have a bit of a temper when someone pushes or threatens someone I care about. I'm not a danger to anyone who doesn't deserve it. You fuck with my family or friends, and you'll see my rage."

"Rage?" Daisy said, ensuring she heard correctly.

"The world goes red, and you'd better not be standing against me."

"And someone stood against you, right?"

"Dale Talbert, your predecessor. He visited me at my house one night—not here, I lived over on Dutch Lane. Anyway, Talbert kept harassing me about Willa's homicide. He wouldn't stop, and then he printed a bunch of lies. He said our marriage was on the rocks and that I had a history of violence. He was hungry for a story and called me a murderer and a coward. I was still grieving her death, and that little prick pushed me too far. I stormed out the door, kicked him in the chest, and he landed on the sidewalk—split his head open. But that wasn't enough, so I beat him until both eyes swelled shut. I finally let him go, and the idiot took off running—right in front of a moving car."

Daisy cringed at the picture Cody had painted in her mind. "Oh my God, how did he survive that?"

"It was a small car going slow. But he spent three weeks in the hospital and months in physical therapy. I was charged with assault and given four years, but I got out four months early. I didn't mean to hurt him so badly. I just...reacted...to his ludicrous accusations."

Daisy set her beer aside and studied his face for a moment. She closed her notebook that was sitting on the table and gripped her phone.

Cody mimicked her action, pushing his own beer aside to ease her nerves.

"I know how that can be," Daisy said in almost a whisper. Cody noticed she was now hugging herself and staring at the rough wood grain of the kitchen table. "My ex-husband. My ex was a violent man. Especially when he was drinking." Cody wanted to take her hand, but his courage with women was still locked up in Dalton County Prison.

"I'm not the same man I was back then, Daisy."

"I'm sure that's true," she guarded herself. "Still, it's getting late, and I should get home."

"Okay."

Daisy walked to the door with Cody following. As she opened the door, she turned abruptly to face him, as if she had something important to say, but when his gray eyes met hers, the thought vanished like smoke in a windstorm.

"May I walk you home? It's getting late, and there are some crazy people out there."

Daisy politely turned down his chivalry.

They stepped onto the porch, the outdoor light glowed off her skin, and Cody admired a beauty he'd not seen in years. "If you have any more questions, you know where to find me. And it just so happens that I'm free tomorrow evening."

"I think I have all I need, Mr. Savage."

Damn, Cody thought to himself. 'Mr. Savage.' She sounded like his high school English teacher, who used to refer to him like that when he was in trouble.

"But, if I think of anything else, I'll be in touch," Daisy stepped off the porch and walked out of sight. She remained on foot, staying on the sidewalks as she made her way through town in the dark. Alone with the streetlights to guide her home, she thought about the interview and the man who intrigued her. She wanted to know more, but knew that she might be treading in dangerous water.

She needed to regain her focus and concentrate on the priority. She needed to write the story of Darcy Poole's disappearance.

*****

Cody picked up the beer bottles and drop cloths and put away the cans of paint. He took one last look at the bare canvases that surrounded him. "A fresh start." Alyse's words danced in his head as he started up the stairs to the bedroom.

Without warning, the doorbell chimed, calling him back to the front door. He bounded down the stairs, hoping Daisy had returned. He flung open the door, but instead of seeing Daisy, he saw nothing but the dark. On his front lawn, a small flame erupted. It was difficult to discern what was burning. His eyes, still used to the interior lights, watched the fire grow until it illuminated a figure standing on his property. The figure, dressed in dark clothing, hurled a burning brick toward the open door.

Cody jumped to the side and landed on his hip. He rolled across the kitchen as the flaming brick bounced off the linoleum and smashed against a wooden hutch. The hutch was instantly ablaze, and the hungry flames snaked up the wall.

Staying on the floor, Cody crawled on his elbows, opened the kitchen sink cabinet, and fumbled for an old fire extinguisher. Please still work! He pulled the pin, squeezed the trigger, and gritted his teeth as a geyser of fire retardant spewed from the nozzle. He sprayed the little inferno, but as he did, a round of small-caliber bullets riddled the walls, and the frantic homeowner had to take cover. The barrage of deadly lead kept coming, perforating the walls and cupboards of the kitchen. The flaming snakes reared their heads again and crawled vertically once more.

Cody heard the bullets thump against wood studs in the wall and perforate the Sheetrock. Shards of glass cascaded onto the floor next to him as the windows shattered. He stayed against the dishwasher, hoping it was solid enough to shield him from the hail of gunfire. Smoke filled the room, refusing to exit the open door.

The shooter emptied two magazines into the house before Cody heard two car doors slam shut. Tires squealed, and the assailants sped away. Eight seconds later, a second vehicle—possibly a big truck based on the engine's sound—left the scene, following the first.

Cody stayed low and out of sight as he pointed the old fire extinguisher at the growing fire. Once the last of the fire's life had been doused, Cody stepped outside and dropped the extinguisher on the porch. He sucked fresh air into his lungs and coughed out the smoke he'd inhaled.

The back of his arm burned, but he didn't recall getting that close to the fire. He twisted his arm to get a look at his injury. Blood ran down his triceps, around his elbow, and dripped off his left hand. The burning sensation he felt was from a bullet that had tagged him.

Back in the kitchen, he wrapped the wounded arm with a dishtowel. He donned a pair of oven mitts and dragged the smoldering cabinet with him. The hutch came off the porch with a loud crash as Cody kicked it from the top step, just like he'd done to Dale Talbert four years prior. The wooden furniture stayed mostly intact until Cody grabbed the used-up extinguisher sitting idle on the porch. He roared like a raging bear and swung the extinguisher as if he were trying to bust through a door. The extinguisher bashed the wood hutch repeatedly until nothing was left to break. He tossed the extinguisher like a baseball bat after a home run hit, and it bounced off the ground and struck the side of the house. The hutch had no resemblance to furniture any longer and was nothing more than a pile of splintered, smoldering wood.

All he could do now was sit on his front steps and wait to see if anyone had called the law. His beer buzz was now diluted from the double shot of adrenaline, and a calm descended over him. A few silhouettes appeared in the neighbor's windows and doors, like shadow puppets, and sirens would soon break the silence of the night. He waited, letting the rage monster return to its slumber.

*****

Sheriff Bourbon and Deputy Birchcraft pulled up and parked on the edge of Cody's front lawn within twenty seconds of each other. They talked to one another for what seemed to Cody like an eternity. Bourbon walked down the driveway, his deputy following in his steps. Strobes of blue and red lights illuminated their path to the house.

"We've got a few calls about shots fired at this address, Savage," Bourbon grumbled. He was still exhausted as the search for Darcy continued.

Cody didn't say a word. He just nodded toward the house, and Bourbon could see the holes. The smell of burning wood invaded Bourbon's nostrils as he kicked at the pile of wood that had once been an ornate piece of furniture.

"What the hell happened here?" Bourbon asked.

"Some asshole tossed a flaming brick into my front door and then used my house for target practice." He pointed toward the perforated vinyl siding and broken windows.

"Did you see anything? A vehicle or the suspects?" Birchcraft asked.

"No. I was too busy ducking for cover behind the dishwasher."

Bourbon walked up onto the porch and peeked his head inside. He poked his index finger into a bullet hole, surprised by its small size. "Jesus." Fresh drops of red liquid, spattered by gravity, stained the floor. Bourbon took a mental picture of the damage and turned back to Cody.

"Anyone else with you tonight?"

"Not at the time. A reporter left about fifteen minutes before the shooting started."

Bourbon stepped off the porch and spoke to his deputy, "Birch, go check with the neighbors. Make sure they're okay and see if anybody saw anything. Maybe somebody has a doorbell camera that caught the action."

The obedient deputy back-stepped twice and spun toward the road. He cut through Cody's yard and followed the road on foot to reach the closest neighbor's house.

"Think a doorbell camera could have recorded that?" Cody asked.

"Most new houses have them, but this is an old neighborhood. Closest house is pretty far away, too. What's it, about seventy-five yards to Mr. Santino's house?"

Cody stood, holding the back of his left arm. Bourbon knew the ex-con was bleeding, but just now noticed the blood dripping from Cody's fingers.

"Is that a bullet wound, Savage?"

"Nothing serious. I'll survive."

Bourbon led Cody to his truck and retrieved the first-aid kit. He re-wrapped the bloody wound with sterile gauze, but Cody needed a few stitches. The bullet had pierced the skin, inflicting minimal damage to the muscle, but the exit wound was ugly and needed an appropriate dressing.

"Come on. I'll run you down to the ER," Bourbon ordered.

"To hell with that," Cody said. "I'll be fine, Bourbon, just go find those sonovabitches before they get too far."

"Relax. Birch will find an eyewitness—probably a plate number, too. We'll have those guys locked up by breakfast." He pointed to Cody's injury. "Let's go before this gets infected. You wouldn't want to lose your arm, would you?"

Cody applied pressure to the wound to keep it from bleeding all over Bourbon's patrol vehicle. When the door slammed shut, an uneasy feeling choked the ex-con, and a torrent of old memories returned to him. Although this was a different vehicle, it produced the same effect as Bourbon's previous car. Cody studied the interior as he sat in the rear seat. Long before his release from Dalton, Cody swore he'd never see the inside of the sheriff's vehicle again.

Memories of prison drifted through his exhausted and half-drunk brain while the sheriff chauffeured him through town to the hospital. He especially thought about Thomas, the Uber driver who'd picked him up and driven him to the bus station. Thomas's advice seemed to make sense now, and Cody could hear the kind old man's words: "We all choose the direction we go and the roads we take."

Maybe he shouldn't have come back to Stoneville. Perhaps he should have taken a right at the intersection that day and headed toward Vermont.

Now, he was here, with a house full of holes and a couple of friends who could have been killed. All because he just wanted to make Stoneville his home again. How could he live in a town where all the residents held such contempt for him? If he stayed, he would live with a target on his back—at least until he found Willa's real killer.

"You still alive back there, Savage?" Bourbon asked, looking in the rear view mirror.

"Yeah," Cody whispered, "Just thinking, I should've turned right."

12

SCAREDY CATS 

Jesse Lewis left his lights off while trailing the truck that left Cody Savage's home. Just in case he lost visual contact with the vehicle, he memorized every detail of the truck as it drove under the streetlights. The vehicle turned a dozen times, making its way down alleys and back streets, trying to avoid the main routes, before parking at a small house on the outskirts of town. The house was old and in a state of disrepair. If it weren't for the truck parked in the gravel driveway, the dwelling could have been mistaken for abandoned property.

Two men exited the truck carrying an assault rifle that Jesse couldn't identify. They entered the garage, which seemed larger than the house. The perimeter of the garage was littered with old tires and broken wooden pallets stacked waist-high. When the fluorescent lights flickered to life, the bright glow of light beamed through the windows, illuminating portions of the driveway.

Jesse drove past the house and parked one hundred yards down the road. He was certain he'd seen only two men exit the truck and enter the garage. That was good. Any more, and he would need a firearm. He pushed the truck seat forward and retrieved his weapon of choice: an improvised ax made from a cut hockey stick. Two figure skate blades were bolted to one end of the four-foot hockey stick. They mirrored one another, facing away from the handle to form a double-bladed cutting edge. Jesse had sharpened both blades so they were more suited to slice skin rather than ice. He tried to find a real ax to carry, but the heft slowed his swing, and the deadly device required too much force to stop its forward momentum. His homemade hockey ax could be swung quickly and change direction in an instant. He gripped it tight, ready to confront the two men who attacked Cody Savage minutes ago.

Jesse stayed hidden in the shadows as he crept around the side of the garage like a junkyard thief. He anticipated a dog's barking as he approached, but instead, he was surrounded by two meowing cats. More cats darted in and out of the shadows, climbing through pallets and tires, no doubt on the hunt for mice exploring the rubbish. He knew what it was like to be a hunter tonight as he circled the garage in the dark. He tripped over an empty gas can but remained steady on his feet.

He saw an enormous bat fly across the light of the window. No, not a bat. Was that a bird? His observation was confirmed when he heard a couple of caws from a crow, perched somewhere on the roof of the garage.

The cool night air produced dew on the tall grass. His pants absorbed the moisture from his ankles to his knees, but the wet grass muffled his steps as he moved, making his way to the back of the garage. Fewer windows in the back meant less light cascading onto the lawn. He could hear the two men talking through a single window.

"Holy shit, that was intense," said a tall, bearded man. He retrieved two beers from a rusty refrigerator that hummed loudly. A greasy ponytail hung on the back of his head, and tattoos covered his arms. A black T-shirt with the logo of an eighties rock band covered his muscular build and protruding belly. Passing a beer to his buddy, he took a seat on an upside-down bucket used as a stool for working on a nearby motorcycle.

The second man cracked open the Budweiser and took a big drink, "Hell yeah! Jesus, that was insane, dude. Ever done anything like that before?"

Black T-shirt, already high on adrenaline, lit a joint for a double high. "Once, in Texas. My brother had some trouble with a couple of assholes who owed him eight grand." He took a long drag and passed the joint to his buddy. "We threw a Molotov cocktail into their camper and took their truck. Sold it for parts."

The second man, wearing a blue T-shirt with a truck logo, looked around the garage. "Where'd you stash the gun, man?"

Black T-shirt pointed to a sizable toolbox with wide drawers.

"Think that fucker will get the hint? Think he'll leave town?" Blue T-shirt asked through missing teeth.

"Hard to say. I remember Savage. He was a stubborn sonovabitch."

"Man, I just hope we didn't go too far. Think you killed him?"

"No, he's probably fine. I just want to scare him—let him know he's not welcome here anymore. Stoneville tolerates a lot of shit, but not wife killers."

"And if he don't get the hint?" Blue T-shirt handed the joint back.

"Then I'll have to get me a quarter-stick of dynamite," Black T-shirt laughed.

"Where the hell you gonna get dynamite, dude?"

"We got some at work—for blasting beaver dams," Black T-shirt said. He sucked on the marijuana joint and then snuffed it in an ashtray.

Blue T-shirt stood and headed out the garage's back door, a small man door that creaked on its hinges and slammed hard when it closed. The loud noise scattered the cats, but only momentarily. He stepped to the far side of the garage to relieve himself in the shadows.

Jesse ducked under the light of the window and stood just four feet behind the urinating man in the blue T-shirt. A tingle of pain crept up his neck and gripped his brain, a familiar pain only brought on by being in close proximity to a sinner.

The crow cawed somewhere in the dark, dropped from the gutter, and flew in a circle before settling back on the garage's shingles.

"He's guilty," a raspy female voice whispered into his brain, a woman he'd never met, but come to loathe. And then he saw the woman from the dock.

What was her name, again? Flesti. Flesti Thaed. What the hell kinda name is that?

Jesse's migraine worsened with each slow step. Jesse could sense the sins of the man in front of him and hungered to take them away, while the woman from the lake ushered him on. He didn't know if she was real or a product of his aching mind. But he could hear her clearly. "Well, go on now. Take his goddam head off."

Blue T-shirt finally heard the pastor approaching but thought little of the sound. "You damn cats get out of here before I piss on your heads."

He finished, zipped up, and turned to cuss the cats some more. Instead of frightened cats, he stood face to face with a shadow.

Blue T-shirt opened his mouth to yell, but Jesse was too fast with the ax. He swung from the side, the blades arching from the right, and never slowed as they cut through the man's throat. The target stumbled backward as his blue T-shirt turned purple. Even as he drifted into the shadows, the man's eyes were visible in the dark, like the felines around him. He tried to speak, but only a gurgle left the open wound where his voice box used to be. He clutched his throat with both hands, confused about what had just happened, trying to figure out who had unleashed the deadly attack. He lost control of his body and felt himself melting into the dark.

The dying man fell into a pile of disassembled scaffolding, rattling the metal and making a loud crash like an entire kitchen of pots and pans falling onto the floor.

Inside, Black T-shirt laughed out loud. "Jesus, Pete, you only drank one beer." He waited for a response and for Pete to re-enter the garage.

"Pete? You okay out there?"

Black T-shirt walked to the back door and opened it to check on his companion, but all he saw was a dark void. There was no sign of his buddy or even a sound to follow. Pete was already in the past tense.

Black T-shirt stepped back inside to retrieve a flashlight, but not before Jesse Lewis had snuck around the garage and entered from the front. He was waiting for Black T-shirt to come back inside. They met near the motorcycle.

"Who the fuck are you?" Black T-shirt said. His hands turned to fists. Then he saw the blood on Jesse's hockey ax. His eyes narrowed in anger. "What did you do to Pete?"

"Pete's dead, asshole."

"Dead? What the fuck do you want?"

"Your sins!" Jesse swung the hockey-ax straight at Black T-shirt's head, but the big man was faster than Jesse had anticipated and an experienced fighter. He blocked the hockey stick with his left forearm, sacrificing a bone that cracked loudly from the impact.

Black T-shirt threw his right fist forward, landing it squarely in

Jesse's chest and sending the smaller man reeling backward. Losing his grip on the hockey-ax, Jesse tripped over a tire on the floor and fell flat on his back, knocking the air out of his lungs. His opponent lunged for the large toolbox, and the top compartment popped open. Black T-shirt pulled out the semi-automatic rifle, fumbling the gun with a broken bone in his forearm, and finally managed to rack the first round into the chamber.

"You're dead, you bastard. You're dead!" The man with the gun screamed.

Jesse propped both feet against the heavy Harley-Davidson between them and pushed with all his strength. The motorcycle fell onto the legs of Black T-shirt before he could turn around. He went down but held onto the large toolbox to prevent himself from dropping to the floor. Jesse recovered, picked up the spare tire he had tripped over, a rubber motorcycle tire not yet mounted on an aluminum rim. He hooked it around Black T-shirt's face, and pulled as hard as he could, nearly breaking the other man's back, and looped it to the handlebars of the fallen motorcycle.

Black T-shirt struggled to free himself, forced to drop the gun in his hands. He managed to twist his body and escape the tire trap, but the heavy motorcycle had him pinned down. Jesse was on him in an instant with the hockey blade to his throat.

Black T-shirt stopped struggling, conceding defeat. He was in a push-up position, the Harley pinning his legs, and his weapon was out of reach.

"Who the hell are you, man?" Black T-shirt asked.

"You tried to kill Cody Savage."

"We weren't trying to kill him. I swear, we just wanted to scare him, is all. He's a fucking *killer*, man. He killed his wife and got away with murder. What do you care about that piece of shit, anyway?"

Jesse applied a little pressure to the big man's throat. "Because nobody gets to eat his sins but me."

Outside, the crow hopped on the windowsill and watched the performance, while its head bobbed up and down and its wings flapped in anticipation.

"What the frig are you talking about?" Black T-shirt was nearly sobbing now, unaware that a stream of urine ran down his leg. He didn't understand. How in the hell could a sin be eaten?

Jesse's arm was numb, and his head throbbed from the smell of the evil that lingered in the garage. "Your simple mind wouldn't understand. Your worthless life and poor judgment have brought you here. To me. I'm sorry, but I must feed the lake."

"You going to talk him to death? Get on with it."

Before he could say another word, Black T-shirt's body jerked as the hockey-ax struck the back of his neck and broke two vertebrae.

The crow cawed three times and vanished in the night.

Jesse picked up an oil-soaked rag and wiped the blades of his weapon clean. Within the clutter of the garage, five cats had witnessed his wrath and shrank away to hide. Jesse left the garage, turned off the lights, and drove home.

*****

Jesse lay awake in bed, sweating, tossing, turning, and sated by the sins of the two men he'd murdered. Their faces flashed in his mind, and he envisioned their heinous crimes. Blue T-shirt was a child predator, and Jesse's abilities allowed him to see the man's innocent and helpless victims. Black T-shirt had been a car thief when he was younger, and made extra money selling meth on the streets. Jesse could see so much.

His power—if he wanted to call it that—was getting stronger.

Jesse couldn't tolerate the taste of their sins any longer, and he needed to free himself of the nightmarish visions. There was only one way to wash the sour experience from his skin. He abandoned his bed and drove to Cain Lake. The moon had risen in the last hour, casting its natural light across the lake's surface. Jesse parked his truck behind the church, shining the headlights toward the beach, and walked the path through the little field of wildflowers to the lake.

The water was cold on his naked skin as he waded into the lake, but he endured its frigid temperature until the blue bugs of light came and took his pain and the sins he'd stolen in that cluttered garage. The water glowed with life below him, and the little organisms swirled and raced in hasty effort to consume the guilt Jesse had brought them.

Feeling lighter, he floated higher with each passing minute. Time was as lost to him here as it was when he slept. He could have been there for minutes or hours; he wasn't sure, and he didn't care. There was no leaving the lake until the purge was complete.

Alone in the dark, he watched a satellite pass under the stars, and he wondered if the satellite saw him. They were two solitary objects floating aimlessly in space, surrounded by little lights. Once the purge was complete and the lake satisfied, he swam back to shore, drained and tired.

Two fewer sinners in town. Even though Jesse could easily justify his actions, the guilt choked him like ragweed pollen with each breath. The irony wasn't lost on him: he knew he was a sinner, too, and the day would come when he would pay his toll.

He thought about Flesti Thaed hiking the woods alone, searching for something, and possibly having the same experience. Was she a killer—a sin eater like him? Or did his loneliness merely conjure the illusion that she was like him? He wondered what had happened to the lone hiker and if she'd found her dog.

He gathered his clothes and carried them to the car. So many questions about Cain Lake and its power wrestled with his mind. Who else experienced this feeling? Who else was seduced by the lake's influence?

But mostly, he wanted to know how long it would be before he got to devour the sins of a killer. When would he feed on Cody Savage?

13
THE LAST DONUT

Cody leaned against the window of Bourbon's SUV. "You always drive this slow, Sheriff?"

"No sense causing an accident. You're not going to die," Bourbon said.

"You mean I'm not worth causing an accident, don't you?" Cody said.

Bourbon signaled left and made his way through a green light. "No, that's not what I mean. You're a complicated guy, you know that, Savage?"

"How's that?"

"You're still the main suspect in a murder investigation that's been going on for four years, and you choose to come back to the scene of the crime. You buy a house—"

"It was inherited."

"You inherit a house and start fixing it up like you're going to spend the rest of your life in Stoneville. The problem is: if you stay here, you'll probably be killed within a year, but if you leave, then everyone will assume you're guilty. So, maybe you're staying because you believe the people in this town will change, or maybe you're staying so you won't look guilty."

"What's really bothering you?" Cody leaned toward the front seat. "Is it that you have to protect me from being killed because you don't know if I am guilty or not?"

"Maybe. I'm dedicated to this job. If that means protecting you from harm, then I guess I have to protect you from harm. I try not to form opinions about people's guilt until I have the evidence, and right now, there's no evidence to prove you killed Willa."

"You know I didn't. You've always known. You just pretend it could

109

have been me because you can't find her real murderer?"

Bourbon was silent. Thinking of Willa now was a distraction, and he had a missing girl, a killer, and two shooters to find.

They pulled into the Emergency Room parking lot, and Bourbon escorted Cody inside. They sat in the waiting room across from one another, Bourbon checking his watch every thirty seconds, which was about as often as he stretched or yawned.

"I'm a big boy; you don't have to wait with me," Cody said.

"I know," Bourbon replied. "I'll stay until they take you back. You're a gunshot victim, so they'd call me to start an investigation anyway. As soon as they finish with me, I'm going home. Tomorrow, the rescue dive team is coming up from Albany. They're going to do a thorough search of the lake for Darcy Poole's body. It's our last resort before we call off the search. Besides, Birch is meeting me here. He's got a lead on the suspects that shot up your house."

"You still haven't found that girl?" Cody's concern was genuine.

"Nope. I'm sure it's a recovery mission now."

"You think she's dead? Jesus, Sheriff, that's not a very positive outlook. You just give up on everybody, don't you?"

"Watch your mouth, son. We've had a hundred volunteers out there looking for Darcy since she went missing, but now people are more worried that there's a murderer on the loose since Brody Sherwood was killed at The 'Shaft. Some people think it's you. I haven't seen you out there searching." Bourbon was visibly discouraged by the topic, and Cody knew he'd struck a nerve. And Bourbon was right: Cody hadn't been out there searching.

"No, I just heard about it tonight from AJ and Alyse. I've been at my house all weekend with no television or radio. I had no idea, or I would have helped."

"Ah, bullshit. There were too many people searching who would have protested if you'd shown up. Your presence would just distract the other searchers."

Red and blue lights from the hospital parking lot illuminated the foyer walls, redirecting Bourbon's attention to a patrol car parked outside. Deputy Birchcraft rounded the front of the vehicle and walked toward the emergency room entrance.

Bourbon stood when he saw his deputy approaching the sliding glass doors. "There's Birch—let's see what he's got. He looks happy about something."

Cody saw no expression on Birchcraft's face. "How can you tell?"

Bourbon ignored the question.

Eli Birchcraft walked through the glass doors, filling the frame with his broad shoulders. Cody joined Bourbon, standing to greet him, but Bourbon motioned for Cody to sit back down. They began their discussion as Cody listened.

"Whatcha got, Birch?"

"We got lucky," Birchcraft began. "Neighbor did have a video doorbell which showed two trucks leaving the scene. However, the second truck left eight seconds after the first. An eyewitness, Mr. Whitney, saw the whole thing." Deputy Birchcraft opened a tattered notebook and started reading his notes from the interview. "According to the witness, a fire began on Savage's front lawn, and a burning object was then hurled into the structure. The man who threw the flaming brick retreated to the first truck and climbed inside. The driver of the same truck exited with a military-style firearm and began firing at the residence."

"Jesus," Bourbon interrupted. "What the hell is this town coming to?"

Birchcraft continued, "The first truck then sped away, seemingly unaware of the second truck."

"You mean they were being followed?"

"It appeared that way to Mr. Whitney."

"Anything else?"

"Oh yeah," Birchcraft almost smiled, "Turns out Mr. Whitney got both license plate numbers. The first truck, that did the shooting, belongs to Darin Cloudwater. He lives out on Allison Road. He's got an extensive rap sheet from Texas."

"And the second truck?"

"That's where it gets interesting. The second truck belongs to Connor Bayley—Darcy Poole's boyfriend, that we've been trying to contact."

"Connor Bayley? Where the hell has that little prick been?" Bourbon said. "If he's still in town, why isn't he answering his phone? We need to find him and question him about Darcy. He must know something about her disappearance."

The deputy looked around the waiting room and then lowered his voice. "I don't know, boss, but that shoots down our theory that he and Darcy Poole might have run away together. No one's reported him missing, but he has been."

"Well, if he was driving that truck, he's not missing anymore. Think Darcy could have been in the truck, too?"

"I don't think so," Birchcraft answered. "Whitney was right across the street, walking his dog, and got a good look. He was sure that there was only one person in the second truck. He also said that Connor's truck had been there for an hour—like he was surveying Savage's house."

"Damn. Call Archer and wake his ass up. Meet me at the judge's house in thirty minutes to grab the warrant. Tell Archer you'll meet him at Darin Stinkwater's house afterwards."

"Cloudwater," Birchcraft said.

"Yeah, whatever his friggin name is. Text me the address, would you?"

Birchcraft bolted toward the door. He was already on the phone calling Archer when he got to the exit. By the time Bourbon got to his patrol vehicle, he had received Cloudwater's address on his phone from Birchcraft.

Bourbon left Cody sitting in the hospital and headed straight for the judge's house to secure the search warrant and hand it off to Birchcraft. Then he was going to pay a visit to Connor Bailey's trailer. Hopefully, Connor had returned and would have some information to help him track down Darcy Poole. And if the little pecker-head didn't cooperate, he was going to bring him in for questioning.

*****

Deputy Charlie Archer was at Cloudwater's house within twenty minutes of Birchcraft's call. He waited inside his personal vehicle for Birchcraft to arrive with the search warrant. The cluttered property's lights were off, but Archer could see the front man-door to the garage was open. He peered through his windshield with a set of Nikon binoculars, but the scene was as quiet as a cemetery. The only noticeable motion was a few feral cats climbing through the debris. Forty minutes later, Birchcraft finally arrived. The two men met at the back of Birchcraft's patrol vehicle.

Birchcraft gave Deputy Archer the details over the phone while he drove to the judge's house. Archer was out of uniform but displayed his badge on his belt. After the exhaustive search they'd endured looking for Darcy Poole, Archer was irritated to be called back into work and was in a miserable mood, but that wasn't unusual.

"Fuck is this all about anyway, Birch? If the assholes in this house shot up Cody Savage, then they're damn heroes in my book. Judge should be serving 'em a medal rather than a search warrant."

Birchcraft stayed professional. "These men are reckless, Archer. They could have killed innocent people. Savage had company just before the bullets started flying."

The two deputies walked toward the house, side by side, disputing amongst themselves. Archer was always griping if the job caused him any inconvenience, but Birchcraft seemed to live for his career.

A black truck with oversized tires was parked in the gravel driveway. Birchcraft pointed to the truck's license plate, a match to the number that Mr. Whitney had given the officer.

"That's Cloudwater's truck, all right."

They were at the correct address. They drew their service pistols in unison and popped the safeties off. Birchcraft moved until his back was against the trailer wall, and motioned Archer to approach the front door. Archer gripped his gun with both hands as he climbed a long ramp built for a wheelchair or scooter. Birchcraft stayed six feet behind, pistol pointing to the ground, but ready to draw if necessary.

Archer banged on the front door of the house with a fist. Birchcraft watched the garage and truck for movement in the dark.

Archer banged again. "Open the friggin door! This is Stoneville Sheriff's Department with a warrant."

Birchcraft felt something rub against his ankle and knew, without looking, it was one of the cats. He kept his eye on his impatient partner until the cat lay on his foot. He pulled his foot out and noticed the thick red liquid that covered the gray tabby's belly. "Archer, check this out."

Archer saw the cat rolling over, "Where the hell did that come from?"

"Garage."

When they turned on the garage's lights, the grim scene shook them. They had come here expecting to arrest the two suspects in a drive-by shooting and arson case. Now, they would need two body bags.

They called Bourbon on his cell phone and gave him the news. Bourbon had struck out as well, finding Connor Bayley's trailer on the other side of town, empty. Bourbon had sifted through Connor's mail that was overflowing from the mailbox at the end of the driveway. On the porch, a dog's water and food bowl were bone dry, and the grass hadn't been cut in at least two weeks.

Sheriff Bourbon then knew that he was searching for two people. But what he didn't know was whether Connor was a victim or a suspect. If he had hurt Darcy Poole, then he had a hell of a head start.

"What do we do now, boss?" Birchcraft asked over the phone.

Bourbon climbed into his truck. "I don't know, Birch. I don't know."

*****

Cody came out of the Emergency Room with a few stitches and a written prescription for a painkiller he couldn't pronounce. The night air chilled his skin, but he knew the long walk home would warm him up.

He tossed the written prescription in the outside garbage can because he didn't want to get hooked on some narcotic just to evade a couple of days of pain. He believed pain stimulated the body to heal faster, and the only benefit of most medication was to enrich the doctors and pharmacies.

"Aren't you going to need that?" A familiar voice asked from beside him. "It's going to hurt like hell tomorrow."

Daisy Torrez leaned against the wall, smoking a light menthol, getting negative looks from a man waiting for his wife to be discharged.

"How the hell did you know?" Cody asked Daisy.

"I'm a reporter. I have a keen sense for these things, and nothing gets by me."

"Really?"

She laughed. "No. My boss called me and told me to get my ass over here. He heard something on his police scanner."

Cody took a minute to admire her in the dim light of the hospital entrance. Even he was surprised at how happy he was to see her.

"Need a ride?" Daisy asked. "I didn't walk this time." She lightly jingled a set of car keys.

"Sure. If you don't mind." Then it occurred to him. "Jesus, I'm so glad you left when you did. You could have—"

She cut him off with a finger to his lips. "Don't worry about it. Makes for an interesting story, right?"

She walked him to a beat-up Subaru Outback in the parking lot, and Cody guessed it had a million miles on it. When she put the key in the ignition and turned it, the car sputtered to life, and they accelerated down the road with only one headlight. It was difficult for them to have a conversation over the noise of the Subaru's Boxer engine and a loose exhaust pipe. They rode without conversation for less than a mile, stopping at their destination in the heart of Stoneville.

Cody exited the vehicle and shut the car door, which popped back open. Then he closed it again and a third time before it latched.

"Don't say a word. It was my mom's car," Daisy said. "I haven't gotten a paycheck yet. I can't get a loan for a car of my own. Plus, my mom doesn't like to drive, so...."

"Hey, it's nicer than my car."

Daisy thought he was teasing until she realized that he didn't own a vehicle. She gave him a wink.

"I thought you were taking me home," Cody said. They hadn't driven very far from the hospital when Daisy stopped at a nineteenth-century commercial building made of rugged sandstone blocks. The entire first floor was occupied by a pizza restaurant owned by an Italian family.

The aroma of burnt cheese and spices filled the air, even though the restaurant had been closed for an hour. "This used to be Willa's favorite. But back then, it was called 'Slice of Sicily.'"

"When and if I finally let you take me out on a date, we can go here." She nodded at the neon sign that read "Pizza Primo."

Daisy led Cody to a heavy steel door beside the restaurant with a different street address sign. She unlocked the door and revealed a rickety old stairwell that ascended to her second-floor apartment.

"Don't you eat here all the time if you live upstairs?"

"You'd think so, but no. Still no paycheck, remember? The smell drives me crazy, though."

Cody hesitated at the bottom of the stairs. "Do you want me to come up?"

"You're not going home tonight, Mr. Savage." She was still talking like his English teacher. "It's way too dangerous. You may sleep on my couch, and when you wake up, you owe me some answers."

"You mean, I owe you a story."

"You catch on quick," she laughed.

They climbed the stairs together until they reached her third-floor apartment, which wasn't much cleaner than his house. She brought him a pillow and blanket, which smelled like her hair. Daisy disappeared into another room, and Cody heard her brushing her teeth. He tried to stay awake so he could thank her and say goodnight, but the two painkillers a nurse forced him to take, mixed with the alcohol in his blood, knocked him unconscious.

*****

He slept great for six hours, then the sound of a spoon stirring coffee in a ceramic mug woke him.

"Sorry, did I wake you?"

She wore less makeup and was wearing a long NY Giants jersey that Cody assumed she had worn to bed. Her hair was a little messy—How cool was it that she didn't even try to fix it? And she was already hard at work on her computer.

Cody rubbed the sleep from his eyes. He could get used to this. He made his way into her little kitchen nook. "You're a morning person, too, huh?"

"5:30 every day."

"Cool. Me too," Cody said under his breath, not wanting her to hear his presumptuous comment. He joined her at the small table, where she had set up a makeshift office.

"So," Daisy said, "who do you think shot up your house last night and burned it down?"

"Okay. First of all, no one burned my house down. It was just a flaming brick that caught a hutch and one wall on fire. Second, Good morning to you, too." He took a big drink of coffee and waited for her reaction.

"Good morning," Daisy said just before sticking out her tongue.

Cody laughed. "You need a nickname for your reporting career."

"A nickname?"

"Yeah, something like the Shark, or the Piranha." He snapped his fingers in revelation. "The Chupacabra. Daisy 'The Chupacabra' Torrez."

"Are you finished? Do you think you're funny, Mr. Funny Guy?" Daisy said in a serious tone, but struggled to contain her laughter. She stood, pushed past him, and opened the refrigerator door. When she returned, she was smiling behind a box of day-old donuts. Opening the lid, she presented the baked goods to her guest. "Breakfast?"

Cody let her have the maple cream, even though it was his favorite. "Aren't you supposed to be writing the Darcy Poole story?"

"Yes, but there's not much to report. The sheriff's hit a dead end. Volunteer search teams are losing hope, and they're too afraid of being the next victim of whoever killed Brody Sherwood. The searchers have almost completely given up. And rumor has it she ran away with Connor Bayley." She saw the confusion on Cody's face. "He's the boyfriend."

"Connor Bayley couldn't have run away with Darcy. His truck was at my house last night."

"What? You mean he hasn't vanished, too? Why didn't you tell me that?"

"Because I just found out there was a connection. The deputy came to the hospital last night to report to the sheriff. An eyewitness got both license plate numbers, and one of them belonged to Connor Bayley."

"What did the sheriff think of that?"

"I don't know. I was in too much pain to try to keep up. I know that the other truck belonged to some guy who lives outside of town."

"So, if Connor's truck is in town, then he's in town. Guys like that love their trucks more than their girlfriends. They don't leave without taking their vehicle, am I right?"

She didn't wait for an answer. "Of course," Daisy continued, "this proves that Darcy didn't run away—at least not with her boyfriend. I have to write this up for today's update. Maybe this will inspire the volunteer search teams to keep looking."

Daisy rapped on the computer keys, the screen reflecting in the round-rimmed glasses balancing on the bridge of her nose.

Cody felt a little ignored now and made an attempt for her attention, "Hey, I got shot last night. Remember that? That's a good story, too."

"*Deja de ser un bebé*. It's just a little flesh wound," Daisy responded, her eyes fixated on the laptop's monitor like a cat watching fish in a bowl.

Cody served himself a refill of coffee and then took the last donut. "Mind if I use your shower?"

"Sure, go ahead." She poked at the computer keys with hyper-focus until Cody stepped on something in the living room. He picked up a tiny toy car and looked at the woman writing in the kitchen.

Daisy peeked over the laptop and saw Cody concentrating on the little toy car in the palm of his hand. He looked at her, wearing the same glasses as when they first met. His face donned an expression of confusion, as if he'd just solved an age-old mystery.

"You," Cody said. "You were at the bus station with a little boy."

"*Si*, Samuel."

"Samuel?" Cody echoed.

Daisy left her table and computer and picked the car out of Cody's hand. "He is my son. He's four."

"Where is he?" Cody looked around.

"With my mom. I took an Uber to the bus station that day. I was offered this job, but I couldn't afford daycare or a babysitter. So, Samuel and I took the bus to my mother's house, thanks to your kindness."

Cody's cheeks warmed.

"Sammy is staying with her, and I borrowed my mother's car to come back to Stoneville and start working. I'll go pick him up in two weeks."

"When you have a paycheck?"

She nodded timidly. "I couldn't have taken this job otherwise."

"Why didn't you tell me before?"

"Because it was a little embarrassing. But you should know that your small act of kindness, giving me all the money you had, saved my life, Cody. If it weren't for you, I wouldn't have this job. I wouldn't have made it to my mother's house, I wouldn't have had anyone to watch Sammy, and I don't know what I would have done. *Gracias*, Mr. Savage." She was so close now Cody could smell the sweet maple sugar.

He slid his left arm around her waist, leaned down, and kissed her. He was glad she didn't resist. She melted into him, just a little—just enough.

Daisy finally pulled away and looked him in the eye. "I fell for you the very moment you handed me that debit card—but—"

Cody cringed, worried about the ultimatum he was about to hear.

"If you want this to seriously happen...if you don't want this to end before it even begins...you'd better split that last donut with me."

14

THE MORGUE

Bourbon didn't realize how hungry he was until he sat down at the counter of Tabitha's Diner. Connie brought his usual plate and set it in front of the famished sheriff. She patted his hand, knowing how his week had been, and gave him a warning: "Here comes your deputy officer."

Bourbon didn't spin around on his stool because he was expecting Deputy Charlie Archer to meet him at Tabitha's this morning. Archer walked through the door and took the empty stool adjacent to his boss, although he stood in front of it, waving for Connie's attention. She ignored him until she finished pouring four coffees for table nine.

"Is Connie ignoring me?" Archer asked.

"Morning, Arch," Bourbon said.

"She is ignoring me. Damn her. Someday I'm going to be sheriff and—"

"Morning, Arch," Bourbon repeated.

"Huh, oh...Morning, boss. So, what's so important that you wanted to meet during your breakfast?"

Bourbon waited to reply until he finished chewing his bacon. "Lot to do today. The coroner's office called a few minutes ago. You know those two perps you and Birch found last night?"

Archer stared at Connie. "Jesus, I just want a cup of coffee."

"Archer? Are you listening to me?" Bourbon barked. "I've got news from the coroner."

"Yeah, yeah, sorry, boss, go ahead."

"The coroner cut the shirt off those two boys who shot up Cody Savage's house. Both of them had a word carved into their torsos."

"You mean like scarification or some gang affiliation shit?"

"No. It was fresh—from the killer," Bourbon said. "Carved it with a knife or sharp tool. I think it's some kind of message."

"Jesus, what the fuck did it say?"

"I don't know yet. Maybe the killer was labeling his victims, or maybe he was signing his work. The only way we're going to find out is to catch this bastard, and we need to do it quickly. The last thing we need is a town full of carved-up bodies."

Connie finally made her way to Archer and poured a steaming cup of freshly brewed coffee. He stirred in two teaspoons of sugar, "'Bout damn time," he murmured under his breath.

Bourbon put more food in his mouth and thought as he chewed. He finally swallowed, washed it down with the last of his coffee, and had a plan for the day.

"Okay, Arch, I'm going to go down to the coroner's office and check this out for myself. I'm going to have you lead the dive team that's coming to search the lake for Darcy Poole's body. They're on their way here from Albany—left at six a.m.—should be in the water by 9:30."

"I gotta go babysit a bunch of frog faces? Can't Birch do that when he comes in? I've got a tip from the waitress at the AMVETS about some guy selling Oxycontin out of his van."

Bourbon shook his head, "Finding Darcy Poole, dead or alive, is our number one priority right now. Her parents are going through hell and are counting on us for answers. Our second priority is finding what appears to be a serial killer. I'm keeping you and Birch on our missing person. I'll keep working on our serial killer case and try to find out why he seems to be following Cody Savage."

"What makes you think he's following Savage?"

"We've seen the same truck twice, a full-sized black Chevy. Both times, it was following Savage. First, when he left The Mineshaft, the night Brody Sherwood was murdered. The second time was last night. He chased down the men who shot up Cody's house and murdered them in cold blood."

"See, if you ask me, Sheriff, Cody's got himself a guardian angel. Some dumb ass protector who doesn't know what a piece of shit he is.

Put me on that case. I'll find him and set him straight."

Bourbon's phone buzzed in his pocket. Seeing Annabel's number appear, it crushed him not answer since he hadn't seen her the night he left her in the restaurant.

She'd just have to wait.

"Archer, get to the lake and coordinate with the dive team. Show them where the tributary streams create currents and where the deepest holes are. They need someone there who knows that water. Keep me posted."

Archer chugged his coffee and left Bourbon sitting at the counter.

Sheriff Bourbon dropped a twenty on the counter to pay his bill and exited the diner with his cell phone still in hand. His index finger punched numbers as he crossed the parking lot, then leaned against his truck and waited for Annabel to answer. Their conversation was brief, full of ideas about how they wished they could see each other more. Bourbon assured Annabel that there was nothing to fear from Cody Savage, even though she didn't ask. She was more worried about Darcy Poole's safety than her own.

When he hung up the phone, guilt squeezed his chest, and he wasn't sure from which direction it came. Was it guilt for not spending time with Annie or not finding Darcy? Or had this guilt spawned from letting three more murders occur in his town?

He drove his usual zig-zag pattern across town, looking at the way things had changed since he first took office. Jesus, it seemed like forever ago. What was happening here—why were people so different? When he started this job, all he had to do was write a few traffic violations, catch kids out painting graffiti on the walls, and serve court papers for divorces. Now, the streets were overflowing with narcotics and guns. His department was called to more domestic violence cases than he could count, and there had been six homicides in the same number of years—three of them this week.

It was more than he and his two deputies could handle. The Stoneville Sheriff's Department was significantly understaffed.

He stopped his truck at a red light and stared down the quiet road. Three men sped through the intersection on bicycles—fast road bikes with narrow tires that allowed greater speed. Bourbon envied their freedom. They were just riding, not racing, cruising the streets of Stoneville, enjoying their exercise.

Over the last few months, the idea of retirement had started to nag at him. He could just sit by the river and fish, maybe do a little traveling, and he had always wanted to climb Mt. Marcy, the tallest mountain in New York. And he'd hike around Cain Lake with nothing but a backpack and a clear mind. He'd take his time over the course of a week or more and enjoy the different types of wildlife that the east side provided.

Bourbon knew he'd probably die as the sheriff of Stoneville. He leaned to his right and looked at the old man in the Jeep mirror, barely recognizing him. He thought Jeff Bourbon was a young buck with bulging muscles and keen eyes, but the reflection staring back was pale and tired. Crow's feet parenthetically formed at both eyes, which had darkened and sunk over the years.

He thought about the man he used to be, who wanted to backpack around Cain Lake and sleep under the stars. Where was the man who dreamed of hunting and fishing in his free time and playing with his grandkids when he got old? The duties of being a sheriff had taken over his existence, preventing Bourbon from following those dreams and robbing him of the opportunity to start a family.

He knew he was thinking selfishly, but shouldn't—not now—not when Darcy Poole was out there somewhere, waiting to be found. She was probably dead by now, but that didn't mean she was any less deserving of his attempt to find her.

Archer and Birchcraft are good cops. They'll find her.

The traffic light turned green, and he crept through the intersection, crossed town, and parked in front of the coroner's office, a little extension built off the side of the hospital.

******

The coroner was down the hall when Bourbon arrived, so he took a seat in her office and waited. Hand-drawn artwork—marker and colored pencils—covered the walls. The strokes were bold and aggressive, but they composed beautiful scenes of alien worlds with a central theme of water. Bourbon's curiosity made him stand, stare, and wish he could be there now. Maybe the people in that world were pleasant to each other. Perhaps he'd have the pleasure of being out of a job there.

"That's my son's work," a voice called out behind him.

Bourbon turned to see the coroner standing in the doorway. The short brunette in a lab coat smiled at Bourbon.

"Hi, Shari," Bourbon said. "Hari did these? They're remarkable."

Shari laughed. "No, not Hari. Roshan."

Roshan was Shari's autistic son, and Bourbon was amazed by his talent. He wondered why a kid, maybe twelve, would paint worlds so different from our own as if he'd been there before. The pictures intrigued Bourbon, and he wanted to learn more. But he had work to do.

"These are amazing, Shari. The kid has talent."

"Well, I'm not sure where he gets it. His dad is as obtuse as a beach ball, and I can't even draw stick figures."

Shari stepped to her desk and opened a drawer. "I assume you're looking for these?" She handed Bourbon a file with some autopsy photos, and the big cop retook his seat. He set the file on the desk as Shari narrated, pointing to highlights with a click-pen as Bourbon flipped through the pages. The first page was mostly text, formal seals, and case numbers that were standard in Shari's reports. He flipped to the second page to reveal an image that could have passed as a man's untimely mugshot, taken as he blinked.

"Darin Cloudwater," Shari pointed. "Fifty-four years of age. Cause of death was blunt force trauma from a dull blade of some sort. Blunt force trauma to C-four and five vertebrae. Second area of impact was the posterior cranium. Split his head open like a pea pod."

Bourbon flipped to a page with diagrams of a skull and handwritten notes that matched Shari's description. "And what about the other fella?"

"Peter Felton. Forty-seven years of age. Cause of death was from the same unknown weapon. One blow, which severed the carotid artery and trachea."

"Toxicity report?"

Shari's pen pointer circled the page and dropped on a text box at the bottom of the page. "Alcohol and PCB. Felton had a small trace of cocaine in his system."

Bourbon scanned a picture of the wound on Felton's neck. "Shari, how does this compare to the wound on the other victim from The Mineshaft homicide? Brody Sherwood?"

"Appears to be the same weapon, Jeff," Shari said. She was one of the few people who referred to Bourbon by his first name.

Bourbon tapped his thumb on the file. The same mysterious weapon had killed all three victims. The only common thread was their hostility toward Cody Savage. "What about the other issue you called about this morning?"

"The carvings?" Shari swallowed hard as if her disgust were trying to escape via her throat. "Follow me."

They left her office, turned right through a pair of double doors, and followed a short hallway. Bourbon could feel the temperature drop with every step as if he were walking from a warm locker room to an ice hockey arena.

Shari pushed open a heavy steel door with heavy nickel-plated hinges that eased its motion, and she and Bourbon entered the morgue. The cool air, smelling of plastic and disinfectant, was refreshing to Bourbon, who'd been sweating in the summer heat. Shari pulled her lab coat closed, even though she had acclimated to the temperature years ago. She crossed the room and slid a large drawer from the wall—long enough to hold the body of an adult. Under normal circumstances, Shari would give a person a moment to prepare themselves for what they were about to see, but she knew Bourbon had seen his share of dead bodies over the years.

Shari pulled the white plastic sheet to the dead thug's hips. Six letters had been carved into the bulky abdomen.

"What do you think it means?" Shari asked.

"I was hoping you'd know." Bourbon zoomed in with his phone camera and clicked the shutter button.

Shari shrugged in bewilderment. "I'm a scientist. I just collect the data and document the facts in a tidy report. Figuring out this crazy nonsense is your job." She pulled the sheet back over Cloudwater's head and patted Bourbon on the shoulder. "Good luck."

Bourbon tried to visualize the events from last night, imagining Darin Cloudwater and Peter Felton falling prey to their killer. They died while Cody Savage was in the hospital being treated for his gunshot wound. There was no way Cody could have accomplished something this evil before Birchcraft and Archer found the bodies. Someone else was haunting Stoneville. Someone with a sick agenda and a brutal weapon.

Bourbon stared at the image on his phone. Things were moving too slowly. He had to work faster, find more leads and more witnesses, and close this case before any more victims ended up in the morgue with the word SINNER carved into their bodies.

15

CAIN LAKE

Jessie Lewis stood on the back porch of the church and watched the dive team's boat meander along Cain Lake's shore. From a distance, their pace was barely perceptible. The surface of Cain Lake scattered sunlight like expensive jewelry with a hammered finish. Jesse squinted from the lake's assault on his eyes, donned a pair of cheap sunglasses, and continued watching the search parties scour the shore.

Volunteers trudged through the weeds and clay of the beaches, looking for signs of Darcy Poole. Jesse recognized some of the volunteers as they pushed short weeds aside to locate Darcy's body. Luckily, it was still early enough in the summer that the weeds hadn't reached maturity and weren't a hindrance to the search. In the first few days of the hunt, eighty people combed the woods and alleys of Stoneville. But now, fear and skepticism overtook response, and the number of people in the search party had dwindled to a dozen.

They'll never find Darcy at this rate.

Some of the people searching were Jesse's parishioners, but he looked down upon them from his immaculate white church with disdain and contempt.

There were sinners amongst this motley flock. Mr. Zaglin, for instance, was having two affairs behind his wife's back. Jesse only knew because Mrs. Zaglin had confessed that she had hired a hit man to kill her husband. She changed her mind because her husband was diagnosed with pancreatic cancer, but decided to let her husband's disease carry out his sentence. Jesse told her she was forgiven, but he had other plans for her.

Tiger Blaise, a local business owner, had confessed to killing several dogs in the neighborhood because he had acquired a taste for them overseas. Sick bastard. Jesse was going to make sure Blaise paid for his sins when the time was right. He'd never dine on another pet.

Melissa Quillen, the elementary school teacher, also searched the shoreline. She had confessed to raiding her students' lunch boxes while they were in gym class or at the library, taking just enough from each to satisfy her sugar addiction. *Who the hell does that?*

They disgusted him—these phonies and frauds, half-wits and liars—these sinners. They deserved the punishment that was coming. Cain Lake would feed on their evil deeds and be grateful. That was his purpose now, and, oddly, it suited him. He had grown accustomed to the guilt that followed the purge and imagined this must be a similar experience to what addicts feel after a fix. Satisfying yourself with tainted desire, and experiencing freedom and a lack of empathy, only to face the bitter crash when the buzz wears off. That's when you feel low, promising yourself you'll never do it again, but the low remains, so you decide to fight it with one more high. It's a vicious cycle for any addict, and Jesse knew he was no less a sinner than the others.

The pastor held a Bible in both hands while leaning against the porch railing on his forearms. His thumb flipped the edges of the Bible's pages, producing a sound similar to a deck of poker cards being shuffled. He stopped flipping and gave in to his curiosity. He walked down to the little beach to converse with the sinners.

Melissa Quillen was the first to acknowledge Jesse's presence.

"Howdy, Pastor Jesse!" She shouted from knee-deep water.

"Hello, Ms. Quillen." *You snack-pack thieving piece-of-shit.* He wanted to say the words out loud for everyone to hear, but he was sworn to secrecy by the church. All sinners who come to confession are protected by an arbitrary rule that protects their admission. He used to believe in his church's sanctity until Cain Lake revealed the numerous crimes of Stoneville's residents. He felt as though he had a window into their souls, observing the truth and detecting the bullshit and lies. Jesse had lived his life on the straight and narrow. He followed every law with strict adherence.

It had been hard for him to make friends growing up. The other kids would tease Jesse for following the rules and trying to help the community and his teachers. He was bullied and slandered. He had grown up believing that he wasn't like the other kids and that the bullying would never stop unless he held a reputable position in the community that was above judgment.

He studied hard and got good grades, and the other kids teased him.

He played piano and performed at recitals and school plays, and the kids would put tacks on his seat.

He would cry to his parents and teachers, who would advise him to toughen up or fight back, ignoring his pleas for justice.

They were all sinners, and now he was a sinner too.

Jesse made his way to the end of the dock, waving to the volunteers. Some joined him there, and they held hands and said a prayer. They prayed for all the searchers to be safe and that Darcy would be found alive and well.

Jesse wasn't optimistic.

******

At first, Jesse thought nothing of the small Jon boat that came around the rocky point and pointed its bow toward the church. He assumed the two men in the watercraft were probably just more local volunteers searching the shallow bays. They steered the aluminum boat toward shore, focused on the water rather than the man on the dock.

The dive team from Albany had two boats: one pontoon boat with antennas, radars, extra oxygen tanks, and a small crane that could pick up 500 pounds from the water. Their second boat was a sixteen-foot-long rubber raft, bright orange for safety, and a motor that seemed too large. The pontoon boat had disappeared to the eastern side of the lake. The orange rubber raft zoomed away, heading west, most likely to refuel.

The aluminum boat made its way toward Jesse, and he noticed the two occupants were probably fishing rather than searching. His theory was proven correct when he saw the boater raise a fishing pole and cast a baited hook toward shore. The hook, spinner, and minnow sailed through the air and landed with a small splash near the shoreline. The man in the boat reeled the minnow in a zig-zag pattern, stopping and starting with quick flicks of his wrists until something from the water attacked.

A small-mouth bass swallowed the hapless minnow, flicked its tail skyward, and kicked hard at the water. The result took the fish to the bottom of the lake in seconds, and the battle began. The fisherman stood in the boat, keeping his rod high and the line taut, but the fish pulled, stealing the fisherman's line from the spool as it darted through the weeds.

The fish was holding a free meal in his jaws, but this was the fisherman's plan. He let the bass swim hard away from the boat, staying parallel with the shoreline. The fisherman pulled the rod higher, adding tension to the line and hoping it held.

The fish tired quickly, gulping as much water as possible, but its gills could not pump enough water to restore oxygen consumed during the fight. It was too tired to struggle any longer, and the fisherman reeled him back to the boat slowly, sure he was the victor. When the two contestants came eye-to-eye, the second man in the boat reached for a net to scoop up the defeated fish.

In desperation, the small-mouth bass used every bit of its remaining strength to kick itself toward the fishing boat, putting a large loop of slack in the line. Its second kick brought him straight out of the water, and it entered its version of outer space. The bass spun 180 degrees, folded its body like a horseshoe, and swiped at the translucent fishing line with its broad tail, which yanked the treble hook loose from its mouth.

The fish dropped back into his natural environment with a beach ball-sized splash on entry. He could hear the disappointment from the two aliens that had nearly beamed him to their ship and swam to the nearest log to hide and rest.

"Almost had him," Cody said, staring into the clear lake.

AJ Timmons stared over the side of the boat, hoping to get one more look at the trophy bass. "Sonovabitch, Cody. That was the biggest bass I've ever seen in this lake."

"There's a reason he's so big, AJ—he's smart. And the smart ones always know how to get away." Cody sat back down at the bow of the boat, but faced the stern. "Don't worry, my friend, where there's one, there's a whole school. Besides, I don't care how big they are. You know how long it's been since I've been fishing?"

AJ knew the answer but didn't give it up. He changed the subject when he saw Jesse Lewis standing on the wooden dock, watching their failed attempt to catch dinner. "Hey, there's Pastor Jesse. Let's stop and say hi, see how the search is going."

AJ throttled the little engine mounted to the boat's transom, pushing it toward the church property. They pulled alongside the dock, and Jesse caught the front of the jon boat as a courtesy.

He faked a smile, "Hello, gentlemen, how are the fish biting today?" Jesse began tying the front of the boat to the rope cleat bolted to the dock.

"Well," AJ said, "I think all these divers in the water and searchers patrolling the shoreline have them spooked. But Cody just lost a huge bass right over there." He was pointing to a large willow tree that cast a shadow on the water.

"Hmm, that's a good spot. I once reeled in a thirty-five-inch walleye in that same area. There are a couple of large boulders in about eight feet of water there, and the willow tree keeps it shaded."

AJ stepped out of his boat and onto the creaking wooden dock. "Well, you'll have to come out with us sometime, Pastor. Show us the hot spots. Oh, by the way, Pastor Jesse, this is Cody Savage."

Cody wanted to avoid an introduction. Everyone in town knew his name but not his face, and he preferred it that way.

Jesse watched Cody climb out of the boat, nervous with excitement. He hadn't had a chance to get this close to Cody since the man had come home from prison. He knew that any minute now, the throbbing headache was going to come, accompanied by the tingling in his arm. He usually dreaded the sensation, but today, he would welcome it. The pain would be a gift. He watched as Cody wiped his hands on his pants. This was it—the moment when Jesse would get to see Cody's sins. Cody could no longer hide the guilt of killing his wife, and then Jesse would use that vision as motivation to punish the sinner.

Cody wiped his fishy hand on his denim pants and extended it forward. "Nice to meet you, sir."

Like a kid not wanting to open his birthday present and spoil the anticipation, Jesse hesitated. His hand moved forward at an awkward speed, open wide and ready to accept his gift. Their hands clasped like two pit bulls locking jaws.

Nothing.

There was no vision. There was no throbbing migraine or radiating pain down his arm. Jesse felt utterly disappointed and then was distracted by his own voice. "Nice to meet you, Mr. Savage."

"Please, call me Cody."

"Cody," Jesse nodded. "Are you new in town? I see AJ here at Mass every Sunday, but I'm afraid I don't recognize you."

"No," Cody said, relieved that someone in town—a pillar of the community—did not recognize his name or face. "I've lived in Stoneville my whole life...born and raised. I'm sorry, Father—"

"Pastor," Jesse corrected. "I'm a pastor, not a priest."

"Oh, sorry. I haven't been to service since I was a kid."

Jesse nodded that he respected Cody's choice. On the inside, his temper was percolating in disbelief. How was this man, the personification of evil and brutality, standing beside him so calm now? How did Cody, a man who brutally murdered the woman he'd vowed to love and honor until parted by death, trick his senses—his God-given power of perception?

AJ's voice interrupted his thoughts. "Pastor? Mr. Lewis? You okay?"

"Yes, AJ, I'm sorry. I was just thinking about the best place to take you to hook some walleyes. You were saying?"

"Oh, that's cool. I was saying that maybe Cody and I could bring back some food and snacks for the volunteers. Maybe set up a table at your church with refreshments...to thank all the volunteers."

Jesse squeezed AJ's shoulder. "That's very generous of you, son, but the Ladies Auxiliary beat you to it. They've provided an excellent supply of water, coffee, and snacks. Besides, I don't think they'll be using the church much longer. If the dive team doesn't find Darcy here, the search is going to move to—"

His speech trailed off like a child's toy with dying batteries. Jesse focused on the wood line. Movement. Not a volunteer searcher, but someone else.

Flesti, the woman who'd caught him purging in the lake the night he murdered Connor Bayley and Brody Sherwood, exited the dense trees and scanned the scene visually.

She appeared from the same direction she had come days before, as if she'd circled the entire lake. Jesse wasn't sure how long it would take an older woman to walk the lake's circumference, but he was confident the journey would last for over a week if the person stopped to sleep and eat. She was carrying her hardwood walking stick, which protruded six inches over her blonde and gray hair. Her attention was on Jesse and the two men who accompanied him on the dock.

"Excuse me for one second, gentlemen," Jesse said, squeezing between Cody and AJ on the narrow walkway to meet Flesti on dry ground. "Flesti, are you all right? Did you find your dog?"

Flesti ignored the concerned pastor and walked straight past, and began to walk the length of the dock. When she realized the staff appeared threatening, she stood it in the water, leaning against the side of the dock.

"Hello," AJ greeted Flesti, assuming she was with the search party.

She ignored him almost entirely, acknowledging his salutation with only a brief glance and a forced smile. Her attention immediately turned to Cody.

"Howdy, ma'am," Cody greeted Flesti, as her eyes seemed to burn right through him. Cody could feel his face turn red, and he wasn't sure what to do with his hands, and finally opted to cross his arms. Without warning, the hair on his forearms stood on end.

He was sure this crazy-looking woman was about to give him an earful of crude insults and accusations regarding his alleged crimes. Instead, she unfolded his arms, took both of his hands in hers, and studied them. Then she flipped them over and studied his palms. She dropped his left hand and traced an imaginary line with her right index finger in a spiral pattern around his right palm. AJ watched with bewilderment. Cody watched in confusion.

Jesse watched with jealousy. The demon of Stoneville, as he referred to Cody, had this mysterious woman's attention.

"Cody Savage? You've returned to this hell for no reason," Flesti said. "What you seek isn't here, but it's close—very close."

"You mean the fish. Because I'm sure there are more—"

She gave his hand a little slap and smiled. "You know what you seek. Vengeance. Answers."

"I'm not looking to hurt anyone."

"I know. I know," Flesti continued. "But you will. She knows why you are here. She knows what you will do, but you must not."

Cody's voice squeaked when he guessed who she spoke of. "Willa?"

Uneasy with the woman's presence, AJ stepped backward and nearly fell off the dock.

Flesti squeezed Cody's hands a little tighter and, in a more severe voice, gave him this advice: "What you seek will come to you. Soon, very soon. Stop looking, and don't trust anyone but the mountain and the flower."

From a nearby willow tree, a crow swooped down and perched on the bow of AJ's boat, cawing twice as it watched Cody and Flesti's interaction.

In the distance, a dog barked, deflecting Flesti's attention. "My dog," she giggled. "I've been looking for him for days." She turned away from the confused ex-con and the corrupt pastor, retrieved her walking stick, and made her way into the woods to find her dog. She didn't utter another word or say goodbye. When she was out of sight and hopefully too far to hear their voices, AJ stepped closer to Cody.

"Who the fuck was that?"

16

LITTLE BLUE LIGHTS

Cody and AJ climbed back into the fishing boat, started the motor, and put some distance between themselves and the church. Once they rounded the bend in the shoreline and were a quarter-mile away, AJ throttled down the engine and turned it off. They coasted through the still water.

"What the hell was that all about?" AJ asked. He kept his voice low, knowing how well sound traveled across the water.

Cody spun around in his seat and faced AJ. "I have no friggin idea. That woman acted like she knew all about me—like she knew my future. Maybe she's some sort of fortune-teller or a pretend psychic. I'm sure she was probably trying to scam us for money."

"Like a damn witch, man."

"Come on, you don't believe her, do you?"

"Jesus, did you not see the crow fly down to my boat? Like it was on cue or something. That's some spooky shit, Cody. Nobody has a fucking crow as a pet. Nobody. Unless you're a witch or warlock, or maybe she's a goddam ghost. I don't know. She made my skin crawl."

Cody laughed at AJ. He flipped the lid of their cooler and took out two beers. AJ accepted one, and they drifted as they sipped their drinks. They tried to change the subject several times, but they just couldn't shake the image of Flesti preaching her predictions while Jesse had stared in silence.

"That preacher dude was a little strange himself," Cody said.

"Pastor Lewis? He's all right. He's probably the most honest man in town. A great guy, actually. He'd give you the shirt off his back."

"Yeah, well, he can keep it. I don't need to owe anybody anything. I owe you enough."

AJ stared toward the rescue diver's boat drifting on the glassy surface of the lake. "Think we should have been out looking for that Darcy girl instead of fishing today?"

"I don't know," Cody said. "Bourbon told me to keep a low profile. Already been shot at once, and that was enough. I wish I could help, but my presence is more likely to make everyone uneasy."

"You think they'll ever find her? Darcy Poole?"

Cody scanned the glassy surface of Cain Lake. He shuddered when he thought about the secrets possibly hidden under all this water. Was poor Darcy one of them, down there waiting to be discovered? Or was she just a young girl on the run to spite her parents? He was glad the dive team was there and wished they'd find her soon and bring closure to the Poole family.

"Let's cast a few more times and then go get some dinner. I'm starving," Cody said.

AJ nodded in agreement. "Anxious to go see your new hot reporter friend, aren't you?"

Daisy. Cody had been thinking of her all day and hated to leave her that morning, but she needed to write her article. She was enthusiastic and eager to prove herself as she began her new career. He hoped she was thinking of him.

When their beer cans were empty, AJ yanked the outboard motor's pull cord and started the engine. The noisy Evinrude revved as AJ twisted the throttle on the handle, and they accelerated to the next fishing hole. They fished longer than they had planned, catching three more bass and two northern pikes, which they sent back to the lake. Once the bait bucket was empty, AJ steered them toward the little marina on the west side of the lake.

They pulled into the only marina on the west side of the lake ten minutes after one of the dive teams had docked. It was the team with the large rubber raft and huge outboard engine. Two long docks, forty feet in length, occupied the marina. The water's depth at the end of the aluminum docks was ten feet.

The dive team had split into two separate teams, Team Alpha and

Team Beta, with four members per team. The division allowed them to search the area as four quadrants: north, east, west, and south.

Cody watched Team Alpha reorganize, pulling buoys, ropes, and oxygen tanks from their rubber raft. One man, wearing a wet suit and dock shoes, carried a gas can from a parked truck to the moored watercraft. A pop-up canopy shaded a picnic table that held a few fully charged radios and a map of the area. Under the canopy, a female diver with red hair relished the shade as she ate a banana and drank a bottle of water, but she wasn't alone.

Deputy Sheriff Charlie Archer sat with one ass cheek on the table's corner. He was hoping to impress the rescue diver with his biceps and neatly pressed uniform, but the young woman merely nodded at him in politeness as she watched the two fishermen drifting toward the dock in their small fishing boat. Her gaze was on Cody, kneeling at the front of the boat and ready to prevent it from colliding with the aluminum dock.

Archer noticed the woman's attention had shifted to the ex-con in the boat. He left the redhead at the table and marched toward the dock. His stride was casual as he walked and observed simultaneously.

"What are you two shit-bags doing out here? The lake is closed to all recreational watercraft during the search," Archer said.

"We were just helping with the search," Cody lied. He knew this wasn't going to be a pleasant conversation.

"With fishing poles and a bait bucket?" Archer asked.

The redhead waded into the water beside Cody and AJ and dropped a small cooler of refreshments into the dive team's raft. She smiled at Cody and pushed her damp hair away from her face. Archer was the only one to notice the flirtation.

"I didn't think they gave fishing licenses to ex-cons who'd murdered their wives," Archer said loud enough for everyone to hear.

Archer's ploy worked, and the female diver quickly rejoined her teammates under the canopy.

Cody finished tying the front of the boat and began unloading fishing gear.

"Let's see those licenses, boys," Archer said. "This piece of shit boat registered, Simmons?"

"Timmons," AJ said. "It's Timmons with a T."

"I really don't give a horse's ass."

Cody retrieved the fishing license he had acquired when he and AJ stopped for bait. He held it up for Archer to see, but the deputy yanked it from his hands and gave it a quick look. He dropped it on the dock.

"Any drugs or alcohol on this boat? Marijuana? I'm pretty sure I smell pot."

"We split a six-pack of beer," AJ said nervously.

"You drank three beers? Three whole beers?" Archer said, holding up the same number of fingers toward AJ.

"Yes, sir," AJ said.

"You drunk, boy? Cause your eyes are a little red, and you seem drunk to me."

"No, sir. My eyes are always a little red. Aller—"

"Shut up," Archer interrupted. "Where's your license?" Archer stepped past Cody and briefly looked at the small document AJ held.

"Jesus, Archer," Cody said. "I know you've got a beef with me, but stop giving AJ shit. He's done nothing wrong."

Archer's attention snapped back to Cody. He stood just inches away, with his hand on his holstered pistol, looking down at Cody. "Was I talking to you, dirt bag? Shut the hell up, and don't tell me how to do my job."

Cody didn't flinch. Inmates had tried to intimidate him for the last four years, and he wasn't about to let the arrogant officer do the same. They stared eye to eye for several seconds. Cody knew that Archer wasn't like this with everyone, and he couldn't blame Archer for hating him. After all, in the deputy's eyes, he was a man who'd gotten away with murder. That was how the whole town saw him now.

Cody would be hated until he could prove otherwise. He'd just have to live with it. What he couldn't accept was that AJ was becoming a victim—guilty by association—bullied for believing in his best friend and not wavering for even a moment.

Cody felt his right hand curl into a fist, and it took all his willpower not to use it. The world became a blur, and his mind started picking out targets on Archer's body—uppercut to the chin to make him dizzy, kick to the right knee so his gun hip drops too low to draw, left elbow to the skull to finish him.

Cody turned and walked the dock toward shore to put space between them. If he didn't clear his thoughts and remain calm, he was going to do something stupid. Deputy Archer turned his attention back to AJ, as the entire dive team watched the abusive deputy. Cody nearly reached the shore when he heard the splash. He spun immediately to check on his best friend.

AJ was gone, and Archer stood at the end of the dock alone. Cody hadn't seen it, but he knew Archer had pushed his thin friend into the lake.

Cody sprinted back to the end of the dock and pushed past the deputy who stood laughing at AJ. "Man, BJ, you should watch your step. How's the water today?"

Cody sprinted past. "Jesus, Archer, he can't swim!" He knelt at the end of the dock and reached for AJ's hand. AJ's head bobbed below the surface and back to the top. He gasped for air when his head appeared, but sank again, his outstretched hand just inches away from Cody's. Cody plunged his hand deeper, finally managing to grab a couple of AJ's fingers, but the wet skin was too slick to hold. AJ sank again.

"Well, go in and get him then," Archer said. Cody turned toward Archer just in time to see his polished black boot come up and catch him in the face. He didn't see anything after that, but he felt the cool lake water envelope his body.

The red-haired rescue diver, hearing that AJ couldn't swim, leaped into action. She ran down the aluminum dock and jumped off the end, landing just feet from AJ. She dropped below the surface, sinking until AJ was within reach, and pulled him toward the surface. Clasping his chest with one arm, she began swimming toward shallow water with her free hand, pulling AJ to safety.

Underwater, Cody could only hear his heartbeat, as water filled his ears and muffled the rest of the world. He opened his eyes and saw AJ being pulled to shore.

Cody hadn't taken a breath before the boot knocked him into the water, so his oxygen level was quickly diminishing. His nearly empty lungs provided no buoyancy, so he sank like a brick. For a moment, though, he didn't care. There was a peacefulness to his dilemma that couldn't be described. He didn't bother to struggle or kick his way to the surface. The bottom of the lake pushed against his back, and ten feet of water faced him.

The water was cold and dark at this depth, smothering his anger. He'd forgotten about Archer, laughing malevolently on the dock.

In the darkness, a vision suddenly appeared. He saw Willa, his deceased wife, floating above him. Although he knew he was hallucinating, that she couldn't be real, he bathed in her presence. She was so beautiful, and he remembered how attracted he was to her. He'd spent the last four years so angry that he'd forgotten what it was like to feel love. Even Daisy hadn't been able to remind him of that during their brief time together.

Willa's image began to fade, and Cody felt another presence surround him. Small glowing organisms swam in circles and spiraled around his body. He knew that these were not hallucinations. They glowed blue, growing brighter as they neared Cody's skin. He waved his hand, and they followed. Legless, wingless fireflies were the only way to describe them. They numbered in the thousands, far more than Jesse Lewis had ever experienced, and they were not there to purge Cody of any sins he had consumed. The drowning man felt their benevolence, accepted their presence, and marveled at this extraordinary event.

Willa was still fading, barely visible through the lights so close to his eyes. He wanted to scream for her to stay and made a promise that he'd stay, too. Then another face appeared beside his dead wife—a young blonde girl with a long nose and bony shoulders. Both hallucinations gestured for him to swim upward. Willa vanished, but the girl swam downward, her form as clear as if she were tangible. She looked exactly like the girl on all the posters that littered the town.

She was scared. She was Darcy Poole.

Darcy's image exploded in a burst of a million bubbles as someone from the surface jumped into the water. The little fireflies dispersed at the speed of light. The person above, flesh and blood, rather than some ghostly figure, swam downward. When she was deep enough, a balance between light and shadow formed, and Cody could see the face of the female rescue diver. She grabbed Cody's arm, dug her feet into the lake's soft floor, and pushed away, sending them both floating upward. Her athletic legs kicked hard, propelling them to the surface within seconds. Their heads breaking the surface of the water, they gasped for oxygen.

She was a strong swimmer and pulled Cody toward shore. Holding the side of the dock to steady himself, Cody gasped and coughed up water. The female diver smiled down at him, assuring him that he was going to be okay. But Cody looked back at the deeper water, hoping Willa and Darcy would surface behind him. Neither appeared.

He could hear a commotion on shore, no more than ten feet away. Two men yelled at each other, and once the water drained from Cody's ears, he recognized the sound of AJ's voice spewing curse words.

"Get off me, you piece-of-shit, useless fucking asshole!"

Archer had AJ pinned down in the grass, kneeling on his shoulder, and twisting his arm behind his back. He put handcuffs on AJ's wrists and ordered him to relax.

Blood streamed from Archer's nose as a result of two roundhouses thrown by AJ. Cody was confident that the deputy sheriff was the first person AJ had ever decked, and he was proud of his friend for sticking up for himself. But seeing AJ hauled toward the patrol vehicle in handcuffs tarnished that pride. Cody himself was ready to protest, despite his probation, but reconsidered when another police vehicle pulled into the boat launch parking lot.

Sheriff Bourbon steered his rugged Jeep Gladiator off the road as a cloud of dust formed behind him. He parked the truck but didn't exit immediately. He watched through the windshield, then finally lowered the vehicle's window as the dust settled back to the gravel.

Archer held AJ's arm tightly as he walked him to Bourbon's truck, where he and the sheriff chatted through the open window. Once they ended their conversation, Archer led AJ to the back of his patrol car and drove away. Bourbon remained in the driver's seat of his vehicle, speaking on the phone.

Cody thanked the rescue diver who'd saved him, and a few more divers gathered around to tell Cody what had happened while he was submerged. They told Cody how AJ attacked the deputy sheriff for what he'd done. They reiterated how AJ landed a couple of good hits that sent Archer to his knees, but the larger man regained his footing and was able to subdue AJ, putting him in handcuffs. The entire altercation had lasted less than fifteen seconds.

When Bourbon finished his phone call, he restarted the truck and drove a little further into the parking lot. He cut the engine again and stepped out.

"Wanna tell me what the hell that was all about, Savage?" Bourbon barked.

"Well, I could ask you the same, Sheriff."

"Don't get smart, young man. I pull in here to check on my deputy and the dive team, and Archer's hauling your best buddy off to jail for assaulting an officer. Sounds like your attitude is starting to rub off on RJ."

"AJ didn't do a damn thing, Sheriff. Your boy Archer kicked me in the face after throwing AJ in the lake. AJ can't swim—"

"It's true, Sheriff," the redhead rescue diver intervened. "I saw the whole thing. These two men were just coming in from fishing, and Deputy Dipshit started—"

Bourbon held up his palm to quiet the diver from saying any more. "I'll get your statement in a few minutes, young lady." He motioned for Cody to step under a magnificent willow tree and waited for the shade to cool their tempers.

"Start from the beginning," Bourbon said. "And no bullshit."

17
ARCHER'S PAIN

Cody started his story from the beginning, leaving out the parts about blue water bugs and hallucinations of Willa and Darcy. When he finished, Sheriff Bourbon stared across the lake, wishing he were floating in a Jon boat, drowning a worm, and hooking a few fish.

"Well," Bourbon said, "I can't excuse AJ for striking an officer. He'll be charged."

Cody opened his mouth to protest, but Bourbon stopped him with a hand gesture.

He continued, "I'll have a little chat with Archer. This grudge he has against you is going to end. He's been trying to pin your wife's murder on you since the day we found her."

"I'd never even met Archer until she died. So, I'm not sure why he's so convinced that I'm guilty. That sonovabitch seems to be targeting me," Cody said.

"Yeah, I think I might know why."

Cody waited silently for Bourbon's theory, but Bourbon was hesitant to tell him. He bent down and picked up a smooth, flat rock with an oval shape, cocked his right arm like a baseball pitcher, and slung it toward the lake's surface with a powerful sidearm throw. The rock skipped across the surface six times before sinking. Satisfied, he picked up another but just twirled it in his fingers and told Cody about Charlie Archer's first few months as a Stoneville deputy.

"About four and a half years ago, Archer moved to Stoneville with his wife, Charlotte. He was a happy guy and a much-needed addition to the department. One morning, Charlotte was out jogging, like she'd done every morning. She was some super endurance athlete or something."

He tossed the rock, giving it four skips, and picked up another. It was beautifully smooth on top, but sandpaper on the bottom. "Anyway, Archer was working an early shift one morning when he got a call from 911 dispatch about a 480 on South Street."

"A 480?"

"Hit and run," Bourbon explained. "Archer responded to the call—not far from here—and found that Charlotte was the victim. She was jogging along when—" He stopped talking and used his fist to strike his palm. Cody jumped a little, surprised by the loud sound of the effect.

Cody's face went from shock to a solemn expression, and then he grimaced as he imagined finding Willa in such a gruesome accident. He began to empathize with Charlie Archer.

"So, you see, you and Archer have something in common. It's the worst possible thing you could have in common, but still—"

Seven skips and Bourbon picked another stone. "Archer was crushed that he'd lost his wife in such a tragic incident. He'd give anything to change what happened that day. You see, he can't understand why a man would kill his wife when he misses his so much. Charlotte was his whole world. Everyone talked about the lovely new couple in town."

"And what happened to the guy who hit her?" Cody asked.

"See, that's just it—they never found him. Archer lives with that mystery every day, just like you. You're both trying to figure out who killed your wives and probably never will. I think Archer figures that if he can't bring Charlotte's killer to justice, he sure the hell can find Willa's."

Two skips.

"So," Bourbon continued, "we have two unsolved homicides in Stoneville: who hit Charlotte Archer and killed her, and who stabbed Willa Savage to death while her hands were tied. My gut tells me we're never going to find the answers. But I hope that if we find the answer to one of those mysteries, it will lead us to the other."

Bourbon looked Cody up and down. "Listen, I know your driver's license expired, but you're not getting in my car soaking wet."

"I can walk home."

Bourbon shook his head. "If you've got the keys to that Charger, then take it back to your friend's house. Get it out of the rescue team's way."

Cody nodded. "I will, thanks."

"Don't go anywhere else or drive another vehicle until you get your license back."

Cody walked away, collected the fishing gear, and secured AJ's boat properly. He thanked the rescue diver again for saving his life and politely refused her offer to buy him a beer later to forget his rough day. He piled all of the fishing gear into the trunk of AJ's car and headed home.

Bourbon, still twirling a perfect skipping rock in his hand, waited for Cody to leave when Marissa, the 911 dispatcher, came over his radio. He dropped his skipping stone to listen to his radio.

"Stoneville Sheriff's Department, this is Dispatch."

"Dispatch, this is SSD-1. Go ahead."

"SSD-1, we have a report of multiple 187's at the boat launch on Grandview Road."

"Dispatch, did you say 'multiple'?"

"That's correct, Sheriff."

Bourbon sprinted up the gravel parking lot, jumped back into his truck, and fired up the engine. Two Cooper tires spun in the loose stones as he accelerated away from the boat launch. The rubber wheels hit the blacktop and squealed for another two seconds before they found their grip and launched the vehicle down the road. Grandview Road was on the other side of Cain Lake, and Bourbon was sure the other half of the dive team was there now.

18
GET SHORTY

Cody piloted the muscle car home rather than parking it at AJ's house. The Dodge Charger would be useful if he had to get across town or run an errand. Besides, AJ lived across town, and he didn't want to walk the four miles back in damp clothes.

Learning about Archer's wife had cooled Cody's temper a few degrees, but he was still hot about AJ's arrest. The deputy sheriff had gone too far, and now, AJ would always be bullied by Charlie Archer.

The smell of Cain Lake—fish, mud, and clay—had saturated Cody's wet clothes and hair. Entering his house, he saw the bullet holes in the walls and reminded himself he still had a target on his back.

In the kitchen, he stripped off his wet clothes and let them fall to the linoleum, then gathered them together and stuffed them into the washing machine before climbing the stairs. It took a long, hot shower to dilute his disappointment in today's events, but it wouldn't wash away the memory of AJ being handcuffed or the vision of his wife at the bottom of Cain Lake.

After the shower, he redressed and made his way to the kitchen, where he counted the money that remained from the sale of his uncle's furniture. He crumpled it in disgust and slammed his fist against the kitchen counter. The car keys hanging from a teacup hook by the door jingled from the impact, beckoning him to go for a ride. Snatching the keys in defiance of Sheriff Bourbon's orders, he headed to the driveway.

Cody climbed back into AJ's car and made his way across town. He drove north, taking the back streets, and was cautious to obey all the traffic signs and signals. He wanted a drink, something with a little bite and a smooth finish. The Mineshaft had reopened today, and Cody and

AJ had planned to go there after their impromptu fishing trip. That was before Charlie Archer ruined their plans.

******

Alyse was working the bar, so Cody planted himself on a stool at the far end. That's where he wanted to stay until he ran out of money or they kicked him out. Alyse poured him a shot of Hornitos with a side of lime, which she paid for. By the time he'd swallowed the tequila, she was back with a bottle of Busch beer and a smile. It was happy hour, and the bar was bustling with cheap tippers still in their work clothes. She moved fast while trying to keep up with the crowd's orders—pouring drinks, grabbing bottles, collecting money, returning change, running credit cards, and updating tabs.

The jukebox was free during happy hour, and the volume was always high when Alyse worked, which helped her concentrate on drink orders rather than engage in conversation with customers. The music machine played a variety of country music and classic rock, and one brave soul even dared to select a pop song.

On her next trip down the bar, Alyse stopped and patted Cody's hand, "Where's your partner in crime?" Her hand stayed until she got an answer.

"Been arrested."

Alyse twisted her ear toward Cody as a sign she didn't think she heard him clearly. He spoke much louder when he repeated his answer.

"What? No fucking way. Are you serious?" She popped the top off three Canadian beers and marched them back in the opposite direction. She stopped to concoct a whiskey sour and a Jack and Coke. After putting the money in the till and her tips in a jar, she returned to Cody. A couple of grease monkeys watched her walk away, elbowing each other and making remarks that Cody couldn't hear, but sure they were about him. Or her. Either way, he could sense they were inappropriate. His eyes burned with the heat of the tequila as he glared at the two patrons.

Alyse leaned on the bar with her elbows. She was close to Cody to hear his story, but also because she just liked being near him. "So, what

150

the hell happened?" She stirred a tall glass of Coke with a red stir-straw to break up a clump of ice. Her perfect lips gripped the straw as she drew a mouthful of the cold sugary beverage.

Cody retold his story of the day and how it concluded with Charlie Archer handcuffing AJ and hauling him to jail. When he finished the story, Alyse's mouth was open wide, but she was not surprised by AJ's loyalty to Cody, like a little brother willing to take a beating to defend his sibling's honor. She just shook her head and got up to serve an accountant who had been waving to get her attention for three minutes.

On the way back, one of the mechanics grabbed her arm with thick fingers and dirty fingernails. He was tall and slender, with sinewy muscles that rippled beneath his tight skin. Even though he sat on a barstool, his head nearly touched the lights above. His right arm was like a crane reaching out to grab the pretty bartender, but Alyse quickly broke his grip by twisting her arm in a circle. She cocked the other arm back, threatening him with a fist and fiery eyes. The young man knew he'd crossed a line trying to get her attention. His older and much shorter partner, wearing the same company uniform, leaned over the bar and pointed a thumb at Cody.

Cody was sure he could read the man's lips correctly. "Don't you know who that is? That's Cody Savage. He killed his wife."

Alyse leaned into the mechanic's face. Her perfect eyebrows were inverted like vulture wings as she stared at the man in front of her, who would be dead meat if he said another word. The jukebox went silent when an Eric Church song finished playing, and Alyse leaned even closer to the short mechanic, saying something inaudible so that no other patrons could overhear. The man stood straight and gave Cody a dirty look.

Alyse returned to Cody, picked up his empty beer can, and replaced it with a fresh one.

"More fans of mine?" Cody asked.

"Don't worry about them. They just can't stand me giving you all the attention. Fucking toddlers. How about a cheeseburger, sweetie? With extra, extra pickles?"

Cody remembered how much cash was in his pocket. "Oh, thanks, but I'm not that hungry. I'll just drink my dinner tonight," he said, lifting the fresh beer to his lips.

"Oh, come on. You need to eat. It's on me."

Cody's stomach encouraged him with a growl. "You don't have to do that."

"I insist. Besides, I get a free meal during each shift, but I had a Cobb salad before work. This bar food goes straight to my ass."

"Can't blame it," Cody joked.

She snapped her wet dish towel at him and left for the kitchen to place his order.

Cody didn't need to turn around to know that the two mechanics stood right behind him, encroaching on his personal space. The tall one, built like a torque wrench, stood with his arms crossed, looking down at Cody. He looked like he could throw a punch from a mile away, so Cody would need to get close if this got ugly.

The short mechanic was the same height as Cody as he sat on the stool. He was probably the same weight as the tall guy, but several scars across his nose and brow suggested he was an experienced fighter. His right ear resembled a head of cauliflower—scar tissue on top of scar tissue—a wrestler. Cody made a quick mental note: don't let this guy take you down to the ground.

Shorty was the first to speak. "This isn't someplace you want to be, my friend." His accent was slight but distinguishable. Cody knew a Brazilian in prison who spoke with the same enunciations.

Not just a wrestler. Probably Jiu-jitsu. *Fuck.*

"I beg to differ," Cody said. "This is the best seat in the house. There's no glare on the TV screen," he nodded to the flat screen. "And I can see everyone who walks through the door." Cody swiveled on the stool and sat with his back to the bar. "It's perfect."

Shorty addressed Cody again. "Maybe you'd like to go to Full Throttle, on the other side of town? They seem a little less particular about their clientele."

Cody pointed east with his thumb, the direction of Full Throttle, as he responded. "The biker bar? No, I don't think so. Those guys seem pretty tough over there. I'll stay right here with you two snowflakes."

He was ready to fight, but this was Alyse's place of employment, and he didn't want to get her in trouble. He poured a quarter of his beer down his throat to quell the heat building under his collar.

Shorty elbowed Torque Wrench with his right arm. "Did he just call us 'snowflakes'?"

"Mmm, hmm. He sure did," Torque Wrench replied while pushing his thick glasses up with an index finger.

"Look," Cody said, "I just want a few beers and a cheeseburger. Then I'll be gone. So why don't you two just mind your own business and go back to your end of the bar?"

Shorty spoke through his teeth this time. "Why don't you go back to prison, where you belong, asshole. Murderers aren't welcome here." He pushed his left elbow into Cody's right shoulder, trying to dislodge Cody from his stool.

Cody's rage had been building like a geyser ever since he'd watched Archer handcuff AJ. He was nearly ready to blow, but suppressed it again. He stood, freeing himself of the menial position, and faced both aggressors, who were pleased that Cody would not heed their words. Shorty put both hands into Cody's chest and pushed hard. "Do you need me to show you the way out?"

Cody stumbled a couple of steps toward the exit but regained his balance almost instantly.

The geyser finally blew. Cody stepped forward into his original position and mirrored Shorty's two-handed push. Cody's shove had more kinetic energy than Shorty's, and the stocky bully fell back against the wall with a loud crash, surprised by Cody's power. The entire bar went silent except for Credence Clearwater Revival singing on the jukebox.

Torque Wrench started to swing with his right fist—a big roundhouse. The punch came so slowly that Cody nearly felt sorry for what he was about to do. He raised his left arm high to block the big man's swing, spun 180 degrees in a counterclockwise direction, and threw his left elbow into Torque Wrench's abdomen. The tower of a man had no body fat to absorb the blow and doubled over as the air left his chest. Cody slammed the man's forehead off the seat of the barstool. When his head bounced upward, Cody reversed direction, lifting Torque Wrench by the throat, stepped through with his right leg, and planted it behind his opponent to trip him. Both legs supporting Torque Wrench's weight came off the floor, and the mechanic landed on his back with a room-jarring thud, gasping for air.

Shorty watched his friend become neutralized in fewer than four seconds while recuperating from the impact with the wall. He stood, stepped over Torque Wrench, and resumed his attack. Cody braced himself in a defensive stance.

But the attack never came. A small fist crossed in front of both men and caught Shorty in the jaw. His head twisted so fast that his brain lost consciousness, turning his legs to jelly, and Shorty dropped to the floor without knowing what hit him.

Alyse stood huffing in anger, gently shaking the pain out of her right hand. She dropped the second mechanic with a punch she'd learned from her father years ago.

Cody wasn't sure if he was next, so he took three steps away from the furious bartender.

Alyse picked up a knocked-over bar stool and whispered to Cody, "That was awesome." The adrenaline fueling her temper began to dissipate as she assessed the damage.

When both mechanics recovered, Alyse gave them a verbal thrashing that was almost as furious as her right punch. The two men pushed past Cody with an evil glare, and he knew their paths would cross again someday.

They shuffled to the door, squeezing between the onlookers who had witnessed the altercation. Cody watched them leave until a petite woman holding a laptop computer against her body diverted his attention. She seemed scared or surprised—Cody didn't know her well enough to tell. And then she shrank away and walked back out the door she had come in.

"Daisy!" Cody called out, but the pretty journalist ignored his call.

Cody picked up another stool in his path, set it upright, and made his way through the small crowd. The parking lot was full, but Cody could see the noisy Subaru speeding away.

<h1 style="text-align:center">19</h1>

BLOOD BOAT 

Jeff Bourbon had never seen so much blood. Bold red strokes, diluted with water, painted the floor of the pontoon boat, creating an ugly abstract design, surreal to the mind. Three members of the dive team were the source of the crimson canvas. The boat rocked gently on the waves of Cain Lake, free to drift whichever way the wind blew, as the Sheriff waded up to his knees in the cool water, retrieved the mooring line, and reeled the nightmare toward him. There was no dock at this boat launch; instead, there was a concrete ramp that allowed trucks to back down into the water and release their vessels.

"Sonovabitch," Bourbon said. He was standing alone in the shallows and had never seen a crime scene with three victims. The brutality turned his steely stomach into a sponge that squeezed in a painful effort to expel its contents. He kept himself from vomiting and avoided looking at the victims' faces.

"What the hell is happening in this town?" The words came aloud, although no one else was around to hear them. He'd called Eli Birchcraft on the drive over and was anxious for his deputy to arrive at the scene, but Birchcraft was at the scene of a motor vehicle accident and would be a few hours. Charlie Archer would be on his way back to the station to process AJ Timmons, and then he was supposed to go back to the lake in case the dive team found anything.

Bourbon scanned the water and shoreline with his sharp eyes. There were no volunteer searchers on this side of the lake, perhaps because of the remote access to the shoreline and rough terrain. He saw no fishing boats ignoring the order to stay off Cain Lake during the search. Glacial boulders and sandbars littered this side of the lake, which kept water skiers and large boats away. If it hadn't been such a grisly scene, Bourbon would have sat and admired the beauty for an hour.

He shuddered. Even though three people lay in front of him, he'd never felt so alone in his life. He could sense the emptiness of their bodies and prayed their souls were off to a better place, a safe place far from Cain Lake.

The afternoon sun reminded him of the time. He checked his watch and realized the day was more than half over. There was a lot of work to do to process the crime scene. He needed to get busy.

"So, who the hell called this in?" He asked one of the dead rescue divers, not surprised when they didn't answer. He continued pulling the mooring rope. When the two pontoons on each side of the craft scraped against the concrete ramp, he stopped pulling and tied the rope to a small tree and then carefully climbed aboard.

Bourbon stood in the center of the boat trying not to step where the carpet was stained crimson, but it was a difficult feat. With one hand on the steering wheel, he tried to deduce what had occurred. There was no need to check for pulses or perform first aid. It was evident that he was too late.

A strong blend of odors assaulted his senses—bile, blood, urine, and the lake. He knew these people must have been horrified when they died.

The person who'd murdered the dive team was thorough and brutal—savage. Not Cody Savage, though. He was on the other side of the lake, almost drowning, thanks to Charlie Archer. Bourbon squatted to get a closer look at the injuries on one diver. Blunt force trauma, maybe, but something sliced them open too.

He moved to the back of the boat, and when he did, the deck tipped downward, sinking the stern deeper into the water. His weight caused a small pool of diluted blood to trickle into Cain Lake. He paid no attention to the liquid spilling overboard, and never noticed the thousands of little blue, glowing organisms appear and devour the blood. They were indistinguishable in the daylight that reflected off the water's surface and were gone again in fifteen seconds.

He heard a vehicle racing up the road and was eager to greet Birchcraft, but the arriving vehicle was not the deputy's car. A large Ford van drove toward him, and he could barely see the person behind the wheel.

Shari Kapoor drove the silver van toward the boat launch's parking spaces, nearly hitting Bourbon's truck. The word CORONER, in gold vinyl letters on a black stripe, spanned the vehicle's side in reflective vinyl letters. She backed the van down the ramp and parked at an awkward angle. Bourbon had forgotten Shari was a lousy driver and figured that was the best she could do.

With the back doors open, she retrieved a large, gray plastic box that seemed to weigh as much as she did. As usual, Shari was smiling, unaffected by the horrible scene.

"Hello, Jefferson."

Bourbon gave her a half-hearted wave. "Hey, Shari. You got here fast."

Shari pulled a pair of latex gloves from her pocket. "I was out getting supplies when you called. Well, this looks like a fucking mess."

Bourbon watched her struggle with the tight gloves. Once she snapped the gloves over her wrists, she pushed her hair back and formed a ponytail with a burgundy-colored hair tie.

"What have we got?" She asked.

Bourbon stepped to the front of the boat and helped Shari climb aboard. He motioned with his hand at the three dead scuba divers. "See for yourself."

"My goodness," Shari said nonchalantly. "Someone sure made a mess."

She worked slowly, as both pathologist and crime scene investigator, picking through the carnage and taking pictures. Using tweezers and a magnifying glass, she studied the wounds and collected DNA samples. After thirty minutes, Bourbon finally asked his questions.

"Think this is the same weapon that killed our last three homicide victims?"

"Nope."

"Really?"

"Yup. These people were attacked with something else. Look, there's a splinter of wood in this woman's skull and in the console where the assailant must have missed. A piece of finished wood with a lacquer finish. Extremely hard."

"A baseball bat?"

"Possibly, or something similar. I can analyze these pieces at my lab, and maybe tell you more later. Our previous victims had tiny metallic shavings in the wounds, and the cuts were much cleaner. These people were attacked by something wooden that appears to have broken during the attack."

Shari gently rolled one man onto his back. "No carving in the abdomen. I think we have a new killer, Jeff."

Bourbon shook his head, feeling defeated before the investigation began. He huffed a little when he spoke.

"Maybe the murder weapon is in the water." Bourbon looked over a railing and took his phone from his pocket. "I'll have to notify the other half of their team. I may need one of them to search the water in this area, because there should have been four rescue divers here, but we only have three."

Shari looked around. "So, we're missing a victim?"

"A victim, or maybe, the killer?"

******

Deputy Sheriff Eli Birchcraft hit Grandview Drive with his lights flashing and tires spinning. After making an arrest, writing tickets, and overseeing the clean-up, the motor vehicle accident he had responded to took more time than he expected. He took the curves at a dangerous speed, but the veteran driver kept the vehicle centered on the pavement. There were no painted lanes on the rural road, and a wrong turn could cause a forty-foot drop down the rocky slope.

He was about a half-mile away from rendezvousing with Sheriff Bourbon at the boat launch when movement ahead caught his attention. Pumping the brakes hard, Birchcraft managed to stop the heavy vehicle before a large black bear ran across his path. The big bear crossed the road in three bounds and climbed the steep bank on the other side.

She'd come from the lake, and her fur was still wet and glossy. Birchcraft watched her until she vanished in the late-day shadows as quickly as she had appeared.

He took a deep breath, relieved he hadn't hit the heavy animal. He put the vehicle in motion and drove very slowly for the first fifty yards to ensure no bear cubs were following their speedy mother. He didn't go far when another dark figure trotted up the road in the same direction Birchcraft was traveling. Not a bear, but a man walking the road in Birchcraft's path.

Birchcraft flashed his lights and hit his siren for a single whoop sound.

The figure stopped but continued to face away from the deputy sheriff. Birchcraft put the truck in park, stepped out, and approached with caution until he was eight feet away.

"Sir?"

No response. The man stopped and supported himself with a tall staff. Both hands gripped the stick, his elbows bent, trying to keep himself upright.

"Sir, are you okay?"

The man, obviously a scuba diver, wore a black wetsuit. He gently turned toward Birchcraft as if he sensed his presence rather than heard his words. Wet hair, long enough to reach his shoulders, was naturally colored with equal parts black and gray. A thick beard matched his hair. But the beard and the rest of his face were covered in thick red blood. Most of the blood was still wet and slick, with the exception of vertical paths that had dried after running down his face. Two large eyes stared at Birchcraft through the mess.

His wetsuit was splattered with red biological fluid.

Birchcraft wondered if Sheriff Bourbon were aware that one of the rescue divers was this far from the crime scene. Clearly in shock, this man must have escaped and run into the woods.

"Sir, are you hurt? Stay there, sir. I'm going to help you."

Birchcraft reversed direction and sprinted to the rear of his patrol vehicle, and opened the rear hatch door. He keyed a lock to open a large metal compartment and retrieved his first-aid kit. He closed the rear hatch, which locked automatically. Once he had the kit, he stepped out from behind the Tahoe, but the man in the road was gone. Birchcraft scanned the road ahead, looking at both sides of the rural route. A scuffing sound behind, like feet dragging, spun him around. The rescue diver had circled the vehicle and approached from behind.

A weapon flashed as the diver lunged forward in attack. Birchcraft had no time to react other than to step backward. A streak of color made a sweeping motion across the deputy's field of view and connected, creating a two-inch gash in Eli Birchcraft's throat.

The first-aid kit crashed onto the ground as Birchcraft let go to cover his wound with his left hand. As he fell toward the middle of the road, the man in the wetsuit pulled the weapon above his head for the next blow. Birchcraft stumbled back to put distance between them as he drew his taser from its holster and fired a shot into the man's abdomen. Two electrodes fired 1,200 volts into their target. Every muscle in the attacker's body convulsed as the electricity overwhelmed his nervous system.

The rescue diver grunted as he fell and urinated in his tight outfit. He dropped the weapon, which Birchcraft recognized as a broken canoe paddle with a sharp, splintered edge. He didn't have time to subdue the man in the wetsuit. Instead, he grabbed the first-aid kit and made his way back to his driver's seat. He bled badly in the SUV and dressed his wound while watching in the rear-view mirror. Trembling hands struggled to apply gauze and wrap the laceration. It was impossible not to think about all the blood—his blood. After several layers of gauze and a sterile bandage that he gently wrapped around his neck, he forced his shaky hands to type a text message to his boss, praying that Cain Lake's shitty wireless service was working.

Please, go through. Please, please, please.

The message was challenging to type with bloody fingers that kept smearing the screen. The text finally launched, and Birchcraft stared at the screen, waiting for a response. The screen continued to dim, its glowing green light fading in his vision. He watched the signal strength icon on his phone go blank as he lost service. Night dropped on the burly deputy, and the world went dark. Just before he passed out, he saw a shadow of a man standing at the Tahoe's tailgate, tapping the glass with a broken canoe paddle.

20

BURN THE TIRES 

Cody watched Daisy drive away, hoping to see brake lights and a change of heart. But the taillights disappeared down the street, so he gave up on any hope of her returning. Cody couldn't blame her. Daisy saw him at his worst—violent and reckless—and he feared their connection had been severed.

He climbed the short set of stairs to The Mineshaft. He could still smell Daisy's perfume, but when he lumbered up the stairs and opened the bar door, the sweet scent was quickly overpowered by stale beer and fried grease. A married couple, hand in hand, stumbled out of the bar. They were so engrossed in each other that they didn't notice Cody staring, thinking that he'd blown his chance for that level of happiness.

He re-entered The Mineshaft, ready to face the consequences of his temper.

The bar occupants had settled back into their seats and ate and drank as though nothing had happened. Alyse was busy sweeping broken glass scattered across the floor, which Cody had never heard break. That was typical for him—to break something without knowing.

"Want me to do that?" Cody asked Alyse.

"No. No, don't worry about this. Happens all the time."

"How's your hand?"

Alyse stopped sweeping and tried to make a fist. "Hurts like hell. But it was worth it. Those two come in a couple of times a week and give me a hard time."

Alyse set a dirty dustpan on the floor and guided the broken glass onto it while Cody retook his stool. She had a slight look of disappointment on her face.

"Did you catch your girl?"

"Hmm?"

Alyse dumped the broken glass into the garbage. "Your reporter friend. Did you catch her?"

"No. No, she probably won't talk to me again."

"I really like what she wrote in this morning's edition of the news. She managed to convince the whole town to keep searching for Darcy and not lose hope that she was still alive. That's pretty special."

Cody wanted to forget about Daisy, or rather, his failure to impress her.

"Can I get a Coke, Alyse?"

"Sure, sweetie." She poured the soda and disappeared into the kitchen, returning a half-minute later with Cody's cheeseburger. He bit into the juicy beef, glad his mouth had something better to do than get him in trouble.

While Cody ate, Alyse scrolled in her phone for a minute, then set the phone in front of her favorite customer. "Here. Some heavy reading while you eat."

The phone had an article displayed from *The Stoneville View*, the town's online news site. The bold headline read, "Don't Give Up Stoneville: By Daisy Torrez."

Cody gave Alyse a little smile, then turned his attention back to the phone.

He read the article and ate his cheeseburger, and when he scrolled down one screen, he was staring at a picture of Darcy Poole. It was the same face he'd seen that afternoon when he had been submerged in Cain Lake. Darcy returned to his mind, alive and not so well, and she called out to Cody by name. Cody knew he was still in the bar, but the images of Darcy alone in the dark felt as real as Alyse standing in front of him.

"I'm scared. Help me, Cody," Darcy cried. Her clothes were dirty, and her hair matted and tangled. She spoke one last time. "You have to follow the mountain."

The vision vanished as quickly as it had begun. Cody thought about the words and debated whether the mechanics had given him a concussion during their fight, or was he simply remembering Flesti's words?

Cody couldn't understand it, couldn't believe it. He'd been seeing visions of Darcy ever since he'd fallen in the lake. The words in the article came back into focus, and he kept reading. Beautifully written and persuasive, Daisy's words had inspired an entire town to continue searching for Darcy and to believe she was alive. She also wrote about Connor Bayley's truck being sighted and how they couldn't have left town together.

Cody knew he needed to get in on the search. He had some connection to Darcy Poole that couldn't be explained, didn't need to be explained, as long as he could help find her.

He was about to give Alyse her phone, but the screen refreshed, and another article popped up. Again, the author was Daisy Torrez. "Serial Killer Keeps Sheriff on His Toes."

Cody read the article, skimming on occasion to get through it faster. It spoke of the murders that had occurred in the last week, since Cody had returned from prison. Lucky for him, there was no mention of his name, but he knew the local community believed there was a correlation. He kept reading.

The detailed article described how the murderer seemed to be targeting people with criminal records or those found to have violated the law. It also painted a gruesome picture of the carvings on the abdomens of two of the victims. By the end of the article, the author had dubbed Stoneville's first serial killer the "Sin Eater."

"Sin Eater," Cody read aloud, his voice inaudible in the noisy environment. A slight tingle traveled up his spine, and he hoped his shudder went unnoticed in the busy bar.

As Cody chewed the last bite of his burger, Alyse leaned on the bar, supported by her elbows, and stole a few fries from his plate. Pushing his plate a couple of inches toward her, Cody surrendered the last of his greasy spuds to her. She pushed the last two fries through a puddle of ketchup and bit into them.

"So, we're calling him the Sin Eater?" Cody said.

"Sounds fitting. Maybe you'd prefer 'The Cody Savage Stalker'?" Alyse wiped her mouth with a napkin, revealing a smile.

"I'd rather call him 'The Locked-Up Psycho.'"

"I'll drink to that," Alyse lifted her glass, and Cody raised his soda.

Alyse looked at the empty barstool next to Cody. "What are we going to do about AJ?"

"I have no idea. Maybe we can go down to the station tomorrow and talk to the sheriff. Maybe the people on the dive team who witnessed the whole thing can provide an eyewitness account of what an asshole Archer was."

"Well, you certainly have the bruise to prove it," Alyse said. She touched Cody's cheek gently, and he felt the sting from Archer's boot again. His cheekbone had puffed like a marshmallow, and the skin had turned blue. He leaned slightly into her hand, not wanting the attention to stop.

"I'll pick you up," Cody said.

"You? Will pick me up? Are you going to be on your magic carpet?"

Cody ran some fingers through his hair and then pulled AJ's keys out of his pocket. "I've got AJ's magic carpet, actually."

Alyse chuckled and gave him a fist bump, and then she disappeared to the far end of the bar to mix a couple more drinks for five female teachers celebrating a birthday.

Cody stared at the keys sitting beside his dinner plate. It would be so easy to jump into AJ's Charger and just drive, never looking back. Just point the vehicle south and push the gas pedal until he didn't recognize the terrain.

Until palm trees and sand filled the windshield.

Start over.

A new life.

Forget about Stoneville.

He grabbed the keys, threw a five-dollar bill on the counter for Alyse, and headed for the door. He hugged his beautiful friend on the way out but didn't say goodbye. "I'll pick you up tomorrow around eleven." He turned and made his way to the door and exited the building.

Outside in the parking lot, the Dodge Charger growled when Cody pushed the start button. The deep thumping purr of the Hellcat as it idled reverberated in his chest. He could feel his heart rev, seemingly in tune with the V-8 engine under the hood. He pushed the gas, and his frustration poured out the exhaust pipe in a hot, gaseous form. For a moment, he held himself from crying, as every emotion tried to let go at once. It was just too much.

Seventeen dollars remained in his pocket.

AJ in prison.

Daisy gone.

The town ready to see him burn.

Outcast from the Road Barons.

The Sin Eater taunting him, stalking him. Why?

There was only one way to let it all go right now. One way to get away: burn the tires. Pulling the gear shift lever into drive, he switched his right foot from the brake to the gas pedal. Two wide tires squealed with excitement, and Cody felt his chest crushed by the acceleration. The Dodge Hellcat was the fastest thing he'd ever driven, and the power was similar to a jet launching down a runway. Within seconds, The Mineshaft and his memories of the night were far behind.

21

GOODMAN

Half mile. 10-53. 1199. Bourbon read the text message from Birchcraft. He shook his head, trying to make sense of it. He had to decipher the codes out loud to convince himself that what he was reading was true. "Man down. Half a mile. Officer needs help."

Bourbon grabbed Shari's arm and pulled her to her feet. "Shari, we gotta go!"

"Jeff—"

"Birchcraft's in trouble. I think he needs a doctor or backup. Move your ass, woman!"

She jumped off the bow of the boat behind him. "What happened?"

"I'm not sure, but Birch might have found our fourth diver."

The pair sprinted to Shari's vehicle. She'd inadvertently parked in front of Bourbon's patrol vehicle, and there was no time to move the coroner's van out of the way. Bourbon jumped in the driver's seat. He hated leaving the crime scene unattended, but in this remote area, he was sure it would be undisturbed. He pushed the Ford van hard down the rural road, as Shari pushed her feet hard against the metal floor, one hand gripping the door handle and the other on her seatbelt. She almost screamed as they rounded the corners, but Bourbon refused to let up on the gas.

The van worked hard for forty-seven seconds, which was a long time for Shari, who listened to her equipment fall from the shelves and slide around the vehicle floor. In an instant, they went from sixty-five miles per hour to a near stop, as Bourbon jumped on the brakes while rounding a right-hand turn and parked twenty feet from the Birchcraft's bumper. Parked in the middle of the road, Birchcraft's patrol vehicle windows were fogged over, and the headlights glowed in the low light of the evening shade. The sun still had a little time left to hang in the sky, but Bourbon's location was shadowed by the mountains to the south, and a thick canopy created by the deciduous and evergreen trees. Night crept into the scene early in the valley.

Bourbon knew Birchcraft was inside the vehicle, and Shari must have sensed it as well. Her hand covered her mouth, and a look of fear and sadness formed on her face.

Bourbon jumped out of the van and sprinted toward the vehicle, holding his flashlight that was still powered off. Blood covered the door handle, and broken glass was scattered on the road at the rear of the SUV.

He heard a creaking sound behind him, only to turn and see Shari exiting her van. She took a few steps closer but froze in fright. Seeing a dead body was nothing new to the middle-aged woman, but knowing that the killer could be hiding behind the vehicle scared the shit out of her. She knew she needed to get to Birchcraft, but she would wait for Bourbon to clear the scene.

Bourbon reached for the Tahoe door and yanked it open.

Shari screamed behind him, and Bourbon turned to see her running, one shoe missing, toward him. Hiding in the shadows adjacent to the road, the killer was camouflaged by the dark wetsuit, and now he came for Shari.

Bourbon stepped toward the assailant as Shari ran away. She spun and shielded herself behind the big sheriff who'd taken an offensive stance. The diver walked forward briskly, canoe paddle in one hand, ready to strike anyone within reach, as Bourbon stepped toward the assailant like a one-person army, prepared to defend his two friends with his life.

"Shoot him!" Shari yelled.

Bourbon ignored the coroner's suggestion. He could see the crazed look in the man's eyes, eyes that didn't focus or change when Bourbon hit them with the beam of his flashlight. Eyes that made it clear the man had no plan and couldn't react to orders. The killer pulled the canoe paddle back as if he were standing at home plate. He swung hard, and the makeshift weapon stopped in Bourbon's left palm. The diver tried to pull the canoe paddle away from Bourbon, but the angry sheriff had a grip like alligator jaws.

Bourbon balled his right hand into a solid fist and let loose with a punch that sent the rescue diver on his ass and out cold for an hour. He rolled the wayward diver onto his belly and quickly snapped a pair of handcuffs to his wrists. Bourbon leaped into a sprint as he made his way to Birchcraft's Tahoe.

Shari was already assessing Birchcraft. She held two fingers on his wrist, "His pulse is weak, but he's alive."

"Thank God."

"We've got to get him to the hospital and fast."

Bourbon took out his phone and called for an ambulance. Then he dialed Archer's phone, but his cell phone signal died before he sent the call through. Dammit, Arch, I could really use you right now.

"Let's get him in your van," Bourbon said. "You drive. Meet the ambulance on the way."

It took all their strength to transfer the half-conscious deputy to the back of the coroner's van. Shari jumped behind the wheel and drove northwest.

Bourbon opened the back of Birchcraft's Tahoe, put the back seats down flat, and hoisted the unconscious killer into the back of the vehicle as carefully as he could, but couldn't help dropping the dead weight twice. Once the unconscious man was loaded, Bourbon sat sideways in the driver's seat, feet on the rocker panel, elbows on his knees, trying like hell to catch his breath. Once his heart rate had nearly returned to normal and he wasn't sucking hard for oxygen, he started the Tahoe. He reluctantly drove back to the boat launch to continue processing the scene. He'd have to stay there until Shari could come back, which could be hours.

*****

By the time Bourbon arrived back at the pontoon boat, darkness had taken over the crime scene, obscuring the macabre deaths of the crew.

Although the sky still glowed with the sun's energy, Bourbon was nothing more than a shape among the shadows. Even in the dark of twilight, he could still see the gory scene and smell the stench of death. He closed his eyes for a moment, but the boat had left a bad stain tattooed on his brain.

He went back to Birchcraft's vehicle and sat in the driver's seat while filling out paperwork. The vehicle's headlights illuminated the pontoon boat. When his phone got a sporadic signal, he'd call Charlie Archer and leave a message to meet him at the boat launch, or shoot a message off to Annabel. Neither of them replied.

Bourbon rolled the Tahoe window down, and the frogs serenaded him from the edge of the lake. Somewhere on a ridge, a pack of coyotes howled in the distance, and not far away, a barred owl hooted. All the usual nocturnal sounds one would expect to hear until he heard one animal noise that seemed more suited for the daylight.

A crow squawked from the canvas top of the pontoon boat. Bourbon slid out of the parked vehicle and approached the watercraft. He picked up a small handful of pebbles along the edge of the concrete boat ramp and tossed them at the feathered intruder.

"Get out of here!" Bourbon yelled at the crow. He knew crows were usually the first scavengers to show up at a murder scene, plucking away at eyes and the soft flesh of corpses. He was going to make sure the dive team arrived at the morgue fully intact.

He tossed two more. "I said, get!"

A pebble bounced off the canvas, causing the bird to jump, but it was adamant about staying. It didn't seem interested in the bodies below but kept its eyes on the lake's surface. Bourbon followed the bird's stare and, for the first time, noticed a backpack and some clothes hidden behind a rock near the water's edge. Earlier, he'd walked around that same rock and had seen nothing.

Someone had arrived while he'd gone after Birchcraft.

A soft splash caught his ear, and Bourbon shone his flashlight toward the center of the dark lake. A gentle wind crossed his face, bringing with it the smell of rotting human flesh. He took several steps backward to escape the putrid odor.

"Hello?" Bourbon said. His voice was slightly louder than usual.

The night grew quiet again, and Bourbon stepped lightly toward the water. It took him a minute to realize the pounding he could hear was coming from his chest. The crow cawed in excitement, and Bourbon wanted to pull his gun for the first time and shoot the obnoxious creature. It flew down and landed on the rock beside him and fell silent.

The figure surfaced ten feet in front of the anxious sheriff.

A woman with gray hair and a devilish smile stood in waist-deep water. She shook her head to expel the heavy water that saturated her hair and stepped forward, using both hands to squeegee the liquid from her face. She wore nothing more than a bracelet on her wrist and a hemp necklace that hung between her breasts, both adorned with several square beads featuring tribal symbols.

Her face suggested she was older than Bourbon, but her square shoulders and muscular body would have made a thirty-year-old woman jealous. She strode from the water like a movie star, and Bourbon turned his flashlight toward the ground.

"Jesus, lady, what the hell are you doing here?"

Flesti picked a small towel from her backpack and began to dry herself, unfazed by her exposed body. The crow cawed again, seemingly excited by the woman's return from the depths.

"Hello, Sheriff," Flesti said as she stuffed the towel under her hair. "Beautiful night, isn't it?"

"Yeah, it's fuckin' gorgeous out here, lady. Great night to be skinny dipping in the middle of a goddamn crime scene."

"I'm sorry. I startled you, didn't I?"

Bourbon pointed the light at Flesti's backpack. There didn't seem to be anything unusual or suspicious about it, and he didn't suspect she had a weapon. She certainly wasn't carrying one on her person.

He illuminated the pontoon boat. "You know anything about this shit?"

"The people over there—?"

"The *dead* people over there. Yeah. Did you see what happened here?"

"No, but I suspect your man in custody can tell you all about it. He's awake now," Flesti pointed her chin toward Deputy Birchcraft's SUV.

The sheriff was tired and agitated, just wanting this night to be over. He hoped the night swimmer was right and that the man in custody would have some insight into today's events.

"How the hell do you know that?" Bourbon asked the swimmer, but she ignored the question.

Flesti began pulling her clothes on, and Bourbon wasn't sure if he should keep shining the light to help or turn away. He compromised and shone the flashlight toward her feet—surprised that even they were attractive.

"Why are you out here swimming in the dark all by yourself?"

"Because I was here, and the lake called me."

Bourbon searched the sky for a full moon. "Did I miss someone passing out the fucking crazy juice today?" He murmured to himself. He shone his flashlight at his truck and then directed it into the deep woods. "Do you live around here?"

"This lake is my home. Has been for a long time," she stretched out the word 'long' and finished dressing. Then she pulled her backpack onto her shoulders.

Bourbon had seen some strange shit since being elected sheriff, but this was a first. This woman seemed lucid enough. She certainly didn't appear hungry or thirsty, and her clothes were semi-clean, and her teeth were perfect. She could obviously take care of herself. Bourbon decided she was neither a threat to him nor herself.

He spoke again. "I'm going to ask this suspect some questions, and then, if you want, I can give you a ride somewhere."

Flesti laughed. "I appreciate the gesture, Sheriff, really. I don't need to go anywhere. Besides, I'm looking for my dog. He's around here some- where, and I'd never leave without him."

Bourbon just nodded. He turned his attention to the man in the back of the SUV.

He marched to the back of the SUV and opened the rear gate. Broken glass fell to the ground and bounced off the concrete. The scuba diver was sitting up, with a look of remorse upon his face.

"Hello, Sheriff." He seemed to be a completely different person from the one who attacked Bourbon earlier.

"Gotta name, asshole, or should I just call you Scuba Steve?"

"Wilson. Wilson Goodman."

Bourbon wanted to punch him again solely for his name. "Well, Mr. Goodman, you wanna tell me why the hell you hacked up your three friends?"

As the memories of his crime rekindled, Goodman began to fall over, and the dry blood on his cheeks was re-wet by his tears. He caught himself from tipping over altogether, and then he looked over his shoulder toward the pontoon boat. He wanted to look but couldn't muster the courage. Night's black curtain covered the scene, although it could not mask the images still fresh in his mind.

"Hey, Goodman, I asked you a question." Bourbon banged on the vehicle to get Goodman to snap to attention. It worked as intended.

Goodman sniffled, swallowed hard, and corrected his posture. "I...I...Don't know what happened—"

"Bullshit!"

"I mean, I did it, Sheriff. I won't deny it. I just don't know why."

"Cause you're a psycho murdering dipshit, maybe that's why," Bourbon barked.

"No. No, that's not like me." He sniffled. "The lake made me do it. I know, I know, that sounds crazy, Sheriff, but it's the truth. When I came out of the water, I heard a voice."

"A voice, huh? Let me guess: the devil made you do it."

"Yes! Yes, it was the voice of evil. A woman's voice. I had to do it. I had to kill them for the lake."

Bourbon gave Goodman a little jab in the nose. Goodman's head snapped backward and then forward. Fresh blood trickled from his left nostril.

"Sorry, Goodman, a voice told me to do that. Now they're telling me to drag your ass out of this truck and kick it across the parking lot." Bourbon took a handful of wetsuit and chest hair in his grip. Goodman winced in pain.

Goodman opened his mouth to sob, but the sound refused to come out. A multitude of emotions were drowning Wilson Goodman—fear, remorse, confusion, and sorrow. He was speechless, but the sheriff was determined to get the truth.

"Why, Goddammit?"

"Because. Don't you see it?" Goodman caught his breath. "They're all sinners."

Bourbon reeled backward and released his grip on the suspect as another image appeared in his mind, and he remembered the word carved into the abdomens of Darin Cloudwater and Peter Felton. He stepped back and listened to the singing frogs. The coyotes had gone quiet, probably feasting on their kill. The hooting owl wasn't making a sound. Bourbon enjoyed the serenity for half a minute, composing himself. His pulse slowed, and he stepped back to the suspect. His voice was calm and serious. "What did you say?"

Goodman peeked at the boat again. "All of them. They're sinners. The lake wanted them dead for their sins." Goodman started to sob uncontrollably.

Bourbon turned away, denying the fact that the man from Albany could have the same motive as the serial killer haunting Stoneville. He spun on his heels and returned to the interrogation. "What did they do, Goodman? What do you—or this stupid lake—know about their sins?" He pointed toward the water, jabbing the air with his index finger in anger.

"I could see them," Goodman tried wiping his tears with his shoulder, but couldn't quite reach. "Tara is having an affair behind her husband's back. Jim—Jim is the fat one. Jim has a hidden camera in the girls' locker room at the college where he teaches. Robert, the little blonde man, he's been embezzling from his boss for years. I don't know how I know these things. I just do. The lake showed me."

Bourbon stared at the boat. Flesti was at the front of the Tahoe, half illuminated by the headlights. She was silent as she intently listened to the interrogation.

Bourbon wanted to go to the victims, tell them he was sorry, sorry he couldn't protect them in his jurisdiction. Sorry that this was their fate. He stepped back to the police SUV and grabbed Goodman by the throat. He stared deep into his eyes and asked the question that was burning him.

"What about my deputy that you may have killed?"

Goodman's brow drooped as he shook his head in confusion. "Your deputy? I don't remember—"

"You slashed his fuckin' throat with a broken canoe paddle! Down the road, less than an hour ago. What was his sin?"

Bourbon saw Flesti's hand sliding along the side window of the SUV. He paid no attention to her as she came toward the back of the vehicle.

Goodman stammered. He thought about Deputy Birchcraft, the muscular officer who stopped him in the road. His eyes rolled to the ceiling in an effort to recall what he had seen. "The deputy? I remember, now. I think—"

Goodman arched in agony. His eyes widened. He tried to gulp oxygen, "My chest." The words were barely audible. Then a gurgling sound emitted from his throat, as if he were drowning.

Bourbon snapped his fingers in Goodman's face, "Hey, Hey. You're fine, Goodman. What is the deputy's sin?"

"It hurts. Oh my God, it hurts."

"Goodman. There's a doctor on her way back. Focus on me. What's the deputy's sin?"

"He knows."

"Knows what, Goodman? What does he know?"

Goodman didn't say another word—ever. Blue water began running from his mouth and nostrils, and then the liquid changed to a purplish hue as it mixed with Goodman's blood. Goodman collapsed on his side and died in the back of Birchcraft's vehicle. Bourbon performed CPR for four minutes, but the body just grew cold.

Bourbon finally conceded that his attempt to save Goodman's life was futile. He kicked the vehicle's bumper so hard it nearly came off, and then sat beside Goodman's lifeless body, defeated. He wondered if Birchcraft was still alive. What sin could Goodman have seen in one of the most decent people Bourbon knew? Would he ever know, or would Birchcraft die, too, and take his secret to the grave?

Flesti put a hand on his shoulder and said she was sorry, and told the sheriff she was leaving. She started to march away with her tall walking stick in hand, as a silhouette in the night sky followed.

"Wait," Bourbon stopped her. "I may have more questions for you later. What's your name again?"

"Flesti."

"Got a last name, Flesti?"

"Thaed. Flesti Thaed."

22

SAY A PRAYER 

C ody stopped by his house and picked up a six-pack of beer—minus two—from his fridge. The cold bottles looked lonely in the refrigerator, so Cody thought he was doing them a favor. He popped the top off one bottle and started drinking it at the kitchen counter. Two bullet holes in the Sheetrock stared back at him, and he realized that those could have been in his skull if he hadn't been so lucky.

He was still breathing, and as shitty as his life seemed right now, that was something.

His pinky finger nearly fit into one of the holes, and he began to count the rest. He quit at thirty-one but guessed there were twice that number. Home was the last place he wanted to be right now. AJ's car had a nearly full tank of gas, so he decided to put it to use. Back outside, he climbed into the driver's seat and pushed the start button. The engine awoke.

He drove toward Cain Lake, the beer bottles riding shotgun, and Tracy Chapman joined in through the radio, singing about a fast car.

When he reached Cain Lake, Cody turned down a long gravel driveway full of potholes. The muscle car rolled over the rough path with ease and kept the ride comfortable. A lone building loomed at the far end of the driveway, the steeple reaching toward the heavens like an antenna to communicate with a higher power. Stained glass windows looked dull and dirty from the outside, not a hint of the beauty they produced from the inside.

Cody parked the Dodge Charger in the gravel parking lot and got out of the car. He gently closed the car's heavy door, careful not to disrupt the serenity of the setting. He walked a semi-circle around the struc-

179

ture and back again.

The little white church was quiet and dark. The building was narrow, with a tall belfry that housed an iron bell. The paint on the siding was chipped and peeling due to exposure to wind and rain. The doors were painted black, but Cody remembered them as bright red on the day he and Willa were married. Most of his memories of that day were as foggy as the lake below, and all he remembered was how lucky he felt. She was such a beautiful bride.

Willa had been nearly as tall as he was, and living on the farm meant working on the farm. She helped Annabel morning and night, before and after work, and Cody admired her strong work ethic. She was strong and resilient, wild and devoted. She loved her family, her church, and her friends fiercely.

And then, one day, she was stripped from his life. It was a loss to the whole community.

How was such a person taken from this world? Who had the will to see it all end?

Cody finished his beer and squeezed the bottle so tight he thought it might break in his hand. He would have welcomed the pain. It would have been mild in comparison to his current anguish. He threw the bottle without thought, and it smashed against the double doors of the church.

He walked in the opposite direction of the church, a three-pack in hand, up a hill. Two intricate metal gates were open and rusted in place. They were wide enough to drive a car through, but Cody stayed on foot. He ascended a hill until he was almost as high as the church steeple.

Looking down, he could see seventy percent of Cain Lake. It was the size of a small city, illuminated only by the three-quarter moon hanging in the sky. Twenty or more summer homes and cottages dotted the shoreline, and miles away, he could see someone burning a bonfire. Even from this distance, the heat of the flames was inviting. A singular boat was anchored toward the middle of the lake. It was probably some kids spending the night or fishers jigging for walleyes. Music carried across the lake with ease, and Cody could distinctly hear the lyrics from a Luke Combs song.

On the eastern side of Cain Lake, where the forest was still thick and the land undeveloped, he could see the headlights of a vehicle parked at the boat launch.

The truck faced the lake, and Cody thought he could make out the silhouette of a pontoon boat in the headlights.

Has to be the other dive team, wrapping up the search for today.

Cain Lake was alive, but behind the ex-con, the opposite was true. He turned 180 degrees to a different view—tall stones engraved with names and dates in nearly perfect rows. Cody walked the plateau of land that spanned two acres. Time stood still here, and little ever changed, like Stoneville itself. From time to time, a new resident would move in, but no one ever moved out. Visitors came in waves, depending on the weather or the holiday.

The cemetery had four streetlights on the property's perimeter, so he made his way through the rows of stone and flowers with ease. He passed by a double headstone he vaguely recognized and only paused long enough to read the last name—the same as his. The couple had died together fifteen years ago in their garage. He greeted them aloud, "Hello," as if he were passing strangers in town. They said nothing back, but he wasn't surprised.

He stood long enough for them to get a good look—to see what a disappointment their son had become.

He observed the date and wondered how many couples died on the same day.

He moved along, searching for the one stone that mattered. His loneliness seemed to wane once he found it and read Willa's name softly to himself, just to confirm that this was her final resting place. For some reason, he felt it necessary to do the math in his head to establish her age. Cody had aged four years since he'd last seen her, but she was still twenty-four.

Cody set the two-pack on the ground.

He brushed some debris from the top of the granite monument and straightened a vase full of fresh daffodils. Tulips grew around the memorial, and there were signs that somebody had scraped moss from the stone. Annabel. She made sure her daughter's gravesite was maintained year-round. A little statue of an angel, sitting cross-legged, watched him as he took a seat beside the stone. He remembered Levi, her brother, placing the angel there at her funeral.

The ground was cool but went unnoticed. For an hour, Cody talked to his wife. It was a one-sided conversation, but he didn't care as long as she was listening. He apologized a hundred times for not being able to protect her. He cried when he talked about their future and laughed when he spoke of their past.

Then he told her about Daisy. It was only fair that he be honest, but he also needed to reassure her that she was the love of his life. Besides, he wasn't even sure he'd ever see Daisy again.

He finished their conversation with a few more promises. He promised to find the person responsible for her death and make him pay. He promised that the truth would come out and his innocence would be proven.

When the last beer was gone, he debated whether to stay longer or go home. A cricket chirped somewhere beside him, and a dog barked in the distance. He wished he were a nocturnal creature that could hide in the shadows of night and never be seen by another human. Everyone in town had their eyes on him, watching, waiting to see how he'd fuck up again.

With his head swirling from the emotions and the alcohol, Cody wasn't in any condition to drive, and there wasn't anywhere he wanted to go anyway. He liked being here, in the solitude of the cemetery, alone with Willa, listening to the other wild animals of the night. He put his head back and drifted into a light slumber. He dreamed of Darcy Poole and a murder of crows carrying him to the lake, of being swallowed by a whirlpool, and a cow stuck in the mud.

*****

Pastor Jesse Lewis stared down at the man sleeping against the tombstone. The morning sun warmed Jesse's back, and his blood was hot with anger. Cody Savage leaned against the rock monument with his eyes closed and his head down, reeking of sweat and alcohol. Jesse didn't

182

have his hockey ax with him, but if he did, the kill would be clean and somewhat merciful. Cody's head hung low, relaxed, exposing the vertebrae in his neck.

Jesse had been waiting for this moment all week. A moment alone with Cody Savage. A moment when Cody wasn't anticipating his death. A moment when no witnesses could see the weapon swing and the blood spill.

What a perfect place to rid the world of the sinner—here among the dead. He could strike Cody down, and Willa Savage would see it all happen. She would thank the pastor for avenging her murder.

The town would thank the Sin Eater, their hero. They would see that he was making Stoneville a better, safer place.

Stupid people.

Jesse considered sneaking back to his truck to retrieve his hockey ax. Would there be time to climb down the hill and back up again before his prey awoke?

He closed his eyes to see if Cody could trick him again. When they had met on the dock, Jesse could not sense the sins of the sinner. He put his hand toward Cody's head, fingers open and tense, like some wizard about to cast a spell. Even with his hand just inches away from Cody's hair, he could not sense the evil.

Cody was tasteless.

He tried again and again, hoping to get a glimpse of what Cody was hiding. Finally, he had to accept the truth that there were no sins in this man to devour. No evil deeds that would satiate Cain Lake's appetite for years. Stalking Savage all week had been a waste of time, and killing the two men who nearly stole his prey—well, they were just a bonus, he decided.

Jesse looked to the sky, ashamed of his misjudgment. He had fallen into the same state of mind as the rest of Stoneville and believed Cody Savage murdered his wife. But Jesse had faith in his ability. He knew his power to discern the innocent from the sinners was as accurate as a dog's ability to find bacon in a backyard. They should have dubbed him the Sin Hound. He nearly chuckled out loud at the thought.

Jesse was doomed to continue his murderous spree unless he found someone to take Cody's place. He gave his next move some thought, deciding what to do next.

He kicked Cody's foot with a light touch of his shoe.

Cody stirred, took a moment to open his eyes, and get his bearings.

"Good morning, Mr. Savage."

Cody squinted, waiting for his eyes to adjust to the bright light of the sun. The ground was still slightly wet with dew, and the morning birds singing had replaced the owl hooting. Their notes were high and crisp as they darted around the lawn collecting seeds and insects.

"Is Mr. Timmons with you?" Jesse asked.

"No. No, I drove his car here last night."

"I assume you are the one who smashed the beer bottle against the door?"

Cody fought stiff hips and an aching back as he struggled to stand. He flexed his tongue, trying to produce saliva in his mouth, and stood, using Willa's headstone to give him something to grip and pull himself to his feet. He leaned gently against her monument as he stretched and rubbed his neck muscles.

"Shit. Yes, sir," Cody said. "I'm sorry. I'll go down and clean that up. I shouldn't have been so careless. Just got a little emotional, is all."

"No. I'll take care of it," Jesse said. "I understand. Happens to all of us from time to time. God gave us emotions, but he never taught us how to control them."

Cody agreed, knowing that's why his rage sometimes got the best of him.

He pushed himself off the headstone and stood as straight as a board. "Can I ask you a question, Reverend?"

"Pastor," Jesse corrected. "Of course."

"Do you believe God can give people...special abilities?"

The question took Jesse by surprise, and his astonished expression showed it. He usually got the typical questions about heaven and hell, the afterlife, atonement, and reincarnation, but no one had ever asked him about special abilities.

Is he like me? Can he sense things? Can he sense my sins? *"Of course. Everyone is unique in their own way—"*

Cody waved his hand as if the pastor wasn't understanding. "I have a friend who's having these visions. And you hear about people who can see the future, or sense when something bad's about to happen. This guy I knew in prison said he could see dead people, and I remember a girl in high school who would kill plants with just one touch of her finger."

"Your friend with the visions," Jesse inquired. "What does he see?"

Slowly, they walked down the hill toward the church, side by side. Cody described his visions of Darcy Poole and how he thought his "friend's" dreams indicated that Darcy was still alive. They talked about how horrible her situation was and how the entire town tried to pull together to find her, dead or alive.

When they reached AJ's car, Cody peered out over Cain Lake and asked a question that surprised them both.

"I'm not a religious man. But would you pray for me? I have no job, no money, and only a handful of friends, and I'm afraid of losing them. Everything I touch falls apart. I'm not even sure I should be in Stoneville."

Jesse wasn't sure how to react, except with professionalism. He was, after all, the pastor of the church and a man of God.

"I'll pray *with* you. Would you like to go inside?" Jesse asked.

Cody could see Willa standing at the church's doors, in her wedding dress—not a vision, but a memory. "No, right here, thanks. "

The two men bowed their heads in front of AJ's car. They prayed for Cody, Darcy, and the town. They prayed for their health and gave thanks for all they had. And before they finished, Jesse added a little prayer that Cody would find the answers he was looking for and that Cain Lake would become a place of peace.

He meant every word.

Cody thanked the patient pastor and apologized again for the broken beer bottle. Then he left the church and the cemetery behind.

Jesse watched the Dodge Charger tiptoe out of the parking lot, the driver easy on the gas. It disappeared down the gravel driveway, and then he heard the motor produce a gentle roar. The sound faded fast, and Jesse could no longer hear or see Cody Savage.

He climbed the short stairs to the church. The broken glass crunched under his weight as he opened the door. The building was empty, and Jesse made his way down the aisle until he stood at the altar. He whispered another little prayer, this one was for him alone.

He was angry with himself. The interior of his church always overwhelmed him with remorse, and the weight of his sins crushed his soul. Guilt wrapped him like an itchy wool blanket as he thought about Peter Felton and Darin Cloudwater taking their last breaths in front of him. He hated Cain Lake and its power to possess him. Now, because of him, the whole town was too scared to search for Darcy Poole. Too frightened because of the Sin Eater. Because of his actions, Darcy was doomed.

He opened a wooden door at the back of the church and stepped through. Creaky old stairs led upward, and he began to climb dizzily in a spiral. It had been over a year since he'd made this ascent. He was tired, and the Bible in his right hand felt like an anchor trying to keep him on the ground level. With each step, the heft of the book increased until he arrived at a square room. The room was void of anything other than an electric panel. A yellow label, faded and cracked, on the outside of the metal box read "Danger: High Voltage." A single rope, similar to the one that used to hang in his barn, descended through the ceiling. Stowed in the corner, a wooden chair from the early 1900s collected dust and cobwebs.

This room was once where the bell ringer sat and waited to perform his duties until the job became obsolete. Like many other tasks in the world, it became automated, programmed into a computer with just a few keystrokes. The person who once rang this bell was likely a volunteer, performing the mundane task because of their charitable heart.

The room lacked any decoration or even drywall. This part of the church, constructed of severely spalling bricks, was off-limits to the public. In the corner of the room, a ladder made of hemlock timber leaned against the wall. Jesse carefully climbed the ladder, Bible still in hand, until he reached a hatch to the next level. He pushed the hatch cover upward, and it disappeared into the room above. Then, Jesse squeezed through the narrow opening.

He was now in the belfry, home of the church's heart. The pastor had reached the highest accessible point of the building. In the center of the area, a massive bell hung from an axle with an ornate border wrapping around the sound bow. Two heavy wooden beams supported the axle, and a pulley, three-foot-wide, was bolted to one end of the axle. The belfry was thick with dust and pollen.

Absent of solid walls, the belfry contained Gothic-style openings on each of its four sides, echoing the design of the cathedral windows. Jesse stepped to the south side of the belfry and peered out at Cain Lake. A cool spring wind, born of nothing more than ambition, plowed across the lake and headed straight toward the pastor. The calm surface of the water rippled. The ripples turned to waves, churning the lake as though an angry pod of whales had made their way to Stoneville.

He reached into the open air with both hands straight out and dropped the holy book, watching as it fell and spun. The wind from the lake collided with the falling publication, dislodging the pages. The loose pages scattered like leaves in the fall. The book landed on the sidewalk with a hard thump as ivory pages nestled softly around it.

The wind picked up the dislodged pages, carrying them somewhere to be forgotten.

A gale pushed Jesse away from the opening. He circled the iron bell, reading its ornate pattern as if he were blind, and something extraordinary was written in Braille. Unable to fight the temptation, he rotated the pulley from left to right and back, like a ship captain at the helm, steering his vessel through a storm. The movement swung the bell in a slow rhythm until it struck the clapper and gonged softly. A pair of pigeons watched from above until the noise drove them out. They took flight, swooped through the glassless window, and disappeared in the wind.

For whom the bell tolls.

Jesse completed his circle around the bell and returned to the tower's opening. The Gothic-shaped space included a railing to prevent anyone from falling thirty-eight feet to the ground.

He stared across the lake and could see parts of town from his high vantage point. He loved this town and many of his parishioners, but he'd single-handedly destroyed it. No longer would Stoneville be considered a beautiful lake town, but rather, hell on water.

The wind made his eyes water, so he pointed his face downward. A tear was blown from his eye, down his cheek, and around to his right ear.

It was time to kill the Sin Eater.

He put one foot on the railing and then stepped up. The Gothic opening framed him, its pointed arch toward the sky—toward heaven.

He was going in the opposite direction.

Interrupting his intentions, his cell phone rang.

Goddamit. He'd forgotten to leave it at the altar. The caller identification lit up. Annabel Thompson.

He hit the decline button, hoping that was the end of it. "Not this time, Annabel." But the phone rang again. Maybe she needed help.

"Hello, Annabel," he said with a defeated tone.

"Good morning, Jesse," Annabel blurted in her peppy voice.

"Good morning," he drew in a deep breath. "What can I do for you?"

"I was just out feeding my animals, and when I saw Pearl, it made me think of you."

"Pearl?"

"Yes. You remember Pearl. You and Connor pulled her out of the mud last week."

"Oh, yes. The cow."

"Yes, my cow. Anyway, when I saw Pearl, it reminded me of our date today."

"Our date?" Jesse asked.

Annabel laughed. "I knew you'd forget. Yes. Lunch at The Mineshaft."

"Oh, I'm sorry, Annabel. I don't think I'm going to be able to make it today." Jesse stared down at the concrete sidewalk below. He imagined his body spread across the surface as his crimson blood seeped into the cracks.

"Oh, come now," Annabel prodded. "You wouldn't cancel on a woman who hardly gets to leave the farm, would you? I've been looking forward to your company all week."

The wind vanished, and Jesse was silent. A single crow appeared on the opposite side of the belfry, perched on the railing. Jesse took a couple of steps toward the ebony creature and tried to shoo him away. The bird finally cawed and disappeared into the sky.

Annabel thought they'd lost the connection. "Hello? Jesse? Are you there?"

Jesse looked to Cain Lake for an answer and noticed that the waves had settled. He thought about the day Annabel had picked him up and brought him to his tractor. Jesse sensed something—a sin within her. He wasn't with Annabel long enough to have a vision, but she was hiding something. Could she have killed her deceased husband? Maybe she cheated on her taxes or committed theft. Perhaps she was planning to kill Cody Savage to avenge her daughter.

He needed to know.

He finally gave his response. "Can you pick me up?"

Annabel assured Jesse that she would pick him up at his house. They agreed on a time, and she disconnected the call just as the two pigeons returned to their nest in the belfry.

Jesse felt a knot in his stomach that was as tight as the rope around the bell's pulley.

The Sin Eater was hungry, and Cain Lake was famished.

23
COFFEE & VISIONS

Cody parked AJ's car in the driveway, stumbled into the kitchen, and downed a big glass of tap water. He collapsed in a kitchen chair, unlaced his boots, and stripped off his dirty clothes. The dry air felt good on his skin. He marched the dirty clothes to the laundry room and set the washing machine to do its job.

The shower cleansed the cemetery dirt from his hands and face, and he relished the hot water that pummeled his neck. He then turned to feel it against his chest, the water bouncing off his stiff muscles, and cleansing his tattoos. The steam rehydrated his sinuses and lungs, and Cody could feel the effects of last night's drinks fade away.

Without warning, the water began to whisper to him, stirring visions and memories that whirled in a high-speed blender. He tried to concentrate on what he saw, but the images passed like a film reel running at the wrong speed—sometimes forward and sometimes backward.

He started to think he'd been drugged with a powerful hallucinogen that was just now taking effect. His vision commenced with a muddy cow walking away from a swamp. From that same mud, a man's hand pointed toward the sky. The camera, following these visions, panned skyward to a dark crow the size of a private jet, flying in a circle. The view dropped back to the ground, where Darcy Poole sat, hands tied, with a police car parked behind her. Sheriff Bourbon exited the police car and ran past Darcy. Cody wanted to yell, "Save the girl!" but he was nothing more than a spectator here, forced to watch without interfering.

The vision continued. Bourbon gripped the muddy hand protruding from the ground and pulled a young man from the earth. The thick black dirt hid his identity until the rain fell from the clouds, slowly washing the man's mask away. A human skull took form as the mud dripped away. Bees flew from its eye sockets in thick formation and attacked Darcy. She tried to scream, but the bees filled her mouth until she began to choke. The insects swirled around her, like the blue organisms in Cain Lake, and then flew upward to the sky. They merged with the crow, which accepted them with a deep, guttural caw, and then the ghostly form disappeared into the thick clouds.

Cody saw a female figure cut through the night, absent of shadows and as beautiful as anything he'd ever seen. Willa stepped like a dancer as she approached. She came close enough that he thought their lips would meet. But she pulled away and began to rise above him. She only spoke two words before vanishing through a floating door that reminded him of the church: "Go straight." She stepped backward into the door. It closed and folded on itself a dozen times until it was no longer visible.

Cody's shower turned cold, the temperature change snapping him back to reality. White tiles replaced blurred images. The cold was sobering and refreshing, but he cursed it for interrupting the scene playing out in his mind.

What the fuck was that?

What did it all mean? It seemed so senseless, but he felt in his soul that it was somehow related to the Sin Eater.

He stepped out of the shower and aggressively rubbed his skin with a dry towel.

He dressed in a T-shirt and shorts and passed out in his bed, hoping it would provide a more comfortable sleeping position than the headstone at the cemetery.

*****

He slept for three hours before the doorbell woke him. He'd been in a deep sleep, and lumbered down the stairs like Frankenstein's monster until he opened the door.

"Good morning, jackass," Daisy said. She wore a dress as bright as her smile, and Cody knew she'd been up and working for hours. Her makeup was perfect, and the spring breeze carried her scent into the doorway, awakening his senses faster than a double espresso. He took a deep breath to consume her aroma and couldn't stop himself from smiling.

"Come on in."

She could tell that the man who'd affected her heart had just woken up. "I thought you were a morning person? It's…" she looked at her phone, "10:42."

Cody stretched with both arms and then scratched his left shoulder hard. "Long night. Didn't sleep much." He went to the laundry room and began transferring his clothes from the washer to the dryer.

"Let me guess," Daisy said. "Spent the night in jail?"

"No, I did not spend the night in jail. And FYI, those two guys started that fight."

Daisy sat on a hard chair at the kitchen table. "I know."

Cody peeked out from inside the laundry room.

"I came back to The Mineshaft," Daisy said. "Alyse said I missed you by twenty minutes."

"Of course," Cody responded. He carried a small wad of clothes out of the laundry room and set them on the table. He folded a shirt, and when he finished, Daisy stood and unfolded it. She refolded the shirt with crisp and straight lines on each side of the collar.

Cody watched her as she grabbed another and repeated the process.

He stepped to the counter and filled a tea kettle with tap water. "So, I'm guessing Alyse told you what happened?"

"She did. I'm sorry I didn't give you a chance to explain yourself. I just didn't like what I saw, and I…reacted." Daisy stopped folding for a moment. "I came to New York because this is where my ex-husband's job brought us. He knew people here. He had friends. All I had was Sammy."

Cody held up a coffee cup without saying a word, and Daisy nodded. She continued folding clothes and unfolding her story. "My husband worked long hours and different shifts. And then he'd go out drinking with his buddies."

"And he was violent when he came home?"

"*Si.* Yes, he would get abusive and call me names in front of Sammy. I didn't want my son to learn his father's behavior."

"I don't blame you. You did the right thing by leaving." Cody leaned with his back against the counter and his arms crossed in front of him. "So, why did you stay? Here, I mean, in Stoneville?"

"Because I like it here. I like the seasons and the snow. I like the people and all the rivers and lakes and mountains. I grew up in the desert and spent most of my life in air-conditioned buildings and crowded malls. I wanted to prove to myself that I could survive here on my own."

They sat in silence for a few minutes, but neither seemed to mind. Daisy finished folding his clothes and pushed them to the edge of the table. The teapot finally hissed with a little geyser of steam.

Cody poured hot water into their cups, dissolving the coffee crystals at the bottom. Daisy took her cup, added a tablespoon of sugar, and topped it off with creamer. She thanked him in Spanish as he returned to the seat across from her.

"Sorry, it's instant coffee," Cody said.

Daisy blew across the top of the hot liquid and hugged the heat with her hands. "It's fine. I'm not high maintenance." She blew a little more on the coffee and took a sip. "Alyse told me you were going to the police station to talk to the sheriff and try to get AJ out of jail."

"Aw, shit," He looked at the clock on the wall. "I almost forgot about that. Yeah, well, I'm sure it will be a waste of time, but I have to try. At least AJ will know I didn't abandon him. I owe him too much."

"I could write an article," Daisy said. "Write something about Archer's brutality—his questionable temper—in *The Stoneville View*."

"Maybe. Can I ask you something? You conceived the title 'Sin Eater.' Do you think Deputy Archer could be the killer that's been following me around?"

"It's possible. Then again, it could be anyone at this point. There hasn't been much evidence to point to any particular suspect. And Sheriff Bourbon can't seem to keep up with everything going on. Now, he's knee-deep in blood from yesterday's killings."

Cody nearly spat his coffee. "What! You're kidding. What killings?"

"At the lake. Three of the rescue divers were killed."

"By who?"

"The fourth member of their team. You don't read my articles, do you?"

"Holy shit," Cody said. "What the hell is going on around here?"

"There's more. The officer who came to help Bourbon was attacked and is in the hospital; his throat was slashed with a broken canoe paddle. He'll live, but he won't return to work for months."

"Archer?"

"No, no, the nice one."

Cody gently hit the table with an open palm. "Birchcraft. Damn, that's too bad. I hope he's going to be okay."

They finished their coffees at the same time, and both agreed that they needed to go. Daisy had some interviews, and Cody wanted to visit AJ.

"Can I see you later?" Cody asked, stepping closer.

"Sure. How about dinner? My treat. I got my last paycheck from my previous employer."

"Whatcha have in mind?"

"How about Pizza Primo? Meet me there at...say, eight o'clock?"

Cody nodded. "I'll clear my schedule."

Daisy wrote her number on the back of a business card, "This is my cell. Call me when you get back from the sheriff's office, and let me know how it went. Poor AJ must be going crazy in there."

Daisy touched Cody's face, tracing the bruise on his cheekbone left behind by Deputy Archer's boot. "Better put some ice on that."

They hugged and pecked each other on the lips, neither daring to get too close, or their day would become more seductive and less productive.

When Daisy's noisy car drove out of sight, Cody finished dressing and wolfed down two pieces of toast for breakfast. He devoured the light meal, hardly chewing between bites, and washed it down with a tall glass of water. He nearly laughed out loud when he realized that he ate better in prison than he did as a free man.

AJ's car was waiting for him in the driveway, eager to get back to its owner. Cody fired the engine and pushed the gas pedal. It was nearly as loud as Daisy's car, but without the skipping and sputtering. He spun the tires as he left the driveway, but drove with caution toward The Mineshaft to pick up Alyse.

24

THE STATION

Sheriff Bourbon was at his desk, shuffling through papers and holding a landline phone to his ear when Cody and Alyse walked into the department. The office was a wreck, and Cody imagined that the mess resulted from the exhaustive search to find Darcy Poole. Papers were strewn about desks and held down with dirty coffee cups. Cody was sure he saw a cockroach disappear under a computer monitor and shot Alyse a disgusted look.

They passed one desk with every sticky note, pencil, and file in perfect order. Every paper edge was organized in parallel or perpendicular lines to the desk. Everything was in its place, not a speck of dust to be found. Cody wasn't surprised when he read the nameplate on the front of the work area: Deputy E. Birchcraft.

On the corner of the desk, a picture frame protected the memory of a rugged man, his smiling wife, and a young boy. Cody could see the ski jumps of Lake Placid in the background, and the family was standing next to a wood carving of a black bear. The burly officer and the bear had nearly the same body structure, although Birchcraft's shoulders were swollen and broader.

Alyse backed away and started to take a seat in a small waiting area. When something sticky transferred from the chair to her palm, she changed her mind and decided that standing against the wall might be a safer option.

The sheriff finally noticed Cody and motioned for him to come into the office, sneaking a schnapps bottle back into its hiding place. Cody didn't miss the sheriff's attempt to hide the bottle but said nothing. He took a seat across from Bourbon, who sat at a cold metal desk and started nodding as he listened to the phone.

"Uh, huh...Okay. Okay. Uh, huh...Yup. Sure, send me the paperwork, and I'll try to have it done before lunch. Okay, thanks again, Phyllis. I'll talk to you soon."

Bourbon hung up the phone and took a drink out of a coffee cup, which didn't contain coffee.

"Mr. Savage." Bourbon greeted Cody without making eye contact.

"Good morning, Sheriff," Cody said. "Hope this isn't a bad time."

"Of course, it is. I'm down one deputy, and the other isn't answering his phone. In fact, that was Phyllis LaValley—the mayor—permitting me to hire two new deputies immediately."

"Think that will help find Darcy Poole?" Cody asked.

"You mean her body?" Bourbon closed his eyes and scratched at his scalp in frustration. That was the first time he had admitted out loud that they might be looking for a body, and it made his skin crawl.

"What makes you think she's dead?"

"Reality, I guess. Darcy's been missing for a week. If she's had no food or water, then she's dead. If someone is holding her captive and is worried about being caught—she's dead. Her boyfriend's truck has been seen around town with only one occupant—"

"She's not dead, Sheriff."

"It's not looking very encouraging."

"Connor Bayley may be the only one who knows where that girl is. Find Connor, and you'll find Darcy."

"Of course, we've been looking for that little shit stain. Connor hasn't been to work all week, and Annabel's been trying to call him. He's lost in the wind and not answering his phone."

"Sheriff, I know she's alive. I think someone's holding her in a basement. Don't give up looking for her. Please."

Bourbon spun in his chair, looking out the window. He finished the liquid in his coffee cup and turned back. He stared at a picture of Annabel on the corner of his desk.

"How is she?" Cody asked. "Annabel? Is she—?"

"You don't get to ask that question," Bourbon growled. "She's the toughest damn woman I've ever met. If you really want to know how she is, then go ask her yourself."

"She'd shoot me on sight if I tried to talk to her."

"You're probably right about that," Bourbon said. "So, why are you here?"

"Because AJ shouldn't be," Cody responded. "Sheriff, please, let AJ go."

Bourbon rolled his eyes. "He assaulted my deputy, Savage."

"I know. But Archer was way out of line. He was harassing us and then kicked me in the face. Look." Cody turned his face to reveal the bruised cheekbone from Archer's boot. "Sonovabitch kicked me into the water, and I nearly drowned."

Bourbon dismissed the bruise. "For all I know, you could have gotten that from the little scuffle you got into at The Mineshaft last night." He peeked around Cody to see Alyse biting her lip. "Heard you and your sassy girlfriend out there were both involved."

"Alyse had nothing to do with it. Two guys at the bar were giving her a tough time. They deserved what they got."

"Seems everybody's giving you a hard time since you came home, Savage. Maybe you should take the hint."

Cody's stomach punched him, and a surge of adrenaline flooded his bloodstream. A fire erupted in his torso, and the flames tickled at his throat. He prepared to spew words that burned. Once spoken, the words would cut Bourbon's skin, but the tough Sheriff wouldn't let them go any deeper. Cody knew that.

He swallowed the fire back down, extinguishing it with cooler thoughts. He was here to help AJ, not to get into a verbal altercation with the one man who could destroy his life. Cody sensed Alyse behind him and then felt her calming hand on his shoulder.

"Come on," Alyse urged. "We're wasting our time here."

Cody stood, pushing the chair across the linoleum floor with the back of his legs, which made a high-pitched scratching sound that hurt their ears.

"Sorry to waste your time, Bourbon," Cody started for the door, following Alyse.

Bourbon's steely husk softened a little. "Listen."

Cody stopped in the doorway.

Bourbon picked up a file on his desk and tapped it with an index finger. "AJ will be arraigned this afternoon. Depending on his plea, he could be looking at a year or more in prison."

Cody glared at Alyse and swallowed the curse words that wanted to leap from his tongue.

Bourbon continued, "I'll speak with the judge first and recommend he be released on his own recognizance. But this is a class C felony, so I can't make any promises. I'll also speak to the dive team and get their account of yesterday's events, but that won't be anytime soon. They have enough to worry about right now, and they're already back in Albany. Except the one that saved you. I think she stayed. Turns out, she's the daughter of Dale Kelly, our District Attorney, so he's probably already heard about this. Now, if you don't mind, I have a pile of paper-work to do after the massacre of the dive team."

Cody nodded. "I heard. Three dead?"

"Four, actually. The suspect who went crazy passed at the scene." His face went hard, and his brow collapsed in anger as he looked at Birch-craft's empty desk. "But not before he slashed a good deputy's throat."

Alyse asked, "How's Birchcraft doing?"

"He's going to be all right. There was some damage to his vocal cords that will affect his voice, but the man was a terrible singer anyway."

"What the hell would cause the diver to do that? To go crazy like that and attack the other divers?" Cody asked.

The sheriff pushed his chair away from his desk. He went blank for a moment as he turned away from his visitors and stared out the window. He clicked the button of a pen, watching the images of last night's murder flash through his mind on some sick carousel. Each pen click seemed to shuffle the pictures, so he stopped clicking. Then he gave his answer.

"The lake. According to the suspect, Wilson Goodman. Before he died, he was blabbering on about how the lake made him do it. Fucking water's telling secrets now and possessing people."

"What the hell does that mean?" Alyse asked. She took a step closer, curious to hear the answer.

Bourbon looked over his shoulder at her. "Goodman said that the lake made him kill the 'sinners.' He seemed to know all about his dive mates: their affairs, fraud, and corruption. He even thought Birchcraft was a sinner."

Alyse and Cody looked at each other in disbelief.

"I can't say any more. This is still an ongoing investigation, and the state boys are sending in some suits. If the judge releases your friend, I'll give you a call."

Cody pulled Daisy's business card out and showed it to Bourbon. "I don't have a phone. Can you call this number?"

Bourbon noticed the name written above the number and laughed. "You getting mixed up with this journalist girl, Savage?"

Cody shrugged, but Alyse gave a little nod and a smile behind his back that gave him away.

"Figures. You're both a pain in my ass. You ought to be perfect for each other."

"Can we see him? AJ?"

"No, sorry, I'm the only one here, and I have to run out as soon as I finish this clerical shit." He pointed to the papers littering his desk. "I wish I could help you, but I'll let AJ know you were here. I'll give the judge and the DA a call and try to get back to you."

Cody nodded in appreciation, "I'll owe you, Sheriff."

"You bet your ass you will."

*****

Cody and Alyse walked four blocks to their borrowed car since Cody preferred not to get caught driving without a license. Once they reached AJ's Charger, the twosome rode across town, cutting behind the hospital to avoid the main streets, and ended up back at The Mineshaft, where they'd met.

The Dodge Charger rumbled into the parking lot and filled the parking space adjacent to Alyse's car. Every other vehicle in the half-empty lot filled the parking spaces closest to The Mineshaft's door, but Cody and Alyse had opted to park at the far end near the tree line. They were nearly invisible to anyone inside the restaurant looking out.

The pretty Louisianian didn't go for the door handle. She unbuckled her seatbelt and opened the car's glove box, dug through a few papers, and came out with a little bag that contained three neatly rolled marijuana cigarettes.

Surprised about her discovery, Cody shook his head in disbelief. "How the hell did you know those were in there?"

"AJ shared the other night—after we painted your house."

"Damn, woman, you're intent on sending me back to prison, aren't you?"

Alyse lit the end of one of the joints and sucked in a big breath. She passed it over to Cody. His draw was a bit smaller than hers, and he rolled down the windows to exhale the gray smoke. "AJ's going to kill us for smoking his weed."

"Nah, I'll leave some cash in its place," Alyse said, speaking while trying not to exhale. She finally exhaled through the open sunroof. "Do you believe what Bourbon said about Cain Lake? The way it's affecting everyone?"

Cody sipped from a bottle of water, screwed the cap back on, and gave her a concerned look. "I think something is going on with the lake. I can't explain it, and you'll just laugh—"

"What? I won't laugh. Tell me," she said, taking another draw and turning sideways in her seat to face him.

"You'll think it's stupid, but something happened to me when I fell in the water yesterday." He held his water bottle up and looked through the water as if the clear liquid had come straight from Cain Lake itself.

"Yeah, you almost drowned."

"Funny. No, I mean, there were these—don't laugh—visions."

"Visions? What kind of visions?"

"When I was underwater, I was surrounded by these strange blue lights—like little bugs swirling around me. They swarmed me, and I thought I was hallucinating at first, but then I could feel them."

"Blue light bugs? In the lake? Are you sure that's what you were seeing?"

"Yes. And then, I saw Willa—only for a moment, but she was there.

She was just floating as if she wanted to tell me something. The next thing I know, Darcy Poole is there, too."

Alyse's perfect eyebrows flexed. "The missing girl?"

"Yeah, and I'd never seen her before. But since then, I've seen her picture in the paper, and it was, in fact, Darcy. I don't know why or how, but I keep seeing her. I think someone's holding her captive." He took another drink from the bottle, guzzling it down until it was gone.

Alyse held the joint up, but Cody countered with an open hand to resist.

Alyse withdrew the offer and leaned a little closer. "But the sheriff is pretty sure she's dead."

"I know, but I don't believe that, and I don't think Bourbon truly believes that either. I think Darcy Poole is alive, and I may be the only one who can find her. If I keep having these visions, then maybe a few clues will turn up, and I'll be able to tell exactly where she is."

"Where would you even start looking? The whole town has been out searching. They can't even find Connor Bayley's truck, even though the friggin thing has been seen on camera following you."

"I don't know. But I've got to start somewhere. Maybe the lake can show me. Maybe I'm friggin crazy after being in prison for so long. Or maybe Archer's kick to the head did something to my brain, but I have to try."

"If this is true—if the lake can show you this stuff—you're hoping it will also show you who murdered Willa, aren't you?"

He didn't answer. He just started the car.

Alyse leaned over and kissed him for no reason at all. It brought back a flood of memories for Cody, and he wanted to resist. The time they'd spent together in the months after Willa's death and before Cody went to prison was amazing. He'd fallen hard for the dark-haired beauty with big green eyes, but they were different people now. She deserved someone better —someone who could spoil her and take her places, someone who could give her a life and a family, and help her escape Stoneville.

Cody couldn't do any of that.

When she pulled away, Cody scanned the parking lot to see if anyone had witnessed their moment of passion. He didn't want the town hating Alyse for loving him, and he didn't want Daisy to find out.

Daisy, whose smile bloomed like a flower the night they had met.

Flesti had said that he could only trust the flower and the mountain. Daisy must be the flower if it were true. That made him smile. And then he wondered—if Daisy is the "flower" Flesti is referring to, then who the hell is "the mountain?"

Raindrops began to play a slow rap song on the windshield. It was an ugly tune with no rhythm, starting in slow motion until an orchestra of drops joined in, and the music was loud against the car's steel top.

Alyse didn't say goodbye. She just bounced out of the Dodge Hellcat and sprinted for The Mineshaft's door. Once she reached the covered porch, she turned and gave Cody a little wave goodbye. It was time for her to punch in to work, even though her heart was still outside in the Charger.

Cody stayed there, parked, with nothing to do until his rendezvous with Daisy, which wasn't until much later. He searched the various stations preprogrammed into the radio, going through the list almost three times before settling on 105 FM Classic Rock. Bob Segar was singing "Fire Lake." Pretending to know the lyrics, Cody sang along quietly and thought about his next move.

He realized he was no closer to knowing the truth about Willa's death than when he had arrived in Stoneville, and now he wasn't sure he'd ever know. Maybe he'd have to live with that and let the town think he was guilty. Maybe he needed to give up searching for a murderer and put his focus on finding Darcy Poole.

He leaned his seat back just a little, thinking he might catch up on some sleep. A large Chevy Suburban pulled out of The Mineshaft's parking lot, clearing Cody's view of the remaining vehicles. On the opposite side of The Mineshaft's parking lot, an unusual truck was parked with headlights that seemed to stare right at him. The 1965 Ford F100 was backed into its spot, waiting for Willa's mother, Annabel Thompson, to drive it home.

25
STRIKING DISTANCE

Okay, I admit it. You were right."

"I told you. I knew you'd like it."

"I can't believe I've waited this long to try it. I loved it."

"I know. It's so addicting."

"Now, I may be addicted."

"Yeah, but every time I come here, I put on two pounds. My ass looks like two pumpkins kissing goodnight."

Jesse Lewis felt his face turn hot as Annabel's remark made him blush.

She giggled and wiped her mouth with her napkin. "Sorry, I didn't mean to embarrass you. I've just been a little hard on myself since—"

She cut her words short, but the pastor knew what she was going to say. He finished the sentence for her. "Since Willa passed away?"

She nodded her head, and there was silence between them for a moment. Annabel's attention wavered for a moment as she watched the heavy rain run down the outside of a window. Outside, a young woman dashed around the corner, up the front steps, and entered the restaurant's front door. Annabel didn't recognize her until she came inside. When she walked by, late for her shift, she left a faint odor of pot and perfume. Annabel watched her disappear into the kitchen and returned her attention to the overstuffed pastor sitting across from her.

The corner table in the dining area was more secluded than the tables near the bar, so that's where they chose to sit during their meal. The sound of the TV, the pool table, and the kitchen echoed off the walls in their direction just enough to break the silence while they chewed greasy burgers. Jesse and Annabel had both ordered the Ruby Burger—

black Angus beef, fried red onions, barbecue sauce, lettuce, and maple bacon. They both skipped dessert, but the waitress talked them both into a cup of coffee.

Jesse stirred sugar into his cup, watching Annabel over pour sugar into hers. He admired her. She was fun-loving, intelligent, and caring. She managed the busy farm by herself, although her son Levi sometimes helped, and she had two hired hands. She was a member of various boards in town, volunteered whenever possible, and never turned down anyone who needed help.

Annabel finished stirring in her sugar and pulled the bill toward her. Jesse hadn't even noticed when the waitress placed it on the table. "It's on me," she said.

Jesse stared some more. How could she be such a wonderful person? And how the hell could she be such a sinner? His head buzzed, and his arm throbbed, and sometimes it was the other way around. The feeling he'd felt from all his victims had returned when he was in Annabel's presence. He could smell it on her. He could taste it in the air. But she hid it so well.

It took all his control not to scream, *What the hell are you hiding*?

Jesse smiled as Annabel talked. Her words were ignored, and although he watched her lips move, he could only hear himself saying, *Kill her. Kill the sinning bitch now while you can.*

"Are you feeling okay?" Annabel asked. "You look a bit tired."

"Oh, it's the burger, I think."

"Are you sick? Can I get you anything? Water?"

"No, no, I think I just overate a little. I'm not used to such a big meal. It was delicious, though, and I will be back." He tapped the table as if stamping his statement with a promise.

Jesse wanted her to stop being so pleasant. "I'm sorry. You were saying?"

"I was saying...I know the Pooles don't have much money. If, God forbid, they find Darcy deceased, then I would like to take care of her arrangements."

"You want to pay for Darcy's funeral? That's very kind of you, Annabel. I mean, let's hope it doesn't come to that."

"It's no big deal. It's the least I can do."

"Well, that's a lot. Of course, you should discuss this with the Pooles—when the time is right."

"Of course."

"And the funeral home."

"Yes, I planned to go there later today." She put her debit card on the check, and the waitress quickly snagged it.

"Why?" Jesse finally asked Annabel. "Why do you feel it necessary to do that for the Pooles?"

"Oh, I don't know. I guess...I guess it's because I know what it's like to lose a daughter. When Willa passed away, the last thing I wanted to do was to pick out a casket or a burial plot. I didn't want to think about anything but the good memories we had together. All I saw was this little freckle-faced girl trying to ride her bike or a cow." She snorted, thinking about the memory of Willa falling off a cow and landing in a pile of cow shit. The stubborn little girl had climbed right back on and done it again.

"Annabel," Jesse said. He reached over and took her left hand with both of his. She lifted her coffee with her free right hand. "You can confide in me. I feel like there is something you'd like to get off your chest. Anything you tell me is strictly confidential. I can't even tell the police if I wanted to."

"You mean, like a confession?"

"Exactly."

"Oh, I don't have anything to confess—other than I might get dessert to go. But I appreciate your concern, Jesse."

You lying bitch, he wanted to scream and jab his spoon into her eye. Instead, he just smiled and patted her hand, "Are you sure?"

"Mmm, hmm. I'm sure."

The waitress came back with Annabel's receipt. She signed a copy and left it on the table.

As they left The Mineshaft, Jesse held an umbrella for Annabel, and they made their way across the parking lot to her truck. They dodged mud puddles forming in the parking lot until they reached her old Ford. Jesse opened the driver's side door and Annabel slid behind the steering wheel as she thanked him.

Jesse closed the door behind Annabel and mouthed something through the window. She spun the window crank to lower the glass two inches in an attempt to hear the pastor but keep the rain from pouring into the truck's refurbished interior.

"I'll be right back!" Jesse shouted over the noise of the rain.

He marched across the parking lot toward a gray Dodge Charger parked on the other side. The driver's side window was down an inch, and Jesse recognized the man behind the wheel. This was his last chance, he thought to himself. The rain almost stopped for a moment, getting lighter with each stride he took.

When he was just ten feet from the car, Jesse's foot dropped into a puddle. Water overflowed his shoe and drenched his foot in cold discomfort. It pissed him off, but he faked a calm disposition. He even smiled to exaggerate the charade. The cool rain and the wet foot soothed his aching head and throbbing arm. With each step away from Annabel, Jesse lost a sense of her sin. He needed the break.

"Hello, preacher," Cody greeted through the window opening. He powered the window down almost all the way.

Pastor, damn it. Why is that so fucking hard to remember? "Pastor," Jesse corrected politely.

"Sorry. Pastor."

"I'm good, Mr. Savage. How are you?" Jesse put his hand forward, waiting for Cody's response. This was it—his last chance to test Cody's innocence. He was certain that this time, a handshake would send a shiver down his arm. The sinner had tricked him before, but there was no way he could keep up the charade. Their hands gripped firmly, and the result was the same as before. Nothing. Jesse took a deep breath and exhaled slowly, conceding to the truth. Cody was as innocent as he'd feared.

"Isn't this AJ Timmons' car?" Jesse asked.

"Oh, yeah. AJ got arrested yesterday."

"Shut the f—really?" Jesse said. "How does someone like AJ get arrested? He's such a good guy."

"Guilt by association," Cody said. "The deputy sheriff tried roughing us up yesterday at the lake. AJ took a swing at him.”

“I hope he didn’t swing at Eli Birchcraft. That man could move the world if he could get a grip.”

“No, the other—”

A clicking sound interrupted both men. It had come from behind Jesse Lewis, and when he turned around, he saw the origin of the noise.

Annabel was drenched from the rain. Her mascara was streaking down her face, and her hair fell flat. She was holding a small revolver and trying to point it right at Cody’s head. Her shaking arm could have sent the bullet anywhere if she had pulled the trigger.

“Annabel,” Jesse said, trying to corral her attention away from her target. It didn’t work. Her eyes focused on Cody like an owl watching a mouse.

“Move aside, Jesse,” Annabel commanded in a much lower octave than her normal voice. “I got something I need to say to this man.”

Jesse sidestepped. *Do it. Do it, damn it. Blow his Goddamn head off. I will gut you like a fish. I will devour your sin and enjoy the satisfaction for months.*

“Annabel, what are you doing?” Cody asked calmly. He knew this woman, his ex-mother-in-law, and her amazing character. He loved her once, nearly as much as her daughter.

“Shut up! You shut your lying, murderous mouth before I blow it off your face.”

Cody could tell by the diameter of the barrel that the pistol was a .22 revolver. One shot probably wouldn’t kill him, but the pain would make him hope so. If she were going to shoot, he wished she had a pistol more capable of getting the job done.

She stood quiet for a moment as if she had to think of what she was going to say—or do. Most people would have rehearsed this in their minds a hundred times, but Annabel Thompson never thought she’d have the nerve to pull a gun on an unarmed man. Perhaps the pastor gave her a sense of confidence, a spiritual representative who would forgive her for what she was doing. She spoke her demands with a voice that was as shaky as her hand, “I want you to leave town. Tonight. You don’t belong here.”

Jesse half-heartedly intervened. "Annabel, you can't force Cody to leave town for killing your daughter." *What are you waiting for? Shoot, dammit.*

"Oh, yes, I can." Annabel asserted. The wet gun nearly slipped from her grip. "You gave up your rights to be a citizen of Stoneville. You gave up your life when you tied my little girl up and stabbed her to death."

Cody had both hands up in plain view. "I didn't—"

Annabel pushed the gun closer, forcing Cody to swallow his denial. He wasn't sure what to say to convince this grieving mother to heed the truth. He let Jesse Lewis speak for him.

"Okay, Annabel. Cody's going to leave town. Just put the gun down. He's leaving right now." He looked at Cody, and they both nodded in agreement.

Annabel lowered the gun and stepped closer. The rain fell harder now, but it wasn't enough to quell her fire. She bent down just slightly so Cody would be sure to hear her, "If I see you again, I will blow your nuts off." She back stepped a few times, whipped around, and returned to her truck.

"I'm sorry," Jesse said, though he was hoping for a bloodbath. "She's not feeling well, and...."

Cody raised his hand to deflect the excuse. "It's okay, Mr. Lewis. She has every right to hate me. Someday, the truth will come out, and we'll all know what really happened to Willa."

Cody drove away, leaving the pastor standing under an umbrella.

Jesse was convinced. Cody Savage did not kill Willa Thompson. He regretted the time he'd wasted chasing his sin, killing the men who shot up his house, and taking Brody Sherwood's life.

The kill he wanted wasn't there anymore. The sin never existed.

But this new prey—this woman who radiated guilt—was within striking distance. The parking lot was empty, and the rain hid any chance of witnesses. He strode back to Annabel's Ford truck, and the two left the parking.

Jesse was silent and did not mention the incident with Cody. His mind was twisting, and a plan was formulating within.

26
TORMENT

A nnabel quietly cried from the parking lot to the railroad tracks that crossed Main Street. Neither she nor Jesse said a word about what had just happened at The Mineshaft.

The rain came in intervals, much like Jesse's feelings toward Annabel. He was conflicted, as if two voices argued inside his mind, creating the migraine that stabbed his temples. Pastor Jesse loved Annabel and viewed her as a model citizen that the whole town loved and admired, but Sin Eater Jesse hated her for concealing her sin from the rest of the world.

He was determined to pry it out of her tonight.

The old Ford's windshield wipers fought hard to outpace the rain. They were decades old, and the rubber was thin and hard. Jesse's eyes grew tired of trying to see through the rain and out the windshield. He turned toward the driver, his torso twisted to the left.

He was glad to have seen Annabel's true feelings. She buried her hate for Cody deeper than the water at Cain Lake. What surfaced when she had seen the ex-con was raw and ugly.

Annabel was very good at concealing things.

Jesse wanted to get his hands on her gun and try to get a reading from it. Maybe the pistol had a secret and would spill its guts to him. He'd never read an inanimate object before, but it was worth the effort.

"Where'd you get the gun?" He asked. Annabel ignored the question.

"Are you going to be okay?" He tried again.

She sniffled hard and nodded. "Yeah. I'm sorry you had to see that. I don't know what came over me. Surprised myself."

"This is the first time you've seen Cody Savage since his release from

211

prison, isn't it?"

She just nodded again.

Jesse opened the glove box, and Annabel dismissed the intrusion. She was sure the pastor only wanted to help.

Jesse carefully pulled the pistol from its hiding place and inspected it. He caressed the barrel and turned the cylinder, hoping the metal and gun oil would reveal the story he was looking for. It was an ugly weapon for the man who preferred his custom-crafted hockey ax. The pistol had such a profound, impersonal impact on its victims. The gun's mechanics were primitive—pull the trigger, the hammer strikes a bullet, and the bullet strikes a target. Jesse's hockey ax was a weapon to revere—custom-made, one of a kind, get close and think about your strike.

"My husband," Annabel said.

"Sorry, what?" Jesse asked.

"That was my husband's pistol. Before he died, we would go down to the swamp—same place where Pearl got stuck in the mud—and we'd shoot aluminum cans for hours. Then we'd have a picnic in the meadow on the way back. Willa was just a little girl then. She would sit on my lap and plug her ears when her father shot. And then she would clap. She used to say 'Bad shot, Daddy' to him and 'good shot, Momma' to me. It made him laugh."

Jesse pushed the cylinder sideways to open it. The .22 held four rounds of ammunition.

Annabel continued, "When he died, I put this gun away and never thought I'd hold it again. I thought, someday, I'd give it to Willa and Cody, and they could go to the swamp and shoot together."

She began to cry again and then pulled herself together quickly. They made it to the edge of town and continued driving west against the hard rain. Annabel's foot was light on the gas, and she hoped the pastor would forgive the sin he'd just witnessed in The Mineshaft's parking lot. She waited for the words of exoneration.

She kept waiting.

They left the crowded neighborhoods, crossed a short steel bridge, and entered a rural country road. They kept riding the rolling hills until the geography changed and short cliffs formed. Annabel turned south and drove parallel to the cliffs.

The rain glazed the roads with a smooth layer of moisture, cooling the blacktop. The spring rain gave the tiny new leopard frogs the courage to jump across the blacktop and make their way to the pond on the neighbor's property. Annabel slowed the truck as thousands of frogs hopped across their path, but the road was impossible to travel without splattering the tiny amphibians. The smell of the swamp filled the truck cabin. Annabel kept the vehicle moving forward, splattering blood and guts in her path.

Jesse looked out the old truck's back window and then at the windshield. In front of the Ford, life was vibrant, bounding with enthusiasm, eager to make it to the larger pond. Behind the truck, death and mutilation were left in their path. The assault on the little creatures continued for 200 yards until they cleared the swamp's boundary.

When they reached the pastor's hobby farm, Annabel turned right and started up the long driveway.

"Would you drop me off at my barn?" Jesse asked.

Annabel still hadn't said a word.

The driveway split forty yards from the road to form a Y. Steering to the left would lead a vehicle to the small barn. If you kept to the right, you could park in front of the house. However, a vehicle could make a complete circle regardless of the direction it drove in.

Annabel kept the Ford to the left and parked in front of the barn's two large swinging doors. She'd been so preoccupied with the rain, the road, the frogs, and Cody Savage that she just realized that Jesse Lewis was still holding her gun.

He pointed the weapon at Annabel. A grim look came over him that she'd never seen before. "Get out of the truck!"

She began to shake. "Jesse? I don't understand—"

"Get out of the fucking truck, Annabel."

"Jesus, what is wrong—"

Jesse punched her forehead with the heavy gun in his hand. A small laceration formed, and blood began to flow instantly. Gravity pulled the red fluid downward into her eyebrow, which directed it to the bridge of her nose.

New tears formed on her bottom eyelids, and a look of confusion kidnapped her face. She opened the truck door and stepped into the rain. Jesse mirrored her actions from the passenger side. He kept the gun pointed at the helpless woman and directed her into the barn.

The barn smelled like hay, although there were only a half-dozen bales in the whole place. The foundation, poured concrete from nearly a century ago, was shaped like a stubby T. Annabel studied the barn's interior. She recognized the black Chevy Silverado parked in front of the large double doors that were wide enough for a vehicle or tractor to enter.

"That's Connor's truck, isn't it?" Annabel asked.

Jesse was silent.

"Where is Connor?" Her tone was harsh.

"Do you really care? Does anybody care where that piece of shit is?"

"Did you hurt that boy, Jesse Lewis? Please, tell me you didn't harm him. He's an innocent—"

"Bullshit! You know nothing about Connor, or Brody, or Darin, or Pete."

Annabel was taking small steps backward from the man with the gun. She stopped to stand up to the bully. "And you do? What did you do to those men, huh?"

"I devoured their sins."

Annabel's face turned as pale as chrome. She remembered Bourbon describing the word "SINNER" carved into the murder victims. Her legs buckled, and she didn't even try to fight the weight of the revelation that pushed her to the ground. She collapsed to her knees and cried into her hands. "Why, Jesse? Why are you doing this? How could you do this?"

"Because it needs to be done."

He reached into the back of Connor's truck and retrieved the rope that once saved Annabel's cow from the swamp. He cut off a length of it and then began tying her wrists. Annabel didn't put up a fight.

"I'm making Stoneville a better place," Jesse said. His voice was calm, barely audible, as the noisy rain pummeled the metal roof. "I'm ridding the town of all the sinners. Those men deserved to die." He hesitated.

"And so do you."

Annabel looked up, trying her best to look innocent and confused. Jesse finished tying her hands in front of her waist.

"And what about Cody Savage?" Annabel asked sternly. "What of his sin, Jesse? If you're some kind of sin eater, as they call you in the paper, then why haven't you killed him? He's the one who deserves to die! He's the sinner you should be tying up right now."

Jesse was calm when he answered. "Because he's innocent."

"Bull-fucking-shit!"

"It's true, Annabel. I thought he was a sinner. But he didn't kill your daughter."

"Then who the hell did?"

Jesse cinched the knot tight. With an honest and sincere tone, he looked her in the eye and answered, "I don't know." He led her to the other side of the barn, where he'd built a long workbench that spanned sixteen feet from side to side. A multitude of hand and power tools occupied the bench's surface.

Hanging from the beam above was a three-ton chain hoist designed to lift cars, trucks, and tractors. The hoist was more convenient than a floor jack. A looped chain could be pulled in one direction to lift or the opposite direction to lower. The chain merely spun inside the hoist, winding the lifting chain up or down with enough power to hoist a heavy tractor. A thick metal hook dangled from the hoist.

Jesse placed the rope securing Annabel's hands onto the hook. He pulled the lifting chain downward, which caused the hook to rise. Annabel felt her hands pulled upward and over her head. Eventually, Jesse was lifting Annabel, too, and she felt the tension in her shoulders spread to her back. Then, her feet started to rise from the ground. Her toes just touched the floor like a ballerina's when he finally stopped.

The Sin Eater left the barn without another word. He made his way to the house to change his wet clothes and pray. He'd give her time to reflect and suffer. She'd be ready to confess her sin before Jesse devoured it. He could have killed her then, but it would drive him insane to never know why. She had to tell him. He needed to know, so he left her hanging like a butchered cow for three hours.

*****

Annabel used her toes to spin herself around, trying to make sense of what was happening. She heard fluttering in the hayloft above as two pigeons grew frantic. They wanted to scatter and leave the barn—fly to another barn down the road—but the hard rain imprisoned them.

A barn cat, hearing the commotion upstairs, darted out from under Connor's truck and jumped onto the workbench. With her gray ears perked, she listened intently to the prey that fluttered above.

When Jesse returned, he had left the pistol behind in the house and carried the hockey ax, his weapon of choice. He hooked her blouse with the edge of one blade and tugged. Annabel protested as buttons flew off and the shirt parted down the middle. Her torso was exposed, and her large breasts were supported by a white bra. But the only part that interested Jesse Lewis was her soft belly.

Annabel trembled so hard that Jesse could hear her teeth chattering. He stuck the tip of one blade gently against her skin. The cold metal might as well have been a bullet by the way she jumped. Jesse smiled a little.

"I can do this slowly and painfully, or I can make it quick and merciful, Annabel. The choice is yours."

"Just fucking do it then, you coward!" She screamed. Her right eye, filled with blood from the cut on her head, peeked through the red. Her left eye, clean and bright, stared in horror.

The gray cat walked along the top of the workbench, ignoring Jesse and his catch, and bounded onto a hemlock beam. The cat moved to the other end with grace and not a hint of sound. It leaped upward and disappeared through a hole in the ceiling.

"Unfortunately, it's not that easy," Jesse said. "You see, I need to know your sin first. It was so clear with all the others, and usually, I can see—"

"What the hell are you talking about? I'm no sinner, dammit. Except maybe for misjudging you."

The fluttering and cooing from the hayloft grew more frantic. Powerful wings beat the air, stirring dust and hay. Annabel heard the

216

cat jumping in the air and landing on the hardwood ceiling above her, followed by soft thumping sounds as it ran across the boards.

Jesse dug the cold metal into Annabel's warm skin and carved a letter S just below her ribs. The cut wasn't deep. He wanted her alive so she could speak. With her adrenaline levels so high, Annabel easily tolerated the pain slicing through her abdomen. The blow to the head with the pistol had been more painful than the cut.

Jesse thumbed some of the blood off the hockey skate blade and licked it, hoping the taste would stimulate a vision. The crimson fluid refused to give up Annabel's secret and only revived his migraine.

"Dammit, Annabel! Tell me what you're hiding! Tell it to me, and this will all be over."

He carved the letter "I" next to the first letter and backed away to see her reaction. Annabel screamed, but not in pain, but in fear and anger. She began to sob uncontrollably, and the pastor's anger grew.

It went on this way for twenty minutes until Annabel passed out from the stress of her torment.

Jesse stepped back and read his work. The crude lettering forming the word "SINNER" was carved across her belly.

Annabel was still alive, but Jesse wasn't going to kill her or set her free until she admitted what she'd done.

"It must be big. It must be big enough that you refuse to let the world know." He walked to his workbench and analyzed the various tools hanging on the wall and lying on the bench. A pile of saws, pliers, hammers, chisels, and so much more awaited him. It seemed archaic, but it may be necessary to pry his prize from his friend.

He picked up a slightly used rag, torn from a church event T-shirt, and gently pressed it against Annabel's stomach. The shirt absorbed some of the blood but mostly just smeared it. He pushed a lock of hair out of her face and tucked it behind her ear.

"I'm sorry, Annabel, but we're hungry."

He threw the rag onto the bench and decided to be more patient. Maybe another approach would work better. Perhaps if he were kinder, Annabel would crack, and the juicy secret would spill all on its own.

Jesse put the hockey ax in the back of Connor's truck and left the barn again. He made his way across the saturated lawn, letting the hard rain wash some of the blood from his hands. Wet clothes clung uncomfortably to his skin, making it difficult to move, and he pulled both sides of his collar, ripping his shirt from his body. The motion detector on the barn's outside light illuminated as it sensed his presence, its light casting his shadow in a long, distorted shape toward his house.

He stopped for a moment and looked skyward. It seemed to be a habit he had whenever he needed answers. Perhaps it was something all religious leaders did, to look up—and away—from the problem that was right in front of them. Sometimes, the answer would come to him, and he would call it a message from God. Sometimes, there was silence, and he would call it a lesson to be learned. But tonight, the sky was black and void of anything but ominous clouds and occasional lightning. Tonight, the sky was evil, as if heaven and hell had turned upside down. So, he looked down.

Knees to the ground, Jesse prayed that he wouldn't have to make Annabel suffer much longer. He knew there was no forgiveness in this. This would be his last sin. Once he extracted it from her and completed his purge in Cain Lake, he would end this madness.

Tonight, the Sin Eater was hungry.

Tomorrow, he needed to die.

27

ANNABEL

Annabel awakened in a panic. As her senses came back to her, she gasped for breath and rolled her head to loosen her stiff neck. The pain was unbearable, but what choice did she have but to bear it? Blood had formed a crust around her right eye, and her top and bottom lashes were adhered to one another. She scanned the garage with her opposite eye and found herself alone. Jesse had left her, but she imagined it wouldn't be long before his return. With her toes barely touching the concrete floor, she danced lightly, spinning herself in a half-circle as she hung from the chain. A purple hue had painted the skin of her hands. Needles jabbed her fingertips.

Her adrenaline had faded, and she felt a throbbing pain that imprisoned her entire body: the swollen cut on her forehead that finally clotted, wrists that were constricted by thick rope, shoulders impinged in the sockets, and the fire across her belly labeling her a "SINNER."

She couldn't see the letters, but she knew what word they formed.

Her lover, Jeff Bourbon, had told her about the bodies in the morgue. The two men were killed by a blow with a dull-bladed weapon. She'd seen that very blade in Jesse Lewis's hands, like something from a medieval play gone wrong. Were those hockey skate blades?

Those two men were killed because they were a threat to Cody Savage.

Cody Savage. She blamed all of this on him. Just like he'd killed her daughter, he was now killing her. All this horror began when he returned to town. Bourbon tried to tell her that Savage was probably innocent of Willa's murder, but Annabel wasn't convinced. Her only explanation was that Cody Savage and Jesse Lewis were working together. They both must have killed Willa. And now, she would share her daughter's fate.

She began to weep, but not for herself. It was the notion that Bourbon might be the one to find her dead body in this garage. She didn't want him to go through that, or to be alone. Investigating Willa's death, collecting evidence on her dead body, had been difficult enough for the hardy sheriff, so finding Annabel like this would be devastating.

And she thought about Levi, her son. She hadn't seen him in weeks, and the last time he came by the farm, they had argued about something so insignificant that she couldn't remember what it was. She wanted to apologize. Levi had already lost his father and sister. Hadn't he lost enough? Now, he would get the call that *he* was the last of the Thompsons. He'd turn to the Road Barons and drown his emotions in alcohol and drugs and beautiful women and the feeling of the wind on his face speeding down the open road. But he'd also find Jesse Lewis and avenge his mother, which scared Annabel as much as the Sin Eater himself. She didn't want Levi to go down that path of hate and revenge.

Upstairs in the hayloft, the commotion had grown quiet. The cat and the pigeons had tired themselves, or perhaps they just decided their vicious game was a stalemate.

Annabel's toes danced again, turning her ninety degrees. The chain that Jesse had used to pull her up was hooked around a bracket mounted to the wall. When Jesse worked on a car or tractor, the metal bracket secured the chain out of his way and kept it from swinging freely into a vehicle's shiny paint. Above her head, the mechanical hoist rode from one side of the room to the other along a steel beam. Annabel picked her feet up and kicked them forward and then back, like a kid on a swing set trying to build momentum.

The hoist moved, just as she hoped. It was on rollers and could slide freely across the steel beam that supported it from one side of the barn to the other. She repeatedly kicked until she was close enough to the wall to reach the chain with her feet. A smile formed on her bloody face. "Sorry, asshole," she said to Jesse, who hadn't returned. "But I'm getting the fuck out of here."

She reached out with one foot and hooked the chain with the toe of her shoe. Only one side of the chain came off the hook. The other was still secure. Exhausted by her effort, she cursed herself for the extra forty pounds she was carrying, and then she cursed The Mineshaft and their damn Ruby Burgers. Her abdominal muscles had grown weak over the years. Throwing hay bales, carrying wood and grain bags, and all the other chores required to run a farm had given her a strong back and legs, but the front side had been too neglected. If she survived this ordeal, she swore to herself that she'd start losing weight and get her core back in shape.

As her thighs burned from the exertion, she reached again with her right leg, fighting a scream that wanted to burst from her mouth, and finally pulled the remaining side of the chain off the bracket. The chain swung free. Annabel spread her legs and caught the chain between her thighs in an effort to muffle the sound. She took six seconds to rest and still her breathing.

She wrapped her toes around one side of the chain and pulled it down. She felt herself rise higher off the ground. Wrong direction! She hooked the opposite side of the looped chain and repeated the action. It lowered her one inch. She repeated the action, and slowly, inch by inch, she lowered herself until her feet were flat on the floor. A couple more turns of the chain and Annabel was able to push her hands toward the ceiling. Her arms fell free. They were numb and weak, and she cried quietly. Exhaustion nearly overpowered jubilation, and all she wanted to do was lie down and rest.

But that's not what survivors do.

Annabel needed to survive this night. She needed to find Bourbon and kiss his face and then tell him about the church pastor who was possessed by the devil. Jesse Lewis needed to be revealed for his true self.

She wasn't sure what the whole "Sinner" motive was all about, but she was sure Bourbon would figure it out.

Annabel, the survivor, crept through the dimly lit barn and hid behind Connor's truck. She peeked out the window, but all she could see was her reflection in the glass. She eased the truck's passenger-side door open and searched for the keys. They were nowhere to be found.

The thick rope still bound her hands, but as long as she could run, she didn't dare waste time freeing her hands. She squatted and duck walked to stay out of sight, in case Jesse was watching through the windows, and didn't stop until she was standing behind the tailgate.

In the back of the truck, she found Jesse's weapon and took it for her own protection. She wished she had her pistol back, but the hockey-ax would have to do. She imagined burying the blade into Jesse's skull, and the thought gave her some satisfaction.

She crept to the garage door and slowly turned the knob. Cold rain pelted her face as she opened the door, awakening an innate strength she hadn't felt in years. She stood straight, no longer cowering like a scared puppy. The wild weather tried to push her back, but she stepped into it, exited the garage, and closed the door behind her to hide her silhouette. Washing away her fright, the rain drenched her in courage.

An old memory reminded her of another time in her life—a tough time—when she spent her first year as a widow on the farm. She was alone with two young kids and no hired hands. It was an unusually warm October night when she heard one of her smaller cows bellow in pain. Leaving the kids in the house, she darted out the door with a loaded .30-30 hunting rifle. She made her way through the wind and rain, a night just like this, until she reached the barn. The cow was at the back of the field, and Annabel, the frightened widow, was sure it was being attacked.

She shook violently with fear and nearly pissed herself, but the cow needed her, and she needed the cow. She stumbled through the dark, snagged her leg on a barbed-wire fence, and tripped twice, landing in a slick pile of cow manure. Still, she pushed forward until the barn disappeared behind her. The pounding rain tried to dissuade her, but she leaned into it and trudged on.

No artificial light could penetrate that far into the meadow, and when she shined her flashlight toward the noise, drops of water created a static view of the scene. She felt blind and stupid for standing in the middle of her field at night, trying to ward off a danger she couldn't see. She was about to turn and run back, apologizing to the young cow the whole way until a bolt of lightning lit up the scene and zapped her with courage. Letting the flash of light burn the sight into her memory, she visualized her target as the light vanished.

Annabel, the frightened widow, needed to learn to stand and fight for what she wanted, what she had, and what she needed. She raised the Marlin rifle, racked the lever-action to deposit a shell in the chamber, and tried to aim, but her target was dark and the night black. She stepped closer and yelled like thunder, "Get the fuck off her, you bastard!" The rifle fired, and a large black bear howled and grunted in pain. It tore away with a hole in its lung, leaving its prey behind, and disappeared into the night.

Annabel, the survivor, found the bear the next day, dead in the swamp.

Tonight, standing with her hands tied and her stomach bleeding, she summoned the survivor in herself once again. All she had to do was wait in the shadows until Jesse Lewis returned. Take his fucking head off his shoulders. She took three steps to her right and accidentally placed herself within the garage light's motion sensor. An explosive light flooded the driveway and lawn, revealing her location to her captor.

Annabel, now the victim, froze in fear. It was only a couple of breaths before Annabel, the survivor, yelled, *Run!*

She bolted down the driveway, out of the light and into the darkness she once feared. She knew the path well, and if she could get to the road, then maybe she could get to her house, which was only 200 yards away. It seemed so far away, even though she told people that the pastor lived right next door.

By the time she reached the end of the driveway, her legs burned from the exertion, and her stride was clumsy and awkward. She thought she could see her mailbox in the distance, so she focused her attention on the small reflector attached to the post. Her run turned to a slow jog as she gasped for air, certain she wasn't making any progress to reach safety. The mailbox didn't seem to be getting any closer.

Somewhere behind her, an engine roared, and Connor Bayley's truck careened out of the pastor's driveway. Annabel felt as though the black bear had returned for vengeance, but then remembered that she had shot the predator dead.

The bear was a timid mouse compared to the animal that was now pursuing her. The beast's two bright eyes flicked on. Annabel screamed, and then she chased her own shadow that stretched down the road. Her shadow grew shorter, and the road brighter under her feet. The monster was gaining on her quickly.

No way I'm going to make it home.

She veered to the left and jumped over the shallow ditch beside the road. Her knee twisted a little as she fell, but she couldn't let anything stop her.

Get the fuck up and keep running, Annabel the survivor ordered.

She used the hockey ax to prop herself up and resumed running. She darted through a row of box alders, ducking and swerving like an amateur boxer. Headlights from the road shined in her direction, and she could vaguely see where she was going.

A truck door slammed behind her, and a man's voice yelled something inaudible, muffled by the distance and the rain but mostly by her lungs sucking hard and deep for oxygen. She didn't know what he said and didn't care. She wasn't turning around for anything.

She turned her head just in time to avoid a tree limb, but it still smashed against her jaw, and the taste of blood filled her mouth. She spat out the blood and pain and kept moving. She was almost out of the headlights' reach entirely now, and she welcomed the cloak of darkness as she went deeper into the woods. She hoped Jesse would turn the truck around and head for home. If he did, she could turn to the right, cut across her meadow, and make it to her house.

The truck tires spun on the slick pavement, and Annabel stopped to check its direction. The Silverado drove toward Annabel's house and turned into her driveway. No way she could make it home tonight. She leaned against a tree, huffing as if she'd just finished a marathon. She had to rest for a minute. She could see the headlights jouncing into her driveway, and it infuriated her to know how close to home she had come. Sure, Jesse would have tried to break in and "eat her sin," or whatever the hell he called it, but the only thing he would have eaten was a .30 caliber round from her favorite rifle.

The realization that Jesse wasn't stopping at the house fell on her like a tree. He knew his way around the meadow and would patrol it until he found her. She was cut off from her refuge,s pinned between the open field and the deep swamp.

She darted off again, staying wide as she circled the twenty-acre meadow. Her path took her deeper into the woods until she cut back toward the farthest corner of the field. She slid down an embankment, landing in the soupy water of the swamp. She didn't know it, but she was just eight feet from Connor Bayley's bloated body, still buried in the mud. The heavy rain filling the swamp was also thinning the mud. Connor's bloated body floated to the top of the earthy stew. Annabel's nostrils filled with the smell of death, but right now, she didn't concern herself with its source.

She stayed along the edge of the swamp, making it to the south side of her property, and headed east. If she could stay alive and keep moving, she knew that Lake View Drive was about two miles away. Hopefully, she could flag down a car if she made it there.

The house lights and the persistent truck were long behind her now. The rain grew lighter, but Annabel was certain it would stay with her throughout her trek. She found comfort in the white noise of the shower, which concealed all the nocturnal noises that would have otherwise made her jumpy.

The cold rain was no match for her warm blood coursing through her body, although the wounds on her abdomen and head leaked vital fluid. She held her forearms against her body to preserve her heat and modesty, but she wasn't letting go of the hockey ax, whether it was for protection or evidence against Jesse. She gripped the handle tight and cradled the weapon across her chest.

Annabel had to make it out of the forest alive to bring Jesse Lewis to justice and prevent future victims. If she died afterward, then so be it. Her determination to live was greater than the Sin Eater's hunger to defeat her.

She stopped briefly, fell to her knees, and prayed for an angel to save her. But she feared her prayer was in vain, drowned in the rain, like all the other prayers she'd whispered in the last decade.

28

THE DRIVE 

Cody spent the day driving. He zig-zagged through town once and made his way south. He drove the car to the cemetery gates, found an umbrella with a broken spoke in the trunk, and spent forty-five minutes walking among the headstones. Ten of those minutes included his stop at Willa's grave. He wished she could come along. After leaving the cemetery, he turned onto Grandview Drive, which circled the lake's mountainous eastern side. He drove slowly, never approaching the speed limit or testing the car's performance, but he did test the Hellcat's speakers when Eric Church started singing "Sinners Like Me" on the radio.

The rain obscured the view of the lake, but it was still better than sitting at home counting bullet holes in the wall or re-baiting mouse traps.

He'd forgotten just how much he loved to get in the car and push the gas without any destination in mind. It was something he and Willa did at least once a month, usually on a Sunday. They would often drive counterclockwise around Cain Lake, admiring some of the big houses and making up stories about how the rich earned their money. Their journey always led them to a quiet little swimming hole on the northeast side of the lake, where they would stop and eat the lunch they'd packed. Most of their trips didn't even involve swimming. They preferred to cast a fishing line near the weeds or sit with a beer to watch the loons play. They dreamed of buying land, building a house, and filling it with little versions of themselves.

"Someday," Willa would always say, before climbing back into the car, taking one last look at the scenery, and envisioning her dream.

Cody parked the car at an access road that led to his old memory.

A new gate had been installed at the beginning of the road, featuring a "No Trespassing" sign bolted to the metal crossbeams. *So, someone bought the land and stole our dream.*

That was becoming the trend in Stoneville. He used to think the town's name represented strength and determination. Now, he thought Stoneville was a place where boulders crushed dreams and ambitions, and you needed to try and do your best with the pebbles left in the aftermath.

While he was parked at the gate, reminiscing and dreaming, Willa appeared in the passenger seat next to him. She took his hand and forced a smile. She was always an optimist, a trait she had inherited from her mother. Annabel had been widowed in her thirties, raised two kids while running the farm, and was active in the community. She was forced to have a positive mentality to stay alive and feed her children.

By the time the gas tank was half empty, Cody had forgiven Annabel for pointing that gun at him in The Mineshaft's parking lot. He couldn't blame her, so he didn't. Annabel and Willa had been very close, more like sisters sometimes than mother and daughter.

He wondered if she were home right now, sitting in the kitchen, wishing she'd pulled the trigger. Or had she regretted it? She was probably in the barn, talking to the animals, chatting on her phone with one of the neighbor women, or telling Sheriff Bourbon that she wanted Cody run out of town.

He put the Dodge back into drive and continued on his path.

Cain Lake's wild nature was more evident on the east side, where thick forests and cliffs prevented too many houses from being constructed. It was quiet here, and the variety of wildlife was a treat for any nature lover. There was also a secret fishing spot where the walleyes schooled together like kids at a bus stop. This secret location was impossible for motorboats to access from the water due to a string of boulders and cement pylons hidden just below the surface. The obstacle was an old bridge built for horses and buggies in the 1800s, but it was submerged when the dam was built, and Cain Lake swelled to nearly double its size.

Grandview Drive meandered through the mountainous terrain and then swerved back to the north, losing sight of the lake for the next twelve miles. As the road neared the lake once again, Cody passed the area where Birchcraft had been attacked and then drove past the boat launch. The pontoon boat, parked on its trailer, had been covered with large white tarps to protect evidence and sat in the middle of the lot. Yellow crime scene tape cordoned off the boat launch, and two state investigators sat in a van, hoping the rain would soon allow them to resume their investigation. They had taken over the crime scene early that morning. Cody passed them with caution, trying not to draw attention to himself, and the two investigators hardly noticed or paid any attention to the wandering traveler.

Willa was still riding shotgun in silence.

Cody and Willa drove for two more hours, meandering through the thick forest within the Adirondack Park. Grandview Drive took them away from the lake and back again. Cody parked the car on the edge of the road, next to a large beaver pond, and watched as six whitetail deer browsed for nourishment. The pond was thick with grass and cattails. Thick dead trees, a result of the flood waters, reached for the sky with outstretched limbs. A pileated woodpecker chipped away at one of the trees in search of insects for lunch. Once the deer were out of sight, he restarted the engine and moved along.

Cody and his imaginary passenger turned west as they made their way to the south side of Cain Lake. The weather didn't prevent Willa from staring out the window. She glanced at him from time to time but resisted speaking. Cody wanted so much for her to be real rather than a figment of his mind. He wasn't sure if she was imaginary, a ghost, or real, but if she were to come back and haunt him, he would welcome the intrusion.

When they reached the lake's southernmost side, Cody stopped at a gravel parking lot large enough for four trucks. This is where Cain Lake released its water through a powerhouse that generated electricity, forming the Cascade River. The river flowed south briefly before turning west and then back to the north. As Cody's eyes followed the river downstream, lightning ignited the western sky in a dazzling display of nature's power. The rain was lighter now, but dark clouds still occupied the sky, blocking the sun. Soon, he and Willa would be driving into the heavy storm.

Cody retrieved AJ's broken umbrella once more and walked to the edge of the water. A path led the way, created mostly by fishermen but used by many people who wanted to launch canoes and kayaks. The top layer of dirt had been worn away by the eroding rain, exposing the gravel below. The slippery round rocks forced Cody to step with caution. He turned around, disappointed to find that Willa had stayed in the car. Or maybe she'd left him.

The smell of fresh rain and fish filled the air. Tall weeds grew out of the water, bending in the breeze in unison and waving to Cody as he approached. He removed his shoes and socks, placing them under the umbrella on the ground, and rolled up his pant legs until his kneecaps kept them in place.

He had no idea what compelled him to stand in the water during a rain shower. Maybe it was a distant memory from his childhood when he and his friends would ride their bikes here and spend the day skipping stones and drinking Mountain Dew. They'd go swimming and jump off the bridge. They'd fish all day without a single bite, and they'd smoke stolen cigarettes if they had them. This is where he got his first kiss from Stacie Bates and fell in love with her giggle. He'd heard she was Stacie Marten now, married to some jerk from Higley. Maybe he'd look her up sometime. He looked back to see if Willa was listening in on his thoughts, but she was still in the car.

Something tickled Cody's toes. He was expecting to see little minnows playing at his feet, but nearly jumped out of the water when he saw the tiny blue lights had found him. They swirled around his ankles in random patterns, and Cody thought they were even going through him. He bent down for a closer look, trying to determine what the speedy little bugs were.

"The water's quite warm, isn't it?" A voice split the quiet scene.

Cody looked around to find the source. A pale hand waved from below the bridge. It was Flesti Thaed, sitting on the bridge's cement footer, taking shelter from the rain. She was sipping on a bottle of ginger ale, watching the approaching storm with awe.

"It sure is," Cody said. He stepped through the water and then onto the shore, approaching the mysterious resident of Cain Lake. He joined her under the steel infrastructure that blocked the rain.

He pointed to the water's surface. "Have you seen those little blue lights? In the water? They're like tiny bugs that seem to be attracted to people." He felt stupid for not having a more intelligent way to describe the organisms he had observed.

"They're not attracted to people. They seek energy. They feed on your energy, and sometimes, if they choose, they give it back. You have a positive energy about you, Cody Savage. Abundant. Not many can make that claim."

"So you have." It wasn't a question. "What in the hell are they?"

Flesti's cheeks formed a smile. She rose to her feet with the grace of a teenager and stepped barefoot into the water ankle-deep. The water wet her pant cuffs, but she didn't seem to mind. She shaped her hands like a bowl, dipped them into the water, and hundreds of the little blue lights gathered in her palms. She raised her hands, as the little lights vibrated with excitement, a feeding frenzy at a microscopic scale.

"They are the great secret of Cain Lake—older than the name itself. They are the messengers, protectors, and destroyers, feeding on what energy they can find. They can give, or they can take away."

Cody tried to mimic her actions, but the lights were more interested in Flesti, like squirrels in the park that recognized the older woman who always carried peanuts.

"Why have I never seen them before?" Cody asked. "I've been swimming and fishing this lake my whole life."

"Because you didn't need them. And now you do."

Curious and somewhat apprehensive, he asked, "Where did they come from, and how do you know so much about them?"

Flesti didn't have an answer for either question. "Some things are just unexplainable, like life and death, and we just need to accept them."

"Do you think Cain Lake is the only place where these creatures exist?"

Flesti walked a little deeper into the water. "No, but it's the only place I know." She stepped closer, sensing Cody's confusion.

He was intrigued by her knowledge and her ability to survive the rugged landscape, and he wanted to know more. "What did you mean when you told me before to follow the flower and the mountain?"

She cut him off before he could ask another question. "I know you want to know more, but just know this—Cain Lake is a place of miracles and mayhem. It gives, but it also takes. But either way, there must always be a balance."

Cody pretended to understand, but what the hell are you talking about? Ran through his mind.

Flesti smiled. "I know you're thinking, 'What the hell are you talking about?' But time will be your teacher. You will understand more by the end of the day."

"The end of the day?"

Flesti touched his cheek like a proud mother. She made her way back to the concrete footer where she had been sitting, retook her seat, and sipped her soda.

The rain had been falling like a gentle sprinkler, but now someone had turned on the garden hose. Flesti had told him all she could—all he needed to know—for now.

"She's waiting for you, Cody," Flesti yelled back over the noise of the rain. "You have to go, or you'll be too late."

Cody's head swiveled in the direction of the road, but the tall grass and briar bushes hid the car.

"Don't waste another minute. You need to go right now," Flesti said. There was urgency in her voice, and Cody had a disturbing sensation that someone was in danger. The visions returned, surprising Cody, and he nearly fell into the water. He saw the word SINNER carved in human flesh. A figure ran through the dark woods, chased by a bear-like shadow.

He stumbled over the rocks and back to his boots, grabbed the umbrella, and climbed the embankment. As he tied his shoes, he wondered if Flesti was referring to Darcy Poole. Was she free? Could he find her before she suffered the same fate as his wife? Was she being held captive by the Sin Eater?

It was dark now. A bolt of lightning lit up a nimbus cloud a few miles away, and Cody guessed the coming rain would be substantial. He climbed the embankment, jumped into the vehicle, and punched the start button with his thumb. The Dodge's headlights lit up automatically, and he pulled away, crossing the South Bridge he had just been under.

He checked the passenger seat, but his timid passenger refused to show herself.

Cody followed Grandview until he came to an intersection in the road. A little convenience store with a single gas pump was the only commercial property within miles of the location. Once he crossed the intersection, Grandview Drive became Lake View Drive. This route would take him full circle back to the north side of Cain Lake.

He felt a rush of urgency as if someone were waiting for him. Someone needed him. Darcy Poole? The thought of it was crazy, and he considered the notion that Flesti was fucking with his head.

The Mountain. Flesti had told him that he could trust "The Mountain," but he still had no idea what that meant. There were many mountains to the south of Cain Lake—some small, some large—but they seemed too far away to be of importance.

He kept his speed in check to avoid unsolicited attention but still raced the next big round of rain coming.

This side of the lake had more residents than the eastern shore, even though they were still far apart. Once he cleared the residential area, he leaned on the gas. The Charger growled happily, wanting more and happy to perform. Now Cody traveled north. The slick roads were flooded in places, and the car hydroplaned twice, but Cody reeled it back in and kept it under his control. He rounded a sharp corner, pushed the accelerator pedal, and launched himself off the turn.

The headlights caught sudden movement to his left, an animal on the shoulder of the road lunged forward. Cody hit the brakes too hard, and for a moment, the rear wheels locked up. That moment was long enough to send the ass end of the car around. Cody worked the steering wheel like a NASCAR driver at Watkins-Glen Raceway. He could hear laughing from the passenger side, and even though he was too busy to look, he could sense Willa with him again. She was enjoying the ride of her life, even though there was no life within her.

The car finally straightened and came to a stop, but when it did, Cody faced the direction he'd just come.

He gripped the steering wheel so hard his fingers hurt. The engine idled noisily, laughing at the puny human who had nearly killed them both. As loud as the engine was, the sound that dominated was his heart knocking on his chest.

What the frig was that?

Willa's laughing had stopped. She stared out the windshield, frozen in panic. Cody's eyes followed hers.

Forty yards ahead in the lights, standing in the road, was the source of Willa's fright. The animal that had nearly run in front of him was a woman. She stood with her hands tied together, holding a crude-looking ax. She was mud and blood from head to toe, and her blouse was pulled open. She began walking toward him. Stunned, he just watched at first. There was a craziness about her, and Cody didn't dare tempt fate. Best to let her come to him.

The woman stumbled, nearly falling on the blacktop until she regained her balance. Two eyes peeked out from the blood streaking down her face. Her hair, wet and wild, was draped across her cheeks, sticking to her skin like a shower curtain. There was a look of shock about her that no Hollywood actress could mimic. She trembled violently as she sobbed. Once she was twenty yards from the car, Cody recognized the eyes—those eyes, with makeup washed away, but the same shape and color as those sitting in the passenger's seat.

Cody looked over at the passenger side, where Willa was sitting, and his deceased wife finally spoke in a frightened voice.

"Mom?"

29
THE ANGEL

Annabel fell to her knees in exhaustion, overwhelmed by her ordeal. The vehicle's headlights blinded her, but she refused to take her eyes off her salvation, except when she looked to the sky and cried, "Thank you." She anticipated that her angel would exit the gray chariot at any moment and whisk her to safety. In the past, Annabel had prayed many times: for her husband to survive his heart attack, for her children to be healthy, for the bank to approve her mortgage, and for Cody Savage to die in prison. Some of those prayers were answered, and some were not. But tonight, there was no doubt in her mind: her prayer was heard and answered.

She couldn't rise from her knees. She'd pushed herself beyond her limits during her desperate attempt to escape death. But she had done it. She had won.

Tonight, she was going to hold Jefferson Bourbon again. She was going to call Levi and invite him to come for dinner tomorrow. She was going to live—because of her strength and the angel sent to find her.

Annabel was saved.

The angel opened the car door and approached cautiously. Anyone would have been hesitant to get too close to an injured woman carrying a crazy-looking ax. The angel stepped into the light, silhouetted by the intense glow of the Charger's headlights.

Rain bounced off the warm pavement, and the moisture in the air was thick, as fog swirled around the vehicle. The angel walked through as if he were stepping across a cloud.

"You came," Annabel said. Her voice was weak and squeaky.

"Of course, I came, Annabel."

235

Annabel couldn't believe this miracle. Her angel even knew her name. She had a sense of safety that she hadn't felt in a long time. Dehydration had taken a toll on the middle-aged woman. She was tired and wanted to pass out, but the story inside her was gnawing to get out, and she wouldn't sleep until somebody knew what had happened to her.

She raised her hands, but they wouldn't heed her command to let go of the ax. Her fingers were locked in a state of pain and rigor. The angel landed on one knee in front of her and had to gently pry Annabel's fingers from the weapon in her grip. Cold, numb fingers touched the angel's chest, and then she leaned into him.

He was warm. So warm. Annabel felt the angel's wings wrap her in safety.

His gentle voice spoke to her again. "Come on, Annabel. I'll take you to Bourbon."

The angel stood. Powerful arms lifted her to her feet. She felt a tug at her wrists, and then the rope fell loose. Every joint and muscle from her shoulders to her fingertips ached as her arms fell. Somehow, she found the strength to lift them again and hug the angel's neck, but her eyes refused to open as if she were merely acting out while she slept.

The angel led her to the car, and although Annabel sensed something familiar about the Charger, she didn't care. She climbed into its warmth and wanted to curl up in the seat, but her extra weight and stiff joints reminded her that she wasn't a teenage girl anymore.

The angel sat behind the wheel and turned a couple of knobs on the dashboard. Powerful fans blew soothing tropical heat over Annabel's hands. She leaned forward and indulged herself in the gift of warmth, and her hypothermia began to dissipate as her body temperature rose.

"What the hell happened, Annabel? What happened to you?"

Annabel could hear genuine concern in the angel's voice. The car was dark, but she opened her eyes anyway. After the headlights had scorched her retinas, they began to dilate and adjust to the car's dim interior lighting. The angel's face took form and became recognizable.

30
THE PHOTO

Sheriff Bourbon sat at his desk, trying like hell to catch up on paperwork. He had so many reports to write that he felt like a college student a week before finals. He answered calls about the power outages around town: "Call the power company." Calls about flooded roads: "Call the highway superintendent." And Mrs. McClesky called because her dog wouldn't come out of his doghouse. He couldn't remember whether he had given her someone to call or just hung up on her.

He opened his top drawer, only to find his schnapps bottle empty. He thought about going to the store to get another, but decided he'd just stop on the way home. He didn't want to go out in this miserable weather unless it was absolutely necessary.

A message he'd sent to Annabel, asking how her lunch date went with Jesse Lewis, still hadn't received a reply. As tough and independent as Annabel was, he never worried about her, but it wasn't like her not to respond. If she were busy, he'd receive one of those senseless emojis with a kissing face or a heart. It drove him crazy when people didn't use words.

He heard a noisy car pulling up to the front of the building. The vehicle's one working headlight shone through his office window, obscured by the blinds.

Who in the hell's dumb enough to be out driving in this shit? A red umbrella dashed from the car to the front door and then entered the foyer. There was no personnel at the front desk to buzz the visitor through the next door, so he waited for the umbrella to close so he could identify his visitor. He sighed hard when he recognized the woman. His finger pressed a button to activate his intercom. "Sorry, we are closed. Go away, please," he half-joked.

The person in the foyer looked for the camera that was watching her. She stuck her tongue out at the viewer, and then she heard the door buzz. She gave it a push and entered with a huge smile.

"She's lucky she's cute," Bourbon murmured.

Daisy Torrez walked into Bourbon's office carrying a soggy umbrella and a laptop case. She flashed her smile again, as if it were her credentials, and sat in a chair at his desk.

Bourbon stared over a pair of bifocals at his guest. "Have a seat."

"Hi, Sheriff."

"You know, you're becoming a bigger pain in the ass than my twenty-year-old hemorrhoid."

She giggled. "Admit it, you love my company." Daisy took her phone out and looked at a note she had written herself. "Sorry, Sheriff, but you're my best source for information when there's a story. And I might just have a story."

"Lucky me. So, what wild goose are you chasing now?"

"This one." She held up her phone and showed him a picture. In the image, a man stood beside a car with its driver's side window half down. Behind the standing man, an unidentifiable woman pointed a pistol at the vehicle's driver. The photo had been zoomed in and cropped, so it was a little pixelated. The rain also obscured the scene.

"Someone get shot?" Bourbon asked.

"Not that I'm aware of."

"So, where'd this photograph come from? You take it?"

"No," Daisy said. "A reader sent it to me. Do you recognize any of these people, Sheriff?" She moved the phone closer and gave it a slight jiggle.

Bourbon could never mistake the voluptuous figure of the woman with the pistol. He squinted at the screen. "Well, that might be Pastor Lewis. Can't see the other two."

"The witness who sent this to me said the woman with the pistol was Annabel Thompson. That's your girlfriend pointing a gun at my... friend."

"You mean Cody Savage? Annabel was pointing a—" He stopped,

realizing it wasn't as crazy as it sounded. She did despise the man, and who could blame her, but he was sure—seventy-five percent— Annabel would never actually pull the trigger. "Look, Ms. Torrez, I'm sure this picture was taken out of context. I'm also sure that if there were a situation, then it was resolved by Pastor Lewis. He's one of the most respected and cool-headed men in town."

Daisy began tapping the screen on her phone.

Bourbon thought for a moment and then perked up in his chair. "Why is Savage driving around in that car anyway? I told him to park it. His license has expired."

"I have no idea, Sheriff, but it doesn't really look like he's driving to me. In this picture, he's parked at The Mineshaft."

Bourbon rolled his eyes. "Where is he now?"

"I haven't seen him since this morning. I had work to do, and he dro—walked over here to see you about getting AJ out of jail."

"Uh-huh. Sure you haven't seen him?"

"No. We're supposed to meet up for dinner in about fifteen minutes, though."

Bourbon shuffled some papers on his desk. He bound a couple together, banged them on the desk to align the edges, and placed a paper clip on the corner. Then he spun in his chair to face his computer monitor. He hoped Daisy would get the hint that he had work to do. It didn't work.

"Sheriff, what's the situation with AJ Timmons? Wasn't his arraignment this afternoon?"

"Nope. It's been postponed until morning. The judge had a family emergency at the last minute."

"Oh, that's too bad. What kind of family emergency?"

"The none kind. As in, none of our business."

"Have you reprimanded your deputy for the assault on Cody and AJ?"

"No."

"Why not? I think Stoneville would love to read about an abusive officer."

"I doubt that. Archer's been here for four years and doing a great job despite his arrogant and selfish personality."

Daisy tapped a pen on her chin, trying to think of any other questions she had for the sheriff. She had thought for sure that the photo of Annabel waving a pistol at Cody would ruffle his feathers, but the man was an ice cube. She went back to the situation at The Mineshaft. "So, are you going to charge Annabel Thompson with menacing or anything like that?"

"Nope."

"May I ask why? Is it because of your relationship with her?"

"Nope." He looked out from behind the monitor. "You have no proof that the person in that very blurry photo is Annie. Furthermore, Cody Savage would have to file a complaint, and he has not done so."

"Well, what the hell am I going to write about for tomorrow's issue of The View?"

"Honestly, I don't care. Write about the weather. Oh, did you hear that Mrs. McClesky's dog won't come out of his doghouse? You could go interview her," he chuckled to himself.

"*Eres un idiota*. Come on, Sheriff. It's hard enough to be a journalist in this town. Give me something."

"Well, you could write about your boyfriend."

Daisy finally gave up. "Well, Sheriff Bourbon, I'm sorry, but I have to run."

"So soon?"

"Yes. I have a dinner date, remember?"

"McDonald's or Arby's?"

The comment stung a little. "*Muérdeme*." She flashed a fake smile. "Pizza Primo, actually."

Bourbon wouldn't admit it, but he was a little jealous. The restaurant below her apartment did have the best pizza and pasta in town. "Have a good night, Ms. Torrez. Enjoy your meal."

Daisy said goodbye and left through the front door. She popped her umbrella and entered the rainstorm with an empty notepad. Her noisy Subaru sputtered away with one headlight leading the way.

Bourbon rechecked his phone. Now he was a little nervous. Annabel still hadn't responded to his text message. Cain Lake had a history of blocking cellular signals, so he hoped the lack of service was the issue.

But why was she pointing a gun at Cody Savage?

She's fine. She's perfectly fine. Probably went for a drive down by the lake, or she's having coffee with Jesse Lewis. She's fine.

31
THE SINNER

Annabel didn't scream or cry when she finally recognized that her angel—her savior—was a fraud. She watched Cody drive, wondering why he didn't just kill her on the road. But at least she was warm, and if she died now, then her lover wouldn't find her hanging in the barn like a harvested whitetail buck. She thought about that for a moment and wondered if Jesse Lewis would at least have had the decency to bury her on her own property. It didn't matter now. She was out of the barn, out of the wind, and out of luck. She'd run from one killer to another.

She conceded to her fate. Stiff muscles and fatigue would prevent her from fighting off any attack. She was too weak to do anything other than ride, and the loss of blood was affecting her vision and energy. The dexterity of her fingers had partially returned, so she buttoned the one button on her blouse that Jesse Lewis hadn't torn off. She didn't know what direction Cody was taking her or where they were going. Maybe he was taking her back to the Sin Eater.

"Are you going to kill me?" Annabel finally asked. There was stone dust mixed with her voice.

"What? Annabel—Jesus, no. I'm not your enemy." Cody reached toward the back seat and retrieved a bottle of water. He opened the bottle enough to break the seal and handed it to his passenger. Annabel took a few sips of water. Now, she just wanted the rain to stop and the sun to shine on her naked skin.

"Annabel, who did this to you?"

She started to black out again. Her eyes were so tired since her adrenaline had depleted. She cried a little as she spoke, but not about her captor. "I thought you were an angel coming to save me. I thought my prayers had been answered."

Cody adjusted his heat vent. "Well, we both know I'm no angel. But I'm not a monster either. I would never do something like this. And I never hurt Willa."

Hearing her daughter's name woke Annabel. She shifted to sit a little straighter so she could speak. With the warm bottle of water, she washed down some of the stone dust. "Did you kill my daughter, Cody? I need the truth before I die."

Cody looked in the rear-view mirror. Willa sat in the middle of the backseat, her elbows propped on the two front bucket seats. There was sorrow in her eyes as she watched her mother suffer.

"No, ma'am, I did not kill her. Willa was everything beautiful about Stoneville. She was my dream come true, and if I could somehow take her place so she could walk this world again, I wouldn't hesitate for a moment."

Annabel realized then that she wasn't the best judge of character. Jesse Lewis had fooled her for years before carving the word SINNER in her skin. She was fooling everybody, too, and Jesse knew it. It seemed like everybody in Stoneville had their secrets. Everybody had something to hide.

She patted Cody's hand resting on the center shift lever and cried some more. There was no way she would die with hate in her heart. Jesse had tried to tell her that Cody was innocent, and she refused to believe him. Maybe it was the only honest thing he ever said. The words were barely audible, but Cody heard her say, "I believe you."

With the rain pounding the windshield and the tears in his eyes, Cody struggled to see the road ahead and was forced to slow the car. He wanted the whole town to believe his innocence, but he needed Annabel to trust him first. No one else mattered. Willa would want her mother to know the truth.

"Jesse Lewis," Annabel murmured as she leaned her head against the window.

"You don't need a minister, Annabel. You're not going to die."

"No. Jesse Lewis—he's the one who did this to me. He's the Sin Eater."

Cody nearly drove the car off the road. "What? Are you fucking serious? Are you sure that you weren't hallucinating, Ann—"

"Yes, I'm sure," she insisted. Annabel was a little angry now, thinking about the monster that cut her up. "I think he's the one who killed my baby. And if I survive this, I'm going to find him, and I'm going to put a bullet in his goddam skull."

Cody had to remind himself to watch the road and concentrate on getting them back to town. He strained to make sense of Jesse's actions. "Why? Why would he go after you? The two of you seem to be such good neighbors."

"He wanted to know my sin. That's why he preys on people, like some maniacal vigilante who kills anyone hiding a sin. He said he 'ate' them."

Cody shook his head in disbelief. "Well, that's about everybody in town. Everyone's got skeletons in their closets."

"The thing is, he has a way of sensing what you're hiding. He says he can usually see them, like visions, but he couldn't see mine. So, he tied me up in his barn and carved me up, trying to break me to tell him all about it. I think he gets off on making people suffer."

Cody knew his new psychic ability was a result of the mysterious blue lights in Cain Lake, so he suspected that Jesse Lewis must draw his power from the same source. Although this new clairvoyant skill was new to Cody, Jesse Lewis had been exposed to Cain Lake's mystery for years. Maybe too long. Maybe he was going crazy from years of exposure. Homicidal even.

"Jesus, Annabel, I'm so sorry you were put through this. Lewis must be losing his mind to think you, of all people, are hiding a sin worth killing for. He has to be confusing you with someone else."

Annabel scooted down in her seat. She brushed her wet hair away from her face and wiped some more tears. It took her a minute to finally say what she wanted to say.

"He's not." She could see Cody's reaction in her peripheral vision. "He's not wrong. I've been carrying it with me for over four years."

"Carrying what?"

"My sin."

She decided then that she needed to tell someone before she died. Cody Savage, her ex-son-in-law, might be the last person to see her alive if Jesse Lewis found her. So, she began her story, telling Cody everything about the sin she carried. She was hard on herself, but Annabel felt she deserved it. She told him how she covered it up and why no one else knew. When she finished confessing her sin to an ex-con, she cried until she passed out.

Cody couldn't believe her story. It was so out of character for a woman who loved everyone she met and gave her all to the community. Perhaps that was why she was such a devoted church and community member—to atone for what she'd done.

Cody stopped the car at a four-way intersection. To his right, Jesse Lewis's church was down the gravel road. Even though the night was black, he could see the bright white siding. This is where he'd picked up Willa—the imaginary version—and this is where he needed to drop her off. She blew him a kiss in the rear-view mirror, and then she was gone. "Goodbye, my love. I hope I see you again, but I don't want you to see what I'm going to do tonight."

He turned the charger's front tires to the left and headed toward town, but once he'd dropped Annabel off somewhere safe, he was coming back for Jesse Lewis.

32
THE MOUNTAIN

Sheriff Bourbon heard the Dodge Charger rumble to a stop outside his office. The driver blew the horn repeatedly and flashed the lights. By the time Jeff Bourbon made it outside, Cody had gently pulled Annabel from the car. She stood on wobbling knees, every bit of her energy consumed from her two-mile ordeal through the dark woods.

Sheriff Bourbon didn't recognize Annabel until she finally lifted her head, and the wet hair fell away from her bloody face. He felt an earthquake in his gut and a rumble in his heart.

His immediate assumption was that Annabel had been in a bad car accident. "What the hell happened?" He was running down the stairs and yelling at the same time.

Annabel reached out to him, and the two collided in a mash of broken skin, spirits, and hearts. For the second time in one night, Annabel's prayers had been answered. Bourbon reached up and gently pushed her dripping hair away from her swollen forehead.

Annabel bawled against the sheriff's shoulder as he walked her inside to take refuge from the cold and the rain. He still hadn't seen the cuts on her abdomen, but the stains on her clothes indicated further injuries.

"Can you walk?"

She nodded her head against his shoulder, so he supported her as they climbed the front stairs and entered the building. In the foyer, the sheriff punched a code that unlocked the interior door. He was the only one in the building besides the incarcerated AJ, and most of the lights were off. They burst into the warm lobby, with its undecorated walls, and sank onto plastic chairs that formed a row along the wall. Bourbon cradled Annabel, who hugged his chest like a child who'd just awoke from a nightmare.

"Annie. Annie, what the hell happened to you?"

Annabel huddled in the chair, quiet for a few moments. She just wanted to enjoy the safety of his arms before retelling her ordeal. Bourbon looked up at Cody, who was standing near the door, for an answer.

"I found her on the road. On Lake View. Her hands were tied, and she was pretty cut up."

The memory hit Bourbon like a truck: Willa's body lying in the snow with her hands tied in the front, puncture marks in her torso. Annabel's similar condition wasn't the result of an accident. It was an attack.

"Who?" Bourbon growled.

Cody knelt beside the couple. "Show him, Annabel. Show Bourbon who did this."

Annabel leaned back and gingerly parted the lower section of her blouse, and Bourbon stared unbelievingly at the single word carved into her skin. The letters were carved deep enough to bleed but not enough to kill her. There were a few places where the writer's pressure was too much, and the letters still bled a little.

Bourbon knew who the last man with Annabel was. He'd even seen a picture of them together earlier that evening. Of all the people in Stoneville, only one concerned himself with the sins of the population.

Cody could feel the temperature of the room spike as heat radiated off the sheriff. Compared to the hell that Sheriff Bourbon was ready to unleash, the storm outside was nothing. Cody remembered that same storm that had overtaken him the morning that Willa was found dead. He stood up and backed away from the suffering couple.

Bourbon whispered, "Let's get you to the hospital."

Annabel replied with a weak head nod, and Bourbon stood. For Annabel's sake, he kept himself composed and professional. But he was evidently ready to unleash his fury on anyone who crossed him now. He pulled his phone from his pocket and dialed Charlie Archer. It only took two rings for the deputy to answer.

"Archer," Bourbon said. "I need you back at HQ immediately. I need you to take Annabel to the hospital...Yes...Keep your lights on...Get her admitted and meet me at Jesse Lewis's house...Yes, the pastor. I'll explain when you get here. Hurry." He disconnected the phone and called another number.

"Shari? Hey, it's Jeff. Can you meet Charlie Archer at the hospital? He's bringing a patient in...Yes, an attack victim...Please do...Okay...No, it's not Darcy. It's Annabel...yeah...No, she's okay, but she needs medical treatment. I think you should be there if there's trace evidence, and we'll need photos, too. Thank you."

Bourbon walked over to Cody and laid his powerful hand on Cody's shoulder, "Thank you, son." The words were sincere, and Cody couldn't remember the last time he'd heard them.

"Just a matter of luck that I came by, Sheriff."

"Thank God you did. Weather like this, there can't be too many people out on the road."

"Glad to help," Cody said. He was ready to sneak away and find the wicked pastor himself. "Well, if you don't need me for anything—"

Bourbon pulled him closer, "There is something else you can help me with. He stepped back. "Tonight," he placed his badge on an empty desk. "I'm not the sheriff. That means I can't drive county vehicles, so I could use a fast ride if you have one."

"You want *me* to drive you to Jesse's house?"

"I'm going to find that sonovabitch after what he did to Annabel, and he's going to pay. Cancel your dinner plans, Savage. I could use a little of that rage you keep hidden."

Cody watched the front door for Archer while Bourbon disappeared to the back of the jail. When he returned, he wasn't alone. AJ followed Bourbon through the hall.

"Get the hell out of here, Timmons. And try not to take another swing at one of my deputies."

AJ and Cody gave each other a quick slap-on-the-back hug. AJ couldn't keep himself from smiling until he felt the dread in the room and noticed Annabel sitting in pain. "Jesus, what happened to her?"

"It's a long story, bud. I'll explain everything later. I need to borrow your car tonight, though."

AJ nodded tentatively, "Yeah, okay, sure. Whatever you need, man."

"Call Daisy and fill her in. She can come get you."

"What if she asks about you? What do you want me to tell her?"

"Tell her....Tell her I went to get her a story."

Outside, a set of police lights flashed on the street. Archer waited in the car—most likely so his hair wouldn't be ruined by the heavy rain—while Cody and Bourbon half-carried Annabel out the door and into the back seat. She gave Bourbon a three-second kiss, transferring a streak of blood to his brow and down one side of his face. The police car spun in a tight U-turn, and Archer sped away toward the hospital.

Bourbon strode to his SUV and retrieved a shotgun and a box of shells. He locked the vehicle and made his way to the Dodge Charger, where Cody was already sitting behind the wheel, anxious to go. Bourbon took the passenger seat and buckled his seatbelt.

AJ appeared in the passenger-side window. "Cody?"

"Yeah?"

"Not a single scratch, okay?"

Cody looked at Bourbon and back at AJ, "I promise, AJ. Not a single scratch on your car."

AJ left the two men and sought refuge from the rain under the awning that protected the building entrance. With his phone returned, he called Daisy to tell her what was happening.

Cody turned his attention back to his passenger. "Look, Sheriff—"

"Cody, you can't call me 'sheriff' tonight."

"Okay, then what do I call you?"

"You can call me Jeff, Jefferson, or Bourbon if you want, but Sheriff Bourbon just retired."

"'Jefferson,' like the President?"

"No, Jefferson, like the mountain. I was born in Oregon, where my parents had a little house and a view of Mount Jefferson." He shoved shotgun shells in the gun's tubular magazine. "My mother loved that view, so they named me after it when I was born."

"The mountain," Cody whispered to himself, remembering Flesti's words.

"Yup," Bourbon had heard the whisper. "Let's go see the good pastor. I want this motherfucker before he leaves town."

Cody shifted the vehicle into drive and spun the tires thirty feet down the street. He could see AJ in the rear-view mirror and imagined the look of disapproval he was probably receiving. He hated leaving AJ there, but he'd be safe with Daisy.

As they raced across town, Cody sped through red lights and stop signs on Bourbon's command. They shattered speed limits and slid sideways around corners. Cody worked the wheel hard while Jefferson Bourbon sat quietly in the passenger side like a content dog waiting to reach their destination. When they reached Lake View Drive, Bourbon ordered Cody to slow down. He scanned the church in the distance, looking to see any lights or vehicles, thinking the pastor might have come here to hide.

Bourbon sprinted from the Charger Hellcat at the stop sign. He searched the ground and entrance to the gravel road for tire tracks in the fresh mud, but there were none. That was good. He hated the idea of shooting up a church, but as pissed as he was, he'd shoot up heaven itself to bring the Sin Eater to justice. He climbed back inside the car.

The Charger shot up the road, racing like the lightning flashing around them. The windshield began to fog over, so Cody put the windows down a couple of inches. The opening allowed cool rainwater to pellet the left side of his face. Lightning flashed again.

Cody kept his eyes on the road, but his mind flashed other images. The rainwater, a catalyst for visions, seemed to jump-start his ability to see people in danger. He could see Darcy Poole sitting in the corner of a concrete room. No, it was a basement. Surprisingly, she wasn't crying. She'd accepted her fate, captive to a man like some mistreated pet, alone in a basement prison, broken in spirit. She had most likely given up on any chance of rescue. She'd be better off dead.

Cody's focus returned to the road. "Do you think Jesse Lewis is responsible for Darcy Poole's disappearance? Think he's got her?" Cody asked.

His passenger didn't answer as he pieced together the clues they had missed, which had allowed the misguided pastor to fool them all. How did he do it? How did he manage to commit such heinous crimes under all their noses without revealing himself? The horror that Annie went through kept flashing in his mind. What if she hadn't escaped? Would he have ever known her fate?

"I don't know," he finally answered. "Let's go find out."

33

FUCK PAROLE

ody switched off the car's headlights 100 yards before reaching
Jesse's driveway. The smell of death and frog guts saturated the night
air, so Cody powered all the windows up to barricade the odor. The Charger rolled quietly to Jesse's driveway in the dark, creeping along the blacktop as streams of rainwater chased them down the road. The car was difficult to keep quiet, its tuned exhaust hated to whisper. Bourbon directed Cody to steer the car into the driveway and kill the engine. They blocked the driveway, but there was still room to cut through the lawn and the ditch.

There was no movement on the Lewis property—no escaping vehicles and no one running for the woods.

The pastor's barn was larger than it had appeared from the road. The interior was lit by a single bulb hanging from a retractable extension cord. The house was dark, so Bourbon assumed that was most likely the pastor's location if he hadn't fled. They didn't expect to find Jesse Lewis here, but they had to try their luck. If he did escape, they'd figure out their next move after exhausting their search on the hobby farm.

"I assume you know how to use this," Bourbon said, holding a pistol by its short barrel and pushing it toward Cody.

"Of course." Cody took it by the grip. He hesitated momentarily, "You know this violates my parole, right?"

"Fuck your parole. I didn't see anything. Just make sure you don't shoot me."

Cody checked the safety by clicking it off and then back on. The chamber held a live round, and the clip was full. He set the gun on the center console.

"Wait in the car. Keep your eyes on the place. If you see any movement other than me, honk the horn." Bourbon stepped out of the vehicle and gently pushed the door until it latched. He crept along the ditch, cut through the lawn, using the barn to conceal his approach in case Jesse was watching from the house. Once he reached the barn, he disappeared into the shadows.

Cody occasionally spied Bourbon's silhouette, circling the barn like a wary wolf stalking its prey. He waited for what seemed an eternity. The car windows were fogging over again from Cody's body heat and wet clothes, but he couldn't risk starting the noisy engine. Opening the car door, he stepped into the falling rain, which had diminished to a light shower.

He popped the trunk of the Charger and walked backward until he reached the car's open compartment.

He left the pistol in the car. He'd seen enough of prison to last him a lifetime. Carrying a gun could lead to accidental or intentional circumstances that he didn't want to face. The Sin Eater had never used a gun on any of his victims. He seemed to prefer a blade—intimate, painful, and brutal.

Cody reached into the car's trunk and took out the hockey ax.

Live by the sword, die by the sword. He closed the lid as quietly as possible. While Bourbon focused on the barn, Cody needed to get to the house's basement. Preferring the shadows to the right of the house, he approached with short sprints and ducked behind the mature maple trees.

He was there to support Bourbon and avenge Annabel, and to punish his wife's murderer. However, Cody was there for a more pressing matter as well. The visions and images of Darcy Poole would never stop haunting him until she was found. He had to reach the basement of the silent house and search for the missing teen. Bringing Darcy home—dead or alive—would bring closure to the Poole family and hopefully restore Stoneville to some form of normalcy.

By the time Cody had reached the corner of the house, the rain had stopped completely. A silver moon pierced the thinning clouds, lending a weak light to the scene below. He continued around Jesse's house, finding a back door tucked in a small porch. The doorknob was unlocked—too easy, but not unusual in this part of town. The door swung inward quietly on freshly greased hinges. He stepped inside and closed the door as gently as he'd opened it. A rumble in the room next to him—the clothes dryer—covered any sounds he made. Jesse had shed his wet clothes after his hunt for Annabel and put them into the dryer.

The rumble of the dryer and its squeaky belt impaired Cody's ability to hear anyone in the house. He stood in a mudroom, straining to listen to the dark home. Stepping over a pile of clothes that was discernible in the dark, he thought about opening the dryer's door to turn it off, but that might alert Jesse to his presence.

All right, Sin Eater, where the hell are you?

Cody stepped around the corner of the short partition into the hallway. A half-opened door protruded into the hall. Only a closet or a basement would have a door that opened into the hallway.

He stayed low, stepped lightly down the hall, and entered the open door, where a stairwell led to the basement. His chest drummed hard, and the dampness of his grip was more likely sweat than rainwater. From the bottom of the stairs, a dim light illuminated the room below. Cody considered that Jesse might be trying to lure him to the lowest portion of the house. He believed that it might be a trap. Then again, he didn't care. If Darcy Poole were down there, then he was willing to face the danger. He was ready to risk his life to bring her home.

His foot hit the first step with a dull thump, and he froze, wondering if he'd just given away his position. He was more careful with the remaining steps, but the old hardwood treads had loosened over their lifetime. The sound of his steps might ruin the element of surprise, but Cody couldn't let that deter him from descending the rest of the way.

When he reached the bottom, he was surprised that the basement was much smaller than the house. The entire room was twenty feet wide and thirty feet long. Shelves lined one wall with books, jars of canned vegetables, and some items that appeared to be related to the church. The home's furnace, water heater, and chest freezer obscured the far wall. He hesitantly opened the freezer, but it contained nothing more than frozen vegetables, cheap steaks, and some fish. No Darcy Poole, thankfully.

Today's rain had saturated the ground and raised the water table, allowing water to penetrate the white basement walls. It trickled down, accumulated along the floor's bottom corner, and flowed toward a sump pump. Two small nightlights plugged into outlets on opposite ends of the room illuminated the space. When Cody came full circle, he stopped at a cabinet under the stairs, a gun cabinet. The door was open, and Cody saw that the furniture was designed to hold a maximum capacity of eight guns. It appeared that Jesse only owned six guns, all of which were centered in the middle of the cabinet. But the very center butt plate and barrel rest were vacant. Where a rifle should have rested was a clue that Jesse Lewis was probably armed. A box of rifle shells was open, with two dropped rounds resting on the floor, a result of Jesse trying to load the weapon in haste.

Cody picked up a bullet and inspected the caliber. It was a .223. There was no gun of that caliber in the cabinet, so he considered the variety of gun configurations produced in the .223 caliber. Based on the ammunition, Jesse could be armed with a military-style rifle with a thirty-round magazine, which was illegal in New York. He hoped the "good pastor" probably didn't own such a weapon.

The remaining guns were primarily hunting rifles: two high-caliber rifles, a .410 shotgun for bird hunting, one .22 caliber rifle for small game, and one black-powder rifle. Cody looked into the cupboard at the base.

Zero ammunition. The rest of the guns were useless without ammo. A moment of regret came over him, and Cody wondered if he should retreat to the car and retrieve Bourbon's pistol.

Cody would have to defend himself with the pastor's hockey ax if necessary, but didn't like the odds.

A small LED flashlight lay with Jesse's hunting gear, so Cody grabbed it to avoid having to turn on any lights. He flicked it on and off once to ensure the batteries still had charge. They were weak, but operable.

He tiptoed as quietly as he could back up the stairs. A quick scan of the first floor revealed several vacant rooms in the old farmhouse. The layout was open from the kitchen to the living room, with only a bathroom and a closet partitioned off. He crossed to the other end of the house and found a set of stairs leading to the second floor.

Outside, the rainfall grew heavy again, and Cody could hear the drops tapping on the large windows. As the rain drummed on the house's metal roof, creating a sound like never-ending waves, it covered the sound of his footsteps.

He began his ascent up the narrow and dark stairwell. The steps marched upward in a straight line with no turns or landings. The old farmhouse had twelve-foot ceilings, so the stairwell was quite long and the steps many. Cody took his time, taking each step with caution. The steps were small, with low risers and shallow treads, which made him wonder if people had smaller feet when this house was built.

As he neared the top, he peeked down the straight hallway and saw nothing but darkness. He realized he wouldn't hear the pastor with the rain bombing the metal roof, but he listened anyway. His eyes adjusted to the dark a little more. A cool breeze rushed toward him, punching him in the face and flowing down the stairwell.

An open window.

A light flashed at the end of the hallway, searing Cody's eyes as if they had been hit with gasoline. He ducked back down the stairs and forced his eyelids to open. He peeked over the top stair quickly, expecting Jesse to be holding the bright light, but instead, he saw Jesse's silhouette against a window at the end of the hallway.

The window sash was up, and Jesse knelt on the floor, not in prayer, but in sniper position. The beam of the powerful light had originated from the top of the barn.

A motion sensor light! Oh, shit—.

Before he could yell a warning to Bourbon, Jesse fired the .223 hunting rifle. The sound was slightly muffled as Jesse held the gun barrel out the window and fired into the rain.

Cody lunged up the stairs and sprinted down the hallway.

Jesse racked another shell into the chamber of the bolt-action rifle and lined up for a second shot.

From outside, a shotgun blasted, almost as loud as Jesse's rifle.

Everything went dark again. Bourbon had shot out the motion sensor light, giving himself darkness to hide.

Jesse fired his second shot in a panic, then heard Cody's heavy steps running down the hallway. He spun 180 degrees while racking the gun's bolt. The bullet entered the chamber, and Jesse swung around to his oncoming target. Cody blocked the swinging rifle with the home-made ax. The gun fired, barely missing Cody's waist. The hockey ax and the rifle locked together in deadly competition.

Cody threw his right elbow into the side of the pastor's head, stunning the homeowner momentarily. Jesse dropped the rifle to defend himself. Pushing and shoving each other in the hallway with the hockey ax locked between them, they traded punches and elbows, slamming each other against the plaster-and-lath walls.

Plaster crumbled and fell from the walls, exposing the hardwood lath as the two men destroyed the hallway. They spun 180 degrees, changing sides of the hallway. Cody couldn't let himself lose this fight. Too much was at stake, and he needed to know if this was the man who had killed his wife and held Darcy Poole captive.

After slamming each other off the wall several times, Cody snuck a right uppercut past Jesse's guard. The punch landed firmly on the pastor's jaw, causing his eyes to roll back in their sockets as the effects of a concussion took their toll. Cody spun Jesse ninety degrees this time and pushed like a bulldozer with a temper. Outside, Bourbon could hear Cody's battle cry as the two men smashed against the large open window, crashed through the sash, and fell through the charged night air.

Bourbon had taken cover inside the garage, so he was surprised to find that Cody had made his way inside. He heard the fighting in the hallway, but the lack of light made it impossible to see what was happening until the window on the second floor smashed, and the altercation continued outside. The fall was short as the two men landed on top of the porch. The red metal roof was slick from the rain, and they slid and rolled downward. As Cody dropped over the edge, he wondered where the hockey ax had disappeared to.

Beside him, Jesse slid on his back and headfirst down the roof. When he dropped off the edge and fell, his feet flipped toward the barn. He now faced the ground, like a diver ready to belly-flop. At the last second, Jesse realized the ax had made it to the lawn faster than the two men. One side of the ax blade was stuck in the wet ground. The other side pointed straight up. It gave a little when Jesse landed on it, but not much.

Cody managed to roll with the momentum. He dropped from the roof, landed on his feet, bounced off his ass, and ended up on his back. Even though he'd managed to avoid striking his head or landing on any hard surfaces, he had the wind knocked forcefully from his lungs.

Bourbon pushed the barn's two large swinging doors open and let the light from inside escape to the lawn. From inside the barn, the headlights of a black Chevy Silverado illuminated the scene. Bourbon had turned on the headlights, ensuring he could see his target.

"Is he dead?" Bourbon asked as he made his way to the scene. He was holding his shotgun with the barrel staring at Jesse.

Jesse rolled over, holding his ribs where the ax had broken two. He groaned with pain; his breathing was short and heavy. The wound would only be fatal if he didn't receive any medical attention. Bourbon was surprised by the lack of blood.

Cody sprang to his feet rather quickly to defend himself, not realizing that Jesse was severely wounded. He realized what had happened when he saw the pastor and the ax beside him.

He gave Bourbon a little slap on the left shoulder while gasping for air. "Piece of cake, Bourbon."

Bourbon winced in pain.

"You okay?" Cody asked.

"Sonovabitch got me," Bourbon huffed.

Cody stepped back and glanced at Bourbon's back. The .223's slug had grazed Bourbon's shoulder blade. Bourbon held his left arm close to his ribs in pain, but truthfully, it was his ego that was bruised. He didn't want Jesse Lewis to have the satisfaction of dealing any more pain to anyone.

He stepped closer to Jesse and threw his boot into the broken ribs. "Get up, asshole. Your legs aren't broken."

"Sheriff," Jesse winced as he climbed to his knees. "How's your girlfriend?" He sounded sincere.

Bourbon pressed the 12-gauge shotgun to Jesse's forehead, "Ask again. Go ahead. You mention her again, and I will part your skull like the Red Sea."

"Why?" Cody asked. "Why did you carve her up? And those other men? What did any of them do to you?"

"It's not me," Jesse said. He was breathing heavily, and the words spilled out slowly as blood ran from the corner of his mouth. "I mean, yes, I did it. But I can't help it. I have to give the lake what it wants—the sins of its residents."

"The lake?" Bourbon asked. His head dropped in disappointment, thinking about Goodman attacking the dive team. "Not this shit again." He relaxed his grip on the shotgun, hoping Jesse was ready to confess and clear his conscience.

Jesse nodded. "It feeds on the sins of humans. I'm just the delivery man. Cain Lake gave me the ability to see the sins of everyone I come close to. The sensation gets stronger every day." His eyes filled with liquid, sincere and honest tears. "I didn't want to hurt anybody, but it soothes my pain. The sins of my neighbors are like a drug, quenching my addiction until I purge in the water."

"The blue lights," Cody uttered. "They take the sins away?"

Jesse stood as tall as he could on his knees. "You've seen them?"

Bourbon looked puzzled. "What the hell are you two talking about?"

Cody walked around Jesse and picked up the hockey ax. "Cain Lake has some weird-ass power, Bourbon. I keep seeing a woman down there who knows what it's all about. You should go talk to her."

"Flesti? Yeah, I've met that nut job. I think she's mixing the lake water with moonshine, if you ask me." Bourbon lowered the shotgun and rolled his shoulder in pain. "You trying to tell me that this is all her fault?"

Jesse looked toward the sky. The rain had stopped again, and a few stars had even appeared.

He finally brought his gaze back to earth and looked Bourbon straight in the face, "I don't know, Sheriff, but I think what's been happening in Stoneville—at Cain Lake—is just beginning."

34
THE BARN

Bourbon led Jesse to the barn, where there was more light. It took all his willpower to keep from putting a hole in Jesse's chest with the shotgun to avenge Annabel. The word SINNER, carved in his beautiful lover's abdomen, flashed over and over in his mind. It would leave a humiliating scar to remind her of this day for the rest of her life.

Once in the barn, Bourbon shoved Jesse to sit on the tailgate of Connor Bayley's truck and handcuffed the pastor's right wrist to a tubular bed rail bolted to the truck's bed. The chrome rail was an inch and one-quarter in diameter, and Bourbon knew there was no way Jesse could break it.

"Watch him a minute," Bourbon ordered Cody. Cody set the hockey ax in the back of the black truck. It leaned against the side of the truck bed, blade side down, and far enough forward that Jesse couldn't reach it.

Bourbon searched the truck's cab and then circled the outside, performing a visual inspection. There was no blood or evidence that Darcy Poole had been in the vehicle.

"Why are you driving Connor Bayley's truck? Where is he?"

Jesse had to think for a moment. The death of Connor had seemed so long ago, and since then, so much had happened. At times, his mind was not his own. Cain Lake took control, and his fits of pain and numbness would leave his memories a jumbled mess, fragments of a puzzle shaken in a snow globe.

"The boy who owned this truck?" Jesse asked.

"Yes, dammit. He worked for Annabel. Where is he?"

"The swamp behind Annabel's farm." Jesse's injury inflicted pain when he breathed. "You'll find Connor there, buried in the mud."

"What the fuck?" Cody asked. "What was his sin? That's what you do, right? Punish the sinners. Kill them!"

Jesse looked at him honestly. "Yes. He was a sinner. He hurt the girl."

"Darcy Poole?" Bourbon asked. "Did that boy kill Darcy?"

"No, I don't think so. But Connor beat her, and I believe he sold Darcy to another man. I had a vision." Jesse took a deep, painful breath. "Connor sold that girl like she was a cheap piece of furniture."

Bourbon kicked an empty five-gallon bucket that flew across the barn and bounced off a riding lawnmower. The barn cat, a gray-striped tabby, sprang from behind the hay bales and bolted through the hole in the ceiling.

"Jesus!" Bourbon threw a backhand against Jesse's head. "She could be anywhere by now. Canada, Buffalo, New York City. Why didn't you tell me about this? Maybe I could've found her sooner." Bourbon was irate. Last week had been a waste. The searching, the murder of the dive team, sleepless nights, and wasted resources. It might have been avoided if Jesse had let them know.

"Come on, Sheriff," Jesse said. "Would you have believed me if I came to you and said I had a vision? That I see the evil things people do?"

Bourbon realized Jesse was probably right. He'd never believed in that sort of stuff. Psychic visions and lights in the lake. That shit was for TV and Dean Koontz novels. This was Stoneville. This was a regular place with ordinary, boring people. Nothing ever changed here and everyone liked it that way.

"He's right, Bourbon," Cody said. "You wouldn't have believed him. And you probably wouldn't believe that the lake affected me, too."

"What the hell are you talking about, Savage?"

"The day Archer kicked me into the lake, I saw the blue lights Jesse is referring to. While underwater, they swarmed me, and I had visions of Willa and Darcy. I thought I could see them because I was dying. But since then, I keep seeing Willa, and I've seen Darcy locked up in a basement. I thought it was here in Jesse's house. After what he did to Annabel—"

"I don't have the girl," Jesse interrupted. He was so adamant that it was true that Bourbon and Cody believed him, since there was no evidence that she was there. The pastor seemed to be clearing his conscience and confessing what he knew.

"Okay. Okay," Bourbon paced back and forth. He stopped and looked at the hook on the chain hoist that hung from above. He couldn't imagine how terrified Annabel must have been through that whole ordeal. When he finally spoke, he was calm and expressionless.

"There's only one problem with all this bullshit, Pastor," Bourbon said. "You say that you only punish the sinners?"

Jesse nodded. "They come to confession and practically ask for it. The ones who hide it, I can see their sins, regardless. And then I hear her voice."

"Whose voice?"

"A woman. I'm not sure who she is, or if she's even real, but I have to do whatever she asks. I have to obey, and I don't know why. I sometimes lose control of my own body and do things without thinking, like a puppet on its strings. That's what happened when I cut Annabel."

Bourbon nodded but still didn't understand. "But here's where you fucked up, asshole. You messed with an innocent woman. You went after Annabel Thompson, the purest and most honest person in this whole damn town. She's not a sinner! She's a goddamn angel and nothing less."

There was silence in the barn.

It was Cody who finally challenged Bourbon's theory. "That's not exactly true."

Bourbon's head whipped sideways like a rattlesnake had bitten in the ribs.

Cody explained, "Annabel knew what sin Jesse sensed in her. She refused to give it to him. But she thought she was going to die when I was driving her back to town, and I guess she wanted to confess to someone in case she did. So she confessed her sin to me."

For a moment, Bourbon considered pointing the shotgun at Cody for lying, but he opted to let him continue. He stood there, slowly shaking his head in denial.

Cody leaned on the truck and continued, "Four years ago, Annabel left a benefit fundraiser. She'd had a lot to drink, so she didn't go home.

She went to the bar and had even more to drink. And then she went to your house."

Bourbon leaned on the workbench, remembering the night. He closed his eyes and rubbed the bridge of his nose in concentration. She had shown up at his house, too drunk to drive all the way home, but she had made it to his house. Bourbon had to work early the next day, which is why he couldn't attend the benefit. He awoke at four am, and Annabel was still there—asleep.

Cody continued, just like Annabel had told him. "When she left your house in the morning, Bourbon, she was in an accident. She hit a woman jogging on the side of the road and killed her."

Bourbon's head sank. His voice was barely audible. "Charlotte Archer." His brain flickered with scenes from the accident. Utterly defeated, Bourbon fell into a crouching position and buried his face in his hands.

Cody cleared his throat. "She knew she was still affected by the alcohol in her system, so she fled the scene."

Bourbon's head shook in denial. "That's impossible. She would have told me about it, damn it. I investigated that accident while Archer grieved. He'd just started as a deputy, and the poor friggin guy lost his wife the same month. He responded to the accident, only to find his wife dead. He'll never get those pictures out of his head."

Jesse Lewis was almost smiling. He licked his dry lips, considering how the sin would have satisfied Cain Lake and soothed his pain for months. Then his curiosity got to him. "Sheriff, how could you not see the damage to Annabel's truck? I mean, an impact like that must have done a terrible amount of damage."

"Because," Cody said, "she wasn't driving her truck that night. Her truck was in the shop getting repaired, and she didn't own the Range Rover yet."

Bourbon exhaled with force, "She was driving her daughter's car—Willa's car, a Volkswagen Passat."

Jesse almost laughed out loud. "And now you have to go arrest her, don't you, Sheriff?"

Bourbon knocked Jesse across the cheek with the butt of the shotgun. "Shut the hell up, you piece of shit! I could still hollow out your skull with this shotgun."

Jesse fell to his side, but his right arm, across his body and cuffed to the truck's bed rail, stopped him from falling over. He spat a mouthful of blood onto the barn floor.

Bourbon stared. Something didn't make sense. He realized the error in the story, "But, that car—Willa's car—is parked in Annie's barn. There's not a scratch on it."

Cody nodded in agreement. "Because she had it fixed. She got the best auto body repairman in town to fix it for her. In exchange, she promised to get him a job with the Sheriff's Department. As a deputy."

"Birchcraft," Bourbon said. "That's his 'sin.' The rescue diver who attacked him said that Birchcraft knew something. Birch has kept it a secret for all this time." Bourbon thought about what to do next. Since he was now retired, he'd have to have Archer bring Jesse in—charge him with kidnapping, assault, murder, and about ten other felonies, then he'd have to deal with Annabel and Birchcraft.

Cody squared up to the sheriff. "Bourbon, listen....You and I are the only ones who know the truth. Arresting Annabel for an accident won't bring Charlotte Archer back from the dead. We're the only ones who know the truth."

Jesse spoke with a mouthful of blood, "Well, not anymore."

Bourbon shoved the shotgun against Jesse's ribs, "I can fix that real quick."

"Not me," Jesse said. "Him."

Bourbon never heard Charlie Archer enter the garage through the man door next to the workbench. His pistol, a Springfield semi-automatic 9 mm, was drawn and pointed at his boss. His usual fake smile was replaced by a blank expression.

"Archer." Bourbon stepped toward his deputy. "Put your weapon away, Arch."

Archer ignored the order. "Fuck you, Bourbon." He looked around to assess the situation. He was shaking with anger and confusion. "She killed my wife? Annabel? It was Annabel who ran her over and left her like roadkill?"

"Arch, it was an accident, okay? You know Annie. She would never hurt anybody. Put the gun down, son."

"No. No, all this time, I thought I knew who killed Charlotte. I was sure I had the right person! And all this time…. It was her? Annabel needs to pay for what she did."

"She will," Bourbon said. "I promise. I'll arrest her myself."

"You're lying, Sheriff. You're lying!" Archer screamed. He knew the only way to avenge his wife was to keep Bourbon and Savage from stopping him. He pointed the pistol at Cody but was talking to Bourbon.

"Cuff him."

"What? Why? He's not the enemy here—"

"Just do it, dammit!"

Cody didn't want the scene to escalate any more than Bourbon. He gave Bourbon a nod. Being handcuffed inside the barn was better than being shot. Archer would gladly end Cody's life, so he complied.

Bourbon removed a second pair of handcuffs from his utility belt. He snapped the cuff around Cody's left wrist and then clipped the other side to the steering wheel of Jesse's lawn tractor.

"Happy?" Bourbon asked Archer.

"Almost," Archer replied. He took a pair of handcuffs from a leather pocket on his belt and tossed them toward Bourbon. "Put 'em on. Around the post." Archer pointed with his pistol to a thick wooden beam that supported the second floor. Bourbon obliged, wrapping both arms around the pole and then locking the cuffs on his wrists.

Jesse laughed at their predicament until Archer shoved a pistol in his face, "You find all this funny, Preacher?"

"Pastor," Jesse corrected calmly. "And yes, I do. Don't you see it? All of you are here for the same reason." No one said a word. "You're all in this situation, here in this barn right now, because you seek revenge for the women you love. Cody's trying to find whoever killed his wife. Bourbon wants me for what I did to Annie. And you, Archer, want revenge against Annabel for hitting your wife with a car. You all have the same thing in common. The brotherhood of blood."

Archer clutched Jesse's throat with his strong fingers. No one protested. He didn't say a word—he just stared into the pastor's eyes as if to frighten the man, but it did not have the effect he'd hoped.

Jesse cringed in pain, but not from Archer's powerful grip on his throat. A numbing sensation descended his left arm, and his annoying migraine attacked his head. He closed his eyes as the pain stabbed his brain. He grabbed Archer's wrist with his left hand, and though he couldn't breathe, he managed to say a single word through bloody, grimacing teeth.

"Sinner."

Archer let go, and Jesse inhaled deeply. He could see the sins that Charlie Archer was hiding. Jesse fell against the side of the truck bed and rolled his head back until he locked eyes with Cody. "You can stop looking for your wife's murderer," Jesse said. He spat more blood. "He's right here."

Cody stood straight, leaned toward Archer, and yanked hard against the steering wheel of the lawn tractor, but the handcuffs held firm, and he could not move or break free. Cody reached with his free hand, but Archer was just inches too far away. Cody screamed a bloodthirsty cry, and then his rage conjured a new vision. He could see Willa locked in a basement. Somehow, she had managed to unshackle herself and escape Archer several times. But he caught her every time. The night she made her final escape, Archer cursed how he was sick of chasing her. Armed with a knife, he led her outside, but once again, she broke free and ran fast. Through the trees. Through the rain. Archer chased and caught her, plunging the knife into her back. She rolled over to fight. Enraged, he stabbed her again and again. Willa lay alone, snow covering her body. Gone. And then Cody saw Archer carrying an unconscious Darcy Poole into a dark room. The heavy door slammed, and Cody was back in Jesse Lewis's barn.

"You have her," Cody said. "You have Darcy locked in your basement, just like you had Willa. You sick fucker."

Archer didn't deny it. He just shrugged. With all three men tied up in the barn, there was no one to stop him from going to kill Annabel and then leave town with Darcy Poole.

"Archer. Archer, listen to me. Tell us why you're kidnapping these women," Bourbon pleaded gently. "You're tearing their families apart.

Hell, you're tearing this town apart."

Archer slid his hand into his back pocket and withdrew his wallet. From within the wallet, he revealed a small photo. He held it up for Cody to see, keeping it far enough away that Cody couldn't reach it.

"You sonovabitch. Why do you have a picture of my wife? Give it to me!"

Archer tucked the photo back into hiding. "Now you get it. That's not your wife. That was mine. That's my Charlotte."

Stunned by the uncanny resemblance the two wives shared, Cody saw all the mysterious pieces fall into place. So that was Archer's motive. He had kidnapped Willa because she bore a striking resemblance to Charlotte. She had been a replacement.

"Archer, before the night is over," Cody promised with clenched teeth, "I'm going to kill you and take Darcy Poole home to her family."

Archer scoffed. His arrogance alone was reason enough for Cody to kill the man. "Let me tell you something, Savage. That wife of yours was a hell of a fighter. Pretty little thing like her…. After Charlotte died, I thought Willa could take her place, but she refused to love me."

"Why'd you go after her? How did you even know her?" Bourbon pried.

Archer leaned against the truck bed. "When I was investigating Charlotte's death, I found a plastic Volkswagen emblem in the road, and there were flecks of platinum gray metallic paint embedded in her skin. It wasn't hard to track her down. I took the emblem so it wouldn't go into evidence. There was only one 2006 Volkswagen Passat of that color registered in town. I found it in her mother's barn, and when she showed up, I…I couldn't arrest her. It was like Charlotte had risen from the dead. But she was nothing like Charlotte. It was her own fault for getting killed. All she had to do was stay. If she hadn't run, she'd still be alive."

Furious, Cody kicked the tractor's steering wheel. He twisted his arm trying to break free, as Archer twisted his mind. Wrist bones cracked under Cody's strain, but they were no match for the tempered steel of the handcuffs or the steering wheel. "And you'd still have her locked up! You sick fucker. That's why you've had so much hate for me. It was all an act to hide the truth. Nobody in town would suspect that the poor deputy, grieving over the death of his wife, would commit kidnapping and murder."

Bourbon leaned his head against the wooden beam, trying to assemble the broken clues into one clear picture. "And we couldn't use your DNA in the investigation. The morning we found Willa, you purposely touched her body with your bare hands and contaminated the scene. You knew exactly what you were doing."

Archer half-shrugged with his shoulders. "I had to cover the DNA with my own DNA. And the snow that covered our tracks was just dumb luck. If it hadn't snowed, you and that stupid state trooper would both be dead. I'd have shot you both right there and then. I'm glad I didn't have to, Bourbon. It's been fun watching you all suffer to figure this shit out."

"So, now you have Darcy. A docile little girl, broken in spirit and unable to fight. She's not a fighter like Willa, is she? She won't escape."

Archer circled Connor's truck. "Connor treated Darcy like garbage. I gave him five grand to bring her to me and keep his mouth shut. He must have taken the money and left town."

"Connor's dead! And Darcy's a frightened little nineteen-year-old girl, you bastard." Bourbon's face reddened with anger. "Keeping her locked up in your basement is worse than what Connor did to her."

Archer slammed his fist into the side of the truck. "I would never hurt Darcy."

Cody knew there was no reasoning with Archer. As the deputy's anger grew, so did the odds of him putting a bullet in all three captive men. The man was sick and needed to pay for what he'd done.

Archer finished talking. He had a mission to kill Annabel for what she'd done to Charlotte and disappear with Darcy. They'd go where no one would find them.

Archer searched Bourbon and Jesse, jerked their cellular phones from their pockets, and placed them on top of the hay bales.

A one-gallon gas canister in the corner of the garage contained three cups of fuel. Archer drenched the phones and bales of hay with the gas, went to Connor's old Chevy, and pushed in the cigarette lighter on the dashboard. With the door open, he sat on the bench seat, his knees protruding outward and the Springfield pistol across his lap. The garage was deathly silent, every man thinking about his next move, but the three captives were too far away to help each other.

Archer quickly decided his next move. He'd drug Darcy and take her to the hospital. She'd be unconscious in the car while he went inside to make sure Annabel suffered for what she had done. He and Darcy could reach Ohio by morning and Kentucky by the following evening. They could get lost in the mountains or continue on to Texas.

The cigarette lighter popped out, red and hot and ready to burn. Cody knew that he and Bourbon were out of time.

Archer tossed the cigarette lighter toward the hay bales, pivoted, and strode from the barn that began to burn.

35

THE BURN

Cody tried pushing the lawn tractor toward the door, but two flat tires and a snowblower attachment on the front made the vehicle immovable. Brilliant flames crept up the barn wall, higher and higher, while most of the smoke seeped through the cracks in the ceiling and entered the hayloft above.

Bourbon was also making no progress. He was close enough to reach the workbench with his foot, but the tools lying on the bench were of no use.

Jesse Lewis sat motionless, watching the flames grow. He decided to welcome the fire. Where he was going, he'd have to acclimate to the heat anyway. As death stared him down, the pastor felt a moment of sorrow for Annabel Thompson. Now that he knew her sin, Jesse no longer craved to see her suffer. He no longer hungered to peel her open and reveal the truth. She had been his friend up until that very day. She was the woman who brought him a plate of dinner once a week. She watched his house and got his mail when he was out of town. She was the person who called and checked on him when he was sick. She was the only neighbor who genuinely showed kindness.

He loved her.

Jesse knew he couldn't stop Archer from going to the hospital to kill Annabel, but somebody had to. He jumped to his feet. The wound in his side opened, and fresh blood seeped out. He stretched his body, reaching out with his right foot until he hooked it on the chain hoist. The hoist rolled on the steel beam above until it was where Jesse wanted it. He could now reach the hook with his outstretched hand.

Placing the metal hook around the chrome railing on the truck bed, he began spinning the other chain, the lifting chain. The slack in the first chain began to disappear, and Cody and Bourbon glanced at each other in concern. If Jesse freed himself first, they would be helpless to an assault. Unclear of Jesse's intentions, Cody looked around for a means of escape.

The barn cat darted out from the hole in the ceiling, landed on the workbench, then leaped to the floor. The wild animal was out the door in seconds, free to hunt another day.

The fire had spread to the hayloft upstairs and burned like an inferno. All three men sweated from the intense heat of the blaze and the stress of their dire situation.

Bourbon could only think about Annabel's fate. Somehow, they needed to stop Archer or get word to the hospital.

With a loud snap, a few boards fell from the ceiling. The inferno above cracked and popped as it devoured the old barn boards.

Jesse kept pulling the hoist's chain, and the chain, hooked to the truck, went tight, pulling the truck backward, inch by inch. He worked as fast as he could, while the broken ribs in his side ground together with each pull. He used the pain to fuel his own fire.

As the Chevy truck was pulled across the garage floor, it brought the hockey ax in the bed of the vehicle within Cody's reach. Two tires on the lawn tractor ignited, engulfing Cody in foul black smoke. Coughing hard from the toxic fumes, he knew time was running out. The rage burning inside him made the barn fire seem like a barbecue. He needed to be free. He needed to catch Archer before he got to Annabel, and he needed to leave this barn right now. The hockey ax was the only tool available, and Cody made use of it.

"Cody, don't—" Bourbon yelled.

It was too late. Cody swung the ax over and over. It took four swings with the homemade weapon, but he escaped the entrapment.

Jesse Lewis never stopped pulling the chain that hoisted the truck, but he slowed when he realized what Cody was hacking. He couldn't help but stare at the bloody hand that dropped to the floor. His focus was finally drawn away from the hand by a loud popping sound.

The weight of the vehicle was too much for the bed rail to support.

Just as Jesse intended, the bolts ripped through rusty metal, pulling the railing from the truck. He gave the hoist slack, removed the hook, and let the chain swing free. The damage allowed Jesse to slide the handcuffs off the chrome rail. He, too, was free and still had both hands. But rather than attack Bourbon or Cody, Jesse bolted for the open man-door at the back of the garage and escaped.

"Cody, get the hell out of here!" Bourbon yelled. "You've got to stop Archer, no matter what. Don't let him get to Annabel!"

"Not until I get you," Cody said. Cody pressed his bloody arm against the side of the burning lawn tractor tire. The blood hissed and boiled, cauterizing the severe wound. A sound, something between a scream and a grunt, split the air. The odor of burning flesh mixed with burning rubber filled the room, and Cody hoped he'd never smell it again.

He stumbled to the workbench and rifled through the drawers of a large toolbox. He found wire cutters, but the light-duty tool was no match for the heavy-duty handcuffs. He tried a hacksaw that hung on the wall. Bourbon grew weaker, fading from the smoke and stress. Cody sawed at the chain, but his effort was producing little result. He inspected the tool's blade, only to find that the blade's teeth were worn smooth.

Bourbon fell to his side, and Cody caught his weight. "Cody, you've got to get out of here," his voice raspy and faint. "You're the only one—" he trailed off, barely conscious.

Cody felt a presence above him. Jesse Lewis stood over Jeff Bourbon. Cody thought this would be the last sight he would ever see, his death inevitable. But the pastor was holding a pair of bolt cutters. He closed the blades of the tool over the handcuff's chain. The powerful jaws snapped it like a dog biting a milk bone. Bourbon was free.

Cody gripped Bourbon's arm, but the big sheriff was too much for him alone. Jesse dropped the bolt cutters and took Bourbon's other arm. The two men dragged Bourbon across the floor and out of the burning building, not stopping until they were thirty yards away. Even at this distance, the heat was intense on their skin. The flames illuminated Jesse's entire property inside the tree line.

Cody and Jesse both collapsed in the wet grass beside Bourbon, who coughed harshly as the fresh air gave his lungs some relief. Cody watched the barn burn momentarily and then pushed himself to his knees.

Jesse could see the fire in Cody's eyes. "How are you going to stop him?"

Cody turned toward the driveway. "If you gotta catch the devil, you better have a Hellcat."

36

HELLCATS

Archer had a five-minute head start, so Cody couldn't waste another second. He bolted down the long driveway, his wet clothes still steaming from the fire's intense heat. He jumped into AJ's Dodge Charger, backed out of the driveway, and slammed the transmission into drive.

The car seemed to float momentarily until the rubber tires finally gripped the wet asphalt. Cody felt as if the car was producing three G's of force on his body, and before he knew it, the speedometer was reading eighty-seven mph. He kept the high beams on and headed back to town, hoping Archer would come into sight soon, but doubtful he'd catch the deputy. After racing hard for five minutes, he approached the intersection of the entrance of the church. A left turn would take him to the hospital, and a straight would put him back on Grandview Drive.

As he crested a hill, a woman stood in the road. Cody stomped the brake pedal hard, and the car skidded down the damp road. This time, he managed to keep the vehicle from spinning out of control. The figure on the pavement was Willa—or at least his imaginary Willa. At this point, he couldn't tell whether she was a ghost or a hallucination. She turned her back on him as he approached too fast, and instead of striking her, she just vanished and reappeared in the passenger's seat.

Cody slowed the muscle car until he reached the red octagonal sign at the intersection.

"*Go straight,*" imaginary Willa directed.

He hesitated and turned the wheel anyway.

"*No! Straight. Trust me.*" She put a hand on his shoulder, and Cody closed his eyes for an instant.

An old memory of them swimming at the lake hijacked his mind.

They were at their favorite spot on Grandview Drive, standing in the water, chest-deep, embracing each other. Willa repeated her dream, "Someday, there will be a house there." She pointed to a log cabin built on their dream property. But this house was not theirs, and Cody could see Charlie Archer in the upstairs window.

Archer had taken everything from Cody: his wife, his reputation, his hand, and even his dream home.

Cody's eyes were still closed, and Willa pointed to a window in the house's lowest level. A young girl pressed her hands and face against the glass. The window had barbed wire stretched from side to side. The girl screamed and cried, but Cody couldn't hear her. No one could.

Back to reality, he opened his eyes. In his rage, the full power of Cain Lake took effect. The whites of his eyes now glowed with a touch of blue light that was only discernible in the dark. He didn't previously want the ability to see people in danger—but now he embraced it. It surged through his veins, electrifying his brain. He opened himself to his connection with the lake, and the sensation was incredible.

Willa was gone. He was on his own.

"Straight it is."

The tires squealed with an ear-piercing cry across the blacktop, through the intersection, and down the road. Even on the wet road, the rear wheels left a rubber signature, like a celebrity with a squeaky black marker. Two lazy black lines now crossed the intersection.

The car ascended the gradual hills and took the corners like it was on a roller coaster track. Butterflies flickered in his stomach as the Hellcat cruised over the rolling hills. As he worked the wheel with his right hand, Cody was glad the car had an automatic transmission. His left hand—or where his left hand used to be—still bled, even though he'd cauterized most of the wound. He hoped it had been worth it. Pushing the pain aside, he focused only on his goal ahead.

As he drifted around a corner overlooking the lake, he saw two taillights one hundred yards ahead. He kept weight on the gas pedal and even felt the Pirelli tires occasionally leave the road as the car's velocity sent it airborne.

He quickly closed the gap on the deputy's vehicle ahead, which was no match for the 700-horsepower Hellcat. Archer maneuvered the SUV in the middle of the road, blocking Cody from passing on the narrow, winding path. To their right, the bank dropped off fifteen feet. The cliff's edge jutted in and out from the road, with guardrails appearing and disappearing frequently.

Cody knew the only way to stop Archer would be to wreck him. If Archer made it to his house, there'd be no way to flush him out. He'd have Darcy as a hostage, and it was likely he owned more guns, possibly high-powered rifles. Stopping the murdering bastard here and now, on the road, was crucial. It was the only way to free Darcy and the only way to prevent him from killing Annabel.

Cody punched the throttle, and the Hellcat roared, slamming into the rear passenger side of Archer's SUV. The Tahoe swerved to the right, nearly running off the road, but Archer's police training kicked in, and he managed to keep the vehicle on its intended path.

The Tahoe outweighed the Charger by nearly a ton, and the two beasts fought like a grizzly and a jaguar. Both animals were powerful and fast, and the victor would have to be willing to die for the win.

While Archer worked to collect the SUV, Cody moved right and slammed the jaguar into the grizzly's opposite side. The grizzly couldn't correct its path this time and spun to the left. Cody kept pushing until the bear turned 180 degrees.

Archer threw the Tahoe into reverse and stomped the gas pedal.

The two animals slammed together again, locked in combat and unable to pull apart. They were side by side in a forty-mile-per-hour contest for strength. Archer faced west, and Cody faced east. In desperation, Archer yanked the steering wheel counterclockwise, and the heavy bruin pushed both animals toward the edge of the road.

Both beasts careened off the short cliff and went airborne toward Cain Lake.

37

THE WHEEL GUN

The two vehicles rolled several times, but only one came to rest in the lake. Upside down, with only the rear wheels and bumper of AJ's car were exposed from the shore. The tires still spun, and air bubbled to the surface as water flooded the interior, and the Hellcat began to sink into the marshy shore of Cain Lake with Cody unconscious at the wheel. He'd given his life to save Annabel and to avenge his wife. Before he had lost all consciousness, he'd only hoped that Archer was going to suffer the same fate.

Archer's SUV had come to an abrupt stop before entering the water. Steam and smoke engulfed the vehicle. Inside, Archer was strapped to the driver's seat. The deputy knew he'd been in an accident, but he didn't know what had prevented him from ending up in Cain Lake. He thought he'd been ejected and was lying between two logs. Why else would this tree be pushed against his chest?

When he finally came to his senses and realized where he was, he leaned the seat back, creating enough space to squeeze out from under a tree. His vehicle was on its side, and Archer could now see that the tree had crushed the SUV's windshield when it had spun around. The tree would have crushed him against the bucket seat if he'd traveled six inches farther.

Everything hurt—his head, back, and legs. Blood streamed down his forehead, along the bridge of his nose, and to the corner of his mouth. He reached for something stuck to the side of his head, only to realize it was his ear dangling by a thin strip of cartilage. Pushing himself toward the roof, he twisted until his feet were against the driver's side door. The passenger's side door was torn open and folded against the front fender. Using the center console as a step, Archer was able to exit the wreckage through the open door.

The storm had dissipated entirely now, leaving a cloudless sky above. The moon reflected off the lake's glassy surface, but an inverted Dodge Charger broke the smooth reflection of the water. Archer flipped his middle finger at the dead man in the lake and then began climbing the hillside. He was clumsy and sore, but determined to reach the road. He never looked back at the wreckage or noticed the little blue lights that swirled around the Hellcat.

In the car, little blue organisms engulfed Cody's body. Thousands, perhaps millions of the little anomalies zapped and charged the dead man, sharing an ancient and mysterious power. They were unrelenting in their attempt to revive the lifeless driver.

Upside down, with only the rear wheels and bumper of AJ's car exposed from the shore, the tires still spun as air bubbled to the surface. Water flooded the interior of the Hellcat as it slowly sank into the marshy shore of Cain Lake, with Cody unconscious at the wheel.

But the little blue lights were not alone. Through the broken driver's side window, a hand reached inside, unbuckled the seatbelt, and pulled Cody's body through the opening. After reaching the surface, the two figures navigated the dark water, guided by blue amnient light, and rested in the shallows.

Flesti Thaed held Cody's head above water and whispered in his ear. Completely nude, she had pulled him to shore and held him like a newborn baby across her lap. Cody coughed in a fit of pain and expelled the lake water from his lungs. His eyes finally opened, and he stared, in the pale blue light, at the woman who'd saved him.

"Where....how?" Cody struggled to speak at first as an enormous weight crushed his chest.

Flesti put a finger to his lips. "Just rest. Let the water heal you."

Cody knew some bones were broken, but couldn't tell which ones. The little blue lights had numbed his body, passed their life essence to him, and brought him back from a cold, dark void.

Above the scene, Archer had finally made it to the road. The steep embankment was challenging for the injured man to climb, and he crawled on his belly for the last eight feet. He turned around to see the woman in the water holding his rival, both were surrounded by a blue, glowing soup, which Archer assumed was some fluid chemical leaking from the car.

He contemplated going back down to see if Cody was alive, or maybe he'd try his luck and fire at them with his pistol. It was an impossible shot from this distance of maybe seventy yards, and he was too injured and shaken to hit his mark. Besides, he had a more critical target in mind and needed to get to the hospital. His Tahoe was destroyed, but he could walk the last half-mile to his house and get his personal vehicle. One of the perks of being a deputy sheriff was having a patrol vehicle to drive home. He only used his personal truck, which was parked at his house, on his days off.

Determination dragged him up the road with a severe limp that worsened with every step. He kept his eye on the two figures in the lake, but they were inattentive to Archer's movement. Archer hoped they would still be there when he returned. He'd bring Darcy and a hunting rifle and finish Savage for good. A seventy-yard shot with a Ruger .308 was a guaranteed bullseye.

A bright light interrupted his wicked plan. A vehicle approached from the west, a truck he thought he recognized. The truck slowed, cautiously observing the scene like a fox recognizing a trap. The old Ford's brakes squealed as the driver applied pressure, downshifted into second gear, and then put the truck's transmission in neutral. The driver then shifted back into first, crept slowly toward Archer, and stopped twenty yards away.

Archer knew only one old Ford like this one, and its owner was in the hospital, soon to be in the morgue.

The truck's door creaked open, and Jeff Bourbon stepped out. Soot and blood covered his clothes. His gray hair resembled a dove hit by a car with feathers in all directions. Archer had never seen the man so disheveled, even during the search for Darcy, and truthfully, he was glad to see it. He'd come to hate the sheriff of Stoneville, the man every-one loved, the fifty-something-year-old Boy Scout.

"Archer!" A sandpaper voice called out. "Where do you think you're going?" Bourbon took slow, deliberate steps as he spoke.

"Home, old man. And then I'm headed to the hospital. After I kill you and your new buddy down there." He nodded in the direction of the lake shore.

"I don't think so, son. You're never going to hurt anyone again." Bourbon's body tilted to the left, regained his balance, and stepped right, fighting the effects of inhaling so much smoke and fumes. Through arid eyes, burned from the heat, Bourbon glared at his adversary. The inferno had taken a toll on Bourbon, and Archer sensed his weakness.

"You come to arrest me?"

"No. I'm not the sheriff tonight, son. So, either turn yourself in, or I'm going to put a 150-grain chunk of lead through your heart. I've already called the State Police. "Even if you shoot me dead, they'll be here before my body hits the ground." Bourbon stopped walking and faced his former employee from less than ten yards away. Somewhere in the night, a coyote howled and yipped. Frogs resumed their singing at the edge of the lake, and a male porcupine screeched to find a mate. "So, no matter how this plays out...you lose."

"Go to hell, Bourbon." Archer refused to call him 'sheriff' any longer. "I make my own decisions." Archer threw his badge on the ground at Bourbon's feet.

"Looks like neither of us is law tonight," Bourbon's hand rested on his hip, just above his Smith & Wesson 686.

Archer laughed and turned slightly sideways. He kept his Springfield 9 mm holstered on his left ribcage. "Think you can even shoot that dusty wheel gun of yours?"

"Don't test me, son, you won't like the score." Bourbon fought to hold back a cough. His lungs were on fire, and he knew adrenaline was the only thing keeping him on his feet.

Archer's fingers wiggled with enthusiasm. He glanced behind toward his home, toward Darcy. His heaving chest showed off his strong and athletic physique, but also gave away his agitation. He shouted down the road. "Bourbon, I'll tell Annabel you put up a good fight. Right before I slit the bitch's throat." He drew his pistol so fast that even Wyatt Earp would have been impressed. Bourbon knew the younger man was fast, but Archer had to reach his left side, remove the gun from the holster, and swing back to his right.

For the first time in his long career, Jeff Bourbon pulled his service weapon. His draw was quick and short, and he fired from the hip. Charlie Archer had no time to be impressed by Bourbon's speed, but he hated his goddam accuracy.

Archer felt the lead bullet before he heard the shot. Dropping his pistol, he covered the hole in his throat with both hands. The wounded ex-deputy lost control of his knees and crumpled to the ground. His bladder lost control next.

Bourbon holstered his pistol and closed the distance between the two men with four long strides. Archer looked bewildered, not understanding how this had happened.

Bourbon knelt and picked up Archer's pistol. "Just because I've never drawn my pistol on duty *doesn't mean* I don't know how to shoot it." He ejected the live round that never got the chance to prove itself and yanked out the magazine. He tucked the Springfield into the belt line of his pants, along his lower back.

Bourbon laid a hand on Archer's shoulder and looked straight into his frightened eyes. "I'll tell Annabel you put up a good fight, and what a piece of shit you were. The whole town will know, and then, when they know the truth, they'll stop hating Cody Savage. They'll celebrate Cody coming back to Stoneville. They'll call him a fucking hero."

Archer's face twisted in pain and outrage as he reached out with a bloody hand. He grabbed Bourbon's collar in protest, unable to speak. Bourbon pushed his hand aside and watched the life burn out of Archer's eyes.

Searching Archer's pockets, Bourbon found the dead man's cell phone. He called for an ambulance first, and then he dialed Shari Kapoor's number. She was still at the hospital, just finishing up with Annabel, and said she was on her way. Then he called the State Police for real.

Bourbon stood on wobbly legs and let a few tears run down his face. He cried from disappointment, hating that this story had taken place in his town—the hit-and-run, the kidnapped girl, the dirty deputies, and the evil pastor. The only person who'd been genuine and honest with everyone was an ex-convict caught up in the middle of it all.

He peeked down the short cliff to the wreckage below. He'd seen the Dodge Charger upside down when he pulled up, but he did not see what was happening—until now.

Bourbon could make out the silhouette of the woman holding a body in the blue light. He immediately recognized that form from the night at the boat launch and wondered how she could be there now. Cody was fortunate that Flesti was there to save him. As he watched the blue magic that swirled in the shallows, he realized that what Cody and Jesse Lewis had told him about the lake must be true.

Cain Lake possessed an undeniable power that was tied directly to Flesti Thaed.

*****

She was huddled in the corner when Bourbon broke through the door. There wasn't a mark on her other than bruises on her wrists. She wore a pretty spring dress with more wrinkles than a hobo's pants. It was evident that she had been sleeping in the garment since her torment had begun. She shook in fear as Bourbon stood in the door frame, covered in black soot and blood. In his condition, he must have looked like the devil to her.

She pulled a pillow in front of herself and tried pushing further into the corner by digging her heels into the bed sheets. But there was nowhere for her to go.

Bourbon's voice, though raspy, was calm and soothing, and he promised to take her home.

She was finally brave enough to take Bourbon's hand, and he slowly led her down the basement hallway and up a half flight of stairs. Her knees were knocking together as she waited on the landing while Bourbon fetched a blanket from somewhere in Archer's house. She wasn't cold but welcomed the blanket's softness and warmth, which hugged her without malice.

It was dark outside, but she trusted the sheriff with no badge anyway. Bourbon opened the passenger side door of Annabel's truck, and she climbed in, pulling her knees close to her chest. She wouldn't wear the old seatbelt that only went across the rider's lap. She refused to let anything or anyone ever restrain her again.

When Bourbon drove past Archer's body lying in the road, he said, "Don't look."

But Darcy Poole had to look. She recognized the uniform and the build of the man dead in the road. A pool of blood surrounded his head and glimmered in the taillights. She sat higher in the seat to be sure she had seen correctly.

With a mousy voice that was dry and creaky, she spoke more words than she had in days.

"Thank you."

Bourbon stopped the truck seventy yards past the deceased deputy and turned off the engine. "Stay in the truck. You'll be safe. I'm just going to check on the accident near the lake shore." He exited Annabel's old Ford and descended the embankment to Cain Lake, steep and slick from years of wet leaves and dead sticks accumulating on the ground. He fell twice trying to get to Cody.

The ambulance had not yet arrived. Cody lay on his back, his lower legs still in the water. His left eye was swollen shut, and his nose was broken from the airbag. He couldn't move his legs but said he had some feeling in his toes. All he was concerned about was Darcy and Annabel. He kept repeating, "She's in his basement. She's in his basement."

After several tries, Bourbon finally convinced him, "No, she's in Annabel's truck. We saved her. And Archer isn't a threat anymore. He's lying up there on the pavement like roadkill."

"How did you know?" Cody asked. "You didn't turn to go to the hospital. You must have gone straight up Grandview."

"It was a gamble," Bourbon said. "But I saw fresh tire marks across the intersection that weren't there an hour ago." He shrugged. "I had to trust that you knew what you were doing."

"Oh shit," Cody cursed. He looked at the inverted car to his right and grimaced. "AJ is going to kill me."

Bourbon looked at the flipped car with every panel caved in. "Well, on the bright side, I don't think he's going to notice the scratches."

Cody coughed out a painful laugh, then winced in pain.

Bourbon searched the shore and the bay's moonlit surface, but Flesti was gone. He wasn't sure whether to thank her or shoot her. She seemed to be at the center of everything happening. Linked to the lake, she was there when the rescue diver went on a killing spree, slicing his dive mates up because they were sinners. She might be the voice that pushed Jesse Lewis to carve up Annabel and kill the other sinners. And she was here tonight, not to inflict pain or death, but to save Cody Savage. Whatever evil or mysterious powers Cain Lake possessed, she was involved. But that also meant she was responsible for Cody's new ability. He wanted answers, and he was going to find her. Someday.

In the distance, an ambulance siren wailed and grew louder each minute. It seemed to go on for hours. When the ambulance finally arrived, it took six men to carry Cody up to the waiting emergency vehicle. There was enough help, so Bourbon sat in the truck so Darcy wouldn't be alone.

"Who's that?" Darcy asked when Cody gave them a thumbs-up from the stretcher.

Bourbon took a deep breath. "That's my friend Cody. He's the one who found you. I just followed his lead."

38
RAMIFICATIONS

Cody needed a few seconds to realize that he was in the hospital. He was conscious when they had brought him in, but the potent combination of exhaustion and painkillers knocked him out for twenty hours. He tried to scratch his face with the hand that wasn't being violated by an intravenous needle, but it had burned up in Jesse Lewis's barn. A bandaged stub was all that was left, and Cody was glad the pain was minimal. He remembered how much it had throbbed the night before. Thankfully, a surgeon had done a much better job than he had.

There were cards and flowers in the hospital room and a banner on the wall that read. "Our Hometown Hero." Cody figured that the hospital forgot to remove the last occupant's sign. Surely, that wasn't for him.

The bed by the window was neat, clean, and void of any other patient. Flowers by the dozen sat on the windowsill and blocked his view of a tie-dyed sky. There were greeting cards amid the flowers, and he could only read the cover of some "Thank You" and "Get Well" cards printed in fancy fonts and metallic ink. Centered among the flowers was a three-gallon jar of pickles.

Alyse, only you—

"Hey, you," a delicate voice with a Spanish accent spoke beside him. Cody turned away from the window and saw the room's prettiest flower sitting beside him with a little boy sitting on her lap. She wiped a tear from the outside corner of her left eye and set Sammy on his feet. "You gave me quite the scare, you asshole."

"I'm fine," Cody reassured her. "Please don't cry. I'm not worth the tears." He tried to smile, but a split lip made it painful. Daisy moved to his side and gently hugged him.

Jesus, she even smells beautiful.

It wasn't perfume or laundry soap, although there were faint whiffs of both. It was her.

Sammy hid behind his mother, peeking out shyly.

"Sammy," Daisy urged her son. "Don't you have something for Cody?"

Sammy mustered the courage to step out from behind his mother and place a toy car on Cody's belly. Cody laughed when he realized it was the same car he'd stepped on in her apartment, and the same one Sammy had lost when they first met at the bus station—a gray Dodge Charger.

The split opened in his lip when Cody smiled, but he didn't care. "Thanks, Sammy. I love it, and I'm so happy to see you again."

Sammy shrank behind his mother again, much shyer in the hospital than he had been in the bus station.

"So, how bad is it?" Cody asked, referring to his diagnosis.

Daisy squeezed his arm. "Doctors say you fractured your back, but your vertebrae somehow fused back together. Weird, right? But the swelling is putting pressure on your spinal cord, so you won't be able to walk until that goes down. You have multiple hairline fractures in your face, but they'll heal, and you broke three ribs. Oh, and if you hadn't noticed—some idiot cut your hand off."

"Some good-looking idiot."

"Some okay-looking idiot." She kissed the idiot on the lips. "Don't scare me like this again, okay?" A happy tear leaped off a long eyelash.

"Promise. Maybe. I'll try."

"We'll be right back." She pecked his cheek. "Don't go anywhere," she winked. She and Sammy left the room for two minutes and returned with AJ and Alyse. AJ didn't say a word about the car, even though Cody tried to apologize several times. Alyse carried a bag that contained a Ruby Burger from The Mineshaft, just for him. For thirty minutes, they talked about all kinds of stupid stuff, trying to remind Cody of happier thoughts. He'd been through enough for a while.

Cody ate his burger, even though it hurt to chew. He passed his French fries to Sammy, who sat in a corner chair, content with his treat.

AJ and Alyse brought Cody up to date on the fate of Darcy Poole, who was safely reunited with her parents after a night in the hospital for precautionary observations. The Poole family had come by to thank Cody, but he was still asleep. Darcy was going home to resume her everyday life. Hopefully, with a little therapy and time, she will be able to put the experience behind her.

The door to Cody's hospital room eased open, and a new visitor hesitated to enter. Cody waited, expecting to see a nurse, but the door began to close again. Cody spoke up, "Wait, come on in." Stunned, Cody watched as Annabel Thompson stepped into the room.

She didn't say much. She couldn't say much. Sniffling hard, she tried not to break down like a teenage girl stood up for prom. Alyse handed her a box of tissues. She pulled one out with a "Thank you" and dabbed her eyes as she sat in the empty chair beside the bed.

She squeezed Cody hard and kissed his cheek. Her voice was soft, breath like coffee and a cinnamon candy. "I'm so sorry, Cody. I'm so, so sorry. I should have known you would never have hurt my Willa. I should have known. How can I make it up to you? Anything. You just ask, okay?"

"All I need from you, Annabel, is to accept the truth. Know that I never hurt Willa."

More tears and a head nod, Annabel squeezed his hand, "I know. I do. I know. Jesse was adamant that you were innocent. Then you saved my life. And more importantly, you never gave up on Darcy Poole. I don't know how you knew she was alive, but Jefferson told me everything. He told me how you saved us both. I can't believe Archer...."

They hugged for what seemed an eternity. Cody was glad his ex-mother-in-law had finally seen the truth, but he hated what it had taken to get here. He didn't want to think about Willa right now. Ever since he'd returned to Stoneville, he'd been focused on the past. Mr. Thomas' words in the Uber ride to the bus station played in his ear: "...the past is a place where previous correctional residents, like us, should avoid. Ain't nothin' in Stoneville but the past, and you need to have a future."

Mr. Thomas was right, and Cody wanted to focus on his future.

"Where is he, Annabel? Bourbon. Is he okay? He's been through hell the last week. We all have.”

“I don’t know where he is, honestly.” She shook her head. “He brought Darcy to the hospital, stopped by to see me, but didn’t stay long. He said he was going back out to the barn to finish what he started. Whatever that meant.” She choked on the last three words, and the hurt showed in her eyes. “The mayor called my cell this morning and asked if I had been in contact with him. She found a note on her desk this morning that said, ‘Not fit for duty.’ It was under his badge and pistol. She took it as a letter of resignation.”

“What happened to Jesse Lewis?”

“No one knows. He’s just disappeared.”

*****

Cody left the hospital after four days. The swelling in his back had diminished, allowing him to walk again with crutches, and his ribs were healing nicely. Daisy drove him home. Thanks to AJ, her car sounded great, and everything was in working order.

“He’s pretty good like that, isn’t he?” Cody said about AJ on the quiet ride.

Sammy sat in the back seat, trying to tickle Cody’s neck, and played with the power window that finally worked.

A few minutes later, they pulled around the corner, and Cody’s home came into view. He thought they were on the wrong street. People from across town lined his driveway, and a small crowd had gathered in his side yard. Neighbors, old bosses and coworkers, people from the church, and Darcy Poole’s family—they all cheered when Daisy drove into the driveway and parked.

AJ and Alyse were barbecuing in the yard, and someone had set up picnic tables so they could all enjoy the party.

“What the hell is going on?” Cody turned to Daisy.

She grabbed his hand as they sat in the parked car. “This is the welcome home you should have had—that you *deserve*.”

Daisy got out of the Subaru and opened Cody’s door for him. She then carefully led Cody down the driveway, “Just wait, you haven’t even seen the best part yet." They climbed the steps to the porch, which had been cleaned and painted. The bullet holes in the walls were patched, and the door was new. When they walked inside, Cody noticed that the whole house was clean, and the burned wall had been repaired.

"Where'd all the new furniture come from?" The homeowner asked.

Daisy pointed out the window to the Poole family. "Darcy Poole's uncle owns a furniture store in Higley. When he heard what you'd done, he wanted to help. The whole town pitched in. They were glad to help our local hero—"

"And it was Daisy's article in *The View* that made everyone see the truth," Alyse said, sticking her head between the two lovers, while scooping up Sammy and throwing him on her back. "Let's go get a hot dog, kiddo." Alyse carried Sammy outside while Cody and Daisy watched them go.

"Daisy, this is too much. I don't deserve all of this."

"Yes, *you do*. You do deserve this. Just enjoy it. Besides, I'm sure you'll do something to fuck it up." Her impish smile flashed at him.

"Yeah, you're probably right." He conceded.

Across the river, a Land Rover was parked on the side of the street. Annabel Thompson watched the party. Oh, Willa, I wish you were still alive and that none of this had ever happened. She didn't know how many people knew the truth about her hit-and-run accident that killed Charlotte Archer. She pressed her hand against the bandage on her abdomen, feeling the scars underneath that were starting to form. A lifelong reminder of her mistake. The scarification was justification for what she'd done. The lie she'd been living with was now exposed by a single word etched in her skin.

Lost in thought, she jumped when her passenger side door opened, and a broad-shouldered man slid into the seat. She barely recognized him at first, but once she did, she struggled to hold back the tears.

Bourbon was a wreck. He hadn't shaved or showered in days. He wasn't smiling, and Annabel knew his visit would be brief.

"Hello, Annie." His tone was serious, as if he were interrogating a suspect.

"Jefferson, where have you been?"

"Trying to find him. He's out there, somewhere," he nodded at the horizon.

"You don't need to get yourself killed to avenge me." Guilt consumed her. "I'm sorry. Listen, we can look for him together. We can get the whole town to track him down. I need to be with you."

He was silent for a moment. Looking into her eyes opened an invisible wound inside him. "No, I can't."

She couldn't hold the tears any longer. With stiff arms, she leaned against the steering wheel for support.

"Look, Annabel, I've been thinking. All of this started with you—everything that's happened. I'm not trying to make you feel bad. I need you to see things from my perspective."

Annabel wiped her eyes and stared out her window at all the happy guests across the river.

"You fucked up. When you hit Charlotte Archer, you set off a chain of events that could have been avoided. Archer went nuts when his wife died. He thought it was Willa who killed her, so he kidnapped her. Who knows what the sick bastard did to her during those two days? When she escaped, he killed her. Everyone blamed Cody. Then Cody, still grieving, got pissed at a reporter and put him in the hospital, which led to a prison sentence. Meanwhile, we've got a serial killer who feeds on people's sins and thinks you're the biggest sinner in town—after finally realizing it wasn't Cody."

Annabel put her face in her hands to hide her shame.

Bourbon continued, "Then Archer takes the opportunity to enslave another girl. The sale of that girl gets Connor killed by Jesse Lewis."

Shaking his head gently, he opened the passenger door and stuck one leg out, "You should be in prison right now. I should haul you away. But I'm not the sheriff anymore. I can't come back, or I will be obligated to fulfill my oath as an officer of the law."

He stepped out completely, closed the door, and leaned into the open window.

"I love you, Annabel Thompson. I always will. Maybe things will calm down, and I'll sort this shit out. But right now, I need to focus on finding Jesse Lewis and Flesti Thaed. Goodbye, Annabel."

Annabel couldn't bear to say the words. She kept her goodbye to herself.

Bourbon kept his head down and walked casually down the street, peering across the narrow Cascade River to the party. He was glad that Cody had been redeemed and able to reconnect with all the beautiful people at the party. But he also feared for their safety.

The Sin Eater would return to Stoneville with a ravenous appetite.

Jesse Lewis's power comes from Cain Lake, which poisoned his soul and made him thirst for death. He needs to purge, as he called it, after taking a life. Jesse could run, but the Sin Eater couldn't hide.

Jeff Bourbon thirsted as well. His thirst was for Jesse Lewis's blood, and he would have it if he could find the fugitive.

I'm coming for you, Sin Eater. I'm coming.

THE END

THANK YOU
FOR READING

Enjoyed
SIN EATER?
Don't forget to leave a review and then
pick up your copy of
Cain Lake 2: Phantom Pain

www.TerryFisherBooks.com
Sign-up for announcements and notifications.